I0686195

POLYGAMY

By

Andrew Gurlowski

Pieta Publishing LLC

Michigan

This is a fictional story. All characters appearing in this work are fictitious. Any resemblance to real persons, living or dead, is purely coincidental.

Dedicated to Jesus Christ and The Feast of Divine Mercy

Chapter One

Pierre Bosse woke up at 4:30am every day, put on his uniform, and went to work. He was not a morning person, and he did not like waking up so early. He was slow in the morning. His eyes were slow, and his knees were even slower. He had to force his eyes to open, and it hurt to straighten his legs. He was in his late 30's now, and his large bulky body just kept getting slower. Like most people when they age, he was a little surprised the first time he noticed that he had a gray hair, or the first time his back hurt when he tried to lift something heavy. He was becoming old, and he really did not mind, but his slowing body was somewhat of an inconvenience that he wished could be remedied.

In every other aspect of life besides his aging body, Pierre liked things slow. For him, life was something to be savored like a fine meal. Of course, there were always the great landmark moments of a man's life to think about—a first job, marriage, a child's birth—however, Pierre especially liked to chew on the many precious moments of day to day life that most people let pass by without much thought. As he dressed and brushed his teeth and went through his morning routine, he took time to half-dream in his mind, and contemplated all the routinely good things in his life. He fantasized about making love to his wife. He thought about taking his son and daughter to the beach, and playing in the sand with his little girl, or of kicking the ball with his son. He laughed at how everything was new to his children, and he loved to teach them. He thought about cooking some meat on his barbecue, and drinking a cold beer with his crazy next door neighbor, and talking about the football game with him. Pierre's mind would drift from one cloudy image to the next, and he loved slowing down and taking it all in. The one thing he especially loved to do, before he left the house in the morning, at some point between the coffee maker, and the front door, was to check in on his sleeping children and wife, and watch them for a moment in the stillness of the dark house. Then he would leave, though he would have liked to stay there drinking his quiet coffee in the hallway with the creaky floor, and looking at them. And many times, as he drove his 15 year old car at 5:15am to a job he did not like, and a boss who hated him, he contemplated those children and that woman, and he considered himself blessed by God, and he gave thanks to God.

Pierre did not like his boss. More importantly, Pierre's boss did not like him. Pierre's boss was arrogant, ambitious, and took himself and his work too seriously. He wanted to be a captain. Pierre, on the other hand, was not arrogant, and only had ambition to be happy with his family, and was not terribly enthusiastic about his work. If it could be said that some people are the opposite of others, then Pierre was the opposite of his boss; and in this case, opposites repelled each other violently. In 13 years on the job, Pierre had never been promoted, and his boss looked down on him. In his boss's mind, this meant that Pierre was a follower and not a leader; therefore, he felt that he was superior to Pierre. Because Pierre showed little enthusiasm for his work, his boss thought that Pierre was not a sincere or serious police officer, and was not the quality of man that he wanted on his team. Pierre's boss would like to have fired him, but Pierre was unionized labor. He could not be gotten rid of. Pierre's boss was like a frustrated gardener annoyed with some weed in his plot that just kept coming back—and Pierre was the weed. This fact only made Pierre's boss hate him more.

Pierre lumbered out of the driveway in his tiny, old and rusty car. The car was much too small for Pierre's tall and husky body. He had to push the seat as far back as it would go in order to drive comfortably. He looked clownish as his head nearly touched the roof of the car as he drove. Pierre hated his car, but it was still reliable after all these years, and he could not afford to buy a new one—or even a newer used one.

When Pierre finally did arrive at work and parked his car, he became disappointed. His boss happened to park his car in the next spot just as Pierre was gathering his things together to take into the station, and that meant that Pierre was going to have to talk to him. Of course, Pierre's boss always looked for some opening to make a gibe at him. Maybe Pierre's hair would be out of place slightly. Maybe his uniform was wrinkled. There was always some comment that his boss had to make to belittle him. Pierre could only wonder what it might be today. It was like torture for Pierre to wait for the inevitable insult to come his way.

Like an old man having a coughing fit, Pierre's car continued to diesel after he turned the engine off. As Pierre left the car and closed the driver side door, the engine let out one last gasp and the "old man" finally stopped with a clunk. Pierre's boss stood there watching, and could not resist the temptation to make fun of the car.

"Morning Frenchie," the lieutenant greeted him, "You ever think about buying a car made in this century?"

Pierre stopped walking in front of his boss

"Trying to save some money, huh?" the lieutenant said with a smirk.

Like a man who really wanted to say something back, but who knew better than to give the other person the excuse they needed to start a fight, Pierre just looked down at his feet and laughed nervously, "Yeah, a little bit." he said, and then he just walked past his boss without any further comment, and made his way towards the station. He wanted to get away before his boss could think of another way to deride him.

Pierre stepped into the locker room and tried to forget the entire encounter with his boss in the parking lot. But like all the other little moments in his life, he could not help but go over it again and again—slowly dissecting each little nuance of emotion. He opened his locker and checked his hair in the mirror that he kept on the inside of the door. Nobody else was around so he started to make some funny faces in the mirror as he put on his hat. Next to the mirror taped to his locker door, he kept a newsletter with a large picture of his boss, the lieutenant, with a mustache, goatee and horns drawn on it with marker. "Derrick Murphy of the 3rd Precinct is promoted to lieutenant. ..." the caption read. Pierre frowned at the picture, put the newsletter back into the locker, and slammed the door shut.

"Like I've never thought of buying a new car? Can he be serious?" he thought to himself. "No, no, no, I'm not trying to save any money. Don't be silly lieutenant. I drive old crappy broken down cars in 100 degree heat with no air conditioning for fun! I love the way the steering wheel wiggles when I go above 60 miles per hour. Oh wiggle some more! Oh yeah! I love it! Wiggle baby! Wiggle for me! Oh, it's so nice lieutenant. I love it when it wiggles like that! Oh yeah, lieutenant, I love driving my piece of crap car."

He grabbed the keys to his squad car, tied his shoes, and then went to check in and start his work day. Out in the parking lot, the air was still. It was dark outside, but the birds were chirping. It was cool and quiet, and the streets were empty. The sun had not yet come up over the horizon, but its light was starting to reflect on the distant clouds. Even though he was not a morning person, Pierre loved this part of the day. It was like the world was new and fresh; like it had been given a second chance. He stopped for a moment to listen to the singing birds, and smiled. A little sparrow was startled by Pierre as he walked by, and zipped out of a garbage can, and made a few frustrated chirps at Pierre. "Don't be angry with me my friend. I'm just going to my car." Pierre said out loud. The bird made a few more angry chirps, and Pierre smiled again. "Goodbye my friend," he said as the bird flew off in a hurried rush chirping loudly. "Geesh, even the birds are giving me a hard time this morning." Pierre thought to himself.

Pierre began his shift. He was on the road, and driving. It was 6:15am now. Immediately, the first thing that came to his mind was that is was time for some coffee and donuts. This was not something that only a police officer would think of as most people would suppose, but rather a fairly natural reaction to being awake at 6:15am. Pierre was simply hungry and tired and wanted something to pick him up. He stopped at a local gas station that had a donut counter.

The station was owned by an immigrant Russian family. They were on the front lines, as it were, of a kind of battle with the bad elements in the neighborhood, and were very glad to have the police regularly visit their store the way some beleaguered soldiers might feel at seeing reinforcements arrive. They happily provided free coffee and donuts to Pierre and his fellow officers whenever they came in. Pierre indulged himself every day, and liked to make small talk with the owner's pretty daughter, Sasha.

"How's it going today, Sash?" Pierre shortened her name, but lengthened the pronunciation 'Saauush.'

"It goes good my Pierre." She answered in her slight accent. "Would you like a donut?"

"Oh, how about a Boston Crème?"

Sasha smiled flirtatiously at this handsome and tall and well built police officer who she was very attracted to. She turned her back, and bent down to grab two donuts from the shelf behind the counter. Pierre was happy. This was another one of those little moments that he loved to dwell on. Not only did he love the thought that this much younger woman was attracted to him, but like any other man with a pulse who came in contact with her, he could not help but notice Sasha's intense and exotic beauty. She had a dancer's body. She was skinny, very athletic, and had bleached blonde hair. When she moved, it was like her body was a coiled spring that was always on the verge of popping open. She was full of energy and life. She was something to behold, and when she bent down to get a donut from behind the counter, Pierre was able to behold a great deal. There was more to this little exchange every morning; however, that made Pierre happy. Sasha was only 20 years old, but she was not stupid. Pierre felt like he had come to know her well, and he liked to talk with her every day. She had a quick and ironic wit. She was comfortable with herself, and confident but not cocky. She was used to men flirting with her, and trying to weasel their way into her life, but she was not a fool, and certainly was not deceived by the false impression that men who wanted to date her tried to make. The fact that she liked him, made Pierre feel like he still had something to offer; like he was not stale or uninteresting. With Sasha, Pierre felt the opposite of the way that he felt when he interacted with his boss.

"And here's a coffee for you my Pierre."

"Thanks Sash...how's school?"

"Mmmm...very good. I am almost finished now."

"And then what? Where are you going after that?"

"I would like to work for the State's department of natural resources, but there are plenty of other options."

"Like?"

"There are a number of veterinarian offices in the area that I could work for, and there are many ranchers in the state so there is a good market for my degree."

"That sounds great...how's mama and papa?" Pierre said imitating Sasha's vernacular.

"Mama is here in back, and good. Papa is sick. It's nothing, he has a cold."

"A cold in Texas? In August?"

"Yes, I know. It is ridiculous, but he gets sick like that often. He is not a big strong man like you...with your hunky chest and muscle arms."

Pierre smiled. He liked this talk.

"Sash...take it easy now. I'm an old man."

"You're not too old, I see."

"I'm older than you think, probably. How old do you think that I am?"

"Mmmm....38?"

"Well, okay...you're right...but you don't want some old guy like me, Sash. I'm worn. I'm withering."

Sasha contemplated for a short moment.

"I guess you are right."

"Well you didn't have to agree so quickly...it is true how old I am...but you should find yourself some young guy...but not some crappy guy...A good guy...You know?...Someone who likes you...not just...Well you know...Get to know him..."

"Yes, you sound like mama now...Ah, I have to take care of this person."

Another customer was waiting in line behind Pierre. He moved to get out of the way so that Sasha could serve the next person in line. He waited a minute or so until the customer paid for their coffee and left before he resumed the conversation with Sasha.

"So who makes the donuts every morning if your dad is sick?" Pierre asked Sasha.

"Me. I get here around 4am."

"Wow! When do you get done?"

"Two."

"Two! Really? That's rough...So you what--wake up around three, get here at four, make the donuts, work until two, and then go to class?"

"That's my life."

Pierre paused. He was amazed by this beautiful, intelligent, hard working, and friendly woman. She was some kind of oasis. The surrounding neighborhood was a desert of empty souls and wasted lives, and yet here in the middle of it all was a cool spring of smiling eyes and soothing voice that lifted the spirit and chased away the dark clouds. Her laugh was like a balm and her cheerful words were like a soft and warm blanket on a cold rainy night. Truly, truly, the way to man's heart is through his ears.

"Well, yes ma'am." Pierre started, "You definitely have direction..." Pierre caught himself staring at her in wonder, and had to look down before he embarrassed himself.

"I better leave now...I have to leave anyhow...You know... You're a smart girl...hard worker...I should leave now...Say hello to your mother and father... I hope your dad feels better soon..."

"Goodbye my Pierre!" waved the smiling eyes and graceful pale arms.

"I will see you tomorrow, and will have a special donut just for you."

"Oh geesh. A special donut? Give me a break." Pierre smiled shyly as he pushed the glass doors open with his hip because he was carrying a donut and a coffee. "Okay. I will see you tomorrow. Take care." He left the store, and went to his squad car.

It was now time for work, and Pierre started his shift. Sasha and her family was the one bright spot in the section of Houston where Pierre worked. The police called this part of the city the "Drain Field" because that is all that the people who lived there were to them—the waste of society. Criminals and losers, drug dealers, prostitutes and drunks populated the Drain Field, but at this time of the day most of them were asleep. The thought of these people depressed Pierre. In the 13 years that he had patrolled there, he did not feel that he had made any positive impact. The drug deals, gang fights, muggings, beatings, robberies, rapes, arsons, and stabbings went on incessantly. The drug dealers and drunks, whores, pimps, johns, addicts, rapists and robbers went into and out of jail like ocean waves. And how, by what fantastic contortions of logic, could anyone say that they were individual lives worth saving? What fool could convince himself that the out of control drunk on Tuesday was any different from the heroine addict on Wednesday, or the 17 year old prostitute on Thursday? One pathetic tragedy after another came and went eroding a justice system like a sandy beach. Who could say things would ever be any different? Pierre tried to believe that these people's lives meant something; that they were worth a damn, and the drunk and the addict really were not worthless lumps of flesh and bones occupying space. They were still people. They all had a mother and a father like everybody else. The 17 year old prostitute was young enough to possibly be redeemed even. In any case, it was important to believe that these people—this scum of the earth--had some worth if only because they were human beings. They were not inanimate objects made of wood or something—merely things to be managed, used and then discarded. Pierre tried not to succumb to the temptation to write these people off as worthless even as the same faces came and went, but it was difficult. Over the years he had retreated backwards from one trench to another of excuses and apologies and found it hard to resist the cold hearted conclusion that some people were not worth his effort. Where such a supply of human perversion was so abundant, and the demand for human civilization was so low, human life itself seemed practically worthless. Pierre was getting tired of waging a one man war to try to raise its value. For him, the struggle for these men's souls seemed futile. He just wanted to contain this mess of humanity to this portion of the city.

He was driving on Martin Luther, and turned onto another street to go towards the railroad tracks. It occurred to him that it was still quite early in the morning. He was still feeling good at that moment, and he considered that he might not want to run into the type of people that he knew he would probably see around those railroad tracks. Like a man who pretends he does not smell anything when an infant's diapers are dirty in the hope that his wife will change the mess, Pierre decided that there was nothing to see by the railroad tracks in this part of the city at this time of day, and turned his patrol car around, and decided to do some traffic work instead. Perhaps the next shift would take care of the railroad track people. He went the opposite direction on Griggs, and headed towards a familiar parking spot near US Hwy 90.

Officially, Pierre and his fellow police officers did not have quotas when it came to issuing traffic tickets. It was the same kind of official policy; however, that politicians have when it comes to bribes. Officially, they do not take them. Unofficially, for a price they are willing to be reasonable. How else can they afford their 5 bedroom resort condominium and keep a mistress on the side? A man has to make a living, doesn't he? Pierre did not like it, but he knew that he had a few tickets to write in order to catch up to where he needed to be. He parked his car, and waited.

It did not take long for Pierre to find a motorist to pull over. People were on their way to work. He wrote a ticket for speeding, and another ticket for running a red light. He had "made" $350 for the city—a very productive rush hour. He felt that if he could write one more ticket for the day that it would bring him up to respectability in the police department's eyes, and it was only slightly past 9am. Feeling like he was way ahead of the game because he still had over 5 hours left in his shift, Pierre decided that it was a good time for a little break. He drove his squad car into the nearest gas station, and bought a newspaper. Then he went back to his spot near US Hwy 90, parked his car, and settled in for lunch. Pierre took a few bites of his sandwich, and then opened the newspaper for a little reading.

In the upper right hand corner of page 1A, one could read that some rain would be rolling through the great city in the evening. Further down the same page, one could read about the very important government and corporate sponsored economic development in one of the poorer sections of the city. The event was touted as a new spirit of cooperation between the public sector and private sector. As far as the editors were concerned, it was a day like any other day in the history of the planet. People were married. Babies were born and grew into adults. Celebrations of every sort were held. The sun rose in the east, gave life to the plants and animals, and then set in the west. There was nothing out of the ordinary. On the surface, everything appeared perfectly normal. On page 5E, however, there was one story that did catch Pierre's eye. It was the story—only one paragraph--about a little girl named "Betty" who had been dropped off at the hospital by her mother the previous morning.

Betty was the fictitious name of the girl that the authorities gave to the press. Betty was 8 years old, and was like any other 8 year old girl in the world. She was innocent, credulous and above all curious. She elated in the simple games children her age play to exhaustion like hide-and-go-seek or tag. She still played with dolls, and liked to skip rope. She knew nothing about the world, and blindly trusted the adults around her. In one way, however, Betty was unlike any other girl her age in the world. Indeed, she was unlike any other 8 year old girl on the entire planet. Betty, who had just recently started to learn how to multiply numbers in elementary school, had given birth to a live child and was now a mother. She had complained about stomach pains to her mother, Topaz, early the previous morning. When Betty's water broke, Topaz realized something more serious was wrong, and took Betty to the children's hospital immediately. It took the doctors some time to figure out what the cause of Betty's pain was, and they certainly regretted x-raying her stomach, but they knew of no other way to diagnose her. An obstetrician was rushed in, and Betty gave birth to a full term, 3.5 half pound baby girl four hours later. Both the mother and her baby survived the ordeal, and Betty became the youngest mother in American history. Simultaneously, Betty's mother, who was only 23 years old, and her mother's mother, who was only 39 years old, and her mother's mother's mother, who was only 56 years old, and her mother's mother's mother's mother, who was 74 years old, and her mother's mother's mother's mother's mother, who was 92 years old--five more generations of mothers—became the youngest grandmother, great-grandmother, great-great-grandmother, great-great-great grandmother, and great-great-great-great grandmother in the entire history of the world. The obstetrician who performed the delivery called Betty, "an early pubescent girl," and no one had a clue who the father could be, but the authorities were "looking into the matter." Somehow, in the eyes of the newspaper's editors this incredible fecundity only merited one paragraph on page 5E of the daily Houston newspaper.

In truth, Pierre was a little surprised to see the story in the newspaper at all. As a cop, he heard or witnessed ridiculous stories of crime all the time, but they very rarely ever made the paper. He tried not to think about the reasons why such stories did not make the paper. He did not like to consider how many large drug seizures he personally had been a part of where the drug dealer had walked away free, and the story had simply faded away. In his early days on the police force, these things infuriated Pierre, but now, like a man who works with his hands, which become calloused and rough with the toil and less sensitive to the pain, his heart was calloused and he felt virtually nothing. In any case, there was barely anything else written about Betty, and Pierre turned the page of the newspaper to the big story.

The big story of the day was the planned manned mission to Mars, which was still years away. Even so, the newspaper had a two page spread covering the progress of the mission. Full color graphics showed exactly how the landing was to be accomplished from take off on earth, to a re-fueling rendezvous with the international space station orbiting around the earth, to the final stages of touch down on the Martian surface and the return home. The likely launch vehicles were described, the difficulties were listed, and the work to be performed by the astronauts was summarized.

All of this information was presented in a simplistic, and eye-catching way, but the one detail that was not explained...the one piece of the puzzle that was not provided was the whole purpose of the mission in the first place. Nobody with the National Aeronautics and Space Administration, or the federal government could give an adequate explanation of why the government wanted to send men to Mars at all, and yet hundreds of billions of dollars were going to be spent on the attempt. No journalist working for a major publication anywhere in the country seriously questioned the government's official explanations—at least their doubts were certainly not printed. "Why are we going to Mars?" became a common question, but the common people who asked it did not care long enough or hard enough to force an answer from the people who were avoiding giving that answer. While it is true that you can only fool some of the people some of the time; all that is necessary is that you fool enough of the people enough of the time—thus democracy was born, thus the creation of the senate, thus the endless commissions... Enough of the people went on with their daily lives enough of the time, and could care less about the Mars mission, and all the money that was being spent on it, and the government had a free hand to do as it pleased.

One man, who cared very much about the mission to Mars, however, was the mayor of Houston. There was a story about the mayor on the front page. He gave a long speech to the Economics Club of Houston concerning the importance of the space program to the City of Houston, and how many jobs were created as a result of the program; which is to say, he read a speech written by one of his aides about an incredibly wasteful government project to a group of sycophants and corporate fat cats, who could not even define economic wealth despite all their education and so called expertise.

The mayor talked at length about his many accomplishments for the city--the buildings that he had built, the roads that he had fixed, the port facilities that he had updated, and the budget that he had balanced. And he truly felt that these accomplishments were indeed his to claim; though in reality, he had nothing to do with any of them. He did not lay one brick to build one building. He did not spread any concrete to fix one road. He did not dig one dredge to update one port facility, and he certainly did not plan any budget. Others did these things for him; moreover, the decision to do these things itself had been made by others.

The decision that more roads needed to be fixed was made by road builders who wanted the money. The decision to build more buildings was made by the corporations and construction unions who wanted the buildings to be built. The decision to fix the port facilities was made by the oil refinery corporations that wanted the new facilities. The budget was planned by accountants—the mayor himself could not tell you what a debit or a credit was. Not one of the decisions that the mayor had "decided" upon would not have been made by some other politician that could have been put into office by the same various interests, and party machine that put the mayor into office.

In truth, the mayor was merely a tool, and he was the worst kind of tool—the kind who have no clue that they are just a tool. "No man is more hopelessly enslaved than he who falsely believes that he is free" as Goethe said. Though he played the humble servant of the people, in the mayor's mind, he was a great man of history. His speeches were of great significance; his responsibilities of great magnitude, and his decisions of grave importance. What would the world do without him? Why could his opponents not see his rightness all the time? Why could his critics not see his patent goodness? "Alas, they just did not get 'it'" he thought with a heavy sigh. This incredible ego made the mayor one of the most easily manipulated politicians to come out of the party system in years, and the wealthy interests of the State loved him for it. All they had to do was play to that ego, and make any idea seem like it was his idea, or that his "enemies" were against it.

Never did it occur to the mayor that those ideas had been planned long before he had arrived in office, or that his "enemies" had proposed ideas that were virtually the same in substance. The mayor proposed "x" billion dollars of spending, and his "enemies' proposed "y" billion. The mayor proposed "x" miles of roads to be repaired, and his "enemies" proposed "y" miles to be repaired, but in a different manner perhaps. The mayor could not comprehend that there was merely a distinction without any real difference between him and his "enemies," and sadly neither could the people.

The great event of the mayor's speech to the Economics Club of Houston about the very important mission to Mars, and its benefit to Houston—mission control--was recorded by the newspaper in an article with the headline above the fold on the front page as was its editor's duty —his duty!

Pierre put the newspaper down; he did not want to read anymore. He finished his lunch and thought about the remainder of the day that lay ahead of him. In the next four hours he would write two more traffic tickets before he headed back to the station. An hour later he would pick up his children from school. He might watch a little television or do a little laundry for an hour or so, and around 5pm he would start making dinner. His wife would come home an hour after that, and Pierre and his family would sit together and eat. After dinner, Pierre and his wife might clean up around the house together, or watch some television together. Someone would make the children their lunches for the next day, but since Pierre had to wake up at 4:30am the next morning, he was in bed by 8 o'clock—an hour and a half before his children went to bed. This schedule was nearly the same every day. Pierre's wife dropped the children off at school before she went to work, Pierre picked them up on his way home from work, and they all met together each night for dinner. It was a stable and predictable arrangement, and it worked well for Pierre and his family. It was not a perfect arrangement, but it was one where good things could grow like a tree in good soil.

I scattered some seeds I found in my socks.

Some fell among thorns and by the wayside,

And some managed to descend between rocks.

All by some sorry fate withered and died.

But one landed on earth, mineral rich.

It was nourished as the heavens became

Dark and cried the thunder's rolling pitch.

Seedling became sapling, apple by name.

This apple sapling grew and took root.

I witnessed its branches expand and uncoil

Until it bore bountiful fruit.

Despite nature's whim, it strained and toiled.

What is the lesson for those who will see?

Those who discount it seem silly and snide.

Good men are good soil and their grace a tree.

And this is the Way we aspire to be.

Chapter Two

"Pierre, come with me into my office."

Pierre did not ever want to hear these words from his boss, and most certainly did not want to hear them the first thing in the morning. They were the kind of words that a man knows cannot lead to good things. Why must I see you in your office? What is it that you need to tell me there in your office that you cannot possibly tell me here out in the open? What good news could require such privacy? Pierre closed his locker, and followed his boss with dread like a dog who knows it is going to be punished, but knows it will be worse if it resists. Pierre had no clue what he had done wrong, but he also knew it did not matter. Whatever the charge against him was, he would agree and take the punishment. He had learned over the years that this was the best course, the easiest course, the most expedient course, and the only real course. Pierre sat down in a chair, while his boss closed the office door and then took his own seat at his desk.

Derrick Murphy started his rehearsed statement. "Pierre, I know you've done good work here, and I appreciate your work. All the guys like you…" Pierre knew this to be a lie, but he ignored this talk and focused on his boss's words to find out what the meeting was all about. Lieutenant Murphy spoke the way he always spoke to people he did not respect, which was anybody who could not advance his career. He spoke quickly without any pauses. He was loud. There was no inflection in his voice. He spoke in a way that made it known to the listener that the words that he said were unalterable, and that they must be accepted without questioning. His thoughts were not well crafted. They were stated with the certainty that they were brute facts that had to be dealt with. They were the words of a man who was used to getting his way, and presumed that there would be no objections. "We've had some transfers recently, and we are in need of some extra help on third shift. I know that you have had extensive experience on the third shift previously early on in your career so I volunteered your name to the captain. You are to start on third on Sunday--this Sunday."

Pierre was in shock. His mouth was wide open. This was the talk of a madman—a sick mind with a bramble of worldly worries and cares pricking at every thought and word. Murphy continued and was brazen with his lying.

"It's really a promotion of sorts if you think about it. You will be the senior officer on third. That kind of assignment would certainly put you in line for a supervisor position."

Pierre put his elbows on the desk in front of him, put his chin into his folded hands and just stared at the desktop. Did Murphy really believe these things? Did Murphy think that Pierre was so stupid that he did not know that these were lies? How big of a jerk was Murphy?

Murphy went on with his prepared lie, "When the captain asked me who I thought was most qualified among the available officers, I immediately thought of you and recommended your name. You easily have the most experience...I thought that this would be a good opportunity for you to have a chance at a promotion...I know your professionalism, and wanted some of the more inexperienced guys on third to learn from a guy like you..."

This last comment really bothered Pierre. It was such a bold and obvious lie with a weak attempt at flattery. It was the kind of lie a man tells when he has absolutely no regard for the person he is telling it to, and is too lazy and disrespectful even to think up a good lie. Who cares if the other person knows it's a lie? What does it matter? He will do as he is told. Who cares what he thinks? He will never call this bluff. He cannot do anything about it anyhow. He has no leverage. "I know you're professionalism, and wanted some of the more inexperienced guys on third to learn from a guy like you." It was such a pathetic lie that it was laughable. There was a brief moment of silence. Pierre paused to contemplate this statement, and in this brief moment, Pierre Bosse changed as a man.

In the thirteen years since leaving the academy and joining the police force, Pierre had tried desperately to play it safe. He had managed things well. He had performed his duties as a police officer with honor, but had done everything that he could to steer around the kind of confrontations that would force him to take any kind of stand. He had ignored insults, stayed out of disputes, and made certain not to offend anybody--ever. He did anything he could to stay on the same safe course that he was on—a long steady career as a Houston police officer—which he knew was the best course for his family. This avoidance of confrontation had had its negative consequences for him personally. He had been passed up for promotions that were rightfully his, and at times had taken blame that he did not deserve. He was at peace with these developments, however, because he knew that as long as he did not cause or become involved in any kind of controversy, he was guaranteed a job by the union, and this meant stability for his family. This proposed transfer to the third shift, however, threatened his family's well being. He would hardly ever see his wife or children if he accepted this transfer. He would get home around 7am, and his children would already be leaving for school. He would be asleep when they came home, and they would be going to bed when he woke up. He might see his wife for twenty minutes on his way out to work, but they would be on totally different sleeping schedules and would never share the bed together. This transfer was a knife being stabbed into the heart of his family life, and that was the one thing that could motivate Pierre to challenge the decision. No one would threaten the well being of his family without a fight. He had to confront his boss, whom he despised; despite his fears, he had to adapt. He had to change and be strong, and make Murphy know that he was not going to be pushed around like this. Being put on third shift like this was for a rookie. Pierre was a thirteen year veteran.

"I think I have a problem with this." Pierre started. His heart skipped a beat, and he felt very uncomfortable, but Pierre made the leap into this new man that he was becoming with these simple words. "I don't think that I can accept this."

Derrick Murphy's look of contempt was not masked. He stared at Pierre with anger. Could this pathetic grunt possibly be defying his authority? Could this idiot...this mediocre lump from the academy possibly think that he had a choice in the matter? No, he was not going to allow Bosse to squirm out of this. He would use his leverage against Pierre, and let him know with whom he was dealing.

"You know, Pierre, I noticed that you haven't written any traffic enforcements in a while--"

"That's not true. You must be looking at an old report. I wrote four violations yesterday." Pierre shot back. He was not going to let Murphy take this line of argument anywhere.

"That's not what I saw."

"Well you are looking at an old report. You need to get an updated report. That report you have is old. I did four enforcements yesterday. That gives me seventy for the year, and its only August."

Murphy was cut off from using this stick against Pierre, but he was not going to admit it.

"Well, I don't know about that. It doesn't matter anyhow. You're the only guy right for the position that is available."

"No I'm not. There's Jefferson. He worked third shift before, and I have two years on him in seniority. Brommy's worked third, and actually preferred it to working first. Ask him. Roth worked third as well, and I outrank him too."

"Don't argue with me. We have a need, and you are going to be a team player and fill that spot."

"This is ridiculous. I've got thirteen years on the force. I've only been on first for eighteen months, and you are going to pull me off, and send me back to third shift? There's no way—"

"Look! Damnit! You're doing it. I don't want you here on my shift." Murphy replied, and in his frustration and anger he had overplayed his hand, and revealed too much. Originally, he had stated that he wanted Pierre to move to the third shift because of Pierre's experience. Now, the facade of lies had come off, and Murphy had exposed his true motivations, and that this decision was purely due to his dislike for Pierre. Pierre looked directly into Murphy's eyes, and they both knew that the ceremony of politeness was over.

"Well I don't care what you want." Pierre answered briskly.

"You don't have a choice <u>Bosse</u>."

"I'll take it up with the union--<u>Murphy</u>."

"That's so typical."

"What the hell do you mean by that?"

"Guys like you, Bosse—you come in here and think that all you need to do is go through the motions—"

"What the hell do mean "guys like me"? I did my time on third for five years when I came out. I had more arrests on third shift in those five years than anyone else. I have thirteen years here now. I have a family now. Do you think that I can just ignore them? They are a major consideration here."

"There's nothing that you can do about it." Murphy answered.

"Yes there is. You're not a dictator here. I have options, and I am going to take them."

"No, you can't. You're wrong. You have to go."

But Murphy did not say this last statement with the conviction that it was truth. He said it like a four year old child who thinks that if he just says something over and over again enough times it will become true. In reality, Murphy knew that Pierre did have options. He knew that Pierre did not necessarily have to go to the third shift. Pierre knew this fact as well, and for the first time in thirteen years on the police force he felt that he was in control of matters. He was going to decide what he was going to do. He had made his stand. He had confronted his boss, and had beaten him for the time being.

"Don't you have a family? Don't you understand what this would do to my family?" Pierre asked.

Murphy did in fact have a family, but it was not much of a family, and these last words touched a nerve. Murphy's wife slept in a separate room and was having an affair. Murphy knew that she was having an affair, but he could not prove anything. Whenever he did see his wife, there was an immediate argument so Murphy avoided her. He invented reasons not to go home, and worked late in the office doing tasks that easily could be put off to another day. His son did not talk to him. He had moved out of the house and had taken a job waiting on tables. They had not spoken with each other in almost a year. Murphy wanted badly to patch up the relationship with his son. It tortured him to think about his son working at some menial job when he had the talent and intelligence to do so much more. Murphy could get him on the police force so easily, and he could have a fine career. How could he get through to the boy? How could he make him see? His daughter had run off with some pervert, who rode around in a motorcycle gang and was twice her age. Murphy did not even want to think about where his daughter might be, or what she might be doing. Murphy's home life was a ridiculous madhouse, and he did not like this talk from Pierre about his family. He was not going to take it.

"I have family, Bosse, and they have <u>nothing</u> to do with this. You're going on third starting Sunday." This was said with authority, and in a tone that indicated that the conversation was over as far as Murphy was concerned.

The conversation was over; the fight, however, was only just beginning. Pierre knew that Murphy would go to the captain as soon as possible, and start using his influence to get his way. Pierre decided that he would go to the captain himself—before Murphy got the chance. Then he would file a grievance with the union. Then he would request a hearing with the board of review, and formalize his arguments. He had no idea how long it would take, but the more he thought about it, the more confident he was that he would win.

"We'll see. Is that all that you wanted?" Pierre asked.

Murphy did not immediately answer, and Pierre did not wait for a reply. He left the office abruptly, and started towards the captain's office before Murphy even got out of his chair.

When Pierre arrived at the captain's office, it was locked and the lights were off. Pierre stopped one of the police officers who was walking by, "Hey, do you know were the captain is?"

"He's on vacation."

"Until when?'

"I'm not sure really. Ask Murphy. He'll know."

There was no way that Pierre was going to go back to Derrick Murphy's office, and ask him when the captain returned from vacation.

He walked around asking various people until he finally found someone who knew when the captain would be back. The captain was out of town until Monday. There was no way to talk to him until then.

Pierre felt a little anxious when he found this out. It meant that he would be forced to work at least one late shift in the Drain Field before he could talk to the captain face to face. He contemplated that reality for a moment, and was more hopeful. He could handle one day on third shift. He would just avoid any and all difficulties for the one day— basically do nothing and not take any risks. When his shift was over, he would rush back to the headquarters and corner the captain in his office, and make his case. The more he thought about the matter, the more confident he became, and the better he felt. There was hope. He only had to make it through one late night shift in the Drain Field, which he could do easily.

He decided, however, that it would be best to leave a message on the captain's telephone answering system to give some forewarning. He thought about the message that he wanted to leave for some time, and decided to write down exactly what he wanted to say before making the telephone call. The message was too important to improvise. After about ten minutes, he had formulated what he wanted to communicate, and had written it down on a scrap piece of paper. He went over to an empty desk, made the call to the captain's telephone, and left his message. Then he went to his locker and found the telephone number to his union steward, who worked in another precinct. He called the number, and spoke with his union representative directly. The union representative was completely on his side, and encouraged Pierre. The union would back him. He had seniority. There were others available for the shift. Pierre had paid his dues, and Murphy was in a bad position. The steward told Pierre that if he needed someone from the union to make a call to the captain that all he needed to do was ask. For this, Pierre was thankful. He told the steward that he needed to talk with the captain first, and would

---

let him know how that meeting went before he made any other plans. He hung up the telephone, and as he headed towards the door to the parking lot to start his shift, he felt very good. He had laid the ground work for a good discussion with the captain. He had used just the right words, and had spoken them with just the right tone. He was certain that the captain would lean his way. With a little push from the union, which he had already lined up, and a face to face meeting, he knew that the captain would inevitably decide in his favor. He now felt that he would be back on the first shift within a week—maybe even less-- despite all of Murphy's efforts. He left the headquarters with great optimism.

Pierre went to the parking lot to start his day. It was still dark, and as he walked into the parking lot Pierre searched for his little bird friends, but they were not around. "Hello birds?" he called, but none came flying by. It was strange not to hear any birdsong to start the day. Pierre felt abandoned. Where were all his little friends? Pierre went to his car, and headed in the direction of Sasha's donut shop for his daily morning donut and coffee. When he pulled up to the driveway, he noticed that Sasha was in the back alley feeding left over donuts to a stray Chihuahua. When she noticed Pierre's squad car, she left a small pile of the donuts on the ground, and went inside to the shop.

"Hey, Sasha. Who's your little friend out there?" Pierre asked.

"That is Petya."

"What?"

"Petya. It means 'Little Peter.' I named him after you."

"What are you doing? Me?"

"I feed him."

"Oh..."

"I named him after you because he is so cute."

"Oh please." Pierre replied.

"Do you want a donut and coffee?"

"Yeah…thanks….Uh Boston Crème…two…"

Sasha got the donuts from the trays behind the counter, and gave them to Pierre, and went to the coffee maker to pour him a cup of coffee. She was wearing a half shirt that exposed her midriff, a pair of Capri pants and sneakers.

"You know I don't think that that is such a good idea Saaash."

"What?"

"Feeding that dog."

"What about it?"

"And I don't know about that shirt. I don't think that it is a good idea to feed him. That dog could have all kinds of diseases."

"No."

"Yes. And then he could bite someone and they would get sick. He could bite you."

"Not my Petya."

"Oh yes."

"No, no, no, no"

"Oh yeah. What are you feeding him?"

"Left over donuts. He comes to see me every day. He is so cute. And what's wrong with how I am dressed?"

"You can't go around dressed like that around this neighborhood. You have to know that Saaash. Anyhow... I am just saying that that dog could be dangerous, and that you should let me have the animal services people take care of him."

"NO! My Petya is my friend. Don't do that." Sasha said like a protective mother.

"I won't. I won't. But you should let me."

"No."

"Okay forget it. But think about it--"

"You look sad." Sasha asked as she handed Pierre his coffee.

"I look sad?"

"Yes. Something has happened?"

"Yes, something has happened."

"Well?"

Pierre did not want to go into the matter of his transfer with Sasha. It was not any of her business. He was worried, though, and he knew that Sasha could make him feel better. He always felt better after talking to Sasha. She always gave him more self confidence.

"My boss wants to put me on a different shift of work, which would mean that I would not see my family very much."

"Oh no!"

"Yeah. I would start work at 10pm and finish at 6am."

"No!"

"I would not see my family so I am fighting it."

"What are you going to do?"

"I am going to talk to the captain—my boss's boss. And I think that I will have it straightened out."

"Yes, you must. Your family is too important. Do not let him do this."

"No, I won't."

"Fight him! You can do it." Sasha encouraged Pierre.

"I will."

"Yes, you must. And you will win too. I know you will."

Pierre felt better, and was glad that he had talked to Sasha about the transfer. Her words were like medicine. Pierre felt more confident, and hopeful.

"Are you working Monday?" he asked Sasha.

"Yes, I will be here."

"I'll see you Monday morning then. This is for the paper." Pierre put down some money, and grabbed a newspaper on his way out the door.

"Goodbyeee." Sasha waved cheerfully.

"Bye bye. I'll see you Monday at the end of my shift maybe." Pierre smiled. He left the donut shop, went to his lucky traffic spot, and settled down to read the daily news. He pulled out his newspaper, quietly ate his donuts, and drank his coffee. As he sat there drinking, a group of four teenage boys came around the corner of a building right next to Pierre's car. They were taken off guard, and obviously did not expect to see a police car. Even so, they were laughing about something amongst themselves, and sauntered by Pierre as if he were not even there. Pierre looked at his watch. It was just after 7am. What would four teenage boys be doing in the middle of summer while school was out walking around at 7am? He considered following them for a moment to find out what they were up to, but remembered his plan not to take any risks until after he spoke with the captain on Monday. Pierre resolved himself to do as little police work as possible until after that meeting. He put those teenage boys walking around the back alley of an abandoned building at 7am out of his mind, and went back to his newspaper. After a moment of reflection, he realized that in this section of Houston—even on first shift— things could get very strange very quickly, and that the best way to avoid the terrible violence that was a daily routine in the Drain Field was to do traffic violations to busy yourself. If dispatch called, you could say that you were in the middle of a traffic enforcement, and some other officer would be directed to the call. Pierre decided to spend his entire day writing traffic tickets to keep himself busy, and away from any call dispatch might make. It also occurred to him that whatever tickets he wrote today would pad his already healthy total for the year, and strengthen his case against Murphy. He put his coffee and newspaper down, and went to start his car, but just then a call came over the radio.

"25? Bosse?"

Pierre's heart sank when he heard his name called by dispatch. He waited a while before picking up the microphone. He knew that he had to take the call. He just hoped that if he waited a moment, it might go away. He picked up the microphone and answered the call.

"10-4. Go ahead."

"We have a neighbor reporting a shot fired--domestic disturbance on Newkirk."

Pierre let out a deep sigh, and his head fell down. This is not how he wanted the day to go. First, his boss drops a bombshell on him, and now he had to respond to a terrible call. Newkirk was next to the railroad tracks, and it was a dirty street. This call could only be bad. He reluctantly picked up the microphone, and replied with his head still hanging down.

"25--Affirmative. I'm on it."

He put the microphone in its receptacle on the transmitter, and paused for a moment. "Damnit! Can this day get any worse?" he said out loud to himself.

He angrily shifted the car into "drive" and headed for Newkirk Lane, which was somewhere south of 90 by Martin Luther.

When Pierre arrived at the disturbance, there was a group of neighbors hanging around on the sidewalk in front of the house. It had started to drizzle slightly, and they were huddled underneath an umbrella with one of its spokes missing. As Pierre opened his door, one of these neighbors pointed towards the house.

"Thanks." Pierre nodded to the neighbor. He picked up his microphone, and let his dispatch know that he was at the scene.

The house looked like it should have been condemned. The front lawn was a mess of uncut grass, and weeds with garbage spread about. The windows were filthy with an opaque yellow film, and the roof was badly in need of repair. Much of the aluminum siding was black with dirt, and here and there parts were falling off the façade. The front porch was cracked and uneven. It was difficult to believe that anybody really lived there. It looked like the scene of some horror film.

Pierre went to the trunk of his squad car, and put on his bullet proof vest. "No risks." he whispered to himself. He pulled out his shotgun, loaded it with three shells, grabbed his flashlight, and then leaned against his squad car and waited for back up to arrive. The neighbors huddled underneath the umbrella just looked at him in wonder. Their eyes said, "Aren't you going to do anything?" But Pierre just smiled back at them, and waited. His eyes said to the neighbors, "No, I am not going to do anything by myself today and risk my life because you stupid people decided to shoot each other, and I don't care what you think." About a minute later, another police car was turning the corner onto the street and pulled up next to Pierre. The driver was Jeremy Bromfeld, who everyone at the station house called "Brommy." He was one year younger than Pierre, and he and Pierre got along very well.

"What do we have?" Brommy asked.

"I don't know yet. I've only been here a little while."

Brommy called in to dispatch, and then went to the trunk of his squad car to put on his own bullet proof vest as well. Pierre went to the back of Brommy's car to formulate a plan.

"Why don't you go around the back of the house...I'll go in the front. What channel are you on?" Pierre asked.

"Seven."

Pierre set his walkie talkie to channel seven, and both he and Brommy started towards the front door. There were no lights on inside the house from what they could tell. They went up the front walk that was nearly overgrown with grass which was wet from the rain. Pierre and Brommy had to pick their feet up in an exaggerated way just to make their way through the lawn. Their feet and lower pant legs were wet and muddy by the time they reached the front door. Brommy gave Pierre a funny look as they stood on the tiny front porch that was sunken on one side. Pierre signaled with his head for Brommy to go around to the back of the house. While Brommy was on his way, Pierre pounded on the front door, and shouted, "Houston Police! Open up!" But there was no response, and there was no sound at all from the inside of the house. All that Pierre could hear was the soft patter of the rain. Things were too quiet. Pierre did not have a good feeling about the situation. He knew that there was a death here. Somehow, he just knew. He picked up his walkie talkie, and called to Bromfeld.

"Brommy?"

"Yeah."

"Anything moving back there?"

"No, it's quiet."

"I know. Come up front, and let's go in together."

Brommy came around the house and up to the front door next to Pierre. Pierre nodded to him, and tried the door handle. The door was unlocked and opened with a loud creak. "Houston Police!" Pierre shouted as he walked through the door with his shotgun in front of him. But there was no response.

There were no lights on inside the house, but Pierre could see the living room, and main hallway with his flashlight that he held under the shotgun. The place was trashed. To the unaccustomed eye it might have appeared that it had been ransacked by a thief. Furniture cushions, and dirty clothing were scattered over the floor. There was rotting cheese somewhere in the house, and the smell was overpowering. A broken old television set lay in the middle of the living room floor, and overhead a ceiling fan with only one blade was motionless. None of these things surprised Pierre. The lives of the people in this neighborhood were disheveled and frantic. They were poor, and demoralized and violent.

They meandered through life from one crazy incident to another without much thought or purpose. There were no families with a married mother and father. There were only drugs, gangs, unemployment, prostitution, illegitimate pregnancies, and violence. The state of this house was very much like the state of the entire neighborhood—a total mess. The only thing that surprised Pierre was that the house was so quiet.

"What do you think?" Brommy asked.

Pierre turned his head and cupped his ear, and paused to listen. He thought that he heard something from the back of the house. "There's something back there." He said pointing to the kitchen. Brommy nodded, and Pierre went to move towards the kitchen. He shined the flashlight down at his feet as he walked over the piles of dirty clothes that lay in a pell-mell fashion all over the place until he came to the back of the house where the kitchen was.

"Houston police!" Pierre shouted.

There was no reply. Brommy looked at Pierre questioningly, and for a moment, the two men just stood there looking at each other in complete silence. The only sound in the house was the soft huff of their breathing. Then, Pierre thought he heard something again—like somebody slurping. Brommy heard it too. Like a diver, Pierre took a deep breath, held it in, and walked around the corner into the kitchen with Brommy following from behind.

"Police!" he shouted.

When a person experiences shock or fear, he freezes like a statue. He becomes paralyzed in a way, and cannot move or think. Sometimes he cannot take his eyes away from whatever stimulus has caused the shock. Pierre stood in such a frozen state.

"Oh God...Oh God...Brommy?...Oh...I can't—"

Brommy came behind Pierre, and let out a groan, "Ahhhh... Ohhhh...I—Oh God! Oh my God!"

All Pierre could do was stare at the abomination in front of them. Besides Brommy's groans only a sick, ugly sound breached the silence, the sound of someone sucking. Sitting in the middle of the kitchen floor was a small boy, no more than seven years old. He was naked, and completely covered with blood. In his mouth was the arm of a dead body lying at his feet. Blood was spread in a pool by the head, and was smeared all over the window above the kitchen sink. A throw rug was completely soaked in the red pool. At the foot of the kitchen sink that overflowed with dirty dishes, laid the body of a woman with a large gunshot wound to the back of her head. Its limbs were twisted in a macabre, unnatural way behind the head. She was wearing a nightgown, which had flown up after she had fallen. Her legs were spread apart exposing her nakedness. Parts of her brains were splattered on the window above the kitchen sink. A revolver rested on a chair next to the boy, who stared blankly at the two officers while he chewed at the fleshy arm of his dead mother like a dog gnawing on a piece of furniture.

Pierre came out of his stunned trance, and cautiously leaned over towards the cannibal boy without actually stepping into the kitchen. He did not want to step into the large pool of blood. He bent down and pulled the chair with the revolver on top of it away from the boy, who never took his eyes away from Pierre. It then occurred to Pierre that he would have to do the dirtiest of jobs. As the boy continued slurping on the arm of the dead body, Pierre gingerly put two fingers around the limb, and pulled it out of the boy's mouth, setting it on the floor away from the boy's grasp. As the naked little blood covered boy stared at him, all Pierre could think about was the ridiculousness of it all. Madness! What a senseless waste of humanity! What a total and complete waste! What kind of brutal world was it where a seven year old boy murders his mother, and feeds on the rotting corpse? Was there any sanity left?

Pierre was totally dejected, and hung his head. His heart had been stabbed with the cold, cold cruelty of a world that did not care--a world of throw away people with throw away lives. There did not seem to be any point in trying anymore. As snow on a mountain peak melts and makes its way down the slope, and gathers into a stream, the tough veneer on the heart of a 13 year police veteran cracked and melted into a trickle of soft tears that ran to the tip of Pierre's nose and dripped onto the floor. Pierre rubbed the wet from his eyes. This was his last day on first shift in the Drain Field. Brommy called the murder into dispatch.

Chapter Three

Lieutenant Murphy knew people. In fact, getting to know people—the right people—was his chief occupation. Law enforcement was merely the framework within which he worked. If he had been employed by the public school system, or an organized church, or the military or any of the large institutions that are like wheels upon which our society is governed, Murphy would have made earning the favor of the right people, the people who really decided matters within these institutions, his primary task. If he had been employed by the public school system, he would become friends with a certain administrator or school board member. If he had joined the military, he would have courted a certain general. Murphy was one of those professional bureaucrats who knew that the secret to success in any institution is to court the favor of the few people within the organization who really mattered. Let the actual work be done by others.

Lieutenant Murphy knew that the captain was on vacation, and would not return until Monday. He also knew that Bosse would make his little attempt to out maneuver him as soon as possible. If this simply had been a matter between himself, Bosse, and the captain, Murphy knew that he would lose. Bosse could and would make a successful case and stay on first shift, and he, Lieutenant Murphy, would be humbled. This was not going to happen. Though this was only a simple case of reassigning a staff officer to a different shift, Murphy was willing to go out of his way, and make an extra special effort to make certain that Bosse went on third shift. It was not spite that motivated Murphy. It was a perverted sense of pride that drove him. He was an important person with important responsibilities and important friends. Bosse was a grunt, and a slacker. Lieutenant Murphy was on a path to become a captain one day, and knew people like the mayor by their first name. Bosse was a nobody, who knew nobody and was going nowhere. Even as Pierre was leaving a message on the captain's telephone answering system,

Lieutenant Derrick Murphy was making a telephone call to the deputy chief in charge of south central Houston—the captain's boss.

"Hello?"

"Hello, this is Lieutenant Derrick Murphy. Is Deputy Chief O'Sullivan available?...Pat? It's Derrick Murphy here in the Third."

"Derrick! Good to hear from you. How's the family?" Deputy Chief O'Sullivan said cheerfully.

"Good. Good...everything's great. [Murphy lied] How's your dog? The last time I talked to you he was having...ah...digestive problems..hey, hey..."

"Yeah, the little bastard. That was a mess. He was crapping everywhere. Crap by the Jacuzzi. Crap in the sun room. Crap in the library. Some sort of infection. The vet gave him some pills, and that took care of it. I'm taking him quail hunting next week. You should come. You know I've had him specially trained."

"What day is that?"

"Next weekend—Friday."

"That's sounds good. I'll bring that over-and-under I was telling you about, and you can try it. Count me in...." Murphy was happy to be invited to a hunting party, but wanted to end the small talk, and get to the business at hand. "Hey Pat, the reason I called was to discuss a little problem that I am having down here."

"Oh yeah?"

"Yes sir. I have some dead weight here that I am trying to move to a spot on our third shift that opened up. His name's Pierre Bosse, and he's not going for it. Nothing but a complainer—bitching about the inconvenient hours. You know. He is going to make a stink about the whole thing with Nicholas. And if I know Nick, he's going to play it the union's way for sure."

"So this guy has a case with the union?" O'Sullivan asked looking for an excuse to get out of helping Murphy.

"Yes sir….sort of. You know. He's got maybe a year of seniority over the next available guy, but I have to tell you he does not belong on first shift. He does only the minimum. He never volunteers. I don't think he even contributes to the fraternal order of police fund here."

This last comment caused Deputy Chief O'Sullivan to raise his eyebrow, "That's not good. How is he on traffic for the year?"

"Well, that was the first thing I checked. The report I have shows him a little short, but he says that he just wrote four enforcements yesterday. I guess I have to believe it, but I have to check into it too. So maybe he is on track for the year, but he really doesn't care about the force. You know what I mean? Even today, he just pulled the union card on me right away for no real reason." Murphy was careful to manage the tone of his voice here. He wanted to sound like he was under stress, but did not want to come off like a whiner.

"Have you talked to Nick at all about it?"

"He's on vacation until Monday, and I know that this guy, Bosse, will be on him the first chance that he gets." Murphy purposely let out a heavy sigh for O'Sullivan to hear. "I thought that I would give you a call, and get your advice on how to handle it. I figured you could probably point me in the right direction."

This last comment was totally obsequious, but was said with such subtle flare that a man of Deputy Chief O'Sullivan's arrogance could not detect the guile. In the Deputy Chief's mind, here was a good and faithful subordinate, Murphy, an up and comer—much like he himself was when he was younger—coming to him for some honest advice on a tricky matter. Yes, this was the Deputy Chief's area of expertise. This was why he was deputy chief—to give such counsel, and guidance to the officers below him. This was where he earned his money. He leaned back in his chair, lit his illegal Cuban cigar with his special carved ivory lighter that he had bought in Fiji on his last vacation, and scratched his chin in deep thought for a moment.

The unfortunate reality; however, was that Deputy Chief O'Sullivan had no counsel to give in this instance. Pierre Bosse was in the right as far as the transfer was concerned. If his record was clean, which it was, there was no way, according to the rules, to move, that is demote, him like this. The lower seniority man would have to take the spot. All Deputy Chief O'Sullivan could offer Lieutenant Murphy was the raw power of his political connections on the police force. He knew who he had to call to make the transfer go through, and what he needed to say. The question was whether the matter of this transfer was worth the trouble to call in such a favor. In the twisted world of society's governing institutions where the only thing that was produced and traded was political capital, how one spent that political capital was the main thing. The rightness or wrongness of Pierre Bosse's objections was irrelevant. His spotless record and merits were irrelevant. The agreed upon rules with the union were irrelevant. Pierre's family life was irrelevant. The law, logic, and decency, all were irrelevant. The only thing that was going to decide whether Pierre Bosse was going to be transferred to the third shift or remain on the first shift was whether Deputy Chief O'Sullivan deemed it worth the trouble to help out a man like Lieutenant Murphy. O'Sullivan scratched his chin some more, and took a few more puffs on his cigar, and weighed the matter on the scales of politics, and agreed that such an up and comer like Murphy, who would certainly be grateful, should be assisted.

"Let me make a few calls, Derrick. I think that I can probably help."

"Really?" Murphy said in feigned surprise as if he were impressed with the Deputy Sheriff's ability to make something like this transfer go through with just a few telephone calls, "That would be great. I surely would appreciate the help."

"Oh, no problem. I can't promise anything, but there's a good chance that we can get this guy, Bosse, to third shift. What's his first name again?"

"Pierre."

"French...very French...nobody likes the French anyhow...Let me make a few calls."

"That's good to hear, Pat. And uh...I guess that I will see you next weekend?"

"Yeah, I want to try that gun."

"I need to know the where and when."

"Hey, call my wife. You have my home phone right? Yeah, call her, and she will give you all the details as they say."

"Okay, great. I guess that I will wait to hear back from you about this Bosse transfer?"

"Yeah, I will call you after I make a few calls—probably tomorrow or Tuesday. I will talk to Nick about it too on Monday, and then I will get back to you."

"Sounds good. And I will see you next Friday."

"Absolutely my com—how to the Italians say it—compadre?"

"Yes sir. I think that's it."

"I will talk to you my compadre."

And that was the end of it. Pierre Bosse would move to the third shift regardless of his efforts. No amount of pleading with the captain or anyone else would change that. Nothing would stop it. Murphy smiled as he hung up the telephone, and leaned back in his desk chair—he felt like smoking a cigar.

When Pierre arrived home at the end of the day, he was a troubled man with the weight of the world on his mind. It was 3:30pm. Lost in his thoughts, he picked his children up from school without even greeting them. On the drive home the boy and girl in the back seat of the car were loud and obnoxious, and squabbled the way that children just out of school for the day do. Pierre thought about the transfer, and thought about having to explain it to his wife and about the terrible crime scene that he had witnessed, and about how much he hated his boss, Lieutenant Murphy. The children continued to fight and shout in the back seat, and Pierre became more and more angry and annoyed. Traffic was terrible. The car in front of him came to an abrupt stop, and Pierre almost ran into it from behind. The children shouted in surprise from the violent stop. Pierre's patience reached its breaking point. He turned around and shouted at his children, "SHUT UP!" When a 6' 5' 230 pound muscular man tells his seven year old boy, and five year old daughter to shut up in such a way, they shut up. There was no more noise the remainder of the trip home. When they arrived home, the children quickly unbuckled their safety belts, and ran into the house ahead of their father.

In another hour, Pierre's wife arrived home from work, and she could immediately sense Pierre's agitation. He was fidgety, and complaining. When she spoke to him, his mind seemed to be off in another place. She knew there was something wrong, and it had to be about work. What else was there? As the two of them prepared dinner in the kitchen, she asked him about his day.

"So how was work?" she started.

Pierre glared at her, "After dinner we need to talk."

"What is it?"

"After dinner."

"What is it? Let's just talk about it now."

"Irene, I don't want to talk about it now...after dinner...not in front of the kids."

"Why? What's wrong? What's happened?" she pressed.

"After dinner, Irene."

"I don't understand. Why not now?"

"Damnit Irene! I said after dinner! God Almighty! How many times do I have to say it?"

Irene was a little shaken by Pierre's tone, and his imposing bear like frame that was shaking. She knew that she had pushed him too far, and immediately became quiet, and finished preparing the meal. The Bosse's ate dinner in silence, and it was very awkward. The children could sense the tension between their parents, and did not make a sound. Pierre's mind was racing. His frustration simmered, and he wanted to relieve it by talking things out with his wife. He needed her help. He decided to break the silence, and begin the conversation even though they were still eating with the children.

"They want to move me back to third shift at work starting tomorrow." he said in a robotic monotone.

This was, of course, a bombshell, and Pierre did not deliver it with any tact. His wife stared at him in shock as the implications of such a move were played out in her mind.

"I'm trying to fight it, and I think that I will probably have a good chance of winning and staying on first." Pierre tried to reassure his wife, but as is often the case with married couples—she did not listen to what he said or necessarily have faith in his efforts.

"Who will pick up the children from school? When will we ever see you? "

"I said that I am trying to fight it."

"How can they do this? You've already worked on third shift. Can't you transfer to another precinct?"

"I said—I'm trying to fight it."

Pierre kept trying to explain to his wife that he was trying to fight the decision, and his wife kept ignoring what he was saying, and continued to bombard him with questions. She could not help herself. Pierre's thoughts, and plans and reassurances really meant nothing to her mind at the moment. The only thing important to her was how she and the children would cope if this transfer went through. Pierre and his wife, Irene, had a great argument over the thing. The children were dismissed to their bedrooms. The fight escalated and turned into a yelling match. They were saying the same things over and over again to each other. Neither of them listened or absorbed the other's thoughts or feelings. Pierre wanted to slap his wife. Why would she not hear what he was saying to her? Could she not understand that he was trying his best? Pierre's wife wondered at her choice of husband. This kind of thing would not have occurred if she had married differently. And so Pierre and Irene went on and on arguing over the same question that husband and wife have argued about since the first man and woman were put on this earth

—"who was to blame?" The fight ended with Pierre storming out of the house wondering why life had to be so damn complicated.

Why things like this happen in their lives is a mystery to most men. Why anything happens the way it happens always has been a mystery. Priests, philosophers and poets throughout the ages have applied their great minds to the hardest question of them all—"why?" What is God's plan? Is there a plan? Is there a God? What is the meaning of all of the strife and pain on earth? Just when all is in order, and everything seems to be in place, our world is turned upside down, and we are caught flat footed trying to adapt. The world is not static, but is constantly changing into something different, and we cannot help but be carried along with it and become something different ourselves.

As the Catholic catechism describes: God created a world in a state of journeying, or transforming. Some parts of the world are transforming for the better, and some parts are changing for the worse. People too are going through this process. Some of us are becoming something better, and some of us are becoming something worse. This journey of "becoming" generates the presence of certain beings and the extinguishing of others, the simultaneous existence of the more perfect alongside the less perfect.

We often look at the degenerates of society—the bums, prostitutes, beggars and drug addicts—with contempt and mock or scorn them, but the reality is that each one of us could just as easily have transformed into such a state ourselves without the help of God. We might see others who are imprisoned by their addictions and attachments, and ask how we managed to go up, and how they managed to go down? Maybe things will reverse in the future. Maybe they will start going up, and we will start going down. Maybe one day we will end up in a prison of addiction, and they will look down at us. So what is there to mock? We should really pity such people, and try to help them become something better rather than pretend that we are superior to them by our very nature. The true way of viewing ourselves and others around us is to recognize the truth that all of us are constantly in a state of transforming. We develop attitudes, dispositions and habits that are either more perfect, or more imperfect. We become more virtuous or less. We become more like God, or less like Him, and who would not want to be like God? Satan tempted the first man and woman as such, "For God knows that when you eat of the fruit of the tree of knowledge your eyes will be opened, and you will be like God, knowing good and evil." And in truth, we did become in part like God knowing good and evil, but Satan lied because to really be like God involves more than this. **To be truly like God, to have a heart like God's heart, is to let yourself be nailed to a cross for the sake of another's well being. This is the purpose of our lives—to become like God in this Way. What started in Eden is not finished until we reach Calvary. This is the meaning of all the struggles and difficulties we face. This is God's plan for us. THIS IS THE MEANING OF LIFE—TO GROW A HEART LIKE GOD'S HEART, TO BE WILLING TO SUFFER FOR ANOTHER'S WELL BEING WITHOUT ANY REGARD FOR OURSELVES.**

Pierre did not return home until 5am the next morning. He had his thoughts to work out, and he had to change his sleeping habits to conform to his new hours anyhow. When he came home, his wife was asleep. Luckily, it was Sunday and she did not have work and the children did not have school. Even so, when Pierre awoke at noon, his wife and children were gone. They had left for church. Pierre looked at the clock. He had to report to work at 9:30pm. He had a little over nine hours to prepare. He felt much better after a night's rest, and the first thought that entered his mind was to reconcile with his wife. He rose out of bed, and went to shave his face, and take a shower. When he came out of the shower, his wife and children had returned. He put on his robe, and went into the kitchen. Pierre's and Irene's eyes met briefly, as he walked up to her by the kitchen sink.

"Irene." He whispered. Then he simply hugged his wife. She melted in the warmth of his embrace, and buried her face in his chest, and that was it. The fighting was over. "I promise you, I will do everything I can to stop this move. I will talk to the captain the first chance that I get." Irene nodded and smiled, and trusted her husband. She was crying and wiped the tears from her eyes. Pierre lovingly stroked her hair. He had resolved in his mind not to let his boss's stupidity come between him and his wife. His boss was the enemy, not his wife. Pierre spent the rest of the time before work, watching television, or doing yard work and going over his arguments to prepare for his talk with the captain. He almost forgot about the actual work of being on duty on the third shift until he got into his car, and headed for the station.

His plan for the third shift work that he would perform was very simple—he would take no risks. He recalled his first days out of the academy in which he worked on the third shift in the very same precinct. He had been bitten on the hand on two different occasions while arresting a suspect, and had to receive a tetanus shot, and an AIDS test each time. After the second bite, he started wearing leather gloves when he made an arrest. He had almost been stabbed once, and had been spit on more times than he could remember. Third shift work was extremely difficult, and depressing. He was dealing with the scum of the earth. The police did not call this precinct the "Drain Field" without good reason. Pierre had a family now, and was not going to take the same risks that he used to. He absolutely had to get transferred back to the first shift. He would simply not respond to any call by himself. He would always wait for a back up, and take every precaution that he could.

After he reported in to work, and almost the very second he got into his squad car and got out on the road, dispatch called to him to respond to a domestic dispute. Everything on third shift seemed to involve a domestic dispute. Pierre did not immediately respond. The first thing he did was call the next closest officer on the radio to confirm that he was responding to the call as well. They both arrived on the scene at the same time. Pierre immediately went to the trunk of his squad car, and put on his bullet proof vest, leather gloves and his pepper spray. The other officer looked at Pierre's over-reaction to a very routine call for third shift. What was this guy so afraid of? Pierre pretended not to notice the look that the other officer gave him, and they both went up to the house together.

Although he wished that it had not been so, the inside of the house was exactly what Pierre expected when he took the call. In the middle of the living room there was a large trash can overflowing with rotting garbage. The stench was so disgusting that Pierre and the other officer had to cover their noses. There was a large swarm of ants at the base of the garbage can. At first, Pierre thought that it was a pile of black clothes, but saw that it was actually ants when he took a closer look. Ripped furniture cushions, and other debris was scattered all over the floor. Two men were shouting at each other at the top of their lungs. One man was completely naked. The other man was walking around in his bikini brief underwear with no shirt or pants on at all. Small tabs of methamphetamine were on the top of a coffee table in the living room. Pierre and his fellow officer watched for about a minute as the two lovers continued to shout incoherently at each other. Pierre had difficulty understanding either of the men, who were both very high, but apparently they were arguing over the bikini underwear that the other man was wearing. Finally, Pierre and the other officer separated the two men, and about twenty minutes later were able to quiet them down, and convince the one completely naked man to put some pants on. Then, the two arguing lovers were told to shut up, and keep quiet for the rest of the night, and that if the police had to return that they would both be arrested and put in jail. There was little point in arresting either man for drug use or possession. The great disturbance that they were causing was the chief thing. As overcome by drugs as they were, the two quarreling lovers understood that if the police had to come back to this house, they would both be put in jail. This threat was enough to keep the peace for the night. This was police work on the third shift in the Drain Field. Pierre hoped that all the calls that he made were this easy. As ridiculous as the situation was, it was not violent.

Unfortunately, the next call Pierre responded to was more typical of the physical violence that occurred in the late night hours. About an hour after this first call to Pierre, dispatch sent him to respond to a stabbing in another domestic dispute. Again, Pierre called another officer to make certain that he was also responding to the incident. Luckily, when he arrived at the scene of the crime, Pierre was not alone. Three other police officers had responded. On the front porch of the house where the stabbing occurred was an extremely fat woman sitting on the front steps in her bra and underwear. She had blood on her right shoulder and was rocking back and forth and crying in pain. Her panties nearly disappeared into her flabby roles of blubber so that if you looked at her from a certain angle it appeared that she was not even wearing any panties at all. Her enormous breasts blended in with her fat rolls so well that if she had not been wearing a bra it would have been difficult to say for certain if she was a man or a woman. Pierre already had his gloves on, but made certain to make the trip to the trunk of his car to put his bullet proof vest on. This time he also pulled out his Taser weapon instead of the pepper spray. Two officers were already talking to the woman, and two others were inside the house looking for the man that had stabbed her. Pierre walked onto the front porch to listen to the interrogation of the woman, who had been caught in bed with another man by her "boyfriend." Suddenly, Pierre heard a scuffle inside the house and officers shouting "PUT IT DOWN! PUT IT DOWN!"

Pierre rushed into the house to help his fellow officers, who were confronting the boyfriend, who was the physical opposite of his obese girlfriend on the porch. His bony shoulders looked like they might pop through his skin, and his silly bird legs looked comical. He had scary

---

looking bug eyes that exaggerated the look of his drawn face with its sucked in cheeks. He had been hiding in a bedroom closet to avoid the police, and held a large butcher knife in his hand. The two officers had him cornered in the closet, but the man was not coming out without a fight. One officer had his pistol drawn, and the other officer had a Taser weapon similar to Pierre's. Immediately, the officer with the Taser weapon fired at the boyfriend, who dropped to the ground and screamed in pain as the high voltage electrical charge conducted through the two wires of the weapon electrocuted his chest and upper torso. Pierre and the two officers were soon on top of the man. They removed the knife, dragged him out of the closet, and handcuffed his hands behind his back. Pierre kept his knee on the back of the man's head. They decided to cuff the man's feet as well, and subsequently carried him like a captured animal to the back of one of the squad cars. An ambulance had arrived to attend to the wounded woman.

The whole event had consumed about four hours. There were statements to take, reports to write, and notes to copy. Four police officers and an ambulance with two paramedics were occupied for those four hours to manage the situation. The man would be appointed a lawyer, who would plea bargain with the assistant prosecutor to avoid a trial. Ultimately, the man would spend about two months in jail only to be loosed once more. It would be his third time in prison. He was not yet 40 years old. The woman was taken to the emergency room of the local hospital, and waited an hour before an intern stitched her wound. She would return to her home, and in eleven months would be pregnant with the child of the man who had just stabbed her. The whole situation was ridiculous, and this was typically how matters went in the Drain Field.

Pierre really could not understand why the state had prisons when the reality was that this entire section of the city was virtually a prison already. Wild gangs of violent young men roamed the streets without purpose and were constantly causing trouble. Simply to be a

---

young male between the ages of 16 and 30 in this section of the city was almost a guarantee that you were either on probation, wanted by the police or eventually destined for jail. The women continually gave birth to a seemingly endless supply of these young men. They raised these boys all alone, and their only relief from the dreariness of their lives was occasional drug use, and a chain of lovers, who occasionally impregnated them. The more cruel of these women went off and had an abortion—even multiple abortions. It was a polygamous society. A relatively few dominate men went from woman to woman, and took no responsibilities for the children. The women raised children by themselves or in groups, and could not manage the discipline. When these children grew up into adolescence, they were completely unmanageable because they had never known discipline, and had no respect for any kind of authority. They became street criminals, and gang members and were a constant source of chaos in the city. The stronger or more ruthless of these youths grew up, and took the place of the dominate males that conceived them, and the whole cycle started over again. The weaker of these youths, without access to women like this, simply caused trouble. If they wanted a woman, they either went to a prostitute or simply found a vulnerable woman that they could rape—the younger the better. The whole nightmarish scenario was produced by the abandonment of any commitment between one man and one woman in a stable relationship. Pierre felt that the city and the state would have been better off if they had simply built a wall around the place. It would be far more cost effective. The lawyers, and bailiffs and judges and clerks, and maintenance staff of the jails could all be dispensed with. What was the sense in hauling these people into prison for a few months every three or four years, and then letting them go? They never stopped committing crimes after their release. You might as well just build a huge wall around this section of the city, and let them do what they wanted. What was the point of maintaining the huge apparatus of a criminal justice bureaucracy that was totally overwhelmed, and ineffective?

The officials governing the affairs of state had another solution in mind for the overcrowded jails, and the heavily burdened courts that was a little more elegant if not as defeatist as a giant wall. Their solution was to offer voluntary sterilization for these women if they were of a certain age. The woman needed only to sign a consent form, and then a device would be implanted in their abdomen. The device released a hormone into the woman's body that made it impossible for her to ovulate more than one or two times a year, and was effective for 15 years with no side effects, that is except for the possibility of severe liver disease, unnatural hair and bone growth and possible ovarian cancer—other than that it was perfectly safe, and the state paid for everything. It was considered a major medical breakthrough. In fact, this measure was really available to any woman of any status. It was therefore hoped that medical science would provide the solution to a problem that the churches and the jails seemed incapable of solving. Nobody really objected as long as the measure was voluntary. And so it always goes.

> The blind man sees the devil's work
> always in this light. As long as no one's
> forced to do it, who's to say what's wrong
> or right?

Pierre only had one and a half hours left on his shift, and then he would wait for the captain to arrive, and make his case to be moved back to the first shift. He pulled up to the donut shop to visit Sasha, and hoped to avoid work for the remainder of his shift. It was still very early in the morning. Pierre saw that Sasha's car was the only one parked in front of the store. He was certain to be her first customer of the day. He parked next to her car in the lot. All the lights were on inside the donut shop, but the front door was still locked. Pierre guessed that Sasha was in the backroom still getting the store ready for business, and would come out to the front counter shortly. He went back to his car, and waited for her to come out and open the front door. After a minute or so, he saw Petya, the little Chihuahua that Sasha fed, running past the front door to the alley in the back where Sasha normally fed him. Pierre got out of his car to follow the little dog.

When Pierre found Petya in the alley, however, the back door to the shop was closed, and the little dog was barking madly at it. Pierre frowned. He knew something was wrong. He was nervous, and his heart sank. He pulled out his radio to call his dispatcher.

"Gary 25. Dispatch. Code 1." Pierre called.

"Dispatch. Acknowledged."

Pierre thought a moment as he considered Petya barking at the closed back door of the donut shop.

"Gary 25. I'm at the donut shop at 610 West exit 35. Possible 603. I'm Code 6."

"10-4."

As Petya barked, Pierre went to the back door of the shop, and tried to turn the knob, but the door was locked. He wanted to believe that nothing was wrong, but when he looked behind him at the Chihuahua that was hopping around and barking he knew that there was a problem. The dog had seen something. It did not make sense for Sasha to come out to see the little dog, and go back inside the shop without leaving him any treats. Something was wrong. Pierre half jogged, and half walked to the front of the donut shop.

"Gary 25. Code 1."

"10-4."

"10-108 at the donut shop."

"Acknowledged."

Pierre ran to his patrol car, and opened the trunk. He fumbled around inside the trunk until he found the small battering ram that he carried. As he ran over to the front door of the shop, he could still hear Petya barking from the alley. He smashed the front glass door of the shop with the battering ram, and reached inside to undo the bolt.

There was no sound inside the shop as Pierre slowly opened the door. Certainly, Sasha would have come out to the front if she had heard Pierre break the glass door open. He knew that there was definitely something wrong now. Pierre crept over the broken glass crunching it beneath his feet, and walked up to the front counter with his gun drawn. He was terrified. Sweat was dripping down his forehead, and trickling from his armpits, and he was out of breath from running. He put his free hand to his chest to feel his pounding heart, and realized that he did not have his bullet proof vest on. Why was he taking this kind of risk? He was mad at himself for not remembering to put on the vest, and badly wanted to go back to his patrol car to get it, but then he heard a noise from the back of the shop.

Pierre was stuck. He was unsure of what to do. He really wanted to go back to his car and get his bullet proof vest, but he knew that his friend, Sasha, was in some kind of immediate trouble. Pierre's mind was in two places, and it paralyzed him. Part of him wanted to preserve his own life, and the other half would rather die than to have to live with the knowledge that he ran away in fear when a friend was in deep trouble. It seemed like a no win situation.

Just then, he heard another noise from the back of the shop, and then saw a head poke out from around the corner behind the counter.

"POLICE!" he shouted.

There was a commotion from the back of the shop.

"25! CODE 30!" Pierre called on his radio, and jumped the front counter without thinking. His heart made the decision that his brain could not come to. He could not leave Sasha in danger. He had to jump that counter with or without a bullet proof vest.

Pierre heard the back door to the alley open, and little Petya's barking became louder. He made it to the back room in time to see three boys running out the back door leaving it wide open. A fourth boy was standing nearby with a gun to Sasha's head, and using her as a shield.

"LET HER GO!" Pierre shouted as he aimed his pistol at the boy.

The boy was around 15 years old. He was sweating, and was frozen with fear. He did not make a reply. His eyes darted around the room and towards the back door where his friends had run out.

"LET HER GO!" Pierre shouted again. He could hear the sirens of his back up coming.

Sasha's bruised face was covered in tears, and blood. Her mouth was covered with tape. She was naked from the waist down except for her stockings.

"LET HER GO! NOW!"

The boy was not going to move.

The sirens were in the parking lot now. Pierre felt some relief. It would be over soon.

Suddenly, Petya came running from the alley into the room and was barking insanely at the gunman in front of Pierre. In surprise, Pierre glanced down at the dog for a moment, and in that moment Pierre Bosse was shot in the chest by the boy, who dropped Sasha and ran out the back door.

Pierre Bosse, loving husband of Irene, dedicated father of John and Sarah, thirteen year veteran of the Houston police force was dead. He had taken a risk that he did not want to take, but felt that he was morally compelled to take. The world that he lived in had forced him to make a choice. He could have gone back to his car for his vest. He could have waited 30 more seconds for his back up. But his friend was in trouble, and Pierre had confronted the threat. He died giving his all for his friend's well being. He was redeemed.

Chapter Four

A long dark blue column stretched across the road from the car, and onto the grass leading up to the grave where an honor guard stood poised to fire a salute. A small group of mourners sat under a canopy that had been erected to shield them from the hot sun. A flag was draped over the coffin, and the priest read from the Bible. Tears rolled down the widow's cheek. Simon Bosse sat next to his sister-in-law and her two children in a stupor of confused anger. Had he not just spoken with his brother only a week earlier? Simon's mind flashed back to all the great times he had shared with his brother, Pierre. A wave of sadness came over him suddenly. He remembered his mother, who had died ten years earlier, and his father, who had died six years before that. Now, the last member of his immediate family was dead. He was the only one left. He would never see his wonderful brother again. He was all alone in the world with no family.

The flag was folded, and handed neatly to the widow by the Lieutenant, who knelt down beside her and offered her his prepared remarks in a half whispered voice.

"On behalf of the City of Houston, and the State of Texas please accept this flag as a token of our respect for your husband. He died in faithful service to us all, and we honor his memory."

The widow looked at the flag without expression. It changed nothing, and the words that were spoken to her were themselves empty. They were background noise, and nothing else. But then she looked up through her tears at the man speaking these words to her, and there in his face she found meaning. His face was a mask that covered a dead spirit. In a way, one could say that the widow was looking at death itself, and death had a name.

"Are you Murphy?" she whispered.

How did she know that it was him? Was it a guess? Or, had she absorbed his image from the years of talking about him with her husband?

"Yes, I'm Murphy."

"Why?" the widow squeezed as she looked into his eyes.

"I don't know." The Lieutenant answered wagging his head in mock concern, but he had misunderstood the widow. Because his soul was dead he could not understand her. The widow had meant, "Why did you put my husband in this situation? Why were you so mean?" But the Lieutenant, who could never consider the possibility of fault within himself, had understood her on a different level. He understood her to mean, "Why did it have to happen? What is the meaning of it all?" which was a question that he did not know how to answer, and really did not care about anyhow. He tried his best, however, to seem sincere, and answered, "I don't know." only because he felt that this would move the drama along like a bad actor delivering a line from rote without feeling just to keep the play moving.

The priest gave one last counsel. The bugler played taps, and as the casket was lowered into the grave, seven guns were fired in synchronicity in three successive waves. The widow rose, and bravely led her children down the dark blue column that stood at attention all the way to the road where a car was waiting.

Simon Bosse rose from his seat to follow his sister-in-law. Periodically along the way towards the car, the officers standing at attention would catch Simon's eye and nod at him to show their respect for his dead brother. There is not one state among the nations on the earth where it is ever an easy thing to kill an officer of the law, and get away with it. All governing officials recognize that these men bear the brunt of the burden of trying to keep order. Special consideration is given, therefore, when one of these men is killed in the line of duty, to finding their killer, and bringing him to justice. There is perhaps no place on earth where this is the case more so than the State of Texas. Within 30 minutes of Pierre Bosse's murder, his fellow officers had cornered his killer in an alley behind a local restaurant. There, they found him "brandishing a pistol" and he was subsequently shot dead on the spot. There would be no reading of rights, and no arrest. There would be no booking, or arraignment. There would be no need for a defense lawyer, a prosecuting attorney, witnesses, or a jury or a judge, and there would certainly be no plea bargain. This boy had killed their friend, and now he was shot dead himself. That was justice. When it came to the killing of a police officer, in Texas justice was swifter than any other state on earth. The coroner, upon examining the dead body, noted that there were over thirty bullet wounds, and could not decide which one had been the fatal shot so he picked one at random, and wrote, "gunshot to the heart" on the death certificate—there were four gunshots to the heart from which to choose...and from four different guns.

Simon Bosse went straight home after the burial of his brother, Pierre, because he did not want to talk to anyone. He hated the world, and he hated himself. He just wanted to let the anger fester inside his mind. When he arrived home, he grabbed a beer from the refrigerator and settled down in his recliner chair. Silently, he absorbed the darkness of the room and waited for something to happen, but nothing did happen. Birds chirped outside beyond the drawn blinds of the window, but Simon could not hear them. The dark thoughts of his brother's violent death drowned the birdsong. He did not think clearly enough to take more than one beer at a time out of the refrigerator. He made eight more trips before he fell asleep. When he woke up four hours later, he became anxious. He wanted to do something, anything. He just did not want to sit in the thick quiet of the dark room anymore. He moved around for about an hour without a clue, and then decided to go out for a walk. The sun was setting by this time, and outside it was a beautiful and mild evening—the kind that is perfect for a walk. The air was still and cool, and the sky was clear and full of stars. Simon walked in a rage, however. His hands were thrust deep into his pockets. His head was bowed down with his chin in his chest, and his shoulders were hunched over. He looked straight at the ground without ever bringing his eyes up to watch where he was going. He could not see how beautiful the dusk around him was— even if he had looked. Tears wanted to flow as he began to think about his brother again, but Simon held them back. Where was Pierre? Was he watching at that very moment? "Where are you Pierre?" he thought. "Oh Pierre. Why? Oh God--Pierre. Where are you Pierre? I need you. I'm the only one left. I'm the only one..." It was too much. He could not keep walking. He stopped and squatted down where he was and burst into tears. Pierre was the closest person in Simon's life. With Pierre gone, Simon's closest family left was his sister-in-law and his nephew and niece. There was an uncle who was very old, and a few cousins here and there, but he barely knew them. Simon had very few friends. He was alone, and had no loved ones, and there is nothing worse than this. "It is not good that the man should be alone." Even in Eden, without love everything else is hollow. When he went back home, Simon flopped onto his couch and eventually cried himself to sleep.

The next day, Simon went to work. He did not have to go to work; he had three days off from his employer to mourn, but he wanted to get over the grief, and he could not see how it would do him any good to mope around for three days without anything to do, but think about his dead brother. He woke up at 6:30am and drove to the airport where he worked as a ramp chief in the baggage operation. Simon enjoyed his job, and he did it well. He loved the smell of the jet fuel, and the roar of the engines. He shared camaraderie with the other ramp agents, and even the plane crews. Even during the dull routine of the day, Simon would sometimes half-salute the pilot or co-pilot of the plane that he was unloading, and they would casually half-salute back to him from inside the cockpit. Simon directed two teams of six men, and made sure that thousands of pieces of luggage were loaded onto the appropriate planes. Every few minutes when a plane landed and docked at its assigned gate, the men would unload the luggage, and read a unique tag for each bag that indicated whether the bag was a "through" bag, interline transfer bag, city bag or on-line transfer bag.

When someone arrived for a flight at the airport, a similar process took place except in reverse. The ticket agent tagged the passenger's bag, and placed it on a conveyor belt that went to the central sorting room. Workers and machines in that room read the code on the tag revealing the luggage's destination, sorted the bags, and placed them onto carts that hauled the luggage to the appropriate flight. Every few minutes another plane would dock at a gate, and the luggage would come off, get sorted and hauled to the correct place by a cart. New passengers constantly arrived at the airport, and the luggage would again be loaded, carted away and reloaded onto the plane by the ramp agents. Then the planes would be refueled, towed away, and take off. This ballet between two hundred pound men, and two hundred ton machines, and thousands of pieces of luggage went on unceasingly seven days a week. The ramp agents watched the luggage, and the ramp chief watched the ramp agents, and the planes came and went, but when something went wrong, the ramp chief made it right. It was certainly not a glamorous job, but Simon and these men who he supervised were a vital link. For years the airport had sought ways of automating the process, but could not find a reliable substitute for the ramp agents and human sorters. The process was as automated as it could be and remain reliable.

When Simon walked onto the tarmac, his friend Jerry was surprised to see him. Jerry had not been able to take off work to go to Simon's brother's funeral. He walked up to Simon, and the men embraced.

"Let's go back inside." Jerry shouted and signaled to Simon to follow him.

The two men went back inside the terminal where they could talk without shouting above the engine noise.

"I can't believe that you're here?" Jerry asked.

"I wanted to come in. I wanted to get to work."

"Dude, you should take the time off. We can manage here."

"I'm okay. I don't want to sit around. It's okay really."

"Okay." Jerry nodded and dropped the subject. He did not want to embarrass his friend.

Then he smiled, put on his ear protection, and opened the door to the tarmac where the noise of the jet engines was blasting. Simon followed him out the door wearing his own ear muffs, and waved to the other men on his shift, who also knew about Simon's brother's death. They returned a half-salute back in greeting to Simon in respect and went on with their job.

"I love it out here." Simon shouted to Jerry, who really could not hear him, but understood what Simon meant by the smile on his face. Jerry smiled and gave Simon the familiar half-salute. He was happy to see his friend in a good mood.

Unless something went wrong with a piece of luggage, Simon worked very much like a ramp agent himself. It was a physical job, but he had the body for it. Simon was a well built man like his brother, Pierre, only not as big. Simon was more athletic and not as tall. Where Pierre looked like a bulky lumberjack, Simon looked like a sleek sprinter. But he was muscular and strong, and lifting the thousands of pieces of luggage that he and his crews handled each day for seven hours was an intense workout. When a piece of luggage had a problem, it was Simon who had to find out where the bag had come from, where it was supposed to go, and how to get it there. It was an easy enough thing to accomplish when there were only one or two mistakes, but on a rare occasion mistakes could multiply, and Simon would have to scramble to fix numerous problems in a very short period of time so that none of the travelers arrived at their business trip or vacation without assurance that their "lost" luggage was being located and returned to them. Luckily, that did not happen very often, and on this day, there was only one mistake, and Simon cruised through the day. It was not until almost the very end of the shift that he had a problem.

Sometimes a piece of luggage fell apart or broke, and had to be temporarily repaired, and marked before it could go on the plane. This kind of thing happened at the very end of Simon's shift. While he was loading a bag onto a plane, the canvas caught on a piece of metal which tore a large hole in the bag exposing the clothes inside. It was an easy fix, Simon only had to tape up the hole and tag the bag with an incident report that had a telephone number on it for the owner to call and be compensated by the airline.

"Jerry!" Simon shouted and waved his arms to get his friend's attention.

Jerry, who was loading the last few pieces of luggage onto the plane, looked and saw Simon pointing at the bag. He understood and came over to Simon.

"Where's the tape!" Simon shouted.

"There's none here. But there's a roll inside."

"Come on." Simon pointed to the passenger seat on the cart hauler that he was sitting on, and Jerry joined him to get the roll of tape, and fix the bag.

Inside the terminal, Jerry found the roll of tape, and the small plastic patch that the baggage handlers used for this kind of repair and went back to where Simon was waiting on the cart hauler.

"This is an easy one."

"Yeah. Let's fix it and go get a beer."

"This chick's got some big bags, and I'm not talking about her luggage." Jerry laughed. In his curiosity, he had unzipped the bag, and taken a look inside. There he found a brazier on the top of the clothes and he held it up for Simon to see.

"Come on. Put that down, and let's get out of here." Simon smiled.

"Dude, look at the size of this thing. You could fit two small children inside this thing. What does it say?...38 D...oh man, I wonder if their real—Oh wow! Look at this!" Jerry held up some skimpy pink silk panties.

"That's nice." Simon laughed.

"And look at this!" Jerry held up a short pink see through negligee. "This woman is prepared."

"Come on. Put it away, and tape it up."

"I'd like to see the woman this belongs to." Jerry put the clothing back and taped the bag as best he could. Simon tagged it and they carted it back to the plane. It was the last bag of the day, and the new shift was already on the tarmac apron to replace them. It was time for Simon and Jerry to go have a beer. Inside the terminal there was a bar that Simon and Jerry routinely went to after work to have a few drinks. They sat down at the bar and waited for the bartender to come over to them.

"38 D! Damn! And skinny! Damn..." Jerry reminisced about the woman whose undergarments he had gone through.

"If you're a girl, and you have big boobs, and you're skinny, you're 90% of the way there." Simon remarked.

"And if you can't speak, you're 100% of the way there." Jerry replied.

The two men roared in laughter. "If I had a woman with 38 D's, I don't think that I would ever get out of bed."

"I think that you probably would have to at some point."

"No, I don't think so," Jerry said thoughtfully, "I really think that I would just stay there forever."

"Whatever. What do you want? Where's the bartender? I'm buying."

"Whoa...look at this." Jerry said as the bartender approached.

"Hi. I'm Gerry." She smiled as she placed two cocktail napkins on the bar.

"Hey, I'm Jerry too."

"Oh really?" The waitress looked at him skeptically.

"Really."

"Let me see your ID."

Jerry handed his drivers license to the bartender, who studied it for a moment.

"Well, Jerome Sra-"

"Strauser."

"Strauser." She smiled and returned the ID.

"That's what I said."

"Do you guys work here at the airport?" she asked.

"Yeah."

"Where at? I mean what do you do?"

"We're ramp agents."

"The luggage--we handle the luggage for the planes." Simon explained seeing by the bartender's expression that she did not understand.

"Well, I'm Geraldine, but I go by Gerry. And you are?" she asked Simon with a broad smile."

"I'm Simon."

"Simon? I like that." Geraldine said genuinely intrigued. She tried to hide her attraction to Simon, though. "Simon what?" she asked.

"Bosse."

"May I see your ID?"

"Are you kidding?"

"I have to see if you're old enough to drink, don't I?"

"I'm old enough." Simon said.

"Well, let me see."

Simon pulled out his wallet and handed the ID to Geraldine.

She studied it for a moment, admired the picture of Simon's plain but sturdy face, and made certain to note his date of birth, and age. "Okay. You're old enough." She smiled. "What can I get you two?"

"Two beers--whatever you have on tap." Simon ordered.

"No problem Simon." She smiled broadly looking at him as she turned to go get his order.

Jerry waited until she was out of earshot.

"That's nice."

"Yeah it is." Simon agreed.

"She doesn't have no 38 D, but I would still take it."

"Yeah."

"Definitely. Those things are no bigger than an 'A'"

Simon shook his head and laughed.

Geraldine was back with the drinks and put them on the napkins. "Here you go Simon. If you want me, just ask." She suggested flirtingly as she walked away. It was obvious that she like Simon.

"That was not subtle, dude. She wants you."

"I know."

"Well what are you going to do?"

"I don't know right now. I'll think about it. I'm not really in the mood to deal right now." Simon said looking down at his drink.

Jerry understood that Simon was referring to his brother, Pierre, and dropped the entire subject. "Let's drink."

The tiny bar was nearly empty. There were a few people in one of the booths that lined the one wall opposite the small bar where Simon and Jerry sat, but otherwise there was nobody else in the place. A small television set on the back wall was turned off. The two men drank, and laughed and talked the way two good friends do, that is, without inhibition, and without pretension or ceremony. For long moments, they would not even talk at all, but did not feel embarrassed by the silence. Jerry and Simon were best friends. They had met in the army years earlier, and had shared some wild times together. After the army, they had gone their separate ways, but had always kept in touch. A year earlier, Jerry was unemployed, and Simon offered him a job as a ramp agent on his crew. The money was not very good, but it was a steady and reliable job, and Jerry was able to work for his friend. He jumped at the opportunity and moved to Houston. Truthfully, Jerry never had been happier with a job in his entire life. Working for Simon was great. The work day passed smoothly, Simon was always happy to help and provide direction to the crew that worked for him. Jerry knew that when he went to work, his boss would be reasonable and honest with him. And they might even share a laugh. Jerry liked working for his friend; he was glad that he had taken the job even if the pay was somewhat low. In his turn, Simon was happy to be able to spend time with his old army friend again. Jerry always lightened things up. It was fun to goof around with him at work. He was more outgoing than Simon; he helped Simon meet new people. It helped that Jerry was a good worker and never complained or made trouble. Simon knew that he could depend on Jerry to help him get the job done. The two men spent a few hours drinking and joking around that night the day after Pierre's funeral. They never really talked about anything of substance. Jerry knew that his friend was hurting. He wanted to do anything that he could to make Simon forget things; and when they were ready to leave, Jerry paid the bill for his sad friend. Simon thanked him for that. They left the bar together and walked to the tram that took them to the employee parking lot

Geraldine Jankowicz watched the two men leave her lonely bar and wondered about Simon. In her mind she formed an image of him even though she had only spoken with him for a few moments. He was kind and gentle, but strong. He wasn't rich, but he had class and good manners. She loved him already didn't she? In a few years, his boss would see Simon's great virtue, and promote him to greater responsibility, and he would make more money and be happy to support her and a child. They would live in a modest home, but be secure. This was a man to get to know. She could only hope that he would come back to visit. She wanted so much to be wanted.

At the end of her shift, she drove home and thought of what she might say if Simon came to the bar again. She could not formulate the words, but only managed to think of the general idea that she wanted to communicate. That idea was simple. She was available. Then it occurred to her that perhaps he was not. She panicked a little at the idea. She wondered why she had not thought about this possibility before. Maybe that is why he practically ignored her strong hints. She had to find out and resolved to do her best to draw it out of Simon if he came back to the bar. She was a woman on the make, which is the worst kind of woman there is. Vanity and guile, presumption and willfulness would combine within her. She would make him want her even if he was not available— even if he did not want her. She drove home that night, parked her little car in its little space, walked up to her little two bedroom apartment, and tried not to make too much noise as she unlocked the door so that she would not wake up her roommate.

Chapter Five

Each one of us wears a mask, in a sense, as we go through life. We present one face to the outside world, but in our inner life we wear another. Outwardly we try to appear one way, but inwardly we are another. We are afraid of how others may react to our inward self, and we are afraid of having the truth of it exposed. A man can tell us a truth about politics or religion that is unpleasant, and we might be slightly annoyed with him, but when he tells us a truth about ourselves that is unpleasant, we are furious. He shows us in our lives how we are selfish, lazy, or foolish and we lash out at him. The truth hurts us when it exposes us for what we truly are, and rips off the outside mask that we want everyone else to see. Simon Bosse was lonely and sad and weak, but he could not stand to let anyone see him vulnerable like this, that is why he worked instead of taking his work allotted bereavement days. Inwardly, however, he was wounded. When he went home after work, he had nobody to talk to except the four walls, and they did not talk back. With all of his family gone there was nobody to visit on the weekends either. So he found himself at the same airport bar that he had been with his friend the night before, hoping to talk to the bartender, Geraldine, again. She seemed nice, and was easy to talk to, and she did have a great body. Maybe she was not so nice though? Maybe she already had a boyfriend? Could it hurt to talk? He wanted so badly to talk to someone. Talk is cheap, except when you are lonely. No, it did not hurt anything to talk. It could only do good to talk. He was confused and could not think clearly.

From the small kitchen in the back, Geraldine had seen Simon walk into the bar, and she knew immediately that he was not there just to have a drink. She smiled and quickly went to her purse that hung by her coat near the dishwashing machine and pulled out her mirror to check her hair. She had correctly anticipated that Simon may show up again and had prepared for this moment all day. She had her best perfume on. She was wearing her black spandex Capri that showed off her tight butt, and she

---

had her best earrings on. Her hair was down, and she was wearing her best lipstick, and eye shadow. "Remember to touch his arm." Her roommate had advised. The arm touch was important. She practiced her smile in the mirror. No, it was not good enough. It looked too rehearsed —too unnatural. She needed to look more relaxed. She loosened a few more buttons on her shirt and pretended like she was laughing—that looked better. This was the face she wanted Simon to see. The happy, laid back, smiling, tight body, charitable, soft hearted, playful, feminine woman. That was the image she was putting forward. She put the compact back into her purse, and went out to the bar.

"Hello Simon." Geraldine came out to the bar smiling.

"Hey."

"Where's your friend?"

"Oh, he had somewhere to go."

"Really? Where's that?"

"I'm not sure to tell you the truth. He just told me that he had somewhere to go."

"Oh, he's a man of mystery." Geraldine said sarcastically while laughing playfully. She looked up and noticed that Simon was glancing at the television screen above the bar. A football game was playing. "So who are you rooting for?" she asked.

"I really don't follow college football very much, but the Cowboys might take one of these running backs next year."

"Are they any good?" Geraldine asked.

"Well, the one guy—in the purple—makes big plays, but is not so consistent. The runner for the other team in the orange is steady but

---

does not necessarily make the big plays. So I guess it depends on what you want."

"I think that I would want the steady guy. We don't have a guy like that. Do we?" Geraldine flirted.

"No. We don't have anyone steady." Simon replied.

Like so many other things in life, they were not really talking about football, but only used it as a metaphor to talk about something else. In this case, they talked about football to find out what the other person's situation was. Now Geraldine knew that Simon was available, and he knew that she was available. They were both looking—so they said—for a "steady" relationship. This is how people talk. They talk around a subject and rarely confront it directly. The face most people wear for the outside world protects their vulnerable true inner selves and must be maintained at all costs. So they talk about other things, when in reality they are talking about something completely different. They talk about football, but they really are trying to find out if another person has a boyfriend or a girlfriend. It lets them save "face" and prevent embarrassment in case things do not work out the way they hoped they would. Inside they are lonely, and desperate. They long for true love, and companionship. They feel like they might die without it. Who can show this wounded self? Who can expose themselves to others like this and risk embarrassment? It is a side of ourselves that is not for others to see except those who we trust the most, and even then it is difficult to let our guard down and show our true self. Our public self is an invention of our pride that covers our true feelings. Only the truly humble successfully discard this imposter and admit their weakness.

"What can I get you to drink?" Geraldine asked.

"Just a beer. Whatever's on tap."

Geraldine went over to the tap and came back with Simon's drink to talk some more. They spent the night talking. Very few people came into the bar to interrupt them. Geraldine made the most of the occasion. She giggled. She smiled. She tossed her hair, and when Simon finally did say something that was remotely witty, she laughed and touched his arm. She used everything that she had to make him want her. She acted a part that was what she imagined Simon would want a woman to be. This was her face, her mask.

For his part, Simon performed the mental calculus that most men who can attract women perform. What will this involve me in? Who is this girl? Is she crazy? Where will this go? She is very well built, and I do want her—I think. No man really can foresee it all. Honest men know they are always taking a chance, but ultimately, whatever doubts Simon might have had, only one consideration really mattered: he was lonely. Combined with the fact that he was both sexually and emotionally attracted to Geraldine meant that it was inevitable that he would ask her for a date, and so he did.

Geraldine had accomplished her mission, she had made Simon want her. She accepted the date with Simon, but not necessarily for the same reasons. She did not feel a need to be with another person in the same way. She did not feel a need or desire to know them and have them get to know her. She accepted the date because she felt something that is more like the feeling of being unappreciated. She was 21 years old. She was five feet five inches tall, and weighed 105 pounds, and was in perfect shape. She could not understand why a decent man would not want to be with her. She never had been with a "decent" man, but only the kind that were using her for a night, or maybe a couple of weeks. But now she perceived that she had hooked a good one. This would be something new for her, and opened the possibility of a normal life with a house and children, which she frequently fantasized about. When Simon was ready to leave, she happily wrote down her telephone number and gave it to

Simon for him to call her. And later that night, when she returned to her apartment after work, she celebrated her victory by sharing a bottle of wine with her roommate, who was up late watching television waiting for the gossip. They toasted their glasses to Geraldine, and the arm touch. Long live the arm touch! Oh yes, touch the arm and giggle; that always works. They clinked their glasses together and took a long drink of the wine.

The next day, as they were getting ready to leave work, Simon's friend, Jerry Strauser, was talking to Simon about another girl the way one might talk about a new movie one had seen.

"What's her name?" Simon asked.

"Bre."

"Like the cheese?"

"What?" Jerry asked ignorantly.

"Cheese...There's a cheese called brie." Simon explained.

"No. I think it's short for Brianna. It doesn't matter what her name is. You should see her."

"Good?"

"It's all there, dude. It's all there. She's just--. She's built and really stupid, and horny. It's the perfect combination."

"Skinny with big boobs, and doesn't speak is the perfect combination."

"Yeah, if you plan on marrying her. I'm talking for fun." Jerry replied, but he really did not mean this. This was a front he was putting on for Simon.

"So where did you meet her?" Simon asked. "Wait—forget it. I don't want to know. Is that where you were yesterday?"

"Oh, yeah. I'm going to see her tonight; it's going to be one of those nights."

"So you're going to take a shower is what you are saying?"

"Oh, yeah."

"Good, 'cause you really stink."

"Ha ha." Jerry laughed sarcastically.

"No, I mean it. You really stink. Can't you smell it? You smell terrible."

They both laughed, and Jerry put his arm around Simon, "Listen, if it goes well I can ask her if she has a friend. I'm sure she probably does."

"Hey, I don't need your pity. I've got a date."

"Who?"

"That bartender."

"Oh, the bartender. Right...when did that happen?" Jerry asked.

"Yesterday. We're going out tonight."

"Nice, but not as nice as Bre...."

Jerry put his jacket on, and started to walk with Simon out to catch the shuttle to the employee parking lot.

"I'll catch you later." Jerry said went they arrived at the parking lot and got off the shuttle.

"Don't do anything crazy." Simon replied.

"Whatever. Don't _you_ do anything crazy."

"Okay…" Simon said smiling, and he waved goodbye to his friend and went to his car to go home and get ready for his date; this only meant that he would take a shower, brush his teeth and check his wallet to see if he had enough money.

For Geraldine, getting ready for her date with Simon meant getting her hair fixed, having her nails done, picking out an outfit, doing her makeup, practicing her laugh and smile, putting on her perfume, going over the items in her purse, looking at how her butt looked in her tight jeans in the mirror, and thinking about what they might talk about on the date. Even though they were only going to a rodeo, they might as well have been going to the opera as far as Geraldine was concerned. She did not want to blow her chance with Simon, and her preparation was much more involved.

It turned out to be a great date, and a happy time. Simon was very excited by the way Geraldine looked. She looked sexy in her tight jeans, and she smelled nice. Her long brown hair smelled nice. It was great just to be with someone else on the weekend doing something else other than watching a football game on television or getting a drink at the bar. Geraldine was happy for the attention. It felt good to have someone tell her that she looked nice. It felt good to have someone spend money on her, and give her things. It felt good just to have someone take her somewhere instead of going to the mall with her roommate to look at things that she could not afford to buy anyhow. She was out with a man, and that felt good.

They went to dinner and had a few drinks. Then they went to the rodeo and watched the cowboys ride the bulls. They had good seats and were close to the bull riders. Geraldine liked watching them. She found her attention drifting from time to time away from Simon, and towards the cowboys' butts. There was a blonde haired one falling off a bull that she thought was cute; and a muscular one with wavy dark hair, and dark eyes was petting a horse. She was mesmerized by him for a brief time. But then, she remembered who she was there with and went back to talking with Simon even though he did not have much to say. Simon liked being with someone who he could share the day with. When a bull rider fell violently, there was Geraldine to shout with. When a clown almost was gored by a bull, there was Geraldine to grab his arm. The whole experience could be shared, and that was something new for Simon. He had not felt this way for some time. He felt like he mattered, like there was a reason for him to be alive. There was this woman; she liked him. He mattered to her. He did not think that he had ever mattered to anyone. Why would he? It felt good to be needed like this for some reason.

They both had a great time with each other on the date, but for significantly different reasons. Simon was glad to be with someone else, and share some time with them. Geraldine was glad to be out of the apartment and have someone take her someplace else. Simon was happy to have Geraldine as a subject to participate in the date with him. Geraldine's joy was to have Simon as an object to have on the date. He was like a new outfit that she would try on, or a designer purse. He looked good on her arm. He was like a mirror that reflected back her own image. It was not Simon that Geraldine loved, but the sense of accomplishment that she felt. He was something to show her friends. Her feelings did not go any deeper than this. At the end of the date, he kissed her lightly. She kissed back, and the thing became much more lustful, and very exciting. They said their goodbyes, and were each very gratified.

They were still dating each other regularly a month later. By that time, they had had sex twice. Simon was very happy. After work, he

---

would go by the bar and flirt with Geraldine over a drink. They were more familiar with each other now, and would share inside jokes with one another. Simon was much more confident around Geraldine—almost cocky. He was changing in a way. He felt like nothing could hurt him, like nothing could go wrong. He put on like he was so sure of himself and often pretended—even to Geraldine—that he was in total control. He took a devil-may-care attitude. But this was a façade. He was not really this kind of man. Inside, he was really shy and unsure. He was afraid that he might lose Geraldine and very much wanted to please her. Every now and then, he would bring Geraldine some food or some little thing from an airport gift shop. Geraldine loved these little gestures, and the attention that she was getting from Simon. The other girls, who worked at the bar, would tell her how lucky she was. They all liked Simon's taut body. They gossiped about him. Geraldine would share her stories with them like she was letting them in on a little secret that only she was privileged enough to know. She had this "boyfriend" that they did not have. She loved knowing that her "man" would be stopping by to visit her in front of the other girls at the end of the day. He was her prize.

The whole thing between Geraldine and Simon was going along quite well so that one day when Jerry approached Simon with a proposal to meet one of Brianna's friends, Simon turned him down.

"Thanks, but I'll pass I think." Simon answered.

"I don't think you know what you're saying. This is a sure thing, dude." Jerry explained somewhat angrily. He did his best to describe Brianna and her friend, and he did well. They were dumb, they liked having sex. They had great bodies. They were "party" girls. What else needed to be said? He tried hard to talk some sense into Simon, but it was in vain.

"So you're going to pass this up for the bartender? I can't believe it."

"Well, I don't know." Simon said shyly. "I like her. She likes me. I don't want to ruin it."

There was a pause while Jerry stared at his friend, Simon, with a look somewhere between contempt and confusion. This was not the friend he used to know in the army. This was not the man who was his supervisor and ran the ramp crew with such confidence, and authority. Simon had changed. He was weak. He was a homebody. In reality, however, there was always a part of Simon that had been weak, and a homebody. It was only that by dating Geraldine, his guard had come down. His mask was off —at least it was off for Jerry to see. Simon did not feel bad in letting his friend see him as he really was. His feelings for Geraldine compensated for the embarrassment of looking like a fool to Jerry.

"Whatever, dude. You're missing out."

"I know, but it's okay. I'm happy."

Jerry gave Simon a strange look and dropped the subject. It was not worth pursuing.

Simon and Geraldine were still dating a month after this. They were having sex regularly at that point--nearly every time they could. A month after that, Geraldine had moved in with Simon in his trailer home. Simon completely owned his trailer home. There was no loan. There were only the utilities and taxes to pay, and this move turned out to be a very good bargain for Geraldine. Simon insisted on paying all the bills himself even though Geraldine offered to split them. Even though these bills were minimal, she felt like she was being magnanimous in this. Nevertheless, Simon refused her offer. He wanted to let Geraldine stay with him for free. It was just wonderful to have her company; so for the first time in her life, Geraldine had more spending cash than she knew what to do with, and this made her very happy. She bought clothes, and a lot of them, and was putting money away for breast enlargement surgery.

Simon was very happy too. There was someone at home with him to talk to after work, and there was something else to do instead of looking at the four walls.

Simon would come home from work on a Friday, put his beer onto the coffee table and lay on top of Geraldine, who was on the couch watching television. Soon they would be on the floor hurriedly taking each other's clothes off. They would have sex, rest briefly and then start again. Later that evening, they would go out to a nightclub with some friends, drink until they were almost drunk, return home and have sex again. The next day they would wake up around noon, watch television for a few hours, and repeat the whole scenario from the previous night. This was how Simon Bosse and his girlfriend, Geraldine Jankowicz, spent their days off. On Monday, Simon would go to work at the airport, and Geraldine would attend morning classes at the local community college. Later, she would work a few hours at the bar, and meet up with Simon after he finished shuttling the luggage. They were happy, and the whole situation was harmless—so it seemed.

In the larger view, however, the situation was not entirely harmless. True, no one outside of Simon or Geraldine was directly harmed; however, that could not really be said of Simon and Geraldine themselves. Humans cannot escape how the world around them forms their attitudes. Nor can the world at large escape how the attitudes of the people who inhabit it affect the society as a whole. When a person goes to a restaurant and the food is very bad, it affects their attitude towards that restaurant. Maybe the food is so bad that they vow never to go there again, and they tell others not to go either. If enough people have a similar experience, that restaurant will eventually go out of business, and the world will have one less restaurant. In this way, the restaurant affects our opinions, and our opinions turn right around and affect the restaurant. Our attitude is formed by the people in the world we live in and turns right back around and affects those same people. Simon and

Geraldine really were involved in a superficial relationship without any formal commitment that ultimately boiled down to using each other for pure self gratification.

Contracting the attitude that other people can be used as objects for self gratification—that other people are objects to be used and discarded when we are through with them--is like contracting a disease. This malignant attitude leads us to view others like machines that exist for our pleasure. We develop expectations of others that are not reasonable, and when they do not live up to these expectations, we become frustrated and confused. We then develop contempt for them and look for alternatives. "This machine is broken." We reason. "I push this button, but it does not do what it is supposed to do. It's supposed to give me everything I want, but it's not working. I want a new one." But people are not machines. They have their own hopes, desires and feelings. We cannot expect them to always react the way we feel that they should. Eventually, this attitude that people are things to be used will consume the person who adopts it and destroy them. Since they can only relate to other people as objects, they always end up being disappointed by other people when they fall short of expectations.

One should reasonably be able to see that when Simon and Geraldine repeatedly engaged in this kind of relationship over and over again—using each other for their own self gratification—that eventually their attitude towards each other would be to treat each other as objects to serve their own selfish desires. And when this indeed became their attitude, they would come to despise the other person when that person denied or blocked the gratification of their selfish desires. They would each become a flaming narcissist. And this is in fact exactly what happened to both Simon and Geraldine. By treating each other over and over again throughout the duration of their relationship as nothing more than objects to be used for pure pleasure—a means to an end, and not an end in and of themselves—they soon came to despise each other when the other was not compliant. And their contempt for each other eventually spilled out into contempt for other people in general.

Simon came home from work one night and wanted to have sex, but Geraldine wanted to go shopping.

"Why are you so late?" Geraldine asked.

"I'm not really late. I just got out later than usual because we were backed up."

"That makes no sense. Give me your car keys."

"What?"

"My car won't start. I don't know what's wrong with it. Give me your keys."

"Oh well. We can get it fixed." Simon said in a whisper as he came up behind Geraldine, and wrapped his arms around her.

"What are you doing?"

"I just wanted to—you know."

"No, I don't want to, not right now. I'm going to the mall to shop. Give me your keys."

"Shopping? Again?"

"Yeah, I want some new clothes. What about it?"

"I don't know. You have an awful lot of new clothes."

"It's my money!" Geraldine said sharply.

"I know. I know. I just thought that we would—"

"You think that because this is your place, and I don't pay that I can't use my own money for--."

"No, no—"

"You know I offered—"

"I just wanted to—you know—I just wanted--"

"Well, I don't want to. Not now. I'm going shopping." Geraldine said as she broke free of Simon's arms. "Just give me your keys. I've got to go. I'm picking up Cari."

Simon gave the keys to her reluctantly. "What about tomorrow?"

"I'm driving you to work, and then I'm going to come back and have mine towed to the mechanic."

"How will I get home from work?"

"Have Jerry drive you."

"I guess that makes sense."

"Of course it does you silly man." Geraldine said in the way an adult might scold a little child. And that's all Simon really was to her, a little child. In fact, he was even less than this. She gave him a small peck on the cheek, and left in a rush.

Simon flopped down on the couch in frustration, turned on the television and looked out the window to watch Geraldine drive off. Here she was in his place, eating his food and sleeping in his bed totally for free, and she couldn't spend twenty minutes with him? There was no gratitude. She just had to go shopping? He looked around at the piles of clothes that laid about the trailer home. "Like she didn't already have enough clothes?" he thought with contempt. He had forgotten how glad he was to share his place with Geraldine in the beginning. He had forgotten how lonely he was before she came into his life. Gone were the memories of coming home from work with no one to talk to, and nothing to do but stare at the wall. He did not think about how happy he was for Geraldine to have a little money by not having to pay rent. All of a sudden, in Simon's mind, Geraldine was some kind of freeloader when before he could care less that she did not pay him any money to live there, but in fact had been happy to provide for her.

Without knowing how or why, Simon and Geraldine were growing apart; they were each changing for the worse. Geraldine was using Simon, and Simon was using her. Each had become accustomed to viewing the other as a tool for some other end. And like a tool, the other person could be cast aside when they were done using them.

Chapter Six

Geraldine Jankowicz was proud of her new body and stood naked in front of the mirror admiring her newly enlarged breasts. In six months of living with Simon Bosse without any bills to pay, she had saved a significant amount of money, and had made an investment in herself; she had gone to a plastic surgeon and had her breasts enlarged. She could not take her eyes off her appearance. She had always had a good body, but had never had large breasts. She had not grown in bra size since eighth grade. Men were starting to give her new looks now. She loved it. She loved every look, and every leer from every man. She loved watching them look her up and down and knowing that they fantasized about her. She loved the power that she had over them. In truth, they had always looked at her, but never before had so many men taken so much notice. It helped that almost all her clothes were too small because she had bought them when she was much smaller herself. Every blouse or shirt was tightly fitted over her artificially enhanced chest. This gave her an excuse to go out and buy more new clothes.

To say that Simon Bosse was delighted would be an understatement. He could not believe the transformation in Geraldine's body. The surgery had renewed his lust for her, and he could hardly contain himself. He did not even think about Geraldine. He only thought about having sex with her. He fantasized about throwing her around. He almost wanted to hurt her. It would have given him so much pleasure if he could make her cry during sex; that would be the best thing that he could imagine. He smiled to himself at the thought of it. He could not believe how perfect her breasts were, and he was anxious to get back to her. He snapped at Jerry, and the other ramp agents when they got behind in their work, and it looked like he might miss a chance to have sex with Geraldine, who was waiting at the bar for him to finish his shift.

"Come on! Hurry it up dammit!" Simon shouted.

"What?" Jerry shouted back over the noise of the tarmac.

"MOVE! Get that cart over there to the belt and move it. This is the last plane of the day."

"Take it easy, dude. The conveyor only moves so fast."

"Don't get smart with me, Jerry. Just get that last cart over to the belt."

"Yes sir!" Jerry mock saluted.

"Bastard!" Simon whispered under his breath. He wanted to be done so that he could get home and be with Geraldine. He watched the last bags go onto the plane and then rushed off the ramp without even letting the ramp agents know he was leaving like he normally did.

Geraldine was sitting at the bar, waiting for Simon to show up. An off duty airline pilot, who was having a drink, mistook her for a patron. He looked her over and noticed how fantastic her body was. He sipped his Scotch, and looked again and again at Geraldine. As a pilot, he had been all over the world and was used to seeing beautiful women. Moreover, as a pilot making good money and with good looks he was used to having them. He was good looking and rich. He knew what to say to women, and he knew how to say it. And he did not waste his time. If he thought that it would go nowhere, he would leave it alone. He started a conversation with Geraldine.

"Waiting for someone?"

"What?"

"Waiting for someone?" the pilot asked her.

It was obvious that Geraldine was waiting for someone. She was standing at the bar looking out over the concourse. Periodically, she looked at her watch. But this was a way for him to start talking with her.

"Yes. I'm waiting for my boyfriend." Geraldine said, explicitly letting this pilot know that she had a boyfriend.

"Where is he? What's taking him so long?" the pilot asked sarcastically.

"I was wondering the same thing." Geraldine answered.

"He'll be along soon. It's what? Twenty after six?" The pilot said.

Geraldine looked at her watch, "It's six thirty." Then she looked up at the man, and got her first good look at him. He was everything she thought a man should be. His dark eyes and dark hair shined. His hands were strong, his face was bold. He had the kind of exotic good looks that are very rare in a man. He could have been a model. She was close enough to smell his cologne, which was wonderful. His whole presence dazzled her. She felt herself get excited just to be near him, but hid her emotions and pretended not to care much—she had a boyfriend.

Five minutes later, he caught Geraldine's eye, and spoke again, "He'll be here." He said laughingly. His eyes sparkled it seemed to Geraldine. The dimples on his face came out when he smiled. "But you should take a seat while you are waiting." He pulled out a bar stool and invited her to sit down.

If it had been any normal man, there would have been very little chance that Geraldine would have taken a seat. But this man was incredibly attractive to her, so she sat down one seat away from him. She was like a woman who might try on an expensive fur coat that belonged to someone else just to see how it looked on her. There was no harm in looking, even though you knew it was not within your reach to own. And so, she sat down and started to talk with the pilot.

"That's a nice seat."

"What's so special about it?" she asked.

"I wasn't talking about the chair." He said.

"Oh...very smooth." She half laughed happy to have the compliment.

"That's what I'm told--very smooth. I don't know how it came to be. I used to be bumpy...Very bumpy. But now I'm smooth. They call me 'Mr. Smooth' That's what I'm known as." He paused momentarily, "I used to be known as 'Mr. Bumpy.'"

Geraldine smiled and laughed to herself. His talk was cute, very cute, and she liked the attention. His looks were unbelievable.

"Well 'Mr. Smooth' I have to go now, but it was nice talking with you."

Before the conversation ever really got going, Simon showed up at the bar to take Geraldine home. He walked with his arm around her down the concourse. She could not help herself, however, and looked back towards the bar briefly. The pilot, who was sipping his drink, caught Geraldine looking back at him from the corner of his eye. He pretended not to notice her looking back—so that he would not embarrass her. He knew what he was doing. He looked down at his drink again quickly, but now he knew for certain that she was interested, and he knew that he would be back. He understood now that she worked there, and that was good. It made things easier.

Geraldine Jankowicz was 21 years old. When she had graduated high school, she had at first enrolled in college, but dropped out after only one semester. It did not suit her. She was not interested in any of her studies. The parties were great, but that was as far as her interest in college went. Her mother was sad about the matter. She had such high hopes for Geraldine. No one in their family had ever graduated from college. When Geraldine left school, she took a job at a department store. The pay was terrible, but she got great discounts on the clothes. Even so, she was not making enough money to move out and support herself; so she had to find a better job. A friend told her about the tips she might earn as a bartender, and after a few applications, Geraldine found herself working at the airport in a bar. So three years after graduating from high school, she was able to move out of her house and live on her own. The pay, as it turned out, was not as great as Geraldine had expected, and she only just paid her bills. Whatever savings she had managed to scrape together often went into repairing her car. At some point, she decided that she needed to make more money and felt that she had to go back to school so she enrolled part time at a community college. She often dreamed about having a husband and a family. The kind of house that she would live in, the neighborhood, her children, in her mind she had a sense of what they would all look like, and be like. She had an ideal of how it all should be.

The next morning, Geraldine woke up in bed next to Simon and took a good look at him while he was sleeping. He did have a great body. She looked over his hard chest and flat stomach. He was decent to her too. He did let her stay in this place for free for nearly seven months, and he never asked for money. She took a look around at the tiny trailer, though, and wondered if this was all there was to be for her. It was so small, and flimsy it seemed. Was this the future that she had dreamed of? Was Simon the kind of man she had in mind? Should there not be more? Simon was not going to go anywhere. It was foolish to think that he might. She left the bed, went over to the mirror, and looked at herself again. Maybe she should do her face next? Maybe the lips? But her body was perfect. She contemplated it for a moment, and then she

---

thought what it might be like to be with the pilot that she had met at the bar. She fantasized about it—about his strong hands cupping her waist. It would be great. It would be much different than it was with Simon. The pilot had money. He would take her places. They would go to fun parties together and vacation all over the world. It would be so glamorous. She felt like she deserved more. Her vanity--her pride--led her to this frame of mind. Pride is the father of all sins. Pride leads us to want what we do not need, and demand what is not necessarily due to us. Pride bids us to have ambition for more, when we have had enough; and pride even dares us to take from others what is rightfully theirs. Pride makes thieves and liars of us all, and Gerladine was proud. "Look at me!" she thought to herself as she stared at her breasts in the mirror. She looked back at Simon, and then back at herself, and she thought about how tiny the trailer home seemed.

The following day, Simon woke up with a renewed desire to please and serve Geraldine. He would buy her flowers, and candy and clothes, and he would take her out to nice restaurants. It seemed strange that he had never thought of doing such things earlier. He would finally get her car fixed the right way—he would find the right mechanic. He would take her out to that musical she wanted to see. Everything was new, clean, untouched, and unspoiled. He felt like he was going to start everything over again with her.

He went to work with a new sense of purpose, and hope. He apologized to Jerry for snapping at him. Of course, Jerry forgave him. Simon dreamed that he might marry Geraldine. He was seriously considering it now. She deserved a commitment; did she not? Was he not wrong for using her the way he was? She deserved more respect than what he had given her. He liked her. She liked him. They got along well. That was a foundation; was it not? He had never thought about having children before. He had never thought about being a father, but now he did, and Geraldine would be his wife. He would sell the trailer and buy a proper house. She deserved it. He had enough money. He had a steady job. This is what he wanted. She wanted it too. He knew she did. Why had he not given it serious thought before? He should tell her. In almost seven months, he had not even told her that he loved her. He was angry at himself for being such a fool. They would live in a modest house and have a family.

He left work early to go out and buy her some flowers, and some wine; Jerry covered for him on the ramp. Geraldine's schedule was different this day. She was not scheduled to go into work until late. Simon was going home early to surprise her. And he did surprise her. When Simon turned onto the street where he lived, Geraldine was standing on the curb leaning into a sleek black Mercedes and giving the driver a large and lustful kiss. When they were finished, the driver handed her an envelope, and drove away. Then, like a cat that has been caught in the garbage, Geraldine noticed Simon's car. For a moment, they both were frozen like statues, and simply stared at each other for a few seconds. It seemed much longer to both of them. Then, Simon quickly drove past her and down the street. He tossed the flowers he had bought for her out the window as he drove by. She glanced down at the flowers as Simon drove away. Her mind was dull from the shock of it all. It barely registered with her that Simon had bought these flowers for her. All she could think was "Oh well." And then she walked back towards the trailer home without a word, or a second look. It was over. She was almost glad that it happened this way. It saved her the trouble of thinking how she would tell him.

In the end, Simon and Geraldine were merely using each other like playthings. Neither one should have been surprised that the relationship ended this way. They had never really cared about each other as people—as an end and not a means to an end. In the beginning, Simon might have really liked Geraldine as a person, but he became used to treating her like a toy. For her part, Geraldine never really liked Simon at all. She only wanted a man—any man. He was something to have like a new pair of shoes. When a better pair of shoes showed up, she made an exchange. The problem, however, with exchanging people the way one might exchange a pair of shoes is that one can never really know what he is getting in the trade. What is gained, and what is lost is something that cannot be entirely foreseen.

The dance floor was a mob of bodies. Hands swayed in the air and groped below. As drunk as he was, Simon found it difficult to squeeze into a space, but he was soon dancing next to the pudgy girl. The lights flashed rapidly, red and blue, and the music's deep base vibrated his body. The swirl of hundreds of bodies created a strong heat, which was occasionally relieved by a puff of cool vapor from a smoke machine above the dance floor. The girl danced with Simon and smiled at him with glassy eyes. She was high. Soon Simon's hands were around her thick waist, then squeezing her fat butt. She twirled around, and Simon came up against her back side and started to rub her stomach, and hips. She twirled around again, and they were locked in a sloppy, clumsy and drunk kiss that went on as the music's rhythm pounded louder and louder. The vapor machine puffed a cloud that descended onto the dance floor casting the "dancers" and their "dancing" in an ambiguous gray light.

Geraldine was gone. She had been gone for a week. Simon was alone again. He did not care about women anymore. He did not care about what they thought or who they were. He was only interested in having sex with them, and with as many of them as he could. He was going to use them and throw them aside and help himself to as much fun as he could handle. He had enough money. He had a steady job. This is what he wanted. These girls wanted it too. He knew they did. On the weekend, he went to a local bar called "Hooligan's." Hooligan's was a large nightclub. It attracted a young crowd, mostly in their twenties, but here and there some old men in expensive suits sat around looking out of place except for the drink in their hands. Underage girls who mulled around trying to look like adults were equally out of place. They dressed in skin tight mini-skirts, or skin tight blue jeans with skin tight dresses and blouses. They fixed their hair into ridiculously tacky styles and wore almost clownish make-up. The bar was owned by a former airline pilot, who Simon knew from the airport, Brian O'Donnell. Before he retired from the airline, Brian got to know some of the ramp agents like Simon, who he saw on a regular basis. Brian was never condescending to Simon or the other ramp agents. He knew that in the long run snobbery was not practical. In any case, it was not in Brian's nature to act superior. He was not a serious enough of a thinker to act superior. He just wanted to have a good time. He knew Simon by name and wanted him to have a good time too. Simon came up with the pudgy girl to Brian at the bar.

"Are you enjoying yourself?" Brian shouted above the music.

"I'm having a great time." Simon replied with his arm around the girl, "How are you Brian?" he asked drunkenly.

"Good. Good. Everything's great. Have a couple of drinks on me."

Brian turned around and signaled to a waitress who was behind the bar. She handed him two beers, and he handed them to Simon.

"Hey man. Thanks. That's great."

"No problem. Enjoy yourselves." Brian said as he patted Simon on the shoulder and looked the pudgy girl over from head to toe.

"Hey, I want to give you something." Brian shouted above the noise.

"What's that?"

"I wanted to give you this." Brian O'Donnell handed Simon a flyer that advertised an anniversary party at Hooligan's

"Absolutely...I will be here." Simon replied.

"That's great. I'll see you then." Like a breeze, Brian was off shaking someone else's hand.

Simon watched his friend leave and stuffed the flyer into his back pocket, "That's a great guy." He said to the girl. She smiled dumbly.

Everybody liked Brian O'Donnell. He was six feet tall with short dark blond hair. His teeth were perfect, his jaw line was graceful, and his physique was sculptured and proportionate. Women loved his deep voice, and bright blue eyes. He was funny, intelligent, and friendly; but most importantly, he was rich. He had the notoriety of having once been a part of the space program.

Simon turned to the girl and asked her if she wanted to leave. She nodded, and they left the bar in his car a little later. She seemed unconcerned about leaving her friends behind. She only cared about letting this man have her. That is the why she had come to the bar in the first place—to let a man have her. When Simon pulled his car into the drive of his trailer home, he and the girl clumsily stumbled up the stairs to the door and went inside.

Simon's head hurt the next morning. He took his first clear look at the girl lying next to him under the blanket. He did not know if he was sad or ashamed; he only knew that he wanted to get away from the girl as quickly as possible. He purposely nudged the girl to wake her as he rose to his feet and started to get dressed.

The girl wiped her eyes and looked up at Simon, "Will you drive me home?" she asked pathetically as if she would be surprised if Simon would say yes.

"Where do you live?" he asked stoically.

Twenty minutes later, they drove to a small ranch house in a normal looking suburb and tried to make small talk on the way without admitting to each other that they did not even know each other's names.

"Well, we're here." The girl announced as if they had just landed on the moon. She waited for Simon to say something. She was sober now. Deep down she desperately wanted a man to really love her. It seemed so impossible for her to find one. She was so fat. The only way to get a man, it seemed, was to let him have her. Somehow, she hoped that maybe one of these times a man she jumped into bed with might actually want to keep her. It never happened, however. Her hopes transformed into despair, and she often took solace in smoking drugs. She lived in a fantasy world. After a short pause of silence, she pulled out a matchbook, and scribbled her name and telephone number on the inside cover, and handed it to Simon, "Here's my number."

"I'll call you." Simon said consciously not offering his own number.

"Great!" the girl said with a fake smile covering her hurt feelings. She lightly kissed him on the cheek, and departed from the car. The whole thing was very awkward.

Simon watched her walk up to the front door of the house, and then he drove away. He looked at the matchbook, "Gem Walker 579-3421 (Hooligan's)"

"Right." He scoffed as he tossed it out of the window. He knew he would never call her, and so did she.

Chapter Seven

Outside the bedroom window of Simon Bosse's trailer home, in a small bush there was a small sparrow's nest. Simon loved to watch the little birds fly here and there in the morning before he went to work. The mother sparrow sat on the eggs, while the father sparrow went about to find food as far as his little wings would take him. Every morning when Simon woke up he would look out of the window, and there would be the little father sparrow, and the little mother sparrow tending to their family.

"Time to go to work." Simon would whisper to the father sparrow.

The little sparrow would chirp and flitter off to work. The mother sparrow sat upon the eggs and kept them warm while the father sparrow was away. Simon loved to watch these little birds that could not see him through their reflection in the glass window of his trailer, which acted like a double mirror. The day the eggs hatched was such a joy for Simon. These birds were almost like his family. He gave them all names. The mother bird was simply called "Mama" and the father bird was simply called "Papa." But to the chicks, he gave particular names. There were five chicks. The largest, he called "Bubba" because he was big and fat. He hogged all the food that Papa brought. The next largest he called "Bud." There was no particular reason for calling him Bud. He just liked the name. The next two he called, "Humpty" and "Dumpty" because they were almost like twins, and he could barely tell them apart. The last, however, was a small one, and he called him "Baby" because he was so small. And Simon loved Baby the most because he had to struggle the most. Papa would bring home the food, and Bubba, Bud, and Humpty, and Dumpty would take it all, and Baby would hardly have any to eat. So Simon would go out at night and dig up some worms and cut them into pieces. Slowly, in the morning, he would open his bedroom window from the top and softly drop a few pieces of worms into the nest next to Baby, who would somehow sense that food was near and would open his beak, and Simon would drop the bits of worm into Baby's open mouth from the top of the window like it was manna from heaven. Mama was certainly nervous when Simon did this, but she never moved from the nest. The little birds grew, and Simon loved every day of watching them grow. First, they were little fuzz balls, and then they almost had real feathers. Then they did have real feathers, but they could only manage to get a few inches into the air when they flapped their inexperienced wings. But then, there came a day when they were able to fly away, and Simon watched each one of them reach that day. First, Bubba took off and flew across the street. Bud left a little while later. Then—almost at the same time—Humpty and Dumpty flew off. And finally, little Baby managed to fly to the sidewalk, and Papa went to get him and watch over him there on the pavement. With a few more tries, Baby could fly as well. Eventually, Mama and Papa abandoned the nest, and Simon was alone again.

It did not occur to Simon, but if the world of sparrows were not arranged in this way, there would be no such thing as little baby sparrows that grew into maturity, and the trailer park would be without their song. Sparrow life was simply too hard and complex to expect a weak little baby sparrow to go from an egg to a functioning adult that could gather berries and worms on its own without the nurturing of Mama and Papa. What if Papa left Mama all alone to sit on the eggs, and he never came back? Maybe she could manage for a time, and maybe even one or two chicks would make it to maturity as long as there was Simon to drop the little bits of worms from on high into the nest, but if this became the norm for all the sparrows in the trailer park, eventually there would be no sparrows that grew to maturity. Without the exclusive commitment of Mama to Papa, there was no way that each of the five little chicks would go from egg to chick to juvenile to mature adult and fly away and sing their song. The little sparrow civilization would collapse without enough newly mature sparrows to keep it going. If this is how things were among the sparrows, how much more was it among the people of the city. "Are not two sparrows sold for a penny, and yet not one of these falls to the ground without your heavenly Father's knowledge. You are worth many more sparrows. Even the hairs on your head have been counted." How much more fragile were human babies? How much more complex, and difficult was it for a little human baby to go from infant to juvenile to adult? How much more difficult for human society to go on without enough children becoming mature enough to take the place of the aging adults?

Simon was watching a documentary on television one day. It concerned the life of lions. In contrast to his little sparrow friends these animals did not choose an exclusive mate for life. Instead, the strongest male dominated the rest and kept all the females for himself. All the females—strong and weak—were his. The strongest male lions benefited the most in this arrangement. They controlled the group, and most of the females. Whatever they wanted was theirs for the taking. The weak females also benefited because they were able to mate with the strongest males, which they would not normally have access to. The stronger female lions lost somewhat in the arrangement because they did not have the dominate males exclusively, but had to share them with the weaker females. And the clear losers in this arrangement were the weaker males because the stronger males dominated, and possessed all the females. This left a group of bachelor males (usually juveniles) without a mating partner. This gang of bachelors lived on the edge of the social group and basically went around causing trouble. Occasionally, they banded together and stole a female for themselves or even took over the dominant male's harem, in which case the strongest of this band of the weakest would take over and the cycle would repeat itself. In any case, these animals lived a violent life that had little resemblance to the peaceful and civilized life of sparrows. The competition for mating was too intense and interjected itself into all aspects of their lives. Fights constantly broke out, and their existence was an incessant struggle to find their place in the pecking order. The offspring were on their own for the most part. Lions did not sing songs like sparrow's or build nests like sparrows. They mostly lay around all day and slept, fought over food that was killed by another and spent whatever time they had left on territorial disputes.

Simon did not think about how sparrows and lions were different or what it might imply for people as he watched the documentary. He did not have the mind to link these things together. He was happy that Baby had made it to adulthood, and that was as far as his thinking went. As far as his own life was concerned, he was going to have as much fun as he could, and that is why he finally agreed to go out on a double date with Jerry and his girlfriend, Brianna.

"Listen, everyone needs some variety. You know what I mean? Variety, a little spice in your life." Simon and Jerry both cracked up again at the thought of Jerry's only half serious talk. They walked out of the terminal together at the end of the workday.

"I'm in." Simon said.

And so it was agreed. Jerry would talk to his girlfriend, Brianna, about her friend, Roxanne, and see if she wanted to go on a date with Simon. Of course, the outcome was never in doubt. For this woman to refuse a date would be as probable as an ape refusing to eat a banana. It was not in her nature to refuse a date, and that weekend the two men found themselves riding together in Simon's car to pick up the two women.

Roxanne was as stupid as Brianna, and as fat. It was obvious to Simon that Jerry had exaggerated either woman's attractiveness. These were not sleek and trim girls. They both had large chests, but they were sloppy and fat. They were not ugly, but they were each very fat. When Simon made a slight remark in this regard, Jerry shot back.

"What do you want?"

"What do I want? Are you kidding? That girl weighs 200 pounds."

"So you got a little bit more to love."

"You told me—"

"Hey now—just wait a minute. Do you want to call off the date? Do you want to break that poor girl's heart? Is that what you want? Huh? Huh?"

Simon had no retort. He could not argue with Jerry over this point. With the frame of mind that he was in, Simon did not want to argue because he did not care. He had never been with a really really fat girl. Now he was going to find out what it was like. Why not?

"Okay smart guy. Let's just get this over with." Simon said.

Simon drove the car with Roxanne next to him in the front seat, and Jerry and Brianna in the back and every time he said something even remotely close to being funny, the two fat girls roared with laughter. If he said a word that sounded funny, they roared. If he gave a funny look, they roared. Simon looked at his friend, Jerry, in the rearview mirror each time they roared, and Jerry just smiled back as Brianna climbed on top of him and started to molest him in the backseat. By the time they made it to the bowling alley, Jerry was wiping lipstick off his smiling face, and tucking his shirt in.

The two couples drank beer, and bowled. Brianna and Roxanne smoked their electric cigarettes, and ate, and giggled, and ate, and smoked some more. Often, they would whisper something to each other, look at Simon and laugh at their little secret.

"What the hell are they laughing at all the time?" Simon asked Jerry.

"Who cares?" Jerry replied.

When Simon went up to bowl a frame, the two women would whoop and shout.

"Yeah, stud. Go!"

Simon bowled a strike, and Brianna and Roxanne rose from their seats, and hugged him between each other. Jerry leaned back and laughed and finished his beer.

On these kinds of dates, Simon found it hard to take things seriously. Roxanne was the type of date that Simon knew he would have on the first night. He was only interested in bedding the girl at the end of the date. Everything else was just a formality that he had to go through. Even so, he still found himself trying to find out more about Roxanne as he talked to her between frames.

Roxanne ran a child day-care of sorts out of her house. At 8:00am each morning, eleven parents each separately dropped off eleven children at Roxanne's house. She watched the children while their parents went to work. It was a relief for the parents, and it was not unusual. All over the city, women like Roxanne ran day-care out of their homes while the parents went to work.

Together with her grandmother, Roxanne fed the children, made them take a nap, and kept them occupied until their parents came to retrieve them. Each one had his own little play area, and Roxanne established who would play in what area, and with what toys. Every few minutes a child would want to play with something new, and Roxanne would shuffle them around until they were all happy. Every day at 8:00am the eleven cars would pull up in front of Roxanne's house, and drop off the children, who Roxanne would quickly sort into their play areas. Every night at 6:00pm the cars would pull up to the house again to pick up the children. Like a ballet, week in, and week out, the children came and went. Roxanne's grandmother watched the children, and the Roxanne watched her grandmother, and the parents in their cars came and went, and when something went wrong, Roxanne made it right.

She charged $50 per child per day, and demanded paper cash. The payoff came to $2,750 each week—all cash, and therefore "tax free." Roxanne never filed the forms for the state service tax, and the state had no way of enforcing it. All Roxanne had to do was keep the children occupied for about eight hours, which was not easy but she had plenty of experience. In addition to the eleven other children, Roxanne watched her two sons.

She lived with her grandmother and her own two children. None of her two older sisters, or three older brothers ever visited or even called. Roxanne herself had not seen or heard from her mother in ten years, and she never had known her father. At the age of twenty six, she was unmarried, and had virtually no friends. Her life was her day-care business—thirteen children and her grandmother. She was lonely, but for the first time in her life she was earning a good income--very good income. She did not tell Simon, but she was seriously looking at liposuction.

"Do you really like this girl?" Simon asked Jerry while Brianna and Roxanne were bowling a frame.

"It's not a question of liking her, dude."

"Can't we just take them home already?"

"What's your hurry, dude. Relax."

Simon sat back in his seat, and watched Roxanne and Brianna bowl.

"Look at them." He said with contempt.

"Hey? They're not ugly. They're just thick. What am I anyhow? Mr. Supermodel? What about you?"

"Yeah, you're right there on that one."

"Yeah. So she's a little big boned. That never hurt. We get along well enough."

Simon finished his beer, and went along on the date like a robot. Ultimately the two couples decided to go to Simon's trailer for some drinks at the end of the date. When they arrived at the trailer, Simon put on some music, and the two girls danced with each other in a mock striptease act show. They all did shots of whatever hard liquor Simon could find in his pantry. It was not long before Jerry gave Simon a look, which meant that he expected Simon to go to another room with Roxanne. At some point during their "dancing" Simon led Roxanne by the hand to the back of the trailer to his bedroom, and left Jerry and Brianna alone in the living room. Finally, Simon had his way with the girl. At the end of the date, when Jerry and Simon drove the two girls back to Brianna's house and were saying goodbye, Simon strangely found himself exchanging telephone numbers with Roxanne. After Simon and Jerry had said goodbye to the two women, as Simon was going over the whole date in his mind on the drive back home with Jerry, he suddenly realized what he had done and felt a pang of regret. Now he would be forced to talk to Roxanne again, which definitely was not part of his plans. Jerry, on the other hand, was beaming, and already talked about the next time they would take the two girls on a date. "Next time we should get them high." He advised. Simon merely nodded his head and grunted. In his mind, he had gotten as much as he wanted from this girl and saw any further contact with her as an irritating imposition upon his free time. He was already drafting plausible excuses to offer Jerry and avoid a second date.

Later in the week, Roxanne called Simon. When the telephone rang, he somehow knew who it was and was tempted to let his phone mail take the call. He had second thoughts, however, and decided to answer the telephone himself and get the whole thing over with. He was not exactly sure of what he would say to let her know that he was not interested in any more dates with her, and he did not care enough about her feelings to put any thought into it. He made up his mind to be unequivocal about it, and to make the conversation as short as possible. There was a basketball game on television that he wanted to watch, and he did not feel like spending a lot of time on the telephone with her. He picked up the telephone and winced slightly when he heard Roxanne's voice. They made small talk for a while. Simon only half listened to her as he flipped through the television channels with his remote control. Finally, he had had enough and was about to tell Roxanne that he did not want to date her anymore when the conversation took a radical turn.

Roxanne was suddenly telling Simon about all the different sexual perversions that she wanted to pursue with him. She went through a litany of explicit descriptions of what she intended to do to him, and she wanted to do them that night. As he listened intently to Roxanne's whispered voice, Simon was becoming very excited; he knew that he was definitely going to wait until after this night before dumping her. When Roxanne had finished her talk, he got her address and turned off the television. He grabbed his jacket and was quickly out the door on his way to Roxanne's house.

Roxanne's house was a small bungalow in a typical Houston neighborhood. The house was very well kept. The yellow siding, and black shutters were freshly painted. Small and neatly trimmed bushes framed the walk up to the front door that was painted red. A small white picket fence surrounded the front yard. Simon had to open a tiny gate in the fence on his way up the walk to the front door. The place looked so innocent—even quaint. Simon could not help but think about how much nicer it was than his own trailer. The driveway looked like it had been freshly paved. As Simon arrived, a car had pulled out of the driveway and was going down the street.

Simon rang the doorbell and curiously peeked into the small window at the top of the door. He craned his neck and stood on the tip of his toes to see if anyone was inside the house. A small face was peeking right back at him almost as if Simon were looking into a mirror that magically reflected a miniature version of himself.

"Get back to the living room!" a muffled voice from behind the door said sternly.

When Simon withdrew his head, the small face disappeared from the window simultaneously. Then Simon heard the sound of scurrying feet, and shortly afterwards, the door opened with a thud, and Roxanne appeared. She was short with dark black hair that was cut short like a boy's. Her skin was pale, and she wore glasses. She was fat with thick arms. Her waist was meaty. She wore a loose tube top blouse that showed off her large chest. She was not ugly. She had a full face, and a clear complexion. Her teeth were nice, and she had engaging eyes. But she was fat. There was no way to ignore her size.

"Hi!" she said with a broad smile and her eyes fixed on Simon.

"Hey, Roxy." Simon replied as he hugged her and walked inside the house. "So what's up?"

"Nothin' The last kids was just picked up."

"Yeah, I was wondering whose car that was when I pulled up."

"That was one of the last parents."

"So where are your kids and grandma?" Simon asked in a tone that indicated a slight concern that his plans might be thwarted by their presence.

Roxanne sensed his concern, and reassured him.

"They're here, but it will be alright." She said confidently, "I can occupy the kids with somethin', and my grandma is takin' a nap." Roxanne paused a moment, and a knowing smile came over her face. "There's somebody else here too."

Roxanne stepped to one side of the small foyer, and Brianna appeared from behind. She was wearing high heels, and a kind of flimsy chemise that was cut high at the bottom making her thick thighs look somewhat appealing.

"We both want you together." Roxanne said softly.

An awkward pause persisted for a few moments while the three of them stood quietly in the hallway. Simon could feel his heart pounding rapidly in his chest. He felt dizzy. He had been taken totally off guard by this proposition. He was extremely nervous and could not move. Brianna sensed Simon's feelings and took the initiative. She slowly walked up to him, gazed directly into his eyes, took his hand and led him into the first floor bedroom. Roxanne began to follow, but then, as if by some other-worldly sense, she noticed two small faces peeping around the corner of a wall. She whipped around; and the children, seeing that they had been discovered, quickly scattered.

"I'll take care of the boys. Why don't you guys wait for me in there." Roxanne said coolly trying to reassure Simon.

Brianna and Simon looked at each other for a moment as Roxanne went to attend to her two children. Then Brianna led him through the bedroom door. A large waterbed filled up much of the space, numerous downy pillows rested against the headboard, and a soft and thick blanket neatly covered the bed. A large and highly polished wooden dresser lined the wall next to the bed.

Out in the hallway, Roxanne came around the corner with her two boys and set them in front of the television in a small living room which was dominated by a large, and expensive looking black leather couch. Along the wall opposite this couch was a large flat screen television set flanked by large, but elegant looking stereo speakers. Neither of the boys could have been older than six.

Simon and Brianna heard the television come on in the other room, and Brianna took it as her cue to start taking off Simon's clothes. The sight of his muscular chest thrilled her as she unbuttoned his shirt. Her heart raced as she rubbed her hands over his smooth skin and felt the hardness of his body. Simon was frozen, unable to think clearly. He started to sweat from the armpits. He tried to reason out what was happening, but he just could not think. As if by reflex, he simply followed Brianna's lead and started to take off her clothes as well.

Roxy came into the bedroom to join them and closed the door.

Simon partially wanted to leave, but he could not find the courage. "Where did Jerry find these woman?" he thought. Even though he had done some wild things in the army, Simon felt very strange this time as if something was wrong. What was wrong with the current situation that he was in? Could there possibly be something wrong with the situation?

Roxy came from behind Simon sandwiching him between herself and Brianna. She smelled heavily of a perfume that Simon thought was awful. He did not care, though. He only wanted to take her. Simon turned around and was quickly locked with Roxanne in a kiss and fondled her. Brianna kissed Simon's neck and rubbed her hand between his thighs from behind.

Such was the activity at 25606 Sinclair Street in a cute little yellow house with a cute little red door and a cute white picket fence in a typical

---

neighborhood in Houston. A house of thirteen hundred square feet with a two car garage, and four occupants became a house for three, which in itself might be considered bad by some; however, during the heat of the adult activity, and without the adults' knowledge, two small children had become bored with their cartoons and had decided to leave the television set and find something more interesting to watch. What came natural for adults, unfortunately, was not what was natural for children. For children curiosity, imitation and learning were natural, and two little boys were peeping through a bedroom door that was cracked open, and they were learning like two little lion cubs.

Chapter Eight

Simon was sitting at the concourse bar with Jerry—not the same bar where Simon had met Geraldine though. Simon and Jerry did not go to that bar anymore. The two men were laughing and sharing a drink after work like they normally did. For long moments they sat silently drinking their beers and watching the television. Simon was thinking about Brianna and Roxanne. He was not totally certain about Jerry's feelings regarding Brianna. It was difficult to tell if he really cared about her or not. He talked so casually about her—like she meant nothing to him. This is how Jerry always talked about girls, however. Simon had known Jerry for ten years. They had both joined the army at the same time out of high school. In those ten years, Simon had seen Jerry date perhaps seven or eight girls, but they were never serious girlfriends, and they were never the kind of woman that a man would be proud to be out in public with. They were girls of convenience. They were the kind of girls who would go out with any man. Since Jerry was a man, he qualified. It occurred to Simon that these were the only type of girls that Jerry could attract. He was not a beautiful man. He was short, and stocky. He had a thick mustache that was out of proportion for his face. Even though he was only twenty-eight years old, he had significant amount of gray hair. He was not hideous. He was somewhere between homely and average looking (closer to average), but he was also poor and this magnified his homeliness like a lense—exaggerating his flaws and mitigating his strengths. Brianna was the first halfway pretty girl that Simon ever had seen Jerry with, even if she was fat. Simon did not know the exact nature of the relationship that Jerry shared with Brianna, but he wanted to find out.

"So how's it goin' man?" Simon asked.

"Things are good, Simon. I'm glad I've got this job. I'm glad I'm working for you, man. This is really working out for me."

Simon took a sip of his beer, and thought about how to maneuver the conversation towards Brianna.

"Well, it's been a little over a year, right?" he asked.

"Yeah, it's been a good year. It's been a good year." Jerry replied and took a sip of his beer.

Simon paused trying to think of what to say next. He did not want to seem too anxious to talk about Brianna. He thought that maybe if he talked about some of Jerry's other girlfriends, he might eventually be able to spin the conversation towards Brianna.

"Do you remember 'Tooth?'" he asked.

"Oh yeah...Tooth...." Jerry nodded his head as he drank his beer.

Just before Simon and Jerry had left the army together, Jerry had briefly dated a girl who he and Simon had nick-named "Tooth" because she had only about three teeth in her head.

"Maybe she got her tooth pulled." Simon scoffed.

"I know for a fact that she did."

"How's that?" Simon asked.

"Because before I dumped her, I pulled 'em myself."

"What?" Simon laughed.

"I pulled her teeth, dude." Jerry laughed. "She didn't want to pay a dentist so I did it for her."

"Really? You really pulled them?"

"I just pulled them. I got a pair of pliers and pulled them out one by one. I made her do a couple shots first so she was good and drunk, and then I just pulled them out. Those teeth weren't in there very good anyhow. It's not like I had to rip them out or nothin'. And I'll tell you what, dude, she was very grateful afterwards if you know what I mean." Jerry guzzled his beer and winked at his friend.

Simon roared with laughter. His friend could always make him laugh. He always had some story or joke or something that lightened things up. Simon was so glad he had a friend like Jerry.

"I can't believe what I'm hearing."

"Believe it, dude." Jerry laughed.

"You really pulled her teeth?"

"Sure did, dude."

"So what happened to her?" Simon asked.

"She ended up in a mental hospital."

"What? Are you serious?"

"Oh yeah. She was crazy, dude. She was a big drug addict too. But she was wild. I mean wild in bed. I'm just glad I didn't catch a disease. Hell, I'm probably lucky to still be alive after that one."

There was a pause. Simon was trying to think of a way to turn the conversation towards Brianna so he could find out about Jerry's feelings towards her. He really needed to know. Jerry could be so nonchalant about things like "Tooth." Simon hoped that he did not really care about Brianna. That way he would know that he had not totally jeopardized his relationship with his best friend. If Jerry did not really care, if Brianna was just another one of his crazy short lived girlfriends, then Simon's affair with her would not be so bad. Maybe Jerry would get somewhat annoyed or perturbed, but not really angry. Simon hoped that this would be the case; but somehow he knew that it was not, and Jerry was more serious about Brianna than he had ever been with any other woman.

"She wasn't totally nuts at first, but she did go nuts later." Jerry continued talking about Tooth. "I know they put her away. Electroshock therapy...crap like that." There was a pause. Jerry was going over his life in his mind like it was a movie. "I'm glad I met Brianna."

Finally, the conversation came around to Brianna, and Simon pounced on the subject.

"Where did you meet *her*?" Simon asked.

"The bowling alley."

"Where we went?"

"Yup. I was at the bar having a drink one night, and so was she. We talked, and I asked her out."

"Just like that?"

"Well not just like that, but that's the short version. Do you want the long version?" Jerry asked.

"No, not really."

"But I like her. She's wild in bed. I mean wild, dude. And she's really not bad looking. I know she's big...like you said. But she ain't ugly, dude. And she's pretty nice. She's the longest steady relationship I've ever had. She's the only girl I've ever had a serious conversation with. I actually bought her some jewelry a few days ago. I ain't never bought a girl jewelry before. Isn't that crazy? Me? I would never have thought that."

Simon was a little shocked. He could tell that Jerry was much more serious about this relationship than he had anticipated. Jerry spoke like a man who had larger things on his mind after the novelties of adolescence have been exhausted. It was obvious to Simon that it would crush Jerry if he ever found out about the affair. There was no way that Simon could risk that happening. He was going to cut it off with Brianna and Roxanne completely. Jerry was his best friend.

"We need to double date again. You, me, Roxanne, and Brianna." Jerry smiled.

Simon felt a lump in his throat. How could he ever take that kind of risk? He never wanted to see Roxanne or Brianna ever again. He wanted to forget that he had ever met them.

"I don't know—

"What? Are you kidding me? Why? She's too fat? What have you got going on? I don't see you with anyone."

"It's not that. I don't know. I—I..."

"Man, I set you up, and this is the thanks I get."

"No, no. I..." Simon was searching for an excuse, but he did not have one that he could relate. He turned his head to avoid Jerry's eyes, and as he did so, he noticed an off duty pilot sitting at a booth all alone having a drink. It was Geraldine's pilot. Simon's eyes became wide. He turned to Jerry with a surprised look.

"That's him." Simon said as he nudged Jerry. "That's the guy Geraldine left me for."

There was a pause, and Jerry leaned back in his bar stool so that he could see around Simon and look at the pilot "Looks like a jerk." He said as he straightened up.

"Do you think I should go talk with him?"

"That's a bad idea, dude."

Simon shook his head, "I should say something."

"I don't—I don't want to be mean or anything, dude, but Geraldine is a slut. Forget about her. That guy only did what any guy would do. You or I would have done the same thing. Don't do it, dude."

Simon sat there for a moment staring at his friend, and then looking back at the pilot. The situation was somewhat ironic. He wondered if Jerry would have said the same thing about Brianna as he did Geraldine. Would he say Brianna was a slut? Would he say that Simon had only done what any other man would have done? If only Jerry knew. Simon looked back at the pilot and felt compelled to confront him. He did not want to listen to Jerry. He had already made up his mind.

He took one last drink of his beer, put his mug down and went over to the pilot. He could feel the adrenaline in his veins, and his heart pounding rapidly as he walked up to the man. His anger was building. He was breathing rapidly, and his fists were clenched. He had no idea what he was going to say, but he briefly fantasized that the pilot would say something flippant, and then he would punch him in the face. There would be a scuffle, and Simon would grab the man, pick him up and slam him to the ground. But nothing of that sort happened. There was no good reason for it to happen.

"Hey." Simon said curtly as his hovered over the pilot, who was seated at a booth.

"Hello." The pilot said cheerfully. He looked up at Simon with gleaming eyes. He had a confidence about him that was infectious. "What is the trouble? There is nothing in life worth getting so upset about. Have a drink." His smile seemed to say.

Simon realized immediately that this pilot had no idea who Simon was, and probably would not care to learn anyhow. What was Simon going to say to such a man? What could he do? If the pilot was not completely amoral, he had at least reached a point in his immorality where concerns over right and wrong were considered a frivolous waste of time. Simon could punch this man in the face in a rage over the affair he had carried on with Geraldine, and the man would probably laugh. He had probably been punched in just such a way numerous times before. For the pilot, it was all a big joke. What satisfaction could Simon get from thrashing such a man?

"Do I know you?" the pilot asked.

"No. It's my mistake. I thought you were someone else." Simon said.

The pilot smiled that smile that said he did not mean to threaten anybody, lifted his glass to Simon and took a large gulp of his martini. Simon walked back to the bar and sat next to Jerry without a second look at the pilot. He had wanted to believe that the pilot was some malicious interloper who Simon would set straight. The reality was that the pilot was nothing more than an easy going opportunist, who had lost his sense of propriety. Between those two kinds of cads was a large enough moral gap that did not justify pounding the man into oblivion. Simon went back to the bar and finished his drink. His fists were unclenched. He breathing was relaxed. There was no fight in him anymore. The pilot had beaten him without even knowing it.

The next weekend, Simon found himself once again with Jerry on a double date with Roxanne and Brianna. They were going to the anniversary party at Hooligan's. Simon was somewhat nervous about the whole idea. He knew that to scorn a woman was to invite trouble the way a man might court disaster by poking a feral animal, and in this case, Simon had scorned two women. He had called Roxanne the night before the date and had explained in explicit language that he was not interested

---

in carrying on an affair with both her and Brianna. He wanted to preserve his friendship with Jerry and had no intention of doing anything that might jeopardize that friendship. He then called Brianna and gave her the same speech. It was difficult for him to do, but for the sake of his only true friend, he willed himself through it. Neither woman had offered any resistance, and both of them seemed to take the whole matter in stride. It was an easy "break up" of sorts—too easy. Simon was on his guard for any sign of resentment from either Roxanne or Brianna the whole night.

If Brianna or Roxanne were upset, however, they did not show it in any way. They laughed the way they always did—loudly and often. They danced with each other on the dance floor. They playfully danced with Jerry between them—which he thoroughly enjoyed. They drank. They ate. They smoked their electric cigarettes. And they never stopped talking. Simon and Jerry were able to grab a table on the mezzanine of the bar that overlooked the small dance floor where a three piece Irish band was set up playing folk songs. The two couples sat opposite from each other at the table and watched people smiling and drinking beer, and wearing green derby's that read "Hooligan's" on the front. The bar was filled with Irish music, and laughter. Occasionally, Roxanne would slyly rub the inside of Simon's thigh under the table and whisper something dirty in his ear. Simon certainly did not object, but he did not want to give Roxanne the idea that he was putty in her hands. He wanted her to know that he was serious about not wanting to hurt Jerry's feelings and would not be with both her and Brianna at the same time ever again. So he did not reciprocate the way Roxanne might have expected, but he did not reject her either.

The night was about as normal as a date could be until it was near the time when the couples were going to leave the bar. As they were drinking at their table, Simon looked out over the dance floor towards the bar, and saw the pilot, Geraldine's pilot, talking with Brian O'Donnell. At first, he was only mildly annoyed by the sight of this man. His previous encounter with the pilot at the airport taught him that the man was not as malicious as Simon had expected him to be. It was not until Simon saw Geraldine walk up to the pilot, and kiss him on the neck that Simon felt an intense repugnance towards them both. He became hot with anger, and tried not to show it, but his fury built up inside him to the point where he felt the need to get up from the table. He excused himself and headed for the bar.

"Where are you going?" Jerry asked as Simon abruptly rose from his chair.

"I'll be right back."

Simon's tone and body language made it obvious that he was upset about something. Jerry watched Simon weave his way through the dancers on the dance floor towards the bar. When he looked at O'Donnell and saw Geraldine and the pilot, Jerry immediately knew where Simon was going, but it was too late to stop him. Rather than needlessly excite Roxanne or Brianna, he simply pretended like nothing was wrong and kept and eye on his friend in case he needed to interfere.

Simon struggled through the crowd. He was driven—completely focused on Geraldine and the pilot. He had to see them face to face. It made him mad to see them laughing and joking around together. It was like they were getting away with a crime or something. He felt like he needed to let them know that they were not getting away with anything. He approached Geraldine and the pilot from behind as they were talking to Brian O'Donnell.

"Simon Bosse!" O'Donnell said smiling.

Geraldine felt her heart sink. Did O'Donnell just say, "Simon Bosse?" Somehow she could feel Simon staring at her from behind; her spine tingled. She whipped around to see her ex-boyfriend, Simon, glaring at her with a clenched mouth. He did not say a word.

"Well hey there." Geraldine's pilot said with a cheer when he recognized Simon. "We've met before—at the bar in the airport, right?"

Geraldine turned around and looked at the pilot in shock. She turned back to Simon.

"Yeah, that's where Geraldine and I met too—at a bar in the airport." Simon replied.

The pilot quickly understood who Simon was. He was a little stunned by this revelation and was at a loss for words. "Oh, I see."

"Simon, I was going to call you— Geraldine started.

"Shut up." He said sharply.

The bar owner, O'Donnell, did not like how the situation was developing. He gave a look to a bouncer who was nearby, and the man was soon at his side before events could get out of hand.

"So how do you like screwing my girlfriend?" Simon challenged Geraldine's pilot.

The pilot was too cool to react to this taunt. He had been in this situation how many times? It was almost a game for him now. He leaned back in his bar stool, rubbed his chin and stared back at Simon with contempt like a man who knows he is better than another man and is glad to have the excuse to prove it.

"It's not so bad." He replied calmly with a knowing smile.

Simon darted towards the pilot, but O'Donnell and the bouncer soon intervened before anything happened. The last thing O'Donnell wanted was a fight between jealous lovers in his bar on its special anniversary party.

"Whoa, whoa! Just a minute, Simon." O'Donnell said as he put his hand in Simon's chest. The bouncer grabbed Simon's arm, and he and O'Donnell led Simon a short distance away from the pilot and Geraldine. Simon quickly realized the futility of the matter, and offered no resistance.

"Simon, I don't know what has happened here between you two, but I can't have this in my bar." O'Donnell explained, "Do you understand me? Are you here with anybody? Who are you here with?"

Simon looked angrily at the pilot over O'Donnell's shoulder for a while and then nodded his head towards the mezzanine and indicated with his eyes toward Jerry and the two girls at the table.

"How 'bout I take care of your tab, and you and your friends leave? Okay? Just get out of here."

Simon looked down in defeat and nodded in agreement. O'Donnell gave the bouncer a look, and he let go of Simon's arm. They both watched Simon closely as he made his way back to the table on the mezzanine.

"Hey let's call it a night, huh guys?" Simon said when he returned to the table.

Jerry had watched the entire episode from his seat and quickly agreed with Simon before either of the women could object.

"Yeah, let's go, I'm done with my beer anyhow." He said.

"What about our bill?" Brianna asked.

"You guys go ahead. I'll take care of it." Jerry said.

"I already have." Simon said.

"Well, okay then. Let's get out of here." Jerry said as he pulled Brianna up off her seat by the arm. She was a little confused, but she went along with Jerry.

Roxanne—equally confused--got up also. She put her arm inside of Simon's and the four people left the bar together. The date was over. This time the two couples went their separate ways, and said their goodbyes in the parking lot. Jerry drove Brianna back home, and Simon took Roxanne back to his trailer.

By his silence and body language, Roxanne could see on the drive home that something might be wrong with Simon. A deep frustration simmered inside of him. He noticed Roxanne looking at him, and he tried to conceal his feelings from her by making small talk, but he was boiling. When they got inside his trailer, Simon kissed Roxanne deeply and roughly groped her body for a long time. He picked her up with her thick legs wrapped around him and carried her to the bedroom. Simon was a torrent of emotion. He was enraged, frustrated, and full of contempt for all women. He hated the world and himself. He worked Roxanne the way a jackhammer worked the pavement. He wanted to break her. He violently threw her on the bed, ripped her clothes off, and had her with an intense mania that went on and on like she was some kind of flimsy inanimate doll. Roxanne was taken away by Simon's mania as if by a whirlwind. She had not expected this kind of end to the date given Simon's lectures regarding her and Brianna. It was a surprise, but she was not going to complain about it. She surrendered herself to the overwhelming force of Simon's madness and loved every minute of it.

Chapter Nine

"Hey Simon! I think there's a problem." One of the ramp agents was shouting.

"What the hell!" Simon said to himself. He was still trying to solve the last two problems that he had with a bag.

Never before in his work as a ramp chief had Simon had so many various screw ups with the luggage. Normally things went quite smoothly. Perhaps he would have three or four bags a week on his ramp that somehow got lost in the shuffle. For some reason, he was now experiencing four or five bags a day that were a problem, and he could not keep up with trying to resolve each individual incident.

"What's wrong now?" he shouted to the ramp agent.

"This says it's a city bag, but look at the identification tag."

"New York City."

"Yeah man, and this plane came from LA, stopped here and is going on to New York."

"Yeah this is probably not a city bag, but there's no way to tell for certain. Go with what is on the tag and send it to the Sort Room. If no one claims it, we'll send it on to New York with the next flight."

"Okay man, you're the boss. But I'm tellin' ya it's a through-bag."

Simon knew that the agent was right, but he did not have the time to discover the exact nature of the problem with this particular bag because he was still dealing with three other problems from earlier in the day. This was the third day in a row that things had gone badly. There had to be some systematic reason why all these problems were occurring now, but Simon had no clue how to determine the cause. He decided to leave the ramp and drive one of the carts to see the super chief. The super chief was the supervisor of all the ramp chiefs at the airport. Simon almost never talked to the man, but he knew that he had to get to the bottom of the matter with the recent baggage handling problems and wanted the super chief's advice. He called on the radio to a friend and found out that the super chief, whose name was Kelly, was only a few gates away.

"Hey, Kelly." Simon called as he waved to his boss. His boss waved back as Simon pulled up the cart.

"What's up Bosse?" he yelled.

"I don't know. That's why I'm here. I'm having a hell of a time."

"With what?"

"With my ramps. I've had four incidents this morning already."

"What? How?"

"I don't know, but it makes twelve for the week."

"THAT'S RIDICULOUS!" Kelly shouted. "What the hell are you doing over there? Walkin' around with your head up your ass?"

"I—I don't know what's--That's why I came here, to ask—

"I don't want to hear it. I don't have time for this crap. Fix it. Figure it out, or I'll find someone else who will." Kelly shot back. He glared at Simon, and stormed off.

Simon had had very little contact with Kelly over the years and did not know the man very well, but it was obvious that Kelly was the kind of man who did not want to be some kind of coach at work. All he wanted were subordinates who would get the job done without bothering him even though he was the supervisor. He did not care how many of them he had to fire until he had a group that was taking care of the problems on their own. Like a doctor who treats a sick patient by simply telling him to get better, he managed affairs at work by giving orders without providing direction. If his subordinate could not figure out how to carry those orders out, he would find someone who could. Simon took the reprimand very seriously. He was very nervous now, and his mind started buzzing. He jumped back in his cart and drove back to the ramp where he was soon approached with another problem bag.

Simon now had four problem bags in front of him, and one in the Sort Room that would probably have to go on the next flight to New York, which did not occur until the next shift. He looked at the newly mis-sorted bag and read its tag. It made no sense. Simon pounded the bag in frustration. He was losing control of the ramp. He started to experience anxiety. Kelly was going to demote him, and the thought of such a thing hurt. Simon loved his job, and he was confident that he would have been promoted in a very short time if these problems had not started occurring. He looked at the four problem bags at his feet that he had sequestered from the rest of the bags on the ramp. None of the tags made any sense. He felt his best chance was to go through the contents of each bag one by one and look for a telephone number or address. Maybe there was a cell phone that he could call, and he could simply ask the passengers themselves where the hell their luggage was supposed to go. He was getting desperate. The anxiety became stronger. He felt like tears were going to well up in his eyes the more he thought about being demoted. He was losing his confidence and was starting to become paralyzed with fear. He stopped for a moment and tried to collect himself. He took a few deep breaths and ran his mind over the situation, but it was useless. He could not think rationally. All he could concentrate on was the fear of losing his job and being demoted or even fired. He looked at his watch. There were three hours to go in the shift. He muddled through the rest of the day and ended up with four bags that he did not know what to do with at the end of the shift. His relief came, and Simon left the ramp with the bags and spent the next four hours figuring out where they were supposed to go and how to get them there. He went home exhausted, flopped down on his couch and immediately fell asleep.

He dragged himself into work the next day fully expecting the chaos to continue, and it did. Simon was ready for it, however, and managed for a time to stay ahead of the problems. He made a Herculean effort to bring order from the cluster of errors, but he was so tired from the night before that he inevitably fell behind. With four hours left in his shift, he had five bags that were going to take half the night to determine where they were really meant to go.

Simon was doomed, and he knew it. There was no way that he was going to be able to take care of all these problems, determine the root cause and catch any sleep at all. He was going to have to admit that he had no control over the ramp to Kelly who would almost certainly demote him. Simon felt the tears welling up in his eyes again at this terrible thought and decided to lie down in the back of one of the carts. He lay there like a soldier resigned to defeat—waiting for the enemy to overtake his position, and take him prisoner. What did it matter anymore? All his work over the years—his spotless record—was meaningless now. There would be no appeal to the five years of perfect service that he had rendered. Kelly would put someone else in charge of his ramps and would not tolerate any argument. Simon would go back to being a ramp agent, take a cut in pay and never have a chance at a promotion again.

While Simon was staring into space and lying in the back, the cart started to move. Someone had gotten into the driver's seat and had started to drive off without seeing Simon. Simon decided to go along for the ride. There was nothing he could do at the ramp at that time anyhow. When the cart came to a stop, Simon started to get up when he noticed

Jerry getting out of the driver's seat and switching the tags on two pieces of luggage that he was preparing to load into the cart.

A shock of total disbelief rushed over Simon. There were no words to describe his mind. He was watching his best and only friend deliberately sabotage all his work and jeopardize his entire future. A surge of rage welled up inside Simon. His heart was pounding heavily, and he could feel the blood rush to his face. He wanted to tear Jerry apart. He sprang out of the back of the cart, briskly walked up to Jerry from behind and then violently kicked Jerry in his rear end as he stood over one of the bags.

"What the HELL are you doing? YOU CRAZY BASTARD! ARE YOU TRYING TO GET ME FIRED! YOU'RE SCREWING WITH MY LIFE HERE!"

"AND YOU'RE SCREWING MY GIRLFRIEND!" Jerry shouted back. He took the baggage at his feet and threw it at Simon, who managed to step aside to avoid it. The bag had broken open as Jerry threw it, and clothes spilled out over the floor.

Suddenly it all came together for Simon. It should have been obvious, but he had been unable to think before. Now he knew exactly what was happening with all the luggage. For a brief moment, he thought about denying the relationship with Brianna, but he realized that this was impossible and instead decided to confront it head on and get the whole episode over with. It would be better this way. Jerry would just have to be a man about it.

"I can't believe that that is what all this is about." He said with his hand to his forehead pretending like he thought the whole thing was not big deal, and that Jerry was blowing the matter out of proportion.

"Yeah, dude. That's what it's about. What the hell? It's not like she's a big prize. Why did you have to go and screw her?"

"She asked me, dude." Simon tried to explain.

"Don't give me that crap!"

"I swear to you!"

"YOU'RE A LIAR!"

"SHE ASKED ME!"

"ALL THREE TIMES?! ALL THREE TIMES, DUDE?!"

Simon was cornered. There was a long pause. After the first night with Roxanne and Brianna, but before he had broken off the affair with both of them, he had returned to revel two more times in their cute little yellow den. He had wanted it, and had initiated it. It was only after he had given the matter some serious thought that he came to his senses and decided to end the tryst between the three of them. He had no rebuttal to offer Jerry.

"I didn't mean— Simon started as he looked up. He could see tears in Jerry's eyes. He was wounded. "Are you crying?" Simon asked.

"Go screw yourself, dude."

"Jerry—

"SHUT UP!"

Jerry's face was red and wet with tears. He jumped into the driver's seat of the cart and drove off. Why? Why had his friend betrayed him? What did he ever do to Simon to deserve this? Why? Why? Why did Simon hurt him? He never did anything to him. He was his friend. Why was he so mean? Why had Brianna and Simon done this to him? He had lost the only woman that he had ever had any true feelings for, and his closest friend in one blow. In addition, the whole episode had sucked away all the joy out of his work. There would never be anything to look forward to when he arrived at the airport in the morning after this. There

---

would be no joking around with Simon or the other guys, no friendly half-salutes, and no after work drinks. Work was work and nothing more from that point on—just a place that supplied him with a paycheck. What was the point of making any friends when they only hurt you in the end? It was too much for Jerry to take. His hand shook on the steering wheel, and his jaw quivered as he drove away. His love had gone cold.

Simon watched Jerry head back to the ramps. What could he do? He had taken the best relationship in his life—his friendship with Jerry—and traded it in for some short thrills with two fat women he could care less about. The one and only genuine friend that he had in the entire world was gone. The full gravity of the loss, however, had not registered with him yet. He just could not absorb it all at that time. He stood there watching Jerry drive away only wondering how crazy life seemed. He turned around, bent over and started putting the clothes that lay about on the floor back into the open luggage. Things were never the same again between Simon and Jerry

It was all madness. Everything that had transpired between these people was insanity. The chaos and confusion were all caused by an obsession with sex, and the polygamous nature of the structure of relations between these men and women.

In the essay "Monogamy and Its Discontents" written by William Tucker and published in The National Review in 1993, Mr. Tucker made the amoral case for monogamy. Mr. Tucker clearly described the characteristics of a modern society that has abandoned monogamy and established polygamy as the social norm. And many of these characteristics were exhibited by Simon and Gerladine, and the others.

Geraldine thought that she was too good for Simon because she had breast surgery, and ran off with a pilot. She had thrown away any chance of having a normal life with a family and a home. Brianna had squandered the same chance for a family and a home with Jerry because she wanted to experience Simon and his athletic body. Simon had lost his best friend by betraying him for the opportunity to sleep with two women at the same time. He had almost lost his job in the process. The inability or desire to form monogamous relationships and stable families was happening all over the city. There were no sparrows singing to the dawn to thank Heaven for their happy nest and chirping families. Men and women lived like lions in a polymorphous polygamous mating dance where fights broke out constantly and territory was hotly disputed. And at the root of all this strife was the pride that drove these people to seek out the highest level of prestige they could in the pecking order. Instead of being satisfied with having what they needed, and perhaps a few things that they may have wanted and merited, their pride impelled them to grasp at more and more when they had had enough. Their pride even led them to take from others what was never theirs to begin with. So a woman would leave a decent man for one that she thought was better, or could provide her with more prestige. A man might take another man's wife or girlfriend, just because he could and wanted to. People became accustomed to treating each other as objects to be used and cast aside, and not to treating people as ends in and of themselves. There was no trust. People did not live up to their commitments, and did not keep their word. They were only interested in their immediate happiness. This most technically advanced society in history wore the mask of civilization. Outwardly, all appeared ordered and calm. Inwardly, however, the society was falling apart. The relations between people had transformed into an arrangement that could not sustain the order that had been achieved by the countless noble families of husband and wife in previous centuries. There were fewer and fewer solid families within which children were able to mature into full adults. Instead, mating groups like those of a pack of lions existed, and children were like baggage to be managed and had to fend for themselves. And if anyone were to rip the mask off of this whitewashed grave and show the world the corpse within, they would have been hunted down and jailed. They would have

---

been executed. Their dead body would be dragged through the streets. People might even shout for joy and celebrate their death by exchanging gifts. How dare that man tell us how bad our world is! How dare he speak! Kill him! Kill that self-congratulatory, self-righteous lunatic! He is stirring everything up! As the sage, Blair, once said, "In an unjust society, telling the truth is a revolutionary act" But what the sage did not say was that no society that made a mockery out of the commitment of one man to one woman in a marriage ever lasted.

Chapter Ten

Simon was drinking at Hooligan's. It was the middle of the afternoon on his day off. He had been there drinking at the bar by himself for two hours. Once again, he was all alone. His girlfriend was gone; his best friend would not speak to him, and he had hardly any family left. He simply did not know what to do with himself anymore; after three boilermakers, he did not care. Simon had become a regular at Hooligan's and was spending much of his spare time, and money there.

Periodically, he would start to think about the decisions that he had made, and where he might have gone wrong. He even sometimes considered trying to patch things up with Geraldine or Jerry, but the futility of it all was obvious, and he quickly rejected those thoughts and retreated into alcohol. There was no point in trying to break down the past. It was much easier, and it felt much better to lose himself in his whiskey and beer. He did not watch the television above the bar. He did not try to make small talk with the bartender. The bartender did not want to talk to him anyhow. Simon quietly drank boilermaker after boilermaker by himself in the bar two or three times a week. He would walk in, and the bartender would recognize him and have the drink ready to go almost before Simon could even situate himself in the bar stool. It would have been just as easy for Simon to do his drinking in his trailer home, but in his mixed up mind, going to Hooligan's somehow made him feel like he was doing something—like he was not just wasting away in his trailer. Simon did not ever give thought to the other people at the bar, but he was not the only regular. Here and there others who found a drink to be the best company they could find lumbered in and took their seat. Some talked, and some did not say a word; words were meaningless anyhow. All that mattered to them was the sweet, sweet numbness of alcohol that curtained over the mind and its bad memories and made heartbreaks a distant dream. They lived in a world of their own. Outside the sky was beautiful, the sun was shining bright, and a cool breeze was

---

constant, but they sat in a bar for hours and hours feeding their sorrow with alcohol—prisoners of their self pity and oblivious to the felicity of life that was theirs for the taking if only they could look outside themselves.

Perhaps if Simon had cared, he might have noticed that very often while he was drinking at Hooligan's a very stunning woman was also a regular visitor. And if he had remained even a little sober, he might have noticed that she noticed him. She noticed his muscular back and shoulders. She noticed how thin his waist was, and how well developed his arms were. And she noticed that he was there quite often and was drinking alone without talking to anyone. In this ridiculous world, this very beautiful woman sat all alone in her booth with her drink watching Simon drink and wondered who he was, and where he came from. How old was he? How much money did he make? Then, she came to her senses and realized that it did not matter. It did not matter how old he was or what he did for a living. It did not matter what his name was or if he had a wife or was single. His hopes, and cares, and thoughts—his person—did not matter. He had a strong back that showed through his shirt, thick thighs, and strong arms. She could see that he worked with his body. She wondered how those muscular arms and powerful back felt. She wanted to lose herself to them. That's all that mattered.

She rose from her booth and walked passed Simon at the bar on her way to the ladies room in order to get a better look at him. She walked like a dancer with her back stiff but graceful, and her shoulders were pinned back. She was small, but her body was somewhat of an archetype of womanhood. She had long graceful arms and legs and long silky brown hair. Her chest was luscious and full. Everyone watched her get up from the booth, and a little while later everyone watched her come out of the ladies room and return to her seat. They all could smell her wonderful perfume as she walked by. She smiled back at them—especially Simon-- and sat back in her booth. She hoped that Simon would come over to her and ask if he could join her. After a few minutes, it was obvious; however,

---

that Simon would never leave his bar stool, which slightly annoyed her. Did she not smile at him and look at him directly? Did she not make it obvious to him that she wanted him to come over to her? In a way, she understood that Simon was in some kind of funk, however, and excused him of slighting her. Besides, she knew that she possessed the kind of body and looks that no reasonable man would resist, and so with a rare confidence among women, she walked up to Simon and took the direct approach. She paid her bill, picked up her purse and went over to Simon.

"Hi. I'm Jenna." She said as she held out her hand to shake Simon's.

Simon paused, looked at her and then at her hand in disbelief.

"I'm Simon." He said as he shook her hand.

"Simon," she smiled, "some friends of mine are throwing a big party next weekend. You look like a nice guy, and I wanted to invite you." Jenna took out an invitation from her purse and handed it to Simon. "Do you think that you would come?"

Simon was stunned. Nothing like this had ever happened to him before. He was like a man who had hunted big game all his life only to catch little rabbits here and there, and then finally at the end, when he had given up hunting altogether, a wild tiger comes up to him and lays down in front of him.

Simon looked at the invitation dumbly and then looked up at Jenna. He did not know what to say. What was there to say? The woman inviting him to this party was petite and probably weighed no more than 105lbs. She might have passed for a child if it were not for her exotic good looks. Her long brown hair cascaded over the spaghetti straps of her light yellow spring dress that showed off her curvy form and tanned skin. She looked at him with her deep, brown, hopeful eyes, and waited.

"Yeah. Sure. I think I'll be there." Simon was so drunk that he appeared very calm even though he was quite shocked.

"That's great. I will see you there. I'm sure that you'll have a good time."

Then, as suddenly as she had approached Simon, Jenna was out the door. Her perfume lingered in the air to remind Simon, and the others at the bar that what they had all witnessed had not been a dream.

"I can't believe what I just saw." The bartender said as he walked up to Simon to shake his hand and congratulate him.

Simon gave him a confused look and then looked towards the door where Jenna had left. "Yeah, I don't know."

"You're going to go, aren't you? You have to go." The bartender said somewhat exasperated at Simon's lack of enthusiasm.

"Yeah." Simon sighed. "Could you pour me another drink?"

"Sure thing, buddy." The bartender said with an annoyed look on his face. It was as if Simon had been handed a million dollars and was not sure if he would take it. It was insanity. The bartender came back with an angry frown on his face and put the boilermaker in front of Simon. "Here you go." He said wagging his head in disgusted disbelief at Simon's behavior.

Simon paused for a moment considering the party invitation in his hands. His cloudy mind could not comprehend it. What was it all about? Who was this woman? Why did she invite me? And then he realized that it did not matter. It did not matter who she was or what she wanted. Her motives, her cares, and her person did not matter. He gulped down his whiskey, chased it with his beer and put the invitation in his back pocket.

The next weekend, Simon drove south down Highway I-45 to the San Luis Pass Road and traveled west until he came to where the Blue Water Highway ends at Surf Side beach. It took him two and a half hours to get there. He was cleaned up and was wearing his good cologne. He had a difficult time finding the private road even with the map that he periodically checked on his cell phone. When he finally arrived around 3pm, a security guard stopped him at the corner intersection and asked for his invitation. Simon handed it to the guard through the open driver side window. The guard waved an ultraviolet light over the invitation, handed it back to Simon and directed him to the valets about 100 yards ahead. Simon left his car with the valet and walked the rest of the way up the private drive to the large beach house. He was not on the grounds of the party more than a minute before someone had put a beer in his hand. He stood by himself sucking the drink down and tried to take in the setting before him.

A band played on an intricate wooden deck overlooking a dance floor on the terraced back lawn that led down to a private beach. The band's music played through speakers located all over the grounds and inside the house so that no matter where a guest might situate himself, he could enjoy the music. Waitresses, bartenders, valets, kitchen help, and security personnel buzzed about trying to keep up with their work. Drinks were in everyone's hands. Shrimp, steak, lobster tails, and desserts of every kind were set up on a long buffet table underneath a large tent where there were tables with chairs, dinner ware and glasses. It was still early on in the party, and perhaps only half the guests had arrived. Even so, there were nearly 150 people meandering about. On the private beach, young and beautiful men and women with hard bodies played volleyball. Young tan boys and older gray men reclined in lounge furniture and oiled each other's bare backs in the hot sun.

Simon went over to the tent where the buffet was set up. He had eaten a hamburger on the drive to the party, but realized that it would be a long time before he would have a chance to eat this kind of food again; so he decided to take advantage of the situation, and made his way through the buffet line and the sumptuous assortment of food. There was so much food to choose from. Simon would have liked to sample everything and wished that he was hungrier. He went for the most expensive food he could find and ended up having a lobster tail, a cut of filet mignon, and an imported beer. He went back for key lime pie, and vanilla ice cream with pistachio nuts, and another bottle of beer. He sat alone at his table and took his time eating as he watched more guests arrive. A group of party goers was one table over. They were smoking marijuana and laughing at Simon and everyone else who happened to pass by. Annoyed and feeling a little out of place, Simon moved to another table out of their sight so that he could eat his key lime pie in peace.

As he sat eating his dessert, he started to wonder how he would find Jenna in this crowd and what he would say or do once he found her. It was obvious that she was interested in him, but he had no idea how the whole matter would play out. Perhaps he would not meet up with her at all? He suddenly realized that he really did not care one way or the other. As beautiful as Jenna was, she was just some chance encounter. He had no expectations. He was not even sure why he had come to the party at all. Even with such beautiful surroundings, and great food, he would have been satisfied with sitting in his trailer drinking and watching television. He sat at his table for some time staring blankly at the guests in the buffet line and drinking beer after beer.

Simon was stuffed with food and drink, and about an hour later he decided to take a walk around the property to see what there was to see. He got up from his table and went inside the house to take a look around. The house, and its furnishings were unremarkable except for their expense. There was a certain tackiness about the place that indicated an immaturity in its owner. Weird artwork covered the walls. The facade

---

facing the beach was a glass window from end to end. A balcony overlooked the living room. With its high ceiling, and metallic, and oddly shaped furniture that was set out in front of the fireplace, the living room contrasted sharply with the beach front view. The theme of glass and metal carried over to the kitchen that also faced the beach. Bright red stools faced a small bar in the kitchen, and an asymmetrical kitchen table was situated in the corner with strange looking chairs set around it. A sliding glass door opened onto the wooden deck where the band played above the dance floor on the lawn. Simon thought about taking a look through the rest of the house, but the main hallway that connected the front of the house to the back was blocked off by a folding divider with a "do not enter" sign taped to it. Only the living room and the kitchen were available to the guests. Simon had seen all that there was to see here, so he decided to take a look at the beach. One of the ubiquitous waitresses with a tray of drinks was meandering by Simon. Simon grabbed a beer from her and left the house for the beach.

The sun danced on the horizon coloring the sky with soft purple and gold and was sinking into the sea quickly. A cool breeze wafted over the sand. The volley ball players had quit their game and had left, but numerous couples sifted about the small beach and huddled close to each other or held hands as they watched the sun set. The constant swish of the gentle surf washed over their talk, but every now and then Simon would hear the giggling of a girl above the sound of the waves and was reminded that he was alone. He suddenly felt uncomfortable and wondered why he had come in the first place. He turned around and headed up the wooden stairs that led back up to the house. Almost as soon as he had reached the top of the stairs where they opened onto the back lawn, another waitress was stumbling in front of him carrying her tray and a bottle of champagne.

"Would you like a drink?" she slurred as she met Simon face to face. She was very drunk.

Simon was slightly startled. He looked down at the short and plump waitress, but did not say anything.

"Would you like a drink?" she asked again. "I have this bottle of champagne."

She lifted the bottle and showed it to Simon like it was a trophy or something.

Simon paused a moment, and stared at her—sizing her up. She had a halfway decent body, he thought. This waitress was what he needed. This was all he cared about right now. The waitress smiled at him with foggy eyes.

"Only if you have some with me." Simon answered slyly.

The waitress laughed, "I'm not really allowed. I don't think."

"I won't tell anybody."

The waitress looked around and smiled even wider. She tried to look innocent as she took a gulp of the champagne directly from the bottle.

"Let's go drink some more of this." Simon said. He was going to take advantage of this waitress.

"Okay."

Just as he was about to take the waitress by the hand and lead her away, two men came walking up to Simon, and the girl. One of the men was very short and stocky. The other man was more normal in size, but the pock marks in his face were visible even in the dim twilight.

"Where are you going?" The short and stocky man asked as he walked up to the waitress, "You almost got away from us." He grabbed the waitress's hand and pulled her away from Simon.

"Soorrry." She giggled.

"We'll take care of her from here." The stocky man said sternly to Simon.

Evidently these men had gotten the waitress drunk and had their own plans for her. Simon was angry. He wanted the girl. She was his. He had found her. He was not, however, going to fight these two men for her. The man with the pocked marked face stared at Simon threateningly with his teeth clenched. The other stocky man looked at Simon with challenging eyes that dared Simon to object, and Simon was most certainly not going to object. The stocky man half carried and half led the girl to the dance floor. The man with the pock marked face followed behind and occasionally looked back at Simon with an angry stare intending to ward Simon off. Simon followed them from a distance despite the stare of the man with the pock marked face. Simon stopped at the edge of the dance floor to watch what would happen.

The sky was dark now, and the party was in high gear as the two men and the waitress squeezed into a space in the middle of the mass of dancers. The men almost immediately had the waitress sandwiched between themselves and were groping her entire body. She gave in to her lust and was carried away by a wave of drunken ecstasy. Simon stared at the "dancers" and watched with a blank look on his face. Interiorly, he regretted an opportunity that was lost, and he gradually moved away from the dance floor and went back towards the beach to look at the rising full moon that was orange on the horizon.

There were nearly 300 people at the party now, and Simon did not know any of them. He wondered who they were. He wondered whose house this was, and why they were throwing the party. The invitation did not indicate any of these things. These thoughts ran away from his mind, however, as he looked at the spectacular moon rising out of the water. It was gigantic, and seemed so close. As it rose higher it became yellow, and smaller. A lone sailboat in the distance cast a silhouette against the brightness of the moon. It looked like a postcard. Simon stared at the beauty for a moment, but his warped mind could not really enjoy it. He was like a woman obsessed with some blemish on her face as she looked in the mirror. He could not appreciate the fantastic beauty of it all, but was so absorbed in his own frustration and self pity that he only focused on his misery and wanted to leave. He took a last swig of his beer and threw the half empty bottle on the grass and decided to leave.

"We're going there." A voice from behind Simon said.

Simon turned around to see Jenna standing in front of him. He was dazed.

Jenna was stunning. She was wearing a little slinky black party blouse with a low neckline, and a skirt at mid-thigh showing off her graceful and muscular legs. Her long brown hair was combed straight back over her shoulders and looked wet.

"I...I'm--."

"Wondering where I was?" Jenna interrupted.

"Yeah...I'm a little surprised. You caught me off guard."

"Of course."

"Have you been here long?" Simon asked.

"Long enough. That waitress slipped away from you, huh?"

It was the kind of bold statement people sometimes make when they want to test the other person to see how they will react. It comes from experience with the darker side of people. Jenna openly stated that she had seen Simon try to take advantage of the waitress. By doing so, she wanted to put Simon on notice that he should not think that he would be able to play her like that.

Simon did not know what to say to this. At first he was unsure of Jenna's meaning. Then he understood completely, and he felt strange. He had never had a woman speak to him like this.

"What? Well, we only talked a little. She—were you watching?"

Jenna ignored Simon's question. She could see that he was nervous about being exposed as a cad.

"It's wonderful. Isn't it? The moon?" she asked.

"Oh yeah." Simon answered without even listening to the question. He was becoming excited just by looking and talking with Jenna.

"We're going there—"

"The moon?...Right, that's right...No...wait....I thought Mars?" Simon asked.

"But first we have to go to the moon."

"No, I don't think that's right." Simon said.

"To build a base?"

"No, I think you mean the space station. They're going to go to the space station first."

"And then we can go to Mars?" Jenna asked.

"Right."

"Not the moon."

"We've already been there." Simon said.

"Have we?"

"Oh, you're not one of those people, are you? The ones who think the government faked going there?"

Jenna smiled, "No, I'm not, I just wanted to see what you would say. But the pictures only show what it looked like. They can't tell you what it felt like."

"Oh, yeah. I guess you're right."

Simon felt uncomfortable around Jenna. He could sense her self confidence, and strong personality. He wished that he had something to say to her, but he could not think of anything. All he could think about was how beautiful she was and wonder why she was interested in him.

Jenna sensed Simon's unease. She wanted to stay in command of the situation, but at the same time she did not want to scare Simon away. She decided to soften her tone.

"Are you enjoying the party?"

"It's great. Great food. It's a great place."

"I like it too."

"Whose place is it?" Simon asked, "It didn't say on the invitation. What's the party for?"

"It's just a party for the hell of it I guess." Jenna said ignoring the first question.

"But whose place is this?"

"I think some lawyer, or something."

"Do you know him?"

"Not really. Do you want to go down to the beach?" Jenna asked in order to change the subject.

"Yeah. Sure."

Jenna put her arm inside Simon's, and they walked together down the wooden steps to the beach below. Simon felt privileged to have this woman on his arm. It almost felt unreal like a dream, like it was happening to someone else, and he was only watching it as a spectator. When they came to the bottom of the stairs, Jenna took off her high heels, and carried them with her as they strolled together along the beach.

"I love it out here." Jenna said as a breeze came up.

"Have you been here before?"

"I mean here near the ocean...in general..." Jenna said quickly.

"It is great." Simon said.

The two stood there without speaking as they admired the moon which was a bright white, and much higher in the sky. The air was cool, and a soft and steady breeze came over the waves. Jenna had her left arm inside of Simon's right arm. With her other hand she was holding her sandals by the strap and grabbing Simon's strong bicep. It was funny that she should be down on the beach like this with him. She had barely known him more than ten minutes, but she felt safe with Simon. He did not seem like a threat to her. He seemed content just to be around her watching the moon, which was reassuring to her. He did not try to control her. He was not pretentious or bossy, and his body was incredible. She could feel his strength next to her. He was not very cute.

In fact, he was plain looking. But he was very athletic. She pictured him as a construction worker or a landscaper.

"So where do you work, Simon?" she found herself asking. It felt strange to Jenna to hear these words come out of her mouth. "Why do I care where he works?" she thought. But for some reason, she did care and wanted to know.

"I work at the airport. I load the luggage onto the planes." Simon said this without any thought of how it might sound to Jenna. It never occurred to him that his humble occupation might chase away such a beautiful woman, who could obviously find a more prosperous man.

For Jenna, it was refreshing to hear Simon talk about his simple job without embarrassment. She listened to him describe how the men loaded the bags onto the planes, and how the luggage tags indicated exactly what to do with a particular bag or how the pilots saluted him. He seemed genuinely content with his job, and comfortable with himself. He did not have anything to prove to her. She liked that about him and rested her head against his shoulder.

Simon was thrilled to be with Jenna. He could not understand what she saw in him, but he did not care. He was there with this gorgeous woman and was looking at the moon on a private beach. He could smell the scented oils in her hair that made it look wet, and he could feel her soft and smooth arms and delicate and tiny hands. Her warm body next to him was comforting.

They stood there arm in arm watching the waves, and the moon for some time before Jenna finally decided to kiss Simon. She looked up at him, their eyes met, and she leaned in to kiss him. And then they were quiet again and huddled close to each other listening to the waves. They were like two wooden beams leaning on each other for support. If one were missing the other would fall down. Where only a few days earlier,

---

Simon had felt like all he wanted to do was drink; he all of a sudden felt contented. And where Jenna had only wanted to use Simon's body when she first had seen him at Hooligans; now she felt like she had found a true companion. How much of those feelings were real, and how much of those feelings were fantasy neither Simon or Jenna really knew themselves. Their self absorption was such that various emotions and moods came over them and went away like the waves they watched coming over the beach.

They spent the rest of the party sipping wine and people watching. Jenna thought about introducing Simon to her friends, but then backed away from the idea. She kept him sequestered to herself the entire evening. At the end of the night, when most of the guests had left and it was time to say goodbye, Simon put his hands around Jenna's waist and kissed her softly. He was in awe of her in a way; he would have liked to have spent the night with her, but he did not dare ask. He knew so little about her. They had spent five hours together at the party, but he still did not even know her last name. They walked together to the front of the house where the valets were posted to take the guests' cars. Simon gave one of the attendants his ticket and then pulled Jenna towards himself.

"When can I see you again?" he whispered into her ear.

"Give me your cell."

Simon reached into his pocket and pulled out his cell phone. Jenna turned it on, typed in her telephone number and name in the address book and gave the telephone back to Simon.

"You can reach me at that number."

She then stood on the tips of her toes and lightly kissed Simon on the cheek. Then she slowly walked away towards the house looking back once or twice at Simon with a smile on her face. Simon smiled back and watched her walk all the way up the drive until she disappeared around the corner of the house. He took out his cell phone. He smiled when he looked at the number and was totally lost in thought about Jenna.

"Sir, your car." The valet called.

"Oh yeah. Thanks." Simon got into his car, and drove home full of anticipation for his next date with Jenna.

Chapter Eleven

Simon Bosse had called Jenna the day after the party and had arranged a date with her for the following Friday at a downtown bar in the America Center. Simon had suggested picking Jenna up at her home or meeting at Hooligan's, but Jenna insisted on meeting at this bar in the America Center. For a week, Simon could not stop thinking about the date. He thought about what he would say and practiced telling a few jokes that he thought were clean enough to tell on a first date. He hardly knew her, but he got the impression that she was very touchy. He did not want to do or say anything that might jeopardize the chances of bedding her.

Jenna was so beautiful. He wanted badly to impress her. But why should he have cared so much? He did not know. There were plenty of girls that he could have, but Jenna was different. She had a charisma about her. He was drawn to her the way a man might be drawn to a celebrity of some sort. He wanted to be seen with her. Simon had stopped drinking any alcohol, and he had started working out every day lifting heavy weights for two hours or so. He put himself on a near starvation diet. In only a few days he had lost ten pounds off his belly. He felt tight. Simon wanted very much to look his best for that date. He bleached his teeth and got a haircut. He plucked out misplaced hairs off his body. He did sit ups every day until he was exhausted. The end of the work week and his date with Jenna was like an impossible dream. Simon felt like it would never come. Every work day was an agony and dragged on and on. Jerry was still not speaking to him, but Simon hardly cared anymore. He just wanted Friday to arrive so that he could meet Jenna. He was so focused on her. Every time there was a problem or mishap at work, Simon became furious and yelled at the ramp agents underneath him. He was crazed and did not tolerate any mistakes that might keep him at the airport past his shift, and away from the gym. The ramp agents were starting to hate him even as the mistakes were becoming fewer.

On Friday, the workday went very smoothly. Simon kept looking at his wristwatch and noting how much time he had left in the work shift until he could leave and get ready for his date. The day passed without incident until almost the very end of the shift when one of the ramp agents broke the handle off a piece of luggage, which meant that Simon would have to fill out a report of the incident and take it to the airline counter. Simon had blown the incident completely out of proportion and looked ridiculous as he waved his arms wildly, and violently screamed at the poor man. He belittled the man. He called him a "fool" and a "simpleton" in front of the others. He made the ramp agent fill out the report and take it to the airline counter himself.

"I don't have time to fix your stupid mistakes."

The ramp agent, an extremely large man who had been newly hired, thought seriously about taking a swing at Simon and quitting the job on the spot, but he needed the money so he only glared at Simon and went off to the terminal with the damage form.

Finally, the shift ended, and Simon frantically sped out of the parking lot for the gym. He made certain to get in a thirty minute workout before the date, showered, shaved, brushed his teeth and drove down the Buffalo Bayou to the America Center in downtown Houston. He was fifteen minutes early for the date and took a seat at the bar where he had agreed to meet Jenna. Fifteen minutes can seem like a very long time when one is anxious. Simon looked at his watch over and over again. He kept looking at the front door, and the reception area for Jenna to arrive. He had to relieve himself very badly and wanted to go to the bathroom, but he did not dare leave his spot at the bar, and take the chance that Jenna would arrive, not see him, and think that he had stood her up. He felt the pressing fullness of his bladder and had to keep shaking his leg to ward off the sensation until he finally could not hold himself any longer. He rushed to the bathroom and emptied his bladder as quickly as he could.

It was two minutes before 7 o'clock. In his rush, Simon splashed some water on his pants while he was washing his hands at the sink and left an embarrassing splash mark near his crotch. He was furious, but knew that there was no way he could walk up to Jenna with a wet pant crotch. He dried his pants at the automated hand drier looking impatiently at his watch as the minutes went by. It was ten minutes past 7 o'clock when he finished, and he rushed out the bathroom door and almost ran to the bar as Jenna was finishing talking to the receptionist and about to leave.

"Jenna!" Simon shouted as he quickly walked towards the front door with his hand in the air. The other patrons sitting at their tables for dinner looked at Simon with contempt for his loudness.

Jenna turned around. She was a little embarrassed to be seen with Simon and made certain that he knew it when he came up to her.

"What are you doing?" she scolded him.

"I thought you were leaving." Simon said a little out of breath.

"Well, I was because I've been here about fifteen minutes and you were nowhere to be seen." She admonished him.

"I—"

"And now you're shouting like a fool across this restaurant and embarrassing me."

Simon stood there silently. He took this scolding from Jenna like a little boy, "I was at the bar waiting, but I had to go to the bathroom, and by the time I came out you were leaving..."

"Okay, okay, but that's no reason to come running and shouting at me in a place like this." Jenna was being short with Simon and thought about ending the date right there. Somehow, when she weighed his behavior on the one side against the relief she wanted from her personal misery on the other side, the scales tipped in Simon's favor—barely. She feigned forgiveness, smiled and followed the receptionist to a small table in the in back with Simon trailing behind her.

The restaurant was a trendy place with an upscale crowd. The drinks were overpriced, and the food was mediocre. It was one of those places where the waitresses wear ties and aprons for some reason that nobody can figure out. It was the kind of place with a sommelier even though the patrons typically drank beer. In a corner by the bar there was a piano player that nobody listened to. Large ceiling fans slowly turned mostly for decorative purposes only. The brick walls, and wood flooring were pleasing to the eye, but the overall impression of the restaurant was that the owners were trying too hard to be stylish. There was no sincerity in the place.

It was only when they had sat down at their table that Simon could think to really look at Jenna. Her hair was long and wavy, and flowed over her brown shoulders. She wore a sparkling necklace, and pricey earrings. Her loose and dainty blouse showed off her deep and wonderful bust line, which Simon could not help looking at. Her khaki shorts were high on the thigh showing off her glistening and tanned legs. Simon smiled nervously as he took the drink menu from the waitress and ordered a drink. Jenna knew that Simon was nervous, and that he was staring at her chest (like she wanted him to), but she ignored him and looked around the bar as if she could care less what he thought about her. She acted like he was not even there. She ordered her drink and handed the drink menu back to the waitress.

Simon sat there idiotically in silence trying to think of something to say to Jenna to start the date, but before he could speak, Jenna was excusing herself and going to the bathroom. Simon watched her leave the table abruptly. He let out a sigh. Finally, he was able to relax a little bit. This was not how he wanted the date to begin, but he was determined to make the rest of the night much better. He tried to remember his pre-date plans and went over the things he had wanted to talk to Jenna about.

Jenna spent a long time in the bathroom. The waitress had come to the table with the drinks and once more with the dinner menus before Jenna returned. Simon did not dare to ask her what had taken her so long, but only smiled and obsequiously asked her what she might have for dinner.

"I don't know." Jenna sighed, "But I'm sure that you probably can't afford it."

"Well, I think—"

"How much can you possible make at that airport job?" Jenna went further.

"I make an okay living. It's not anything fancy."

"Ha! You could say that again!"

Like a bad poker player, Jenna had overplayed her hand here. She did not know Simon well enough yet. She did not realize how this would go over with him. She had intended to make him feel beneath her. She wanted to hear him tell her that she was worth the sacrifice that he would have to make to pay for the date. She wanted him to fawn over her. She wanted to abase him—unfortunately for Jenna, this last comment had the exact opposite effect. Simon was a simple man, and he was awestruck by Jenna's looks, however, the he had a unique pride in his work. He knew that he did his job well, and he knew that it was important—even though he did not make a lot of money. If there was one thing about Simon's social status that gave him self confidence, it was the knowledge that at the end of each work day, he had earned his money. He had provided a legitimate service to others, and that the position was solid. His mood quickly changed. He frowned, and wrinkled his forehead. He was furious.

"Well maybe I should leave, then, and you can pay for it yourself." he said angrily. He meant it, and Jenna could tell.

Jenna looked up from her menu in surprise. Would Simon walk out on her and leave her embarrassed? Suddenly, she felt a little apprehensive about what she should say next. She had to think about what she could and could not get away with when she talked to Simon. She did not want Simon to leave.

"I work pretty damn hard for my money, and I'm not ashamed of what I do for a living." Simon said as he looked directly in Jenna's eyes.

She had no idea how to react. There were limits to how badly she could treat Simon. It was a new experience for her. She was used to treating men any way she pleased. She became quiet and felt uncomfortable. She stared down at her menu to avoid Simon's stare.

After an awkward silence, Simon relented of his anger—mostly because he still wanted a chance to sleep with Jenna. Now Simon and Jenna were on somewhat equal footing, and they started to talk to each other like real people. The tension between them subsided after a few moments. They ordered their meals and spent the evening getting to know each other better. Simon rarely went downtown and remarked about how neat he thought it all was. Jenna knew the area very well because she only lived a few blocks away, which really surprised Simon.

"That must be— He was going to say "expensive" but he stopped himself because he did not want to bring up the matter of money again. "So what do you do for a living?" he asked instead.

"I'm a model." Jenna answered. She was a little unsure about how Simon would react to this revelation and watched him closely to see the expression on his face. Most men could not hide their happiness and always smiled when Jenna told them that she was a model. Simon was on his guard, though, and showed no emotion. On the inside, however, he was overjoyed, and his heart almost skipped a beat.

"I'm too short to do runway work, but I do a lot of print, and lingerie catalogs."

Simon did not know what to say. He was dating a lingerie model. Was this a dream? He sensed that anything that he might say would give away his true feelings.

"Do you have to travel a lot?" he asked. He felt like this was a safe question and hoped that he did not sound stupid.

"Oh yes. I'm always going out of town to some shoot." Jenna answered awkwardly.

"So do you like it, or—

"It pays really well when I'm working. But sometimes there's a long span where I have no work, and that's not good."

Simon only nodded his head politely. He felt uncomfortable talking about her work because it made him feel inferior. He quickly changed the subject, and Jenna did not seem to mind. They became more relaxed with each other as the time went by. Simon told one of his jokes and really made Jenna laugh, which surprised him because he did not think that it was that funny. He started to laugh too. Jenna smiled at him. She had that same feeling that she had with Simon when they were on the beach. She was so happy to be with him again. Simon was happy too. He was not trying so hard anymore. They finished their dinner, left the restaurant and strolled together arm in arm around the downtown.

It was a cool night. The air was still, and the sky was clear. There were very few people walking about downtown, and the streets were quiet. They walked about without a care. Here and there Jenna would point out a building to Simon and tell him the name of it or pause at a store front and tell him what she liked about the store or what she had recently bought there. They stopped at a bar Jenna liked along the way, and they had a few beers and played some pool. A country band was playing. Jenna led Simon onto the dance floor and tried to teach him how to two-step, and they both laughed at his clumsiness. They were losing themselves in each other for the time and forgot about the personal miseries that they concocted in their own minds when they were alone. They were sharing themselves, and as often happens between men and women who get along so well, they each started to fantasize in their minds what it might be like to be with this other person. Simon was mesmerized by Jenna's fantastic body, and strong personality. She was smart, and beautiful. He could not help, but be attracted to her. He was already thinking about marrying Jenna and buying a real house. He was sure that together they could afford a place in southwest Houston somewhere. And after a few years if he got a promotion, Jenna could quit her job or even just do some part time modeling, and they could raise a real family together. It was quite a leap after only one formal date, but that's what went on in Simon's mind. The whole disaster of his relationship with Geraldine was forgotten. Jenna's mind was very different. She thought about Simon the way one might think about a favorite pair of sweatpants. She truly liked him. She fantasized about how nice it would be to have him around—but the idea of marriage never even entered her thought process at that time. She felt comfortable with Simon. He did not pressure her or seem like he would ever boss her around. He was easy to be with. While they were still on the dance floor, and Jenna had her arms around Simon's neck, they stared in each other's eyes and kissed sweetly. They left the bar holding each other by the hand, and started to walk back to the restaurant where they had eaten.

They stopped along the way to admire a statue of Sam Houston. Simon was explaining something about Texas history, which he knew a little about, and Jenna looked up at him and wondered about him for a moment. What would he be like if he was her boyfriend? She wanted to see him again.

"Simon."

"Yeah."

"I'm sorry about how I was tonight—at the beginning. I was bitchy. I don't know why I was doing that. Sometimes I just do that."

Simon smiled as he listened and wanted to believe that he was graciously forgiving Jenna somehow—but he was not. The truth was that he idolized Jenna. She was a trophy to be cherished, but that was all. Simon made himself believe that he really loved her at that point, but it was only his lust for her body, and sense of awe that bonded him to her.

"It's okay." He said softly. "I'm sorry too."

They kissed again and smiled at each other; then they walked back to the restaurant.

"Where's your car?" Simon asked when they got back to the restaurant.

"I walked here. I only live up the street a little way."

Simon paused; a little unsure of himself, he asked "Do you want me to walk you back home?" He felt like he had to make the offer.

"Next time. Call me this week." She whispered.

She stood on her toes, put her arms around Simon's neck and kissed him deeply.

Simon was lost in her kiss. She had him in a trance. He was quiet and stared in her eyes for a moment before he brushed his lips against her cheek.

"You know. I don't even know your last name." he said softly in her ear.

"It's Park." She said as she slowly pulled away from him.

"Are you sure that you don't want me to walk you back home?" Simon asked again trying to sound sincere, but in the back of his mind (and in the back of Jenna's mind) the possibility of spending the night with Jenna lingered.

"Let's just say goodbye here." Jenna said.

They held hands briefly, and then Jenna left. Simon watched her cross the street and turn the corner. The date had started off badly, but it finished very well, and Simon could not believe his good fortune. He wanted Jenna and was very anxious to see her again.

Chapter Twelve

Simon Bosse was not a religious man. He was too busy living life to think too deeply about such things. It is not from a lack of interest or desire to understand God and man's relation to Him that the majority of men tend to ignore the mysteries of life; rather, it is a lack of time that prevents them from diving into such mysteries. Most men are simple too busy getting on with the business of making a living to invest the kind of time necessary to come to any real conclusion about the meaning of their lives. For them, the central questions of existence "why are we here?" or "where are we going?" only come to mind occasionally—perhaps at a funeral of a close relative—but quickly melt away from their conscious when the more practical matters of their daily affairs need tending to.

So the most important truths that a man could possess pass by the bulk of men as they travel on their way from cradle to grave simply because they have prioritized their time in such a way to spend most of it obtaining the necessities of life. They have their faith, their religion, but they have it the way a man who owns an expensive painting might keep it as an investment. It is there hanging on his wall—prominently. He knows that it is worth something, and it makes him look respectable. But he never really looks at it and sees the truth and beauty in it.

Perhaps there is a significant number of men (a minority, but still a significant number) in the world who do have the time to grapple with such mysteries, however, they really have no desire to find these answers, and would not believe the answers anyhow because they rather have the pleasures that the world can provide. In their pursuit of money, sex and power, these men sacrifice the time they have been given by God that they could have used to seek out the more important matters and end up dying as empty shells. All style and no substance, they are like children who eat only desert and refuse to eat their main course with its meat and vegetables only to find out later that the desert did not provide enough sustenance. But God is merciful. He cannot stand to watch his creation walk away from Him, and the opportunity to learn profound truths. So He has set a curse upon all men that has been handed down from the first man, Adam, to all his fellow males through the generations due to their disobedience. The purpose of this curse is to force each and every man who is born to turn to God for answers at some point during their life. The purpose of the curse is to make a man seek God out and beg Him for guidance and counsel. This curse that all men face at least once in their life is the question, "What do women want?"

It would be better to ask, "What don't women want?" For all women—like all men—are full of wants. Human "wants" are unlimited. No matter how many possessions a human being has accumulated, or how many thrills and joys he has experienced, he will always want more, and so it is that the answer to this question is the real curse. The answer to the question "what do women want?" is simple. Women want it all. Women want everything; in this respect, they are the same as men. Only a woman's concept of what having it all means is different than what having it all means to a man. For a man, having it all means that he is able to have any woman that he wants, and no one can tell him what to do, and his belly is full. For a woman, having it all means that she is able to get any man she wants, and no one can tell her what to do, and she is able to buy all the shoes that she desires. Of the many differences that there are between men and women—and there are many—this is the most significant one. Money, sex and power are the great dream of the vast majority of the human race—for both men and women. How they go about obtaining these false gods is another matter.

But to be certain, there are many who obtain these things. Once there was man who spent his entire life obtaining a great fortune. Very often, he cheated in business so that hardly anybody trusted him. He never made any real friends, and complete strangers inherited his fortune when he died. Another man, perhaps a little less clever, spent his entire life in the pursuit of sex. He spent each night with a different woman. But these were the type of women that one could never have enough confidence in to commit to. And therefore, the man never did commit to any of them. In the end, he died all alone never loving anyone or being loved by anyone. Finally, the least clever man of them all, rose in position by his careful plotting and scheming and became so powerful that everybody feared him. He too had no friends or loved ones. He ruled a land from behind his body guards in a heavily armed fortress. He spent his whole life behind those fortified walls and worried about his possessions. Nobody would talk to him. Together these men counted themselves as the three wisest men in the world.

There was another man, however, Who was wiser. Although He spent almost no time in school, He always knew the difference between right and wrong in every instance, and everyone wanted to hear what He had to say. He was very poor, but He had all that He needed and did not have want for anything else. Everything He came into possession of, He freely shared with others if only He was asked. He never married, or even had a girlfriend, but He was so loving that every women that He met fawned over Him, and only wanted to be in His company. He held no position of rank, but He was so kind that all His enemies were afraid to harm Him because so many people loved Him. He never needed any bodyguards or arms.

Many people, however, consider this man to have been a fool. They point out that when He died, He had no formal learning and had not written any books. They note that He had no possessions and certainly no money to leave to any heirs. They note that He never knew a woman, or had a family of His own. They note that He obtained no official title or authority or rank. In short, when He died, He had nothing to show for His life on earth by any human measure. No one even wanted to admit that they were His friend when they were asked. So by this reasoning, many say this one man was the world's greatest fool.

But they are wrong.

For who is richer than He who has want for nothing? Who has more family than He who treats everyone He meets as His family? Who knows more love that He who is love itself? Who is more powerful than He who has so many friends who love Him that His enemies are too afraid to harm Him? How is it that this one man is considered a fool, and the rich and the powerful are considered so wise when this one man showed that as ends in and of themselves, money, sex and power are meaningless?

Most of humanity chooses to pursue money, sex and power while the religious man chooses poverty, chastity and obedience. In the end, it is the religious man who conquers all because he realizes that he must conquer himself first. He does that by showing true love towards others, which is to say, he risks and sacrifices his own well being for another's sake. When he does this, when he loves truly like this, he finds God, Who is love and truth itself. Then, the religious man who finds God has everything, and his human heart is completely satisfied.

In the corner of a small empty bar, in a booth nearby the entrance to the small kitchen, sat a petite woman in her early 20's who was sobbing softly. She covered her face with her hand and slumped down into the booth as far as she could. Her lover had kicked her out of his house and now refused to take her telephone calls. He was done with her. In fact, he was angry with her. She was spoiling his good time. Now this woman was all alone with this child in her belly, and she had no idea what she was going to do. Her life pursuit of money, sex and power was over, and she was not yet even 22 years old. In her mind, she was a tragic victim and was suffering a terrible injustice. She had done nothing wrong, but somehow it was left to her to pay the price. It was not fair. Why should this thing happen to her? Why should she have to be stuck with taking care of this child while his father went on with his own carefree life? The thought of taking any responsibility for her actions never entered her mind. She never once considered herself partially to blame in any way for her current situation. The man was to blame. The birth control manufacturer was to blame. Society was to blame. Everyone other than herself was to blame. All she could do was sit in her little booth, and weep for herself, and her difficult situation.

"Gerry?"

Geraldine Jankowicz looked up at Simon Bosse, who was standing above her next to the booth. Once she had dreamed of marrying this man —before she had met the child's father. She had dreamed of living with him, and raising a family, and she could have done it, but she left that dream behind for some reason, although she would have difficulty remembering why. If she had remembered why, she would have recalled that she did not think that Simon was good enough for her. He was good enough for her to live with for free for 7 months, and he was good enough to pay to fix her car and take her out to eat at restaurants. He was not, however, rich enough or good looking enough for her and her two fake boobs to marry. She had cast him aside. She had moved on to better things in much the same way as her child's father had cast her aside, and moved on to better things.

Simon did not know what he was doing in this bar on this day. He had once vowed never to go into the place again. He had been walking by, however, and had seen Geraldine slumped in the corner all alone. At first, he kept on walking, but had turned back to take a second look out of curiosity. For a few moments, he watched Geraldine slumped down with her chin in her chest and her hand covering her face. It was obvious that she was miserable. He felt strange just standing there at the entrance to the bar just watching her. Under any other circumstances, he would have walked by her. He never wanted to talk to her again. He knew himself well enough to understand that any contact with her would only turn into an argument. What purpose could it serve? However, Simon had received a promotion at work. The super chief had had a heart attack, and was in the hospital. He would be out indefinitely. Simon had been promoted to acting super chief. He had been given a nice bonus, and if the super chief decided to take an early retirement, which was very possible, Simon's promotion would be permanent. He went into the bar and walked up to Geraldine. He was eager to dangle this news in front of her.

"Simon." she whispered as she looked up at him pathetically. Her eye makeup was streaming down.

"I was just walking by." He tried to explain.

They looked at each other in silence for a moment.

"Simon. I don't know what to say."

Geraldine looked down and wiped her tears. There was a long pause.

"Are you okay?" Simon asked.

"Oh yeah, I'm okay." Geraldine laughed at the ridiculousness of the question. "I'm just great."

Simon did not appreciate the sarcasm in her reply, however. He had no patience for it. There was a tension between them. He did not really want to be there. If Geraldine was going to be flippant, he had no reason to stay around.

"Well I guess I'll go then."

"Wait!"

Geraldine was a little surprised to hear this plea come out of her own mouth. She did not really care about Simon. But somehow, she knew that it would be better to sit with him than to be alone. He would be a distraction and take her mind away from her very heavy thoughts.

Simon stood there silently for a moment and waited for Geraldine.

"Will you sit with me?" she asked.

Simon looked sternly at her. For a moment, the better part of his heart considered being charitable to the woman, and he almost wanted to sit down across from her to help ease her pain. He could hold her hand and help her talk through whatever mess she was experiencing. He could forget the past and just help her. But his mind took him back to the days of her lying and cheating, and how she had used him and left him. He became cautious and skeptical. He folded his arms and remained standing.

"I—I just wanted to say, Simon, that you—that you and I—that you were the best thing that ever happened to me. I didn't want for things to get so stupid. I never—I never—

"Yeah, well that's all in the past now." Simon cut her off. He was uncomfortable now, and he regretted coming into the bar. He started to look around for the exit.

Geraldine continued, "I know that you were hurt. I never meant for that to happen. Things just worked out that way."

This last comment fell flat. There was no sincerity in it. Simon kept waiting to hear an apology, but she never made one. He had been hurt, and "things" had happened, but Geraldine never mentioned why these "things" happened or who did them. She was like a drunk describing a terrible car accident, but failing to mention the fact that he had been behind the wheel all along. Simon was disgusted.

"Right. That's how things go I guess. Well, look I have to go. Okay?" He looked away.

"Okay." Geraldine whispered without looking up.

Simon paused a moment, and then turned around and started to walk away. Inside his mind he was boiling with contempt and repugnance for Geraldine. "Things just worked out that way?" he thought. "Like her cheating on me was some accident?" She had not changed at all. He had come into the bar and approached her to throw his promotion in her face, but in his mind Simon felt that he was the magnanimous one, and all he received in return from Geraldine was some half baked—he did not know what to call it. It was not an apology, though. He knew that for certain. As he walked away, his better judgment kept telling him just to continue out of the bar, and never to think about Geraldine Jankowicz again, but his desire for vengeance was stronger, and he turned back around. In a fury he walked with a bold stride up to Geraldine.

"What is wrong with you? Are you--Don't you ever think about what you did? You did it. It didn't just happen like some accident. How can you say that you did not mean to hurt me? You dumped me for some other guy because he made more money. Do you know that I'm the super chief now? Do you? And you say you didn't mean for me to get hurt? How did you think I would feel? Did you think that I would be happy? Like I would do a little dance or something? You're—you're stupid. You know that? You're ridiculous. I can't even understand you. You make no sense. You—I think that-- You're—

"I'm pregnant! I'm pregnant you bastard. I have nowhere to go. I have no money. I'm all alone. I'm pregnant you stupid bastard. I'm pregnant. Oh my God what am I gonna do?"

Geraldine broke down and cried miserably with her face in her hands. Simon was shocked as he watched her cry. She seemed helpless. Momentarily, she had regained her status as the victim in Simon's eyes, but it passed quickly. He was not sympathetic. He remembered her bold betrayal. He was cold now.

"That's your problem."

He turned away and started to walk out of the bar.

Geraldine Jankowicz was not going to leave things this way. Something inside of her would never admit fault. Something inside of her was so proud that no matter how bad the situation was she would always look to blame others. Something inside of her was so evil, that it would always seek vengeance—even just for spite. Something inside of her took pleasure in watching others suffer.

"I hate you! You're a loser. That's why I dumped you. You're a loser, and you're never going to be anything. That's why I dumped you. I HATE YOU!" Geraldine screamed.

She was happy all of a sudden. The thought that she had hurt Simon made her happy.

Simon stopped and looked back at Geraldine. He was furious. All the blood had rushed into his head. He was shaking with anger, and wanted to go up to Geraldine, and rip her apart. He glared at her with wild eyes, and his fists clenched. He fantasized about grabbing her, and smacking her over and over again in the face and spitting on her, and screaming at her about what a stupid whore she was. "But why should I do this?" he thought to himself. "I am dating a lingerie model. I don't need to justify myself to her."

He regretted the entire episode and wondered at his own silliness in approaching Geraldine in the first place. He left the bar without another word. As he walked on towards the employee parking lot, he thought about the encounter over and over again and became very self satisfied. Geraldine's life had turned into a mess since she had left Simon, and he liked that. It made him feel good. He felt better than her. As he drove home, Simon smirked at the thought of his superiority. Geraldine did not deserve him. The first thing he wanted to do when he arrived home was to call his new lingerie model girlfriend and gloat about his promotion.

Simon grabbed a beer from the refrigerator, confidently plopped down on his couch, put his feet up on the ottoman, and called Jenna's cell phone to tell her the good news about his promotion. He was a little surprised when another woman answered the call.

"Hello?"

"Jenna?"

"Um no. This isn't Jenna."

"This is Simon Bosse. Who's this?"

"Jenna's friend."

"Well, can I talk to her? Is she there?"

"Um...Hold on."

Simon was a little annoyed. The woman was stupid, and sounded almost like a teenager.

"Hello?"

"Yeah?"

"Jenna's busy right now. She said she would call you back in about fifteen minutes. Okay?"

"Well...what is she doing?"

"Um...she's in the shower."

"Oh...okay...Tell her Simon called, and to call me back when she gets out."

"Okay. Bye—

"Wait—

Simon wanted to ask the woman for her name, but she had ended the call before he could ask.

He spent the next two hours waiting for Jenna to call back, but she never did return his call. His telephone rang once during those two hours, and he ran from the kitchen to the couch to pick it up only to find that it was a call from a telemarketer, who wanted him to change his internet service. Simon spent another hour waiting after that call. He was frustrated and decided to go for a walk. He took his telephone with him. He walked to the corner convenience store, read a few magazines, stopped for an ice cream at a small diary shop and walked back home, but Jenna still had not called. Simon was angry and confused at the same time. Like a man standing on the fulcrum of a teeter totter going from one side to the other, he at one moment was furious at this apparent snub and then shifted to being confused. Maybe Jenna had not received the message? Maybe she had forgotten? But then he thought that maybe she just did not like him anymore. Maybe she was through with him, and she wanted someone better and was ditching him the way Geraldine had. He became angry again and was determined to talk to her.

He called Jenna again, and once more the woman with the girlish voice answered the call.

"Hello?"

"Yeah. Hi. This is Simon. I called earlier for Jenna."

"Oh yeah, right. Um."

"What happened? She was supposed to call me back."

"I—um—I forgot to tell her."

Simon was getting tired of being lied to so transparently.

"What's your name?"

"You know. Jenna's—

"Tell her that it's Simon—her date from the other night."

"Oh! Her date! Right. Okay. I'm sorry. Hold on a minute."

Simon was frustrated. This woman was so ridiculous. He waited for Jenna to answer his call, but after a minute there was still nobody on the other end of the telephone.

"Hello? Hello?" he shouted in vain.

For a moment, he thought he heard someone on the other side of the line. He strained to listen.

"Hello? Hello? Is anybody there?" he called.

It was useless. He had been snubbed and hung up the telephone in disgust. He had wanted so badly to gloat to Jenna about Geraldine, and his promotion. He had been so sure of himself, but now it appeared like Jenna did not want anything to do with him. What a joke. He had been such a fool. How could he have thought that she would really want to be with him? He was just some ordinary guy. He was a baggage handler. He felt so stupid.

Three days later, Simon looked at his cell phone, which was vibrating, to see who was calling him. He did not get many telephone calls— especially not at work like this one. Whoever was calling had very little understanding of the nature of Simon's job, and the noise of his work place. He looked at the caller identification on the small screen of his telephone, and saw that it was Jenna who was calling him. He was surprised, and confused. He had been calling her, and leaving messages on her telephone mailbox for three days, but she had not returned his calls. A part of him did not want to answer the call, and wanted to make Jenna do the waiting for a change. Another part of him, the stronger part, desperately wanted to make a connection with Jenna again, and was afraid of losing her interest. He had not seen or heard from her since their last date. He therefore hurried off the tarmac—even though he was in the middle of directing a ramp chief—and went inside the terminal where there was less noise so that he could answer the call. The ramp chief, who was eager for Simon's consultation, would have to wait. Simon took the call as he walked towards the terminal door.

"Hello?"

"Hello?"

"Can you hear me?" Simon shouted.

"I can barely hear you."

Simon ran now towards the terminal door.

"Can you hear me now?" he said as he opened the door to the terminal.

"Yeah. What's all that noise?"

"It's my work. I'm on the tarmac where all the jet planes are."

"Right."

Simon was a little perplexed at Jenna's reaction. Did she forget what he did for a living? Did she not know what a jet powered plane sounded like or the level of noise on an airport runway? It seemed ridiculous.

"So what's up?" Simon asked.

"Nothing—I wanted to say I'm sorry that I missed your calls. I've been out of town, and had not thought of checking my phone messages."

"I see."

"What?"

"I said, 'I see.'" Simon shouted as he closed the door behind him. "Who was that girl who answered your phone?" Simon asked referring to the strange girl who had dropped his original call."

"What girl?"

"When I first called three days ago, some woman answered and said that you were in the shower, and then I called back a few hours later, and she answered again so I told her that I was your date from the other night, and said that she was going to get you, but she never came back on the line. What happened there?"

There was a short pause while Jenna prepared her answer.

"That was my friend, Sheila. She's a little spaced out sometimes. I was in the shower, but when I got out she never told me you called, and then I left town that night so I never got the message. And then I only just now came back and checked my messages. I'm so sorry."

In spite of his skepticism and against his better judgment, Simon accepted this excuse. He wanted to believe that Jenna's friend, Sheila, really was a nut, and he imagined her simply dropping the call out of sheer flakiness. And, of course, Jenna was a busy model and probably did not think about checking her telephone while she was out of town on work. He wanted to believe all this because he wanted to be with Jenna more than he wanted the truth. He wanted there still to be a chance that Jenna might really come to love him, and want to be with him. False hope disguised itself as charity, and whispered in his ear and bade him to accept what would have been patently untrue to any outside observer. It told him to concoct reasons for believing this lie for the sake of obtaining some pretend dream that was held out like a treat in front of a salivating dog. It is the sense of an unfulfilled life that gives false hope its grip on men, and inside Simon's heart was a gaping hole that took in this phantom as its fill.

"I understand." Simon cooed as Jenna had hoped.

"Let's meet again." Jenna suggested.

Suddenly, Simon was thrilled. She really did want him, did she not? It was difficult for him to contain his emotions.

"Yes, I want to meet again."

"Why don't you meet me at the restaurant where we ate, and we can go out someplace or something?"

This is what Simon had wanted to hear for the last three days. His heart was beating fast, and he could feel the adrenaline working through his body. He was very excited. Jenna was reinforcing those false hopes in his mind. "Yes, she really does want me. She really is sincere. She really is interested." He thought. It was clear now. There was nothing to be worried about. How could he have ever doubted? And so three days of waiting for Jenna to return his telephone calls, and her poorly constructed lies were forgotten for the time being, and he enthusiastically accepted the date from this dark flower, who had ignored him for three days and now only suddenly wanted to meet him again.

Oh dark flower,

Among the roses of the garden, where is your equal?

You stand alone, apart from the rest.

Evident to all, your loveliness demands attention.

The sun himself kisses your soft cheeks with his radiant lips.

In his hot stare, you bask,

And feed off of it--

As you do the lusty stare of all who enter the garden.

And yet, what purpose does your beauty serve?

Shape, height and form cannot dull your thorns.

Unique among your sisters, you have no scent.

What good is such a rose?

Dark flower, I weep for thee.

No fruit is found upon your branch.

Cut off from the True Vine, what will you do

When The Great Gardener comes?

Wandering men so hapless in this dismal garden,

To good advice now hearken.

Let your feet continue by this proud flower.

Or her beauty, your mind, will darken.

And then you will do foolish things.

Chapter Thirteen

Although Jenna would have preferred that they meet again in a restaurant, Simon insisted on picking her up at her condominium, and would not let her make an excuse. He drove downtown to the America Center to the address Jenna gave him. She lived in a high rise condominium complex, which was near where they had gone on their first date. Simon felt a little out of place in such an upscale building, and was not certain of how to conduct himself as the security guard stopped him in the lobby to confirm his business in the building. As he rode the shiny elevator up the glass sky scraper, Simon could only think about how different Jenna's life was from his. He lived in a trailer, and shuffled luggage around an airport. She lived in a modern high rise condominium complex and traveled the country as a professional model. Even so, she had wanted to meet again, and that gave Simon all the hope that he needed to ignore these differences and fantasize about a real relationship with her.

He was so eager to share his promotion with Jenna and gossip with her about Geraldine. He wanted very badly to hear Jenna tell him how proud she was of him for his promotion or laugh with him at his old girlfriend. He wanted Jenna to share his thoughts, and dreams and hold him, and kiss him, but it was not to be. Instead, Jenna was aloof and distant on their date. She contradicted everything Simon did or said. When Simon tried to be upbeat and positive, Jenna said something depressing or negative. Simon remarked about how much he loved a certain thing, and Jenna derided it, or went on about how much she despised it. Simon's "yes" automatically determined Jenna's "no." It really did not matter what subject they discussed, she willfully took issue with everything Simon said. Simon knocked on her front door and waited for her to answer.

"Hi." Jenna greeted him at her door without emotion.

"Hey! I got these for you." Simon gave her some flowers.

Jenna was somewhat nonplussed by the gift. She was accustomed to having men give her things, but was not familiar with sincere attempts to win her favor—it was almost quaint, and she did not know how to react.

"Well...thanks. Come on in."

Though this was officially their second date and the fourth time that Simon had seen Jenna face to face, he was still paralyzed by her looks. She was wearing a backless purple halter top that showed off her smooth shoulders, and straight back, and the full breasts that dangled temptingly. She had on a pair of off white slacks that showed off her round and muscular behind, and she wore matching colored high heels that pointed her toes and made her look even more graceful. To see such exaggerated proportions in such a petite woman was almost too rare to be believed.

Jenna took the flowers, cut the bottom of their stems, and placed them in a pitcher of water.

"I'll have to find a vase for them, but they can stay in this for now." She explained.

They did not spend a long time in Jenna's condominium, but Simon was able to get a better understanding of her in the few minutes that he had to look around. Jenna obviously had a great deal of money. Everything about her condominium was plush. The carpeting was perfectly white. The couch—in fact all the furniture—was apparently brand new because it looked like no one had ever sat down in it. It was so crisp, and neat. Everything was white or some shade of white it seemed. The art work on her walls looked expensive, and the decorations scattered on the various tables were elegant. Jenna had spent a great deal of money furnishing this place, but Simon somehow annoyed her when he complimented her about it. She was fidgety and wanted to get out of there quickly.

"Your condominium is beautiful."

"Oh—thanks." She replied in a monotone.

"That view is fantastic." Simon said enthusiastically.

"You get used to it after a while."

"It looks great. You look great."

"Oh—thanks."

Simon was perplexed by Jenna's aloofness, but he kept his optimism. He smiled and led her out the door for their date. Simon had planned for them to go to a local bar where they could watch some weekend warriors ride a mechanical bull. He thought that it would be a fun place. It was within walking distance of Jenna's condominium, and he felt that she would appreciate the convenience. Unfortunately, it was obvious that she had been there many times before and was bored with the place. Simon sensed her displeasure and tried everything he could to engage her mind and keep the date moving along.

"I wanted to tell you that I got a promotion." Simon had been holding this information back just for this occasion and had been burning to tell her. "I'm the new supervisor of all the other ramp chiefs."

Jenna just nodded her head as she sipped her drink. Her reaction was a real disappointment for Simon.

"The old supervisor had a heart attack," Simon continued "And I took over his place. They offered it to another guy, but he did not want it so they came to me. It was supposed to be temporary until the old supervisor recovered from his attack, but he decided to retire early so I am taking the job permanently." Simon smiled broadly as he proudly talked about his success and desperately fought to ignore Jenna's apparent apathy.

They watched a woman riding the mechanical bull. The bar was uproarious. People were whooping and shouting to encourage the woman riding the "bull." The machine swung to her left, and then it quickly rotated back to her right, and she almost fell off. The crowd cheered and clapped wildly. The woman skillfully managed to last the duration of the ride and climbed off the bull to the applause of the bar.

"She's really good!" Simon shouted to Jenna above the applause.

"He was easy on her." Jenna replied referring to the mechanical bull operator.

"I guess," was all Simon could think to say at the incongruity of Jenna's comment with the situation around them. The whole bar was going crazy as the woman rider took a bow.

He could not think of what to say next. No matter what he said, Jenna was determined to strike it down. It was very strange. They sat together without speaking for some time. They sipped at their drinks and watched the people around them. Every now and then, Simon thought of something to say, but stopped himself because he knew that Jenna would disagree with it, and he wanted to get some positive response out of her. Finally, he came upon what he thought was a brilliant idea. He decided to put himself down. Certainly, Jenna would not disagree to this. At the same time, however, she could not enthusiastically agree either. In order for her to be polite, she would have to disagree. Simon was going to trick her into affirming him. He did his best to sound sincere.

"You know, Jenna? I'm an idiot. I don't know what you're doing here with me. You look so great, and this place I've taken you to is so boring. I should have—I don't know. I should have done a better job."

Incredibly, Jenna sat there silently, looked away and took a sip of her drink. In her mind, she agreed. "Yes, you are an idiot. Yes, I don't know what I am doing here with you. Yes, I do look great, and this place is

---

boring..." Jenna thought. She agreed with every word of it, but in order to avoid agreeing with Simon in any way, she remained totally silent. She would not give Simon an inch.

Simon was baffled. There was nothing that he could do or say that was going to make Jenna happy or like him. He wanted her more than anything else at that moment. He wanted to take her physically and have his way with her. He wanted to completely dominate her—even humiliate her. He wanted to totally possess her. The promotion, his increase in pay, his peaceful life and steady job were not enough for him. He wanted more. He would always want more. No matter how many great things he possessed or how many happy circumstances surrounded him there would always be something for him to be dissatisfied with. Like all men, he wanted it all. Since no man can really have it all; however, he would—just like everybody else—find something missing and blame his not having this missing thing on someone else. He looked at Jenna with a distressed face. He was exasperated.

"What does she want?" he said to himself.

Now he was under the curse. He might have asked what he himself wanted while he was at it, though, for neither Simon nor Jenna really knew what they wanted, and could not be satisfied with what they had. That was the real curse. Nevertheless, Simon's outlook was transformed from being focused on himself, and all his wants to being focused on another person and all her wants. He was on the beginning of a path that led to a Gate through which a man might pass—if he has been obedient-- into a higher realm where men come to understand that their wants or desires will always be endless, and that as finite beings with limitations they will be unable to meet all these wants and desires. It is a place where everyone is truly wealthy because they have conquered their obsession with their own self and have stopped craving for more and more. It is a place where power is a meaningless term because each man is so loving and has so many friends that control over others is useless because all the souls are so willing to give to each other freely. Simon was only on the beginning of that path, and there was no guarantee that he would make it through the Gate that led to such a place. Were he to know the truth, Simon might eventually come to realize that no amount of money, sex or power would ever be enough for him. More importantly, were he to receive the Truth, Simon would be completely happy.

At this moment, Simon could not understand any of these things. All he knew was that he wanted Jenna, but for some reason she did not want him. Even though she had been the one to have initiated things, and had invited him to the beach party. Even though she had been the one to have kissed him at that party, and even though she had been the one to have accepted a date—not once but twice—she did not seem to want him for some reason. It did not make any sense. "What does she want?" He could not figure it out. The question nagged at his mind, and it was not going to go away anytime soon. Every time he looked at Jenna's incredible body, the question tortured him because he wanted to have her so badly. It seeped into his bones and blood and burned his whole body. It was driving him mad. His anger and frustration percolated throughout the night. Every time he made a gesture to appease Jenna and she rebuffed him, he became more perplexed, and his anger swelled. Every time he tried to compliment her or start a friendly conversation, and she found a way to reply with a sarcastic remark in mockery of him, his rage would shoot up inside of him, but he would hold it back. He was still furious as he walked Jenna back to her condominium at the end of the night.

They walked without talking to each other and without looking at each other. They both felt awkward, but then something happened. As angry as Simon was about the whole stupid situation, he wanted so badly to make Jenna happy with him again that he was willing to take the blame for whatever it was that was upsetting her even though he knew that he had done nothing wrong and that he did not deserve any blame. He started to make a sincere apology as they approached the front door to Jenna's building.

"Jenna, I just wanted to say that I'm sorry that the night did not go well. I really should have done a better job planning it. I'm sorry."

If Jenna had simply accepted this apology or had remained silent (like she had the first time Simon had spoken this way), the date would have ended without incident. Jenna, however, had not really learned her lesson from the previous date with Simon. She decided to stab at him one more time. She went a bridge too far and again picked the one subject that Simon was absolutely unwilling to let anyone use to insult him.

"Well, I'm so glad we had this chance to celebrate your little promotion, Simon, but was it really that important?"

Jenna had no understanding of what she had done. It was as if she had set off an avalanche on a snowy mountain or had tripped the detonator to a bomb. Simon's anger had been building the entire night, but this last comment by Jenna mocking his work life was the final provocation. Simon erupted.

"You stupid bitch! Do you think that I am going to take this from you!" he hissed.

Simon was shaking with anger, and Jenna was a little scared. She suddenly realized that Simon was potentially dangerous. She started to look around for help, but there was nobody else around, and they were still a block away from the front door to her building.

"I don't know what THE HELL you want. I really don't. I like you. I can't figure out why, but I do, and—and I really would like to get to know you better. You're so beautiful, and it was so easy to talk to you that first time at the beach. I felt really right with you there—when we watched the moon, but you make no sense. You seem to like me, and then you—I don't know. And when you attack me like this, I don't want to be around you anymore. And I don't--I can't figure out what you want. I won't ever, probably. You need to figure it out for yourself. If you ever do—you can call me…"

Simon turned around to go find his car which was parked down the street and left Jenna standing all alone on the sidewalk. He never looked back.

Jenna watched with a stunned and blank stare on her face. It was as if Simon had taken everything that she thought she knew about men and had smashed it with a hammer. Her thoughts were completely scrambled. Nothing made sense anymore. "What did I do wrong? What does he want?" she asked herself. His expectations seemed excessive to her, and yet, deep down she knew that he was a decent man. He treated her well. Perhaps there was something wrong with her? This was a radical thought for Jenna. Such a thing had never crossed her mind before. What could possibly be wrong with her? She turned around and walked in the opposite direction away from Simon towards her condominium. She was convinced that she would never see him again. In reality, they were now on the identical path. They were both questioning themselves and thinking about how to please the other person. It was inevitable that Jenna would call Simon again and beg his forgiveness.

Chapter Fourteen

Jenna was frantic. Had she just thrown away the best man that she was ever going to meet? Had she just destroyed any chance that she might have for love? Why had she done it? Why had she been so stupid? What did she expect from him? Did she think that he was some kind of machine that was going to worship her and do her bidding at her every command? Did he not have his own feelings and cares? Did she expect him to be perfect in every way? Who was she kidding? She hated herself for how she had treated him. It was a first for her. She had never hated herself in all her life. Simon was an honest and simple man. She was attracted to him, and he obviously cared about her. She wanted him. How could she get him back? She called his cell phone and left a message.

"Simon, this is Jenna. I want to apologize for the other night. I did it again. I—please just call me back so we can talk." She did not know what else to say; instead of going on and on, she stopped herself and hung up the cell phone.

She spent the next two hours waiting for Simon to call back, but he never did return her call. Her telephone rang once during those two hours, and she ran from the bathroom to the kitchen to pick it up only to find that it was a call from a machine recording that solicited her vote for some politician. Jenna spent another hour waiting after that call. She was frustrated and decided to take a bath. She took her telephone with her into the bathroom in case Simon returned her call. She turned on some music, lit some scented candles and slipped into her bubble bath. She was depressed and confused at the same time. Maybe Simon had not received the message? Maybe he was at work and could not take the call? But then she thought that maybe he just did not want to talk to her anymore. She became sad again and started to cry. She had blown it with him. She was convinced of it. Why had she been so stupid? Forty minutes later, she got out of the bathtub, put on her bathrobe, and headed for the kitchen for something to drink when her telephone finally did ring. She ran back towards the bathroom and stubbed her toe on the way. She grabbed her foot in pain as she hopped towards the cell phone that rested on the floor by the bathtub.

"Hello? Hello?"

"Hey, it's Simon."

"Simon! Oh, I'm so glad you called. I'm so glad, Simon. I really am. I think I made a mistake. It's the second time. I don't know why I do these things. I've been thinking about it these last few days. You know? I— Simon? Are you there?"

"I'm here."

"Simon. Let's meet again. Please?"

There was a pause.

Simon did not know how sincere she really was. For spite's sake, a part of him wanted to hold her off a few days and make her wait some more, but he thought better of it. He wanted to be with her, but at the same time he wanted her to know that she could not push him around. He did not call her to be coy, though.

"I want to meet again too. But you've got to know that you can't treat me like that."

"Oh—I kn—

"Do you understand?"

"I know, Simon. I know."

"It's ridiculous."

"I know."

Again, they were silent for a moment.

"Why don't we meet for lunch, or something? I'm working tomorrow, but I get an hour off for lunch now. I could meet you somewhere." Simon suggested.

"That sounds great. Let's do that."

"Why don't we just meet at Hooligan's by the airport at noon?"

"Okay."

"Tomorrow."

"Okay."

"I'll see you then."

"Okay."

Simon said goodbye, and he hung up the telephone.

Jenna was sitting on the edge of her bathtub. She hugged the telephone and smiled. She was glad that he had called. For the first time in her entire life, she was looking outside herself and thinking about the heart of another person, and their cares, and their wants. For the first time in her life, she was truly happy.

The next day, Jenna was a little early to her lunch date with Simon. There was a fairly large lunch crowd in the bar, and she waited at the front entrance and let people walk by her. She did not know that Simon had arrived just a little before she did, and was sitting at the bar looking for her to come through the front door. Jenna was a little anxious and looked at her watch. She could not understand what could be holding Simon up. She turned around to look inside the restaurant, and then she saw Simon sitting on one of the bar stools fumbling at his cell phone.

"Simon!" Jenna shouted as she quickly walked towards the bar with her hand in the air. The other patrons sitting at their tables nearby looked at Jenna with surprise.

Simon turned around, and was a little surprised at the reaction from Jenna.

"Simon." She smiled.

Simon stood up, and they looked into each other's eyes for a moment.

"Let's get a table." He smiled.

They went to the receptionist together, who seated them at a booth. For the first time since she had met Simon, Jenna was somewhat modestly dressed. Her appearance was not such a distraction. She was wearing a bra, and her blouse actually did not show any cleavage. She was wearing a black short sleeved turtleneck fluted blouse, and loose fitted khaki dress slacks. There were no high heels, and not very much skin showing this time.

"We've not had a good start, I don't think." Jenna said after the receptionist had left them alone. Jenna was not sure of her own feelings. The whole experience of actually talking with another man, and trying to really know him, and get along with him was totally new for her. She was smart enough to figure out that she had been a little too hard on Simon earlier, and she needed to soften up on him a bit, but that's about as far as her introspection went.

"No, I don't think we did." Simon agreed half laughing.

A waitress came to the table. They ordered their drinks, and then began again after she left.

Simon looked around.

"This is where we met the first time."

Jenna only nodded her head.

Simon looked at her longingly. Even in her modest outfit she was dramatically beautiful. He wondered about her. He did not feel like he deserved her. She was too good for him. He liked her. He wanted to have her. At the same time, he did not want to play the fool. If she was just using him, he wanted to know. Was she serious or was this just a fling for her?

"Why—why did you—why were you interested in me?"

There was no way that Jenna could tell Simon the truth. It was not possible to tell him that when she first saw him, she was only interested in his body and did not really care about him. She could not tell him that she had intended only to be with him for one night; then forget about him forever and leave him behind. She had to lie. Things had changed since that first time she had seen him. It was not just a physical attraction anymore. She wanted something more meaningful.

"I don't know. I was attracted to you so I thought that I would take a chance...I really enjoyed the beach that one night." This was the best reply she could come up with.

"I did too." Simon replied.

They were silent again.

"Why don't you have a boyfriend?" Simon blurted out. He immediately regretted asking the question when he saw the reaction on

Jenna's face. He did not know why he had asked. The question had occurred to him a number of times before, but he had not wanted to ask before because he was afraid of jeopardizing his chances of bedding Jenna. Now, it did not seem so important. Although he still wanted to bed Jenna very badly, he really wanted to understand her. He wanted to know.

Jenna's face showed distress--almost panic. She turned her eyes the other way. She wanted to leave, but she knew that there was no way to dodge the question.

"I'm sorry. I didn't mean to— Simon started to apologize.

"It's okay."

"—embarrass you."

"It's okay. It's okay." Jenna insisted.

"I doesn't seem possible. How can it be?" Simon asked.

Jenna was unprepared for the question. She felt like a fool. She knew that she should have expected it, but she had no answer.

"I'm always traveling—for work. You know? It's hard to get to know someone. And you know? Every time I tell a guy that I'm a model, they get weird, and I don't want to be with them anymore."

It was a great lie, and Jenna spoke it well. She was very convincing.

Simon smiled. He thought that he understood. The first time that Jenna had told him that she was a model, he had almost behaved exactly as she had described. He thought that he was starting to see the world through Jenna's eyes. Maybe it was possible for someone as gorgeous as Jenna to be all alone. It seemed possible, but maybe she was hiding something? He thought that she must have had a bad breakup with an old boyfriend or something.

The waitress came back to the table and took their order.

"So how's your job." Jenna asked.

Simon looked at her in disbelief. He was not sure if she really cared or not.

"It's like my old job only there's more of it, and I get an extra week of vacation."

He smiled, and Jenna smiled back. They felt comfortable with each other again. The waitress came back with their order, and they spent the next twenty minutes like two civilized people having lunch together. It was a refreshing change for both of them. Simon talked about his promotion—like he had wanted to—and Jenna actually listened. At the end, Jenna insisted on paying the bill. Simon did not want her to pay, but she insisted on it. He was amazed again. They went out into the parking lot to Simon's car. They stood face to face and looked into each other's eyes for a long time without speaking—searching for the other's feelings.

"Let's go out again." Simon finally said.

"Yeah."

He bent over and kissed her lightly. They looked at each other again; then, Jenna stood on her tip toes, and Simon kissed her deeply. They stood there looking at each other.

"I have to get back to work."

"Right."

"I'll call you, and we'll set something up."

"Okay."

Simon smiled and got into his car and drove back to work.

Jenna watched him drive away. This was all very new for her. She had never been in a serious relationship before. She wondered if she could pull it off. It seemed impossible, but she felt so good with Simon. She did not want to lose that.

When Simon went back to the airport, he was feeling great. Things could not have been going better. He was looking forward to what would be his fourth official date with Jenna, and was certain that this next date would turn out well. He was very excited. He took the long way through the terminal to his post on the tarmac. Jenna had a spell on his mind. He tried to remember everything about their lunch together. He remembered the way she smelled, and the tone of her laugh. He recalled their entire conversation. He was lost in the whole thought of her until he came to the main concourse.

There was a commotion in front of him. A crowd of people was gathered. There were paramedics. Simon stared momentarily, and then he veered off towards the ramp exit at the next gate. He started to swipe his pass key through the security lock, but decided to go back to the concourse and look at the crowd again. He went up to where they were gathered to take a look.

"What's going on?" he asked one of the people standing there.

"Some girl's hurt."

Simon noticed that he was standing in front of the bar where Geraldine had worked, and he suddenly had a bad feeling. The airport security came out of the bar and started to move the crowd back for the paramedics. They were carting Geraldine out of the bar on a gurney.

"Hey! What happened?" Simon asked one of the policemen.

"I don't know. Please move back sir."

"Is she dead?"

"No, no. She's alive. She's going to make it." Simon watched as the paramedics put Geraldine on the back of an electric cart, and started to drive through the crowd.

"PLEASE MOVE BACK. LET THEM THROUGH." The policemen shouted.

Simon hovered around the entrance for a while, and then saw one of the other bartenders that Geraldine worked with standing nearby. He went over to her to try to get some more information.

"Hey! I used to know her. Do you remember me?" Simon asked the woman.

"I remember."

"What happened to Geraldine?"

"I don't know. She almost bled to death."

"How?"

"I don't know. I've got to go now. Sorry."

The woman went back inside the bar and left Simon standing by himself. It was all so strange. Simon thought about the confrontation that he had had with Geraldine only a few days earlier. He had wanted her dead at that time, but now he almost felt guilty. What had she done to herself? He knew that it was because of the pregnancy. He looked at his watch. He wanted to find out more information, but he absolutely had to get back to work. He headed back to the gate towards the ramp exit and went back to work. Whatever his feelings for Geraldine had been, they were nearly as dead as she was. He quickly forgot about her and lost himself in the routine of his daily work. Where this piece of luggage or that piece of luggage needed to go was soon more important than the life of the woman who he once dreamed of marrying. How that was possible for any human being is the secret to our souls.

Chapter Fifteen

Simon was running about his trailer picking up dirty clothes off the floor, dusting off the furniture (which he had never done before) and vacuuming the carpet. Jenna was coming over to pick him up for their date. They both had agreed that Jenna should make the arrangements this time. She was in control. She chose the time, and the place. She arrived at Simon's trailer right on time, and she was dressed in a fashion that made it clear that this date was going to be interesting. She wore a shiny dark red dress that clung to her body and had a very low v-neckline that exposed half her breasts. She was not wearing any jewelry. Simon was instantly aroused. He almost stuttered when he greeted her at the door, and he knew that he was going to have a difficult time concentrating on anything else for the remainder of the date. Jenna complimented Simon about his trailer in order to be polite. He was relieved to see that she really did not seem to care too much about the fact that he lived in a trailer home. His place was a dump compared to her condominium.

"It's not the greatest place in the world, but this is my place."

"It's nice."

"I cleaned it. I haven't done that in a while." He laughed.

"It smells good. I can tell that you cleaned."

"Do you want a drink? Or, do you want to go right now?"

"I'll have a drink." Jenna said trying very hard to be upbeat and positive.

Simon went to his kitchen, and pulled out the small stash of liquor that he kept above the sink.

"Rum and Coke?"

"Sounds good to me." Jenna said with a big smile on her face.

Simon came back with the two drinks. Jenna took a large gulp, which surprised Simon. She seemed nervous if that was possible for her. How could a woman willing to wear such a small dress in public ever be nervous?

"Have a seat." Simon suggested.

They sat on the couch next to each other. Simon was plotting his next move. He was totally lucid about the situation. He had Jenna—a lingerie model—sitting all alone on a couch with him in his trailer home drinking a strong rum and Coke. She was barely wearing anything. All of her 5'3', 100 pound 'C' cup frame would certainly be drunk with another drink. Simon was already very excited and was almost salivating as Jenna took another long drink from her glass.

"I love this stuff." She said as she smacked her lips provocatively. She was playing with Simon. She could see how much he wanted her. "It's great; isn't it?"

"Yeah." Simon laughed nervously.

He was watching Jenna carefully. She was already half finished with the drink. He very much wanted her to have another one, but he felt that it was too soon to suggest it to her so he changed the subject.

"You know. It seems like I hardly even know you."

"I know. Who am I? Where do I come from?" Jenna said with her sleepy eyes.

"Ha! Right." Simon laughed.

"What about you? I don't know you either."

Simon paused a moment, "You go."

"No, you go first." Jenna insisted.

"Okay...Well, I'm really first from Illinois, but my dad moved us down to Texas when I was eight—to Lubbock. My dad was a cop. He got a job offer there. My mom worked in an office. Dad died when I was pretty young. I was twelve. My mom died a little after I joined the army out of high school."

"They're both gone?"

"Yeah."

"I'm so so sorry."

Jenna said this with great emotion, which seemed exaggerated to Simon. He could not determine if it was because of the rum or if she was truly sympathetic.

"Yeah. Well, they married late. They had me late. I think my mom had me when she was forty two or something. And she died early. She was a big smoker. She was great. She sent me to the corner store once to buy her some cigarettes. Well, you know...I was just a kid. No store owner is going to sell me cigarettes, right? Even if I tell him they're for my mom. So I come back, and tell her that they wouldn't let me buy the cigarettes. She was pissed. She couldn't believe it so she goes with me back to the store, you know? Well, this store had a whole aisle of porno magazines, and things. So she takes me to the store, and she grills the owner, and says, you know, 'What's the problem? Why can't you sell my son some damn cigarettes for me?' Well, the guy explains that I have to be eighteen to buy cigarettes, and he kind of said it in a way that made it seem like my mom was some kind of trashy person because she smoked a lot, and was sending me to buy her some cigarettes—because I was a kid. I don't know. He said something like, 'You shouldn't be sending your kid to buy cigarettes for you.' Well, my mom was not going to have any of that. Like she's a bad mother? She says, 'Like that makes <u>me</u> the scum bag here? You have no problem selling fifty different kinds of porno to a bunch of perverted molesters that come through here every day, but God forbid that I send my son to buy me cigarettes.' She swore that she would never buy cigarettes from that guy again, and I don't think she ever did."

Jenna was smiling. Her mind was a little fuzzy, and she had lost herself in the story. She thought that Simon was cute. She wanted him to kiss her.

Simon could tell by the look on Jenna's face that it was the perfect time to ask her if she wanted another drink.

"Can I get you another?"

"That sounds great."

Jenna gulped down the remainder of her drink.

Simon's heart actually skipped a beat when he saw Jenna finish her drink and agree to another. He knew that they were not going to leave the trailer that night. He was fumbling with the ice, and the bottle of rum. He found it difficult to stay focused. He kept fantasizing about how he was going to take Jenna's clothes off. He went to open a new can of Coca Cola, but in his rush the tab snapped off. He did not have another can so he had to push the tab open with his finger and made a mess. He realized that he was losing control of himself so he paused a while and took a deep breath. He looked up at Jenna who was smiling at him from the couch. She had her high heels off, and her smooth and tan legs were curled up underneath her. Simon's heart was beating very fast. He came back with the drinks and handed Jenna the rum and Coke.

"You're trying to get me drunk." She smiled.

"No I'm not."

Simon wanted to smile, but he kept his wits about him. He knew that it was better not to smile. He denied any ulterior motives, but his tone, and his rosy cheeks were giving him away.

"Yes you are." Jenna said as she took a long sip.

Simon watched her lips caress the glass. He could not help but look at her chest. She was sweating. He could see the beads of sweat running down her cleavage. Her expensive perfume enveloped Simon. He was in a cloud. He was very warm, and he started to sweat. In the silence of the room, all he heard was the clinking of the ice cubes in her drink. They were very close, and he was tingling.

"What about the rest of your family?" Jenna asked softly.

This question killed the mood. Simon's face immediately changed. He paused, looked down and pulled away. Jenna could tell that he was hurt.

"Well, I only had one brother, but he died a few weeks ago. He was a cop—like my dad. He was great."

Simon was quiet. He did not want to talk anymore, but he did not want to be rude. He looked down, and sipped his drink, but all his lustful thoughts about Jenna were gone. He tried not to think about his brother. He did not want to think about anything. His eyes were welling up with tears, however, and he had to look away.

"So you're all alone." Jenna whispered.

"Yeah."

Simon turned towards her. Tears were in Jenna's eyes.

"What are *you* crying for?"

"I understand." She said weakly, "I—understand."

Jenna could hardly speak, and started to cry softly.

"It's okay. I'm okay." Simon tried to reassure her. He put down his drink, and held her hands.

"I'm all alone too," Jenna wiped her eyes and took a long drink with both hands. "I never knew my parents. They abandoned me at a shelter. I never had a family."

Jenna was shaking. Simon took her drink, put it on the floor and hugged her.

"I'm sorry. I'm sorry."

"It's so hard." She cried.

"It's okay. It's okay."

Simon had no idea what she was talking about, but he knew that she was hurt deep inside. He held her in his arms and rocked her as she softly cried into his shoulder. He was crying too.

When she had finished, she pulled back from him. Her eye make up was smeared and running down her cheeks, but she had nothing to wipe it away with.

"I'll get you a tissue." Simon offered.

He rose from the couch and went into the kitchen to get Jenna a tissue, but when he returned, she had passed out. She was lying flat on her back with her legs curled under her. Her satin dress clung to her body outlining her entire form. Simon stood above her with the tissue. Everything in the room was quiet except for the soft hum of Jenna's breathing. Had this happened fifteen minutes earlier, Simon probably would have taken advantage of her in some way, but he felt different about her now. He understood her better. She was just like him. They were both all alone in the world. It seemed impossible to believe that a woman as beautiful as Jenna could be lonely, but she was. He bent over, put Jenna over his shoulder and carried her to his bedroom. As he laid her in the bed and started to pull the covers over her, he was tempted very badly. All sorts of thoughts came to his mind. His mind was racing. She was so sensuous.

As he walked back to the living room, he stopped to take one last look at her. He pursed his lips and shook his head. He wanted her so badly. He was like a man climbing a mountain who was within minutes of the summit only to be forced to retreat because of an avalanche. He stomped his foot in frustration. Then, he turned off the lights and went into the living room to spend the night on the couch.

When Jenna woke up the next morning, Simon was making some coffee. She came out of the bedroom with her hair messed up, and her eyes blurry.

"You're awake. Do you want a bowl of cereal?" Simon asked.

"Okay."

Simon pointed to the kitchen table, and Jenna sat down. He put a cup of coffee, and a bowl of cereal in front of her.

"Sugar and cream?"

"Okay."

Simon took a seat opposite from Jenna and sipped his cup of coffee.

"Thanks for putting me in the bed. I can't drink a lot."

"That's alright. If you want to take a shower, there are clean towels under the sink."

"Thanks."

They sat quietly for a moment while Jenna ate her cereal. She was hungry, and ate quickly. The hot coffee felt good.

"Thanks for— Jenna started. She did not know how to phrase what she wanted to say. Simon had been so nice.

"I think we both needed someone to talk to. Really talk to." Simon paused a moment to think about the situation. He did not want to upset Jenna again so he talked about himself. "My brother and I were really close. He died way too young. I don't know. You do the best you can to get over things. But it is hard when all your family is gone." Simon looked at Jenna and saw that she was deep in thought.

Jenna never had shared her feelings about being an orphan with anyone in her entire life. She did not know if she should trust Simon. How could he possibly understand *her* life? He had a family--once. He knew his mother and father. He grew up in a regular home. She grew up —it was useless. He would never understand. There was no way that he could relate to her.

"It's just hard—not knowing where you came from. How you got here. I shouldn't have broken down like that last night. I think it was the drink, but it's just hard to think about, and sometimes I can't help but cry." Jenna explained.

Lost in thought, Jenna stared into her coffee. Simon could have had his way with her last night. She almost wished that he had. But he was not like that. He was too nice—too normal. After a few moments, she seemed to snap out of her trance.

"I'm going to take that shower." Jenna said as she arose from her chair. She smiled at Simon, and then went into the bathroom.

When she came out thirty minutes later, she looked even sexier than she had the night before. Her hair was wet and slicked back over her shoulders. She was walking around bare footed. Simon just stared at her beautiful legs as she sat on the couch and slipped her high heels on. It was hard to watch her leave.

"Maybe we could meet for lunch again?" he suggested.

Jenna smiled at him from the couch. She sauntered over to him, put her arms around his neck and looked him directly in the eyes.

"I would like that."

They kissed. Simon put his powerful hands around her delicate waist. He wanted to take her on the kitchen counter that instant, but it was not to be. Jenna pulled away, smiled at him and started towards the door.

"I'll call you." Simon said as she walked down the steps towards her car.

"Sure." She smiled.

As she drove away, Jenna glanced in her rear view mirror to see Simon standing all alone on the steps to his trailer home waving goodbye to her. He looked so pathetic. Tears welled up in her eyes. She knew that Simon and she could never really be together. She was too mixed up, and Simon was too normal. Before she had passed out, she had intended to let Simon do whatever he wanted to her. She wanted to be with him. She wanted him to be her boyfriend, but it would never work. She understood that now. She cried harder because she knew she had to let him go. He would never be able to accept her past. The tears were coming faster, and Jenna was starting to shake. She had to pull the car over to the side of the road. The whole thing was a lie. Her life was a lie. There was no way that she could let Simon see behind the façade. It would crush him. She was a freak. How could he ever understand? Jenna Park was not a lingerie model. She was a $5,000 per night prostitute. She had been with hundreds of men. Even though she wanted it with all her heart, she knew that she would never know a loving relationship with a decent man like Simon. It was impossible for her. She would always be alone. She would never really know anyone. She would die all alone. She knew that now. She rested her hands on the steering wheel, slumped down with her head in her arms and cried. It was over.

Chapter Sixteen

"Jimmy called."

"I know."

"You better call him."

Jenna had just arrived back home from her date with Simon, and her roommate, Sheila, was sitting on the couch watching television in the living room. Jenna took her high heels off and went into her bedroom to change her clothes.

"What did you tell him?" Jenna yelled from the bedroom.

"Um—I just said like you said—that you were out."

"What?"

"Um—I said you were out"

"Come on Sheila. I need to know before I call him back."

"Can't you hear me? I just said that you were out," Sheila said louder so that Jenna could hear her. "He wanted to know who you were out with, and I said I didn't know like you said for me to say."

Jenna was annoyed with her friend, Sheila, because she did not think that Sheila was telling her everything.

"You didn't say anything else?" Jenna asked as she came out of the bedroom wearing a pair of sweatpants, and a tee shirt.

"No."

"You're certain."

"Hey, I know what I said. If you're going to be so bossy about it, you can—whatever. Do it yourself next time. Didn't he call you?"

"Yes, he called."

"So, what did you say?"

"I didn't say anything because I didn't answer the phone. I was busy."

"You better call him, Jenna. You have to."

"I will. I will."

"What are you going to tell him?"

"I'm going to tell him the truth. I don't have to lie about anything. I didn't do anything wrong."

Sheila was worried. She knew that Jenna was smart, and that she was right most of the time, but Sheila also knew that Jimmy could be unpredictable, and his reactions were not always what you might expect. Jenna was too confident and was going to push Jimmy too far.

"Who's this guy from the bar you saw? When am I gonna meet him?"

"You're not going to ever meet him because I'm not going to see him again."

"Why? What happened?"

"I don't want to talk about it right now."

"Why?"

"I just don't."

"Why?"

"Why are you pressing me? I just decided that it would be better if we didn't see each other again."

"You're right about that."

Sheila's cell phone rang just then, and she went over to the kitchen table to pick it up and answer the call.

"Hello?"

"Open your front door." the voice on the other end of the call said. It was Jimmy.

Sheila went over to the door, and opened it. Jimmy was standing in the hallway. He flipped his cell phone shut and walked into the condominium.

"I gave Jenna your message." Sheila said as soon as he walked in before anyone else could speak.

Jimmy completely ignored Sheila and walked directly over to Jenna.

"Jenna, you were away last night." he said.

"Yeah, I was with a friend." Jenna started.

Jimmy did not want to talk in front of Sheila and motioned for Jenna to go into the bedroom. He was in a brusque mood. He was always in a brusque mood, and his talk reflected this attitude. Jimmy handled words the way a butcher handles a cut of meat. His contempt for others was such that, as far as Jimmy was concerned, the only point in talking to other people was to tell them what he wanted from them. Everything else was a waist of his time.

"We need to talk in private." He said.

Jenna looked down at the floor and walked towards the bedroom. She was a little scared, but was still in control of herself. Jimmy followed her. He glared at Sheila as he closed the bedroom door.

"Where were you last night?" Jimmy asked Jenna as he closed the door behind him.

"I was with a friend."

"A man?"

"Yeah, I met him at a bar."

"A client?"

"No."

"He didn't pay you?"

"No."

Jimmy stared at Jenna in silence a long time. The only sound in the room was Jimmy's heavy breathing through his nose. He wondered if she could possibly be bold enough to lie straight to his face.

"You went to see a man that you met in the bar. You spent the night with him, and you expect me to believe that he didn't pay you?" Jimmy crossed his arms and turned away from Jenna.

"I didn't—I swear he didn't pay me." Jenna pleaded.

Jimmy turned back towards her, but his arms were still crossed.

"Who is this guy?"

"Just some guy I met in the bar."

"Is this your boyfriend?"

"Not really, but I like him."

"That's sweet." Jimmy said sarcastically. "And he didn't pay you?"

"You know I wouldn't do that"

Jimmy walked right up to Jenna and put his face directly in front of hers—very close.

"That's good, Jenna." He hissed through his teeth. "I'm glad to hear that because if you <u>ever</u> took money on the side—Do you know what would happen to you if you ever did that?"

Jimmy looked down at Jenna. His tone was threatening, but he maintained his equanimity. Inside, however, he was crazed with anger. He wanted to scream at Jenna. He wanted to slap her around a little. She needed more discipline--harsher discipline.

Jenna was a little nervous. She was like a child who had been caught eating some cookies that she was not supposed to touch. She could not look at Jimmy and only stared down at the floor. She said nothing, but she despised Jimmy. She always had. She knew that she was smarter than him. Jimmy liked to think that she was not, but deep down he knew that she was smarter. He did not like it when she showed him up, and Jenna knew it.

"We didn't do anything. I only just talked to him. He didn't pay." Jenna whined. She was becoming more scared.

Jimmy let out a loud sigh through his nose.

"Where does he live?"

Jenna was *really* scared now. Was Jimmy going to visit Simon? Would he hurt Simon? Would he tell Simon that Jenna was a prostitute and that Jimmy was her pimp? She started to regret having ever gone out with Simon in the first place. She had dragged him into a dark place. She opened her mouth to speak, but she could not find the courage to tell Jimmy, and he sensed it.

"I'm not going to go get him. It's not worth my time, but you better tell me now. East side? West side? What?"

"North."

"Like where north?"

Jenna did not want to answer, but she knew that she had to.

"By the airport."

This answer seemed to satisfy Jimmy. He took a step back from Jenna and let down his arms. All the tension in the room was relieved.

"Good. That's good. You need to understand that it's over with this guy. You must do what I say. Do you understand?" Jimmy ordered her.

"It's over." Jenna nodded. She was quiet.

"Is it over, Jenna? Don't lie to me."

"I ended it. We never—we only went out a couple of times. We never did anything. I wasn't going to call him back."

"But it's over."

"Yes. I never told him about me. He doesn't know. I realized it couldn't go anywhere..." Jenna's voice cracked and faded. The terrible reality that she would never be with Simon or any loving man came back to her and weighed her down. Tears were welling up in her eyes, and her jaw quivered

Jimmy could see that Jenna was not lying to him. He was no longer angry. Had she lied, he would have had another problem on his hands. As it was, he could settle the issue immediately. Jenna was showing respect for him.

"Good. Don't call him again. Don't return his calls. Don't go to visit him. Don't let him in here. He will get the message, and he will go away. You will forget about him in time."

There was a long pause. Jimmy walked back towards Jenna and stared her down. She felt uncomfortable and crossed her arms. She wanted to leave.

Jenna was going to quit Simon anyhow, but now that Jimmy was forcing her she almost wanted to see Simon again for spite—almost. In the end, she knew how brutal Jimmy could be, and she had no desire to go down that road.

"I am taking your car keys away from you for a month." Jimmy announced.

Jenna was shocked and started to protest, "Why? It's not fa--."

"YOU ABUSED THE CAR." Jimmy shouted. He was not going to argue the issue with Jenna, "You went off behind my back to be with this guy. You knew it was wrong, and now you have to pay. That's it. Do you understand? Don't back talk me. You're pushing me, and I'm getting pissed off."

Jenna was frustrated, and angry inside. She frowned and folded her arms. Her pride was hurt, but she knew that she had no choice in the matter. Jimmy's word was law. She knew she could not defy him and nodded her head in agreement.

"Good. Let's go back." Jimmy said. He opened the bedroom door and let Jenna go ahead of him back into the living room.

Sheila was sitting in one of the living room chairs. She searched Jenna's face for clues as Jimmy, and Jenna came down the hallway to the main room. Jimmy stood by the kitchen table, and Jenna went over to the couch and curled up with a cushion.

"By the way, you guys have work tonight." Jimmy started.

"Tonight?" Sheila asked.

"It's short notice, but you're both going to a party. I will introduce you to some men. If they want a date, you will go with them and call me whenever you are ready to be picked up. Jenna, you will wear that red satin dress. Sheila, I want you in that yellow dress. The one with the top that's cut off—without the shoulder straps."

"The tube top."

"Yes, the one with the flowing skirt--not the mini skirt. I will pick you up at five o'clock. We're going to the beach house again. Don't make me wait."

Jimmy looked at the two women without emotion. He had spoken. He was not going to speak again. He walked over to the door and left the condominium without saying another word.

"Are you okay?" Sheila asked once the door had shut.

"I'm fine." Jenna said as she wiped away the tears that were in her eyes and clutched the pillow that was in her lap.

"Did you get in trouble?"

"Yes."

"Did he?"

"He didn't touch me."

Sheila became more relaxed, "I never told him. I just said what you told me to say."

"I know. You did fine. It's not your fault."

"What did he say?"

"He doesn't want me to see him again."

"And?"

"And he took away my car for a month."

"A month?"

"It's total bull—

"You got lucky."

Jenna looked at Sheila and gave careful thought to her words. She knew Sheila was right and resigned herself to accept the punishment.

"What about that guy from the bar? Are you going to tell him?" Sheila asked.

"No, I'm not. Jimmy doesn't want me to talk to him. I already decided that on my own anyhow."

Jenna was angry now. She left the couch and walked over to the kitchen counter, "I just don't understand what his problem is. Are we not ever supposed to know anybody for the rest of our lives? We're people too!"

"Um--I don't know about that, but I wouldn't push Jimmy if I were you."

"I'm not going to push Jimmy. I just think it's ridiculous. He controls everything, 'You will wear the red dress. You will wear the yellow dress. I will pick you up at five o'clock. You will go— It's ridiculous."

Sheila did not reply. She only looked at the clock, and saw that it was a little after one o'clock.

"Um—we probably have a little time before we have to get ready. Will you touch up my hair?"

Sheila held up her long and beautiful blonde hair for Jenna to see.

"What's wrong with it?" Jenna asked.

"Nothing—I just want to touch up the color a little. I just bought this stuff."

Sheila happily skipped into the bathroom and came out with a bottle of hair coloring.

"Come on. Please."

"Okay. Let's do it."

Jenna consented, and the two women went into the bathroom to color Sheila's hair.

They were ready at five o'clock when Jimmy came and knocked on the condominium door. Jenna was wearing the same satin dress that she had worn to see Simon the previous night. She was soft and sultry like something out of a dream. Sheila's long and wavy blonde hair was flowing. She was wearing a light colored yellow dress with a tube top pulled low across her full chest showing off her shiny smooth white shoulders. A wide black belt exaggerated her thin waist and enhanced the curve of her hips. Jimmy hardly seemed to notice, however. He was all business and escorted the two women to his car. It was a long drive to the beach house—the same house that Jenna had spent that first night with Simon. Sheila sat in the front passenger seat of the car, and Jenna rode in the back while Jimmy drove. They did not speak much on the way. Sheila played her music on her headphones, and Jenna stared out the back window in a daze.

They arrived early to the party. When they came to the front of the house, a valet took their car, and Jimmy walked with Sheila and Jenna to the front entrance which was open in expectation of the guests.

"Jimmy!" someone called as they walked through the door.

"Wait here a moment." Jimmy said quietly to Sheila and Jenna.

He went over to greet one of the guests, who was grinning at Jimmy and shaking his hand enthusiastically. Jenna and Sheila waited in the foyer by the stairs that went up to the second floor. After Jimmy was finished with his friends, he came back to the women.

"We're going to go out to the bar in the back to look for these two guys."

Jimmy walked through the short hallway that led to the back of the house, and onto the large wooden deck with Sheila and Jenna. There was a bar set up on one end.

"Come with me to the bar." Jimmy said.

"What can I get you?" the bartender asked as they walked up to him.

"Nothing for me." Jimmy said.

"I'll have a Cosmo." Sheila smiled.

"Jack and Co— Jenna started to say, but she was cut off.

"You know that you can't drink like that, Jenna." Jimmy said.

"I want it."

"She'll have a Coke. Just a Coke." Jimmy said to the bartender. The bartender poured the drinks and handed them to the two women.

"Have you seen a tall guy with dark blonde hair, blue eyes--perfect teeth?" Jimmy asked the bartender.

"You looking for a date or something?" the bartender joked.

Sheila and Jenna chuckled, but soon concealed their laughter when they saw the look in Jimmy's eyes. He gave the bartender a murderous look and stared him down. The bartender was put off by Jimmy's demeanor. He was about to apologize when he saw the man Jimmy was looking for standing behind Sheila and Jenna.

"Is that him?" the bartender said pointing past Jimmy's shoulder.

Jimmy turned around and saw the man he was looking for. He turned back around and glared at the bartender.

"Thanks." He said dryly.

The bartender let out a large sigh of relief when Jimmy and the two women walked away. He reminded himself never to joke around with the guests again.

Jimmy walked up to the tall blonde haired man and tapped him on the shoulder.

"Jimmy! Jimmy! Jimmy!"

"Brian!"

The two men embraced briefly.

"Brian, this is Sheila and Jenna. Girls this is Brian."

Sheila was immediately thrilled with Brian. He was very handsome. He had a graceful chin, and large blue eyes. He was tall, and well built. She hoped very much that this was her date.

"Hi. I'm Sheila." She introduced herself, and reached out to shake Brian's hand.

Brian looked at Sheila from head to toe. He was equally excited about her. Her white skin was smooth, and shiny. She had bright blue eyes, and flowing and bright blonde hair.

"And this is Jenna." Jimmy said.

"Hello." Jenna said as she shook Brian's hand.

"Boy, Jimmy, you have some beautiful friends here." Brian said as he smiled at Sheila. "I don't think that there are going to be any ladies prettier than you two here tonight." He kept glancing at Sheila as he spoke. It was obvious that he was very attracted to her.

"I need to talk to you." Jimmy said.

He and Brian pulled away from the two women in order to talk privately.

"He's gorgeous." Sheila whispered to Jenna.

Jenna just nodded her head. She watched Jimmy speaking to Brian. Brian was familiar to her somehow. Brian patted Jimmy on the shoulder and pointed towards the beach. Jimmy nodded his head and came back to the two women.

"Wait by the bar for me. I will be right back." Jimmy said. Then he left with Brian, and the two men went towards the beach. They were soon descending the wooden stairs that went from the grassy terrace to the beach.

"Jenna?" Sheila asked.

"Yeah."

"Is it okay if I take Brian as my date? He's so fine."

Jenna laughed a little, "Sure. He's all yours."

They waited sometime before Brian, and Jimmy returned from the beach. Periodically a male guest at the party would walk up to the bar for a drink and flirt with Sheila and Jenna. They were accustomed to this and politely smiled back, but made certain not to show any interest. They were there for business, and they knew that Jimmy was coming back soon. Finally, they saw Jimmy, and Brian coming up the steps from the beach. They were leading two other men. The four men stopped at the top of the steps. Brian shook Jimmy's hand, said goodbye and walked off in another direction. Jimmy and the two other men walked towards the wooden deck and Sheila and Jenna at the bar.

"Oh my God." Sheila gasped as she saw the three men approaching.

Jimmy was leading two small Indian men, who were very dark skinned. One of them was young, skinny, and wore a mustache. The other man was older and had a beer belly. He was bald and wore glasses.

"I don't think that Brian is one of our dates." Jenna commented sarcastically and threw her plastic cup into the trash can nearby in disgust.

Jimmy approached the bar with the two Indian men, and introduced them to Sheila and Jenna.

"Hello ladies."

"Hi." Sheila smiled covering her disappointment.

"Hi." Jenna followed.

"Jenna, Sheila this is Raji, and Rameesh."

"It is a pleasure to meet with you." Raji, the skinny man with a moustache, said in a very heavy Indian accent.

Rameesh only smiled and nodded his head.

Jenna and Sheila politely shook their hands and smiled.

"Raji likes to play golf like you Sheila. He's a good golfer."

"No, no, no, no. That is only partly true, now. Please, please, Jimmy. I like to play golf, it is true, thank you kindly, but I am only just beginning. I am very amateur."

"That's okay. I'm not any good either. It's very hard." Sheila said.

"It is a very difficult sport. I don't know who invented it, but it is very difficult."

"And what do you like to do?" Rameesh asked Jenna.

Jenna looked at Jimmy. He clenched his teeth and stared at her. She knew that she was expected to perform, but was feeling revulsion inside and had a difficult time concealing her emotion. She could see already that Sheila would end up with the younger Raji, which was not so bad. Rameesh was disgusting, however. His teeth were very bad, and his wisps of hair barely covered his bald head. Incredibly, he had tried to dress like a young American and looked very awkward in contemporary fashion. His collar was open wide at the top, and his designer blue jeans were low on his waist. It did not suit him, however, and contrasted badly with his graying hair and thick glasses.

"I like to drink." Jenna said.

"Ha! Ha! Ha! Ha!" Rameesh laughed. Jenna had made him feel genuinely good.

"Then we too have something in common. I, myself, like to drink. Can I get you a drink?" Rameesh asked.

Jenna looked at Jimmy and smiled. "I'll have a Jack and Coke." she said pleased with her little victory of drinking in defiance of Jimmy's will.

"Fantastic!" Rameesh beamed. He signaled the bartender and handed Jenna a Jack and Coke.

"I am going to leave you guys alone. I will see you around." Jimmy said. He gave another dirty look to Jenna and left as gracefully as he could manage. He did not like the fact that Jenna had ordered the drink, but he understood her position. He was certain that she would do her job.

"Goodbye Jimmy!" Raji said happily.

"Goodbye Jimmy!" Jenna taunted him.

Raji, and Sheila also ordered a drinks, and Raji suggested that they all go to the buffet tent and eat some food.

The two couples left the bar and went to the tent that was set up on the lawn, and put their drinks on a table where they could sit and eat. Then they went to the buffet line, and piled their plates with food.

Jenna was feeling fuzzy from her drink as she ate her meal. It was difficult to think of what was ahead of her for the rest of the night, but she had been here hundreds of times before and knew how to get

---

through it. In her mind, she quickly disassociated herself from her body. She reminded herself that Rameesh was only a john. Her own body was a means to an end. This was her job. She would have her night with Rameesh, collect her pay from Jimmy, and go on. In a week, Rameesh would barely be a memory.

Sheila was even more of a pro than Jenna. She was laughing and giggling already. She could care less about Raji or Rameesh. They meant nothing to her. Somehow, she had entered a frame of mind where she was hardly thinking about what she was doing. She had nothing in her heart. She was empty. All that mattered was the food, and the vodka. Raji could say anything he wanted, and she would have laughed. Raji could have been a wooden post, and she would have climbed on top of him. He was totally irrelevant to her mind. He was not even a person to her. She very easily slipped into this mode of thought—much more so than Jenna. She would use Raji, take his money and be done with it. It meant nothing. All she had to do was laugh at his stupid comments and lie down with him for twenty minutes. Even her own body meant nothing to Sheila. When she had sex with Raji, it almost felt like it was happening to somebody else for her.

The reality, of course, is that our minds and bodies are married together in such a way as to constitute a unified whole. People are not just spirits living in a material world; they are spirits married to a material world. A human person is not a soul with a body attached like some kind of outfit one might wear. Human beings do not wear their bodies like some cloak that they can throw over the back of a chair if they like; rather, it is as if two fabrics—soul and body—were interwoven together so finely that the resulting garment was something completely new. Body and soul are so intimately fused together that they transform into something unique—a human person. A soul created by God is joined to two cells at the moment of conception; in that instant, the spiritual world is married to the material world, and a human person comes into existence.

Jenna and Sheila carried on a conversation the best they could with Raji and Rameesh. A waitress came by, and they all ordered another drink. Jenna was already numb from the first drink, but knew that she would need another to get through the night. They ate some desert and watched the people go through the buffet line. The waitress came back with their drinks.

"You are a very beautiful woman." Rameesh complimented Jenna.

"Thanks."

"You are how old?"

"Twenty-two."

"Ah yes. Twenty-two. Your mother must have been very beautiful. You have inherited such beautiful features."

Jenna was a little put off by this comment. She did not know where Rameesh was going with this. He seemed like he was almost testing her, and she did not like it. She was already intoxicated, and Rameesh was bringing her further down.

"My mother gave me up when I was a baby. I never knew her."

"Oh?"

"I never had a real home—I always wanted—to—to—know my real parents." Jenna was drunk and on the verge of tears.

Rameesh could see that he was ruining the night. The reality was that he had a difficult time talking to women, and had not been able to think of anything else to say. He was only trying to make small talk. He realized, however, that he had picked the wrong subject to talk about; he knew that he had to change the mood of the situation, or risk alienating Jenna.

"It's such a beautiful sunset. Would you like to accompany me to the beach?" Rameesh asked Jenna.

"Sure."

"We will be seeing you." Raji smiled as he held Sheila's hand and watched Jenna and Rameesh get up from the table.

Jenna sluggishly rose from her chair and grabbed her drink. Rameesh led her by the arm towards the beach.

"So what do you do for a living?" Jenna asked as they approached the top of the stairs going down to the beach.

"I am a biochemist. I work for a local laboratory."

"Wow. That's something. What kind of work do you do?"

"I develop drugs."

"Do you work with Raji?"

"No, I do not, but he was a student of mind once. He is working very good in Houston for another lab."

"He's a biochemist too?"

"He is a computer software developer."

"Oh." The whole thing was over Jenna's head. She did not really care anyhow. She was only playing the part that she was expected to act with a john.

Jenna was in a fog as they reached the bottom of the stairs. She put her drink down on the last of the steps and stumbled as they made their way onto the beach. There was no one else around. She stumbled again as they made their way across the sand, and Rameesh had to hold her up.

"Careful. Let me assist you now." Rameesh said as he held her up.

"Those drinks were strong."

Rameesh held Jenna up and brought her close to him. He was very aroused as Jenna's soft body came up against his chest. He started to stroke her bare back and gently rub her thighs. Soon he was all over Jenna, licking her neck and groping her entire body. He was clumsy.

Jenna did not care. She was so drunk; she could barely think, but the memory of the last time that she was at this beach with Simon came back. She remembered how nice it felt to just stand there with him watching the moon with her arm around his strong bicep. But now she was being molested by this disgusting stranger. Was this the way things would be for her for the rest of her life? The question did not penetrate too deeply into her mind. She was too drunk. Like Sheila, she slipped into a mindset that did not care about reality anymore. Rameesh was a thing now—not even real. Her own body was just a thing to her—like a car is to its driver. It was just a vehicle that she walked around in. She had willfully divorced her spirit from her body.

"I must have you." He moaned.

Jenna drunkenly smiled at him. She tried to lead him by the hand back towards the stairs, but Rameesh had to help her walk. They started up the wooden steps back towards the terrace.

"Oh wait!" Jenna shouted. She bent over and made certain to grab her drink that was resting on the bottom step.

Jenna and Rameesh went up the steps and walked across the lawn towards the deck at the back of the house. It was starting to get dark outside, and the moon was just a little over the horizon. Jenna led Rameesh into the house. Someone had set up the dividers that kept the guests away from the front of the house, but they ignored these. Jenna showed Rameesh the way through the hallway that led to the front doors, and the staircase that went to the second floor. She knew where she was going. They went upstairs, walked down a short hallway and entered a bedroom that had a small window that faced the back of the house. There was a low bed, a dresser, an end table, a lamp and an alarm clock in the room. There was a small bathroom that joined the room in the corner.

Jenna shut the door behind her and dimmed the lights until they were almost completely off. Then she slowly walked up to Rameesh, took off his glasses and tossed them gently onto the dresser.

There was still enough light in the room for Rameesh to see Jenna clearly. He stared at her eyes for a moment; then, he looked down at her deep cleavage and quickly buried his face in her luscious chest. Jenna was still holding her drink and took a long gulp just before Rameesh had his way with her. She only just managed to set the drink onto the dresser as he slipped off her dress and pushed her onto the bed. She soon lost herself to his lust and let him do as he pleased as the light from the waxing moon came through the window. This was her life. This was why she could never be with Simon. How could she ever have a real relationship with any man? It was hopeless. Her life was hideous. It was too dark to be revealed. There was no escape, though. She knew that. Her eyes started to well up with tears.

Chapter Seventeen

Simon Bosse looked out of his bedroom window. His little family of sparrow's had long since flown away. Baby was gone. Mama and Papa were gone. Bubba, Bud, Humpty and Dumpty were gone. All that was left was the empty nest in the little bush outside his bedroom window. But when he went for walks in the trailer park, or as he went to his car to drive to work in the morning, the song of the sparrows filled the air and made Simon's world a little better. He knew that somewhere around his home in the trees little Baby was singing for him, and that made Simon feel good. Baby would go on to find his own mate and start his own family. Perhaps, even after Simon had moved from the trailer park, someone else would one day enjoy the bird song that came from one of Baby's offspring, and none of this ever would have happened had not Simon nurtured the little sparrow.

Simon's love of this little bird gave birth to this reality. It was a simple love. It was a genuine love. Simon had not gone out at night, dug up the worms, chopped them up and fed the little bits to the little sparrow because he expected anything back. He did these things because he loved the sparrow so much that he would rather do these things than to see the little sparrow die. He would rather suffer these small inconveniences than to miss seeing little Baby fly, or miss hearing him sing. A part of Simon's love was in that bird song and would go on as long as there were birds to sing. As it was with Simon and this bird, so much more is it with God and men. God reaches down to man with a love so generous that it cannot be described adequately. God is spit on for the sake of man. God is beaten for the sake of man. God is whipped, crowned with thorns, mocked, smote on the head and nailed to a cross for the sake of man. And as God is dying on that cross, He is mocked again and stabbed in the heart for the sake of man. God does all these things so that man might know the truth, and have life—true life. To reject this love is to reject life itself. If little Baby had refused Simon's loving care, this little sparrow would have died. In the same way, we have life because we have the love of God. To reject God's love is to reject life. To reject God's love, is to choose death.

Simon Bosse did not know if he loved Jenna Park or not. He thought that he loved her. Then again, he once thought that he had loved Geraldine. Was it different this time? How was he really to know if it was true love? How could he know for certain if what he felt for this other person was honest love? The one true way--the only way--for him to know for certain would be if he was willing to put aside his own wants and desires for the sake of the other. This is love. It is a decision backed up with an action. It is the decision to forgo one's own wants, needs or well being for the sake of another's wants, needs and well being. To love is to give life to another even if a portion of you must die a little in order to do it. Did he love Jenna in this way? Simon had no idea.

Simon Bosse relentlessly called Jenna Park for five days. He called during work. He called from home after work. Jenna never returned one call. Simon went to Hooligan's where they first met hoping to run into her. He asked around to see if anyone had seen her there. Nobody seemed to know or care. He was like a lost tourist in a foreign country where no one was willing or able to help him find his way. "Who was Jenna Park?" "Sorry, I do not remember her." Even the bartender who had been there the day that Jenna first had met Simon had trouble remembering her. Simon was going mad. He was obsessed with Jenna. He just wanted to understand what went wrong. Did he do something wrong? Jenna was constantly on his mind, but he could not even contact her. After a week of being ignored, his frustration had reached a peak. He could not stand it anymore. He needed an explanation and went to her condominium to face her directly.

Jenna's building, however, had a twenty four hour security guard posted in the lobby. During the daytime—most days—the guard on duty was a very tall and powerfully built man. He seemed to know everyone in the building on a first name basis. Simon knew that he would never make it into the building past this guard, and he did not even try.

Instead, Simon tried to stakeout the front door. On his day off, he decided to stand across the street and watch the front entrance to Jenna's condominium building all day long. It was a futile effort. He had no idea if she was even in the building. He had no idea when she might come out. After five hours of standing across the street, he realized that he was being an idiot and went home. He continued to call her a few days after his ridiculous stakeout, and then finally gave up. She did not want to talk to him. He did not know why. He did not know what he had done wrong, and he was not sure that he cared. He only knew that she did not want to talk to him anymore, and he decided to leave her alone. Perhaps Jenna thought that she was too good for him. Perhaps she never really had been interested in him in the first place. Maybe she had found some other boy toy to occupy her time with. Did it matter anymore? He thought that his feelings for her were true, but he decided to let her go. Whatever her reasons for dumping him were, he would rather be miserable by himself than make her unhappy. This in itself may have been the proof Simon needed that his love for Jenna was real.

He was in the bar again, drinking heavily again—alone again. It was the airport bar. Simon was numb. He did not know what to think or do. He felt worthless. He was empty and listless. How did he always end up alone? He did not know, but he did not want to break it down either. He just wanted to drink.

"Hello, my friend." A confident voice called from behind.

Simon turned around to look behind him. It was the pilot, Geraldine's pilot. The two men were silent for a moment.

"Are you going to hurt me?" the pilot asked.

"I'm not going to hurt you." Simon said softly.

The pilot sensed that Simon was not angry anymore, and decided that it was safe to engage him.

"May I sit down?"

Simon had to think about it for a moment.

"Sure, why not? Have a seat."

The pilot sat down, flagged the bartender and ordered a Scotch.

"You're a pretty serious drinker."

"Ha! I'm not serious about anything my friend. Life's too short." The pilot pulled out an electric cigarette to puff on.

"Do you really like those things?"

"Ha! Yes. I enjoy them."

"Whatever."

The pilot puffed his electric cigarette as the bartender put the Scotch in front of him. The two men, Simon and the pilot, sat next to each other quietly drinking for some time. Simon began to wonder what the pilot wanted. There were plenty of other bars in the airport for the pilot to have a drink. He obviously wanted to talk to Simon for some reason, but Simon really was not in the mood to talk. If the pilot had something to say, he should start the conversation himself, and get it over with. Simon was not going to initiate anything.

"I wanted to make certain that there were no hard feelings between us. Am I correct in saying that?" the pilot finally asked.

Simon looked at him sideways.

"Not really, but it's all in the past now. It's not worth getting violent about."

The pilot absorbed the answer and thought carefully about how he wanted to phrase his next question.

"Do you—have you had any contact with Gerry?"

"I haven't seen her since they carried her out of this place on a stretcher." Simon said in a monotone.

This was the subject that the pilot wanted to talk about. He wanted to know more about the matter, but he did not want to show how eager he was for the information and tried to project a certain insouciance.

"That was unfortunate. I did not mean for that to happen. Have you heard anything more about it?"

Simon was starting to get annoyed. It was bad enough that this pilot was talking to him; he certainly did not want to talk about Geraldine.

"Look, I don't really want to talk about Geraldine, okay? It happened. It's over. You're starting to piss me off."

"I apologize. I am truly sorry. Forget that I mentioned it." The pilot went back to his cigarette.

Simon was silent for a moment and tried to control his temper. He was like a caged animal that was being poked with a stick. What was with this pilot? Why could he just not leave him alone? If he wanted information about Geraldine, why not just call the hospital? Then, a thought occurred to Simon. The pilot did not say, "That was a shame" or "It was a tragedy." He had said that he "did not mean for that to happen." He was involved somehow.

"What did you mean?" Simon asked.

"Excuse me?"

"What did you mean that you 'did not mean for that to happen.'"

"The—uh—the incident of course—the bleeding."

"The bleeding?"

The pilot stared down and looked at the water vapor coming from the electric cigarette in his hand in an attempt to avoid eye contact with Simon. He suddenly realized that Simon might not know anything at all about the nature of Geraldine's hospitalization. He had to be careful not to give Simon any information that might come back to hurt him.

"You know that she went to the hospital because of excessive blood loss? Yes?"

Simon played dumb, "No, I did not know that."

"I just—it was a terrible thing."

"But you said that you didn't mean for that to happen. What did you have to do with the bleeding?"

"Nothing. Nothing. I—my English—it's my English. I worded it badly. I only meant that it was a terrible thing."

Simon looked at the pilot. He looked very closely at the man and examined him. He could see the pilot pursing his lips repeatedly. The pilot was nervous. Nothing else in the pilot's demeanor or bearing gave him away, but the pursing of his lips showed that he was nervous, and Simon saw it.

"Where are you from?" Simon asked.

"Dallas."

"Originally, I mean. Where's your family from?"

"Brazil."

"You were born there?"

"Yes, we moved to America when I was thirteen."

"So you've been here how long?"

"Sixteen years."

Sixteen years was a long time to learn English in Simon's opinion. He knew that the pilot was lying. Simon became fully aware of the pilot's uneasiness. The pilot had approached him to pump him for information and find out if Geraldine was going to cause trouble.

Simon had the pilot, and he knew it. He was like a man in some sport who realizes that he has the upper hand over his chief opponent and has a chance to beat him for the first time. He was going to press that advantage. He was not going to let the opportunity pass.

"Yeah, it's too bad she lost the baby." Simon remarked.

This last comment hung in the air like the smell of burnt toast. The pilot did not reply. He only sipped his drink and made a point to show no reaction. He did not think that anyone had known about Geraldine's pregnancy. It appeared to him that Simon knew more about the situation than he first indicated.

"I said, 'it's too bad about the baby.'" Simon repeated.

The pilot only nodded his head. He knew that anything that he might say would be used against him so he remained silent.

"Was it yours?" Simon pressed.

The pilot took a long drag on his cigarette, put it down again, and shrugged his shoulders in mock ignorance.

"Maybe it was, maybe it wasn't. There is no way to tell. Of course, the girl—she was a 'party girl' I think is how you would say it. It could have been a number of men's."

"Yeah, I suppose so."

The pilot sensed Simon's game and had no interest in playing anymore. He was not going to put himself in a position to be manipulated by Simon. He finished his drink and signaled the bartender that he wanted to pay. Simon was not going to let him leave so easily, however. He was not going to let this pilot slip like slime through his fingers. He decided to take a gamble.

"You know, I talked to her before the bleeding. She said that you had broken up with her; that it was over between you and her."

"Yes. That is true." the pilot sighed as he paid for his drink.

"We talked about the baby too. That's how I knew that she was pregnant. She told me that it was yours."

"Oh?"

"But she didn't tell me that you gave her the pills to get rid of it."

Simon looked directly into the pilot's eyes with contempt. The shock on the pilot's face was very brief, but very obvious. Simon had taken a gamble, and it had paid off.

The pilot, however, was not going to be had like this. His machismo was too strong. No one was going to corner him like this. No, no, he was too good for that.

"I do not understand your meaning, and I don't think I want to, my friend."

"It's alright. She probably won't say anything. I'm sure you have nothing to worry about--nothing at all." Simon said with a self satisfied look on his face.

The pilot's inflated feeling of self importance would not stand for this kind of sarcasm from a simple baggage handler like Simon. It was the kind of challenge that he could not back down from.

"You're right, my friend. I have nothing to worry about. And do you know why? Because she is just a girl—a stupid girl. I have been all over the world. Do you know that? I have had hundreds of girls from all over the world. Rich girls, poor girls, famous girls, powerful girls—I've had royalty. Yes—royalty. And they only have one thing in common, they are so, so stupid. They are just bodies with hardly any brains. Maybe one or two here and there have a brain, but most of them are just stupid things. Even the smart ones are not so smart. They are meaningless."

"Maybe you're right, and maybe you're wrong. There is no way to tell." Simon said mocking the pilot's tone. "But those are foreign girls. This is an American girl under American laws--American courts—Texas courts. Seems wrong that human life should have meaning in one time and place, but not another, but I guess that's the way it is. I hope those pills that you gave her were legal in this country because if they weren't— even a 'party girl' can hire a lawyer. This is Texas--big state—big law suits."

The pilot abruptly rose from his bar stool and stood in front of Simon with his teeth clenched. He did not say a word. Simon looked at him like a man who knew that he was better than the other man--deep down inside at the core of his being where it counted the most. Whatever the pilot's wealth in this world was, and no matter how good looking he was, ultimately, Simon was the better man, and he knew it. The pilot glared at Simon for a moment and then walked off in a huff. Simon had beaten him. In that one moment, Simon had changed as a man. Even if it was only a slight change, it was an important one. He understood that Geraldine had worth, if only just because she was human, and for no other reason—but she still had worth. He had worth too. He may not be rich, have a fancy job, be educated or terribly well off, but he still had worth. It did not matter what his status was; it did not matter what any human's status was—they had worth because they were human. Even though Jenna had apparently dumped him, Simon knew that his life had meaning, and there had to be a woman out there who would appreciate him. And even if there was no such woman, there was always God. God loved him. He pushed his drink away, paid the bartender and left the bar. Outside in the open air as he walked to his car, birds flittered by here and there chirping wildly. He smiled at the bird song all around him and started to whistle his own song.

Chapter Eighteen

It was time to go back home. Although he did not want to go back home, he knew that he had to show his face there. He had been out all night. If he did not make at least a token appearance, his wife would have a fit. Of course, he knew that she would have a fit anyhow. It really was not a question of whether she was going to have a fit or not; rather, it was a question of how big of a tantrum she would throw. Like a man holding a losing stock and contemplating whether he should hold onto it longer and hope for the best, or sell now and cut his losses, he knew that it would go better for him to take the punishment he already faced than to risk greater retribution from his wife by staying out even longer. So he went home, even though he knew that there would be a fight.

Rameesh Verma was born in Mumbai, India. He was from an upper middle caste. He had a bachelor's degree, and a doctorate in biochemistry from Mumbai University where he had met his wife, Sonali, in his second year of graduate school. She was an employee in the library at the university. In those days, Rameesh would go there every day that he could, and check out a book—any book—just to have the chance to talk with Sonali. After his fifth book in five days, it was obvious that he was not there for the books. They started dating and were married before the end of Rameesh's second year. They lived together in a small one room studio flat near the university. Rameesh was attending classes and earning a small salary as a teaching assistant. Sonali continued to work at the library almost all the way up until their first child, Tarun, was born. In his last year of schooling at the university, Rameesh, Sonali and Tarun lived together in the small flat. After work, Rameesh and his wife would take the child together to the park in the center of campus and sit on the grass just enjoying the warmth of the sun. Sometimes they would go to a small playground and put the child on a swing. They had almost no money, so they could not afford to do much else; nevertheless, these were the happiest days of Rameesh's life. No matter how difficult the

---

financial situation was, or how many exams that he had, the love of his wife and child always made him forget his troubles proving that nothing in this world is too difficult to handle if you have the right disposition. It is only self love that makes life difficult. Rich people that possess seemingly every material good, can be miserable. Poor people that have practically no material possessions can find happiness. Only the possession or absence of selfish love makes the difference. A person is miserable in direct proportion to the amount of selfish love that he has. Selfish love makes a person aware of what is lacking in his life, makes him obsess about his difficulties, and turns his heart towards using others like a tool to obtain more and more. On the contrary, unselfish love makes a person aware of the blessings in his life, makes him forget about his difficulties, and turns his heart towards sharing what blessings he has with others. It is a matter of the cup being half empty or half full. For the person full of selfish love, the cup is always empty no matter how much water (or wine mixed with water) that is poured into it.

After he graduated with his doctorate, Rameesh was offered a full time teaching position, and he was able to move into a nicer, but still modest home. While he taught classes at the university, Rameesh earned another degree in Computer Science. Shortly afterwards, while working on a project for a large pharmaceutical company, Rameesh came in contact with a man who offered Rameesh a chance to work in The United States. Rameesh leaped at the opportunity and moved his family to California where his second child was born. Three years later, Rameesh was presented another opportunity with a large biotech firm from Texas, and he moved his family once again—this time to Houston.

Rameesh had worked in Houston for this large biotech firm for fifteen years, and had become a United States citizen along with his wife. He was forty-eight years old, and near the peak of his career. He was making more money in one week than he made in an entire year as an assistant teacher in Mumbai during his graduate studies. For all his

---

money, however, Rameesh was miserable. When he had first met his wife in the Mumbai University library, she was serene and yet playful. When they dated, he loved to talk with her, and go for walks in the park. She built him up and made him forget himself. He loved to give her small knick knacks and cheap jewelry that he bought at small local shops. Their life together as husband and wife with a newborn child in the small flat was a struggle, but they helped each other, and they always had enough to eat. When he arrived in America, however, Sonali Verma seemed to change quite a bit. The sudden and dramatic increase in wealth for the family was difficult for her to handle. She was unaccustomed to wealth. She spent money rashly. She was fascinated—almost obsessed—with the array of goods and services that were available to her. Her shopping took the form of a madness. She bought useless items that she did not need, but caught her fancy. When her ephemeral fascination ended, the item quickly found its way into the trash. She never had enough. There was always some new little item that she just had to have. Years and years of this behavior went on until Rameesh was little more than a paycheck to her. She took him for granted and spent his money freely. When he objected or confronted her, she only had to hint at divorce. Rameesh quickly learned the reality of easy divorce in the West. She would get the house, the car, the kids, and he would have to pay her alimony. It was a license to steal. Rameesh became bitter.

Rameesh daydreamed about those early days at the University with Sonali and Tarun as he drove home from the party. He would have loved to go back to those days if he could. No, the money was not that important to him. He had peace in those days. What was money compared to that peace? When he saw the freeway exit, his thoughts turned to the ugliness ahead of him. Her car was parked in the driveway when he arrived home. She was definitely there. For a moment, he considered driving past his house, and going straight to the office to finish his work. He could delay the whole drama until their flight to India the next day, but he thought better of it. He did not want to go through the big argument, and then have to travel with her for sixteen hours. It was better to get it over with now. He just wished things were different. Things were so great when he was at the University. It was not until later that the marriage became strained. Why? It was the money. The money had changed her. How can money change people? Perhaps it is that the money only revealed something that was already in her? The money had her. She served the money; the money did not serve her.

By the time that they had lived in Houston for five years, Rameesh was buying prostitutes on a regular basis. Sonali had stopped sleeping with him for some time. As his income grew, Rameesh was able to afford some very expensive prostitutes that made Sonali look like a flabby piece of trash. He enjoyed the prostitutes quite a bit. They became a habit that he reveled in. He knew that Sonali knew. At first, he tried to hide his affairs. He did not want Sonali to find out, and file for a divorce. Later on, however, it became apparent that she really did not care. As long as she had her allowance, Rameesh could do whatever he wanted. And he did. He even sometimes dared to rub it into her face. For Rameesh, women had become nothing but toys. He was certain that Sonali had her own little trysts from time to time anyhow, but he did not care either.

He parked his car in the garage and opened the door to the house. She was at the kitchen table drinking some tea. He braced himself for the conflict.

"It's about time you came home. Where have you been?" she started.

"At the office." He lied.

"I almost believe you."

"I don't care what you believe."

"You missed Gollum's soccer game."

"I was busy."

"Right. Busy with— she stopped herself.

"Yes. Yes. I was busy. You know. I was busy making the money that you like to spend so much."

"Shut up."

"I will not!"

Sonali was quiet for a moment. She was tired and not in the mood to fight. What did it matter anyhow? She knew where he had been. It was not anything new. What was the point in arguing about it? She really just wanted him to pack his bags for their trip. They were going to Mumbai the next morning. She had not seen her family in four years. She did not want anything to go wrong.

"You need to pack for tomorrow."

"I know." He said as he went to the kitchen sink for a glass of water.

"Because our flight is at 9am."

"I said that I know."

"You better start packing now."

"I said that I will." He was becoming annoyed now.

"Remember last time you forgot to pack, and we were late for our flight because you had been so stupid." She could not help herself here. She had to remind him of this. She took a perverse pleasure in accusing him.

"That was not my fault! You told me the wrong time, and you know it!"

He was shaking with anger. She could see that she had upset him. It amused her.

"I told you the right time."

"No, you didn't!"

"Yes, I did. You do not remember."

"I—I—do—I" he stammered.

"No you don't. You never do."

"Don't tell me what I remember, and what I don't."

"Who cares? I am telling you clearly now. Our flight leaves at 9am tomorrow. We have to be at the airport at 7am."

"Okay."

"You need to pack now."

"I said okay!" He started to walk to the stairs.

"We don't want to be late for the flight again." She continued to antagonize him.

"Okay! Okay! I said okay! Did you not hear me? I am going to go upstairs and pack right now. Is that good enough for you? Is that okay with you? Is that clear enough for you?"

Sonali rolled her eyes at her stupid husband and watched him start up the stairs. She did not care if he was angry with her. He was a lying cheater. She could hear him stomping his feet and slamming the closet door in anger above her head on the second floor. He came downstairs two hours later with his packed luggage, which he wheeled into the kitchen. He had taken a shower and changed his clothes. Sonali was standing at the kitchen counter cutting some vegetables and watched him. She could see that he had cleaned himself up. She knew what this meant.

"Where are you going?" she asked.

"I have to go back to the office."

"What? Why?"

"I have to finish my work and get it handed in before we leave tomorrow."

"Whores." Sonali said under her breath.

"What did you say?" Rameesh challenged her.

"Nothing! Give me twelve hundred dollars." She demanded.

"What!?"

"I need twelve hundred dollars. I need to do some shopping before we leave." She explained.

"What shopping? What do you need before we go that will cost twelve hundred dollars? I just gave you money last week."

"I need to get some shopping done before we go just like you need to get some work done before we go." Sonali said with her eyes begging Rameesh to contradict her. She knew that he was going to get a prostitute. She was going to blow twelve hundred dollars to spite him. If he challenged her about the money, she would challenge him about leaving for the office to do some "work." She had him.

Rameesh knew that she had him. In reality, he did have legitimate work to do at the office before their trip the next day. At the same time, however, he fully had intended to buy a prostitute as well. He was furious that Sonali was "blackmailing" him like this. He had no choice, however, and had to give her the money. It was easier not to argue with her. His marriage to Sonali had become like a game of chess where each side jockeyed for position and carefully calculated whether they could advance against the other or not. Tonight was a stalemate of sorts. Rameesh would have his prostitute, but it would cost him twelve hundred dollars more just to buy Sonali off. He grudgingly pulled out his cell phone and transferred the money into Sonali's account. They would both pretend that they were still faithful to each other for one more night and reset the game board for another day. Sonali smiled to herself as she watched Rameesh make the transfer. He walked past her into the garage to leave. It had not been as bad as he thought it would be. There was no great fight. Still, he was glad to get away from her. These were the circumstances under which Rameesh called Jenna Park for another "date."

Jenna and her roommate, Sheila, were sitting in the living room eating dinner and watching their favorite show on television together, when Jenna's cell phone rang. Jenna looked down at the floor and put her face in her hands. Jenna's telephone had been ringing like this all week. She had dozens of messages from Simon. After the third message, Jenna stopped replaying them herself, and she had Sheila listen to them. It was too difficult for Jenna to listen to Simon's pleas. He was hurt. He was the first man Jenna had ever met who she felt really liked her, and she could not even talk to him.

"He has to call right in the middle of our show. Doesn't he get it? Where did you meet this guy?" Sheila rolled her eyes in contempt.

"Aren't you going to check it?"

"Why?"

"I— Jenna started to explain, but could not find the words. After five days of calls every few hours like this, there were no words. "Just, could you please see if it was him?"

Sheila shook her head and put her plate down on the coffee table. She leaned over and grabbed Jenna's cell phone off the end table.

"I don't believe it."

"What?"

"It wasn't him."

"What does it say?"

"Verma? Do you know a 'Verma?'"

Sheila handed the telephone to Jenna. The caller identification on the screen clearly read "Verma."

"I have no idea who this is." Jenna said.

"Well, play the message."

Sheila watched as Jenna scrolled through her messages and selected the latest one. Jenna listened carefully and shook her head repeatedly as the message played.

"Who was it?" Sheila asked.

"You're not going to believe it." Jenna said with contempt.

"Who?"

"It was Rameesh from the beach house party."

"Oh, gross."

"How did he get my phone number?"

"What did he want?" Sheila asked.

"What do you think he wants?"

Sheila laughed, "Better take care of business, honey."

"Thanks a lot." Jenna said as she put the phone down on the coffee table.

Sheila laughed, and the two women went back to watching their television show.

"I wonder if he got your number from Jimmy." Sheila thought out loud.

The two women looked at each other, and they both realized at the same time that Jenna had to return Rameesh's call immediately. If word got back to Jimmy that Jenna had ignored a john that Jimmy had sent her way, she would be in serious trouble. Sheila picked the cell phone up from the coffee table and threw it to Jenna without saying a word.

"This sucks." Jenna said as she dialed the number.

"Hello?"

"Hello. Is this Rameesh?"

"Oh, yesssss. Oh. Oh. Yes. Yes. Jenna. Yes. This is Rameesh. Oh thank you so much. Thank you."

"How did you get my telephone number, Rameesh?"

"Oh, Jenna. I must speak with you. Oh, Jenna."

"Rameesh—how did you get my number?"

"I got it off your phone that night at the beach house."

"Jimmy didn't give it to you?"

"No, no. I was able to get it myself from your phone."

"Rameesh, you can't call me like this."

"No, no. Please! Please!"

"Rameesh, if you want to talk to me, you have to go through Jimmy. You understand? I—

"Please, Jenna. Please. I must have you. I must. I need you. I need to have you once again."

Jenna was annoyed and looked at Sheila for an answer. Sheila was humored by the entire situation and only smiled—glad that it was not her that got stuck with Rameesh.

"I must lay with you again, Jenna. I will pay you a great amount."

"Rameesh, you don't understand. I can't see you again unless you go through Jimmy. Jimmy. Do you hear me, Rameesh? You have to go through Jimmy. He makes all the arrangements."

"But I must see you tonight. I leave for Mumbai tomorrow."

"Then, I guess you're out of luck."

"No! No! Don't say that. I need you. I need you tonight. You are so beautiful. I must have you again. I won't be back again for a very great time. My wife's family—

"Your wife? What about your wife?"

Jenna looked at Sheila, who was shaking her head and smiling. It was so typical to hear a john go on about his wife. The two women had heard different versions of the same story hundreds of times. The wife did not satisfy him. She was cold. She was fat. She did not understand him. There were a thousand variations, but the theme was always the same. The john was rich. His wife was a prestige symbol, and not much else. He had enough money to buy a woman like Sheila or Jenna—so he did. Jenna often wondered what the wives of these rich men felt. She would have liked to talk to one of these wives just once and tell them what scum their husbands were. It never occurred to Jenna's warped mind that she was just as guilty as these men. In her self-righteousness, however, she felt the urge to berate Rameesh. If she could not talk to his wife, and set her against Rameesh, at least she would beat him down herself. And since he had gone behind Jimmy's back to get in touch with her, she felt like she had a blank check to say anything she wanted without fear of retribution. She leaned back on the couch and put her feet up on the arm rest.

"Does your wife know that you do this kind of stuff? Don't you care about her feelings? Shouldn't you be with her?" Jenna said in her best holier-than-thou tone.

"My wife does know. She does not care. I give her a big allowance, and that is all she cares about. She's married to a charge account."

Jenna was a little stunned by this revelation. In all these years it had not occurred to her that maybe the wife really was cold and really did not care. Maybe the wife really was a bitch, and the poor man was trying to find some kind of solace in his life. She had wanted to really lord the 'wife' over Rameesh's head, but he seemed to have deflated the entire issue. Jenna did not have enough of a moral sense herself to consider talking to Rameesh about vows, and promises to God. For her, that the wife already knew was enough to put an end to her moralizing. Nevertheless, there was still the issue of going behind Jimmy's back. She had to explain that it was impossible to do anything without Jimmy.

"Well, you still can't do this without Jimmy, Rameesh. You don't understand how this works. He would get very angry—

"I can help you find your parents." Rameesh announced. He was like a desperate swimmer that was afraid of drowning and wildly throwing his hands out for a life line.

Jenna's mind went blank when Rameesh mentioned her parents. She forgot all about Jimmy.

"Remember, you told me you wanted to know your parents? I can help find out. Do you remember? I can help you."

Jenna did not know how to reply. She did want to know who her parents were. Still, this was a john speaking. She became skeptical.

"How can you know about my parents?"

"I can help you. You must listen to me."

"How do I know that? You could just be making it all up."

"I am telling the truth. I am telling you."

"No. No. I don't believe you. You're lying."

"No, I promise you. Please I must be with you again. I know I can tell you. Please. Please." Rameesh went on.

"You'll say anything. I don't believe you."

"No. No. I'm not doing that."

"Forget it! I don't want to hear from you."

"I know about Uncle Rick." Rameesh blurted.

Jenna lost her breath at the name. "Uncle Rick" was familiar, but only weakly so. She was like a person who suddenly awakens from a dream that is so intense that at a later time the sleeper is not quite certain if the experience was real or not. Jenna searched her memories, and found the name Uncle Rick, but it was so slippery that she could not grab onto it with her mind and was uncertain if it was even a real memory. But how could Rameesh know the name? How would he have come up with it on his own? He could not have. He had to have some real information.

"Please, you must believe me. I can help you find out who your parents are."

Jenna did not answer immediately. To go out and see a john behind Jimmy's back was death, but what was the point in living anyhow? He controlled everything she did. Was she going to let him take away her past? The one thing she really wanted? She had always wanted? No. She was not going to let Jimmy take this away from her. He had everything else. He was not going to have this.

"Please. Please see me," Rameesh begged, "I promise you I have some information about your parents here."

"Okay. I'll see you."

"Oh. Thank you. Thank you. You have made me so happy."

Sheila gave Jenna a dirty look that said, "What are you doing?" but Jenna brushed this aside and tried to make the arrangements.

"There is a hotel downtown where we can meet."

"I cannot leave this place where I am." Rameesh declared.

"Why?"

"I am running an experiment, and I must remain here and be ready for the results, but it could finish any time. You could drive over to my office."

"No, I can't. I don't have a car."

Sheila went over to the couch, sat next to Jenna and looked at her intently. She could not let her friend jeopardize her safety like this. She tapped Jenna on the shoulder.

"Wait a minute Rameesh. What?"

"What are you doing? Are you crazy? Jimmy will kill you—literally—if you go see this guy."

"I'm going. He knows about my parents."

Sheila grabbed Jenna's arm, "Jimmy will kill you."

Jenna avoided Sheila's stare.

"No, I'm going. I have to try."

"You're being stupid."

"Let me use your car."

"No. No way. Go and get yourself killed, but not me."

Jenna did not bother to debate the issue. She knew that she would not get anywhere with Sheila and turned her focus back to Rameesh.

"Rameesh?"

"Yes."

"You need to pick me up at my condominium. I cannot drive there."

"I can send you a cab to take you to me. Just tell me your address, and I will have it come for you."

A determined look came over Jenna's face. She did not know what information Rameesh had, but she knew that she had to take the chance. She did not want to look back on her life years from now, and regret that she passed up the only opportunity that she ever had to find out where she came from.

"Okay, but I need your address too—just in case. I'll be waiting in the lobby. Have it meet me in 30 minutes."

"Oh. Thank you. Thank you."

Jenna and Rameesh exchanged address information. Jenna hung up the telephone, and rushed to her bedroom to get ready.

"JENNA!" Sheila yelled.

"Shut up! I'm going." Jenna shot back as she put on her jeans and went over to the bathroom to brush her hair. Sheila followed her.

"I know you're going, but listen to me. Jimmy will beat you if he ever finds out. Is this really worth it?"

"Yes, he knows about my parents."

"Some john calls you in the middle of the night, and says he knows whatever. How do you know he knows Jenna?"

"Because he does, that's all. I know he does."

"You're being crazy Jenna. Please listen to me."

Sheila was not smart, but she knew enough to fear Jimmy. She did not want to see her friend destroyed, but Jenna's mind was set.

"I'm going."

"Then at least give me the address. Take your phone and call me if you get in trouble."

Jenna finished brushing her hair and put on her shoes. She scribbled the address on a piece of paper and gave it to Sheila. She was ready to leave except for one thing.

"Here's the address. Do you have any coke?"

"Jenna, you don't want—"

"Yes, I do. I can't handle the drink, and I need something to get through this. I need an upper."

"But you don't want to be like me, Jenna. You've never done it. I can't stop doing it."

"One time isn't going to hook me."

"But that's what I thought—

"Give me it. I know one time isn't going to matter."

Sheila could see that Jenna could not be stopped. She gave in to Jenna's mania. She went over to her purse and handed Jenna a small vial of cocaine and a straw.

"Don't do so much. You won't need a lot."

Jenna took the vial.

"What am I supposed to tell Jimmy if he calls asking for you?" Sheila asked.

"Just tell him that I'm at the bar having some drinks."

"What bar?"

"Tell him you don't know. Don't worry. This won't take long. I'll be back soon."

Sheila looked at Jenna like she was crazy. She could not understand why her friend would take such a terrible risk like this. The john was probably lying to her. Did she not know this? Jenna was too smart to be doing this. Even so, Sheila knew that Jenna could not be stopped.

The two friends hugged each other. Jenna grabbed her purse and left abruptly.

She did not have to wait too long in the lobby for the cab. As the taxi pulled up to the front door, Jenna came outside the building to meet the driver.

"Are you Jenna?" the driver asked.

"Yes. Let's go."

Jenna tried not to think about anything as the driver took her out of the America Center passed Chinatown, and onto I-45. She pulled out the vial of cocaine from her purse and contemplated it for a few minutes. She had never taken this drug, but she knew that it would make her feel good, and she needed to feel good with Rameesh. She had no clue, however, how much to take, or how long it would last. When the driver pulled off the expressway, she finally took notice of where they were headed.

"Where is this place?" she asked the driver.

"I was told Griggs just past Martin Luther. What are you going down there for this late at night?"

"It's an emergency."

"Must be some kind of emergency."

Jenna ignored the cab driver, and focused on the task ahead.

The driver pulled up to a solid brick building with no windows. An isolated street light was on near the front door. There was a railroad crossing down the street a little ways. Just the sight of such a gloomy place was unsettling.

"Is this really it?" Jenna asked. She was perplexed, but before the taxi driver could answer Rameesh came out of the front door and walked over to the passenger door to let Jenna out of the cab.

"I so thank you for coming." He greeted.

"What is this place?"

Rameesh ignored Jenna, and paid the taxi driver. As the cab drove off, he turned to Jenna and explained.

"This is where I work. My simulation is almost finished. I can take you home in my car when we are through."

Jenna smiled uneasily and fingered the cocaine in her purse to reassure herself.

Rameesh was overjoyed. It was fun time. His wife was like a dark cloud over his head, and Jenna was like a cool wind that pushed the cloud away and brought clear skies if only for a short time. Rameesh led her to the front door and passed his hand over a small plate on the wall causing the plate to "beep." The door unlocked and Rameesh pushed it open.

"How's that work?" Jenna asked.

"That is my key--in my hand. See?" Rameesh showed Jenna his hand, but she could not see anything special. "I also open my car this way so I never can lose my keys."

Jenna was not interested in Rameesh's fancy gadgets, however, and wanted to get right to business. She walked past him through the front door.

The laboratory where Rameesh worked was unremarkable. There were a few computers scattered about, and some medical equipment, but there was nothing out of the ordinary. On one side of the main room, there were a series of small offices with window partitions facing the main laboratory space. Only one of them had the lights on.

"Here is my office." Rameesh said as he led Jenna into the little room where there was only a small desk, and an office chair.

"What do you do here?"

"We develop drugs. I have to complete this computer simulation and have the results on my boss's desk first thing tomorrow before I go back to Mumbai."

Rameesh showed Jenna his computer screen. It was all gibberish to Jenna. Long columns of numbers filled the screen. At the bottom, a small bar was creeping from left to right to show the progress of the simulation. A small counter showed that it was 36% complete.

"But why do you do it in *this* neighborhood?" Jenna asked.

"The land is very inexpensive here. The company I work for is like a sub-contractor to much bigger drug companies, and we cannot afford the high end offices. So we rent out this space, which is very unfortunate, but it helps us to save money. Developing pharmaceutical applications can be very very expensive, and if you can lessen the costs you can win a much bigger bids."

Jenna had no understanding of these kinds of things. She really did not want to know, but felt that she had to ask. She only wanted to get the information about her parents from Rameesh and be done with the whole affair.

"So you said that you had my information?" Jenna asked folding her arms.

"Ah yes, I have it."

Rameesh walked out of the small office, across the main laboratory to a small closet like room. He passed his hand over another plate on the wall, and the door opened up. He went inside the small room, and after a moment, he came back out with a small file in his hands.

"This is the file." He said as he smiled at Jenna.

Jenna went to reach for the folder in Rameesh's hand, but he pulled it back gently.

"What?" Jenna asked.

Rameesh only looked at Jenna. He did not know how to express his thoughts, but Jenna understood immediately. She did not want to argue with him, however, and made up her mind to get this episode over as quickly as possible so that she could look at her file.

"Do you have a bathroom?" she asked.

"Yes. Yes. Of course we do—over there."

Jenna gave a fake smile to Rameesh, crossed the laboratory to the little bathroom and closed the door behind her. As she stared at herself in the mirror over the sink, she was tempted to analyze the whole situation in her mind, but knew that if she began thinking too much that she would get nervous. She needed not to think. She needed to get into the place of mind where all of this was happening to someone else. Where her body was not even connected to her anymore. She needed to be in that fuzzy place that drink put her. She thought about how she loved that place and then remembered her purse and the cocaine. She pulled out the vial of cocaine, and a small mirror. She dappled a little of the cocaine onto the mirror remembering not to use too much as Sheila had advised. But what was too much? Jenna had no idea. She formed what she thought was a reasonable amount into a line and sniffed it into her nose through the small straw. She let out a long sigh when she was done. She waited there about five minutes and then put everything back into her purse and went out to see Rameesh.

"Okay. I'm ready for you." She said as she came into his office.

"Oh. Very good." Rameesh said as he put Jenna's file down on his desk. "We can go over to this place over here."

Jenna stopped Rameesh with her hand. She suddenly felt very alert and confident. She had never felt this way before in her life. Everything was clear to her mind it seemed. She was in total control. She slowly unbuttoned Rameesh's shirt and guided him towards his desk chair. Rameesh let himself be controlled and sank down into the chair.

"Put the arms down." Jenna coaxed him softly with a big smile on her face.

Rameesh pressed the lever under the arm rests that released the latch that allowed the chair's arms to be pushed down completely. He never took his eyes off of Jenna, however, as she slowly unbuttoned her blouse. She was soon straddling Rameesh and letting him have her. After a few moments, Jenna got off of him and started to take off his pants.

Rameesh was spellbound and did not make a sound as he watched Jenna take off her own jeans and panties.

Jenna felt completely in control. It felt like all of her body's senses were elevated. She could distinctly hear all the sounds of the laboratory —the hum of the fluorescent lights, the whirr of the computers--what little sounds there were. It was like she had just awakened from a very restful night's sleep. At the same time, she felt an intense euphoria about where she was, and who she was. She was like a mountain climber on top of Everest having conquered the greatest feat of his climbing career, and drinking in the expanse of the world below as he looked down from the summit of the highest mountain.

She methodically took off Rameesh's underwear and was soon straddling him again.

Jenna was a flurry and grinded on Rameesh relentlessly. She was smiling broadly and closed her eyes in exhilaration. She was hot and sweating and breathing in rhythm. She went on and on and on. Jenna was lost in ecstasy like she had never been before. She kept grinding and grinding, up and down, back and forth, up and down, back and forth. It was some time before she realized that Rameesh had stopped moaning and opened her eyes to look at him. There was no expression on Rameesh's face, and his eyes were closed. His body was limp and motionless.

It was clear. Rameesh was dead.

Jenna's heart was pounding intensely. Her hands were shaking badly as she climbed off Rameesh. Suddenly, she felt a great anxiety.

"No! No! Please, no, no!"

She slapped Rameesh on the cheek a few times, but got no reaction. She put her ear to his mouth to listen for breathing, but heard nothing.

"No! No!"

Jenna knelt half naked on the floor next to Rameesh's dead body that reclined awkwardly in the desk chair. She covered her face with her hands.

"No! No! No! No! No!" she cried as she beat the floor with her fist. But he was dead.

Jenna knelt on the floor crying next to the chair holding Rameesh's dead body. The weight of the matter was too great for her. Her mind suffocated under a thousand questions, and possible scenarios. What would she do? What if the police find out? What if Jimmy finds out? How would she get out of there? She continued to cry on the floor of the office for some time as she rocked back and forth. She was like a sailor on a sinking ship in a storm trying frantically to find a lifeboat as waves of water came over the deck. She was vexed. Even the cocaine in her blood was not strong enough to overcome the foreboding thoughts of disaster. After a few minutes, however, she stopped crying, put on her clothes and started to think more clearly about her options. There were not many to consider. It was obvious that there was only one thing that she could do. She had to leave immediately, get back home and hope that nobody would ever find out that she had been there.

She put on her clothes and opened her purse to take an inventory. Everything was there—most importantly, her cell phone. She realized that she could call Sheila for a ride home; this made her feel much better and more calm. She double checked the bathroom to make certain that she had not left anything in there, and then she went back to the office to take one last look around before she left.

Rameesh's dead body was reclining backwards naked from the waist down. The eyes were closed, but his mouth was open with his tongue loose and some drool spilling over the side of his lips and down his chin from his last moments of ecstasy. It was not going to take a great detective to solve the mystery of Rameesh's death. One of the dead arms dangled at his side, and the other was resting on the top of his desk—on top of Jenna's personal file. Jenna saw the file, but for a moment she was uncertain if she should take it or not. Then, she realized that if her file was left underneath the dead man's hand, that the police would come to her first with their questions. She had to take the file. It was an easy decision. She wanted it anyhow. It was what she had come for in the first place. Jenna contemplated the dead hand for a moment. The dark skin was scaly and the fingernails were yellow and long. There was a very small tattoo on the top that was barely noticeable. She went to pick the hand off the file, but hesitated. She was disgusted by the sight and winced; nevertheless, she lightly put two fingers around the wrist, lifted the hand and quickly snatched the file away. She let Rameesh's dead hand plop back down on the desk and walked out of the room. She paused at the exit from the building and looked back one more time. She had her purse and its contents, her cell phone and her file. She had to make certain that she had left nothing behind because she knew that once she walked out the door; it would lock, and there would be no way for her to get back into the building. She was certain, however, that she had left nothing behind. She opened the door and left. It was over.

When she looked around her and heard the door close and lock behind her, Jenna suddenly felt like she was in danger and wanted to go back into the building, but it was too late. It was around eleven o'clock, and she was in a terrible part of town. A decaying street lamp cast a weak yellow light from the top of an old wooden telephone pole next to her by the entrance. A train was crossing the street a few dozen yards away. Its blaring horn was like an omen in the night. As the sound faded away Jenna heard the strange shouting and laughter of some drug addicts gathered down the road by the corner. Jenna moved out of the light of the street lamp so that the addicts would not see her and pulled her cell phone from her purse. Sheila had the street address. It would take her some time, but she could find the building. Jenna called and waited for Sheila to answer.

"Sheila?"

"Jenna?"

"Sheila—oh my God. Please, you've got to pick me up."

"Jenna I can't."

"Oh my God! What are you saying? Please, please—

"I can't, Jenna."

"I need you. Please. Please!"

"Jenna. Jimmy was here. He knows where you are. He's coming to get you. You can't come back here. You have to get out of there as fast as you can. Leave! Right now! Get out of there! Wherever you go, just don't come back here."

Jenna was in shock and could not breathe. Like a heavy chain, despair wrapped itself around her heart pulling her down, down. What would Jimmy do to her? How would she get away? She was terrified— unable to move. She crouched down and closed her eyes with her hands over her head wishing that when she opened her eyes again that she would magically find herself back in her high rise condominium. More shouting came from the drug addicts down the street. Jenna opened her eyes and could see one of the addicts coming towards her. Did he see her? She ducked behind the light pole. The drug addict passed her without even noticing that she was there, but Jenna hardly felt any better. Jimmy was coming for her. She was dead. He was coming, and he would kill her. She had to get away, but where would she go?

"I GOTS YO' CRACK!" one of the addicts down the street shouted.

"WHAD!"

"CUM N GID DA CRACK!"

Jenna quickly whipped her head around to look. The sweat from her head was trickling down the side of her face. The drug addict that had walked passed her just a moment earlier had turned back and was coming towards her again. She was exposed. Did he see her? Would he notice her! Oh no! No! The blood was rushing to her head. Her hands were shaking. He was coming closer. He would see her. He was only a few steps away now.

Chapter Nineteen

Jimmy Demos visited his prostitutes from time to time without any notice. It was his way of checking on them and making certain that they were not cheating him, or getting into trouble. It was one way for him to maintain control. Even though he did not make these surprise visits often, the girls still hardly ever knew when Jimmy might stop by, and therefore they could never make any plans without taking a risk that he might show up unexpectedly. The girls knew this and made their own plans anyhow. They covered for each other. Sheila was washing her hair in the bathroom sink, when Jimmy came knocking at her door the night Jenna had gone to see Rameesh. She could not hear him over the noise of the water coming out of the faucet, and he was made to wait.

Jimmy knocked and then paused to listen for someone to answer; then, he knocked a few more times and paused once more. He waited a while longer, pounded his fist on the door and stopped again to listen. Still, there was no answer, and he became very frustrated. He stepped away from the door, folded his arms and tried to regain his composure. He felt disrespected. For a moment, he considered using his own key to the condominium, but he did not want the girls to know that he had his own key and put the thought out of his mind. He went to the door once more, made a fist, and pounded on the door with heavy, slow and deliberate blows while he gritted his teeth. One of the neighbors opened their door and came out of their condominium to see who was making such a loud noise in the hallway. When the neighbor came out into the hallway, Jimmy whipped around and scowled at him. The neighbor became scared and quickly retreated back into his condominium without saying a word. Finally, Sheila heard the loud thud of Jimmy's fist on the door, turned off the faucet and went to the front door with a towel on her head to look through the peep hole and see who was there.

"Oh no." she whispered when she saw that it was Jimmy.

She immediately thought about calling Jenna, but she knew that she could not make Jimmy wait any longer. She did the best that she could to brace herself and then opened the door.

Jimmy gave Sheila a stern look and marched into the room without saying a word. Sheila closed the door behind him.

"What the hell were you doing?"

"Washing my hair in the sink."

"Don't make me wait at the door like that."

"I couldn't hear you—

"I don't give a damn! Don't make me wait—ever."

"Okay. Okay."

"Where's Jenna?"

"She's at the bar."

"What?"

"She went to the bar."

Jimmy walked closer to Sheila and stared directly into her eyes.

"What bar?"

"I don't know." Sheila said knowing enough not to look away to avoid the appearance of lying.

Jimmy was quiet, and he did not take his eyes off Sheila, "When will she be back?"

"She didn't say."

Jimmy let out a sigh through his nose and frowned. He went over to the kitchen, pulled some ice out of the refrigerator and methodically went about making himself a drink. The room was quiet for a moment. The only sound was the clink of the ice cubes inside the glass as Jimmy stirred his drink.

Sheila looked about the living room for her cell phone while Jimmy was in the kitchen. She saw the telephone next to her purse on the coffee table in front of the couch. She wanted desperately to call Jenna to warn her about Jimmy. Sheila had no clue what to say to Jimmy. She always felt that it was always better to let him speak first.

Jimmy calmly walked into the living room and sat down on the couch with his drink. In his strange way, he cocked his head and held his glass up to the light looking for something. The whole situation was very awkward. Sheila wanted to leave the room, but did not want to do anything that might set Jimmy off. Should she say something? Should she go back to the bathroom? She was not sure how Jimmy would react.

Jimmy put his empty drink down on the coffee table next to Sheila's purse and pulled out his cell phone. For a while, he played with his cell phone pushing some icons on the screen. He never said a word. He just quietly studied the screen on the phone.

Sheila was stressed. She knew Jimmy was angry that Jenna was gone. She felt that she had done a good job with her prepared lie; but the room was too quiet, and Jimmy was acting weird. Of course, Jimmy always acted weird, but Sheila could see that he had something on his mind. She decided to take a risk and try to warn Jenna before Jimmy did anything crazy.

"I'll get you another drink."

Sheila walked over to the coffee table in front of Jimmy in order to pick up his empty glass. As unobtrusively as possible, she picked up her cell phone and slipped it into the front pocket of her bathrobe. Jimmy pretended not to care. He barely looked up, but in his mind he was full of contempt for Sheila. Who did she think she was fooling? When was the last time any of these whores ever fixed him a drink? He glanced at the purse on the coffee table and clenched his teeth.

The room was completely silent as Sheila fixed Jimmy's drink. She knew that she would have to make the call to Jenna quick. She could not talk long and risk the possibility of Jimmy hearing her. She pre-dialed Jenna's number and had the cell phone ready to send the call before she went back to the couch where Jimmy was sitting. When she handed Jimmy his drink, she would announce that she was going back into the bedroom to change, and dial Jenna on the phone with the push of a button while she was walking down the hallway.

"Maybe I'll wait for Jenna to come back." Jimmy announced breaking the silence.

Sheila's eye's widened. Did Jimmy know that she was lying? Was she in trouble? She studied him in the quiet of the room. What should she do next? She hesitated a moment, and then went over to the couch with the drink and pretended like nothing was wrong.

"Here's your drink."

Sheila handed the drink to Jimmy over his shoulder from behind.

"I'm sure she'll be back soon." Jimmy took the drink without looking at Sheila.

"I'm going to go change into my pajamas." Sheila said.

Was she going to get away with it? Would she be able to call Jenna to warn her?

She turned around and started to walk down the short hallway towards her bedroom. Before she could even push the button on her cell phone; however, Jimmy came running up behind her. He grabbed her by the arm, hustled her into the bedroom, and threw her on the bed.

"WHERE IS SHE?" he screamed.

"I—I—

"TELL ME!"

Jimmy had his belt off. He was whipping Sheila in the legs with it as hard as he could.

"DON'T LIE TO ME! DON'T EVER LIE TO ME!"

Jimmy put the belt down, made a fist and buried it in Sheila's chest. He grinded her ribs with his knuckles as hard as he could.

"STOP! STOP! PLEASE!" Sheila pleaded.

Jimmy vigorously grated his fist against the ribs of Sheila's chest.

"WHERE IS SHE?"

"PLEASE! AHHH! She's with a john. She's with a john."

Jimmy was relentless. He kept gnashing his fist against Sheila's chest. He held her down by the neck with one hand as he pressed his fist deeper into her ribs.

"TELL ME! WHERE?"

"IT'S—IT'S ON MY DRESSER. OH GOD. OH GOD. IT'S ON MY DRESSER."

Sheila was crying in agony. Her ribs in her chest and side were burning with pain. Jimmy went over to the dresser and saw the small slip of paper with the address of Rameesh's office. He was breathing heavily as he put the slip of paper in is front shirt pocket. He went back to Sheila and grabbed her by the hair.

"Don't ever lie to me, Sheila. Don't you ever lie to me. I'll always find out if you lie to me."

He threw Sheila's head down violently, reached into her pocket, took out her cell phone and threw it against the wall. Then he stormed out of the room. Sheila heard him slam the front door shut as he left.

After a few moments of recovery, Sheila sat up on the bed. Her chest was red from her neck all the way down her sternum to her stomach. She had large welts on her legs from the whipping. Jimmy had beaten her in the past. It was nothing new, but she hated Jimmy now more than ever before. She had stuck her neck out for her friend, and in a way blamed Jenna. But her hatred for Jimmy was greater. Jimmy had beaten some of the fear out of Sheila. Now that the threat of being beaten by him for some transgression had been fulfilled, he seemed less terrifying. More than anything, she now wanted to spite Jimmy and see Jenna succeed in defying him. She slowly picked herself up and shuffled towards the wall where Jimmy had thrown her cell phone. It was still working. Sheila dialed the front lobby for the front desk security guard, Terry.

"Terry?"

"Yes ma'am?"

"It's Sheila."

Terry knew Sheila's voice, and was familiar with her.

"Well hey momma. What's up?"

Sheila got right to the point.

"Remember how we always talk about you doing me a favor, and me doing you a favor?"

Terry's eyes widened and he sat up in his chair.

"Yes ma'am. I sure do remember that."

"Jimmy's coming down in a few minutes to get his car. If you slash two of his tires for me, I'll do two of those favors for you."

Terry paused for a moment. He had always wanted Sheila. Every day he fantasized about having her. His real dream was to have Sheila and Jenna at the same time. He had the whole fantasy choreographed in his mind. He knew that Sheila was a prostitute, and that Jimmy was her pimp. He also knew that Jimmy was a killer, and so he was a little hesitant. He was a little like a wise mouse looking at a baited trap. He knew he might die, but the cheese was so good. He decided that he needed more information before he made his decision.

"How do I know you won't back out?" he asked.

"If I do, you can tell Jimmy that I told you to slash his tires."

"Will you say that on my machine?" Terry asked.

"Go ahead. Record it with your machine."

Terry had a telephone recorder on his desk in case he ever took an emergency call, and needed a record of the conversation. He pushed a button on the machine to start the recording.

"Go ahead. It's recording."

"This is Sheila. I'm telling Terry to slash Jimmy's tires so that he can't go get Jenna. I'm giving Terry a freebie in exchange."

This was enough for Terry. He stopped the tape. Rewound it, and played the recording back to double check it. The message had been recorded. The cheese was safely his. A big smile came across his face. This was probably the only chance he would ever have to take Sheila. He certainly could not afford her.

"I'll be up in a little while. Let me go take care of these tires." Terry hung up the telephone, went outside on the street and slashed two of Jimmy's car tires.

Sheila had bought Jenna some time. She plunged herself onto her bed and was about to call Jenna to warn her, but Jenna called her first at just that moment.

Jimmy came down the elevator into the lobby of the condominium complex anxious to get into his car and drive off to confront Jenna. He was focused. His anger focused him somehow. He was going to hurt Jenna. He had to hurt her in such a way that her fear of ever feeling that kind of pain again would never leave her mind, and would prevent her from disobeying him ever again. When he came to the front door and looked across the street towards his car; however, he could see that it was leaning badly to one side. Something was terribly wrong. He trotted across the street and saw that the two tires on the driver's side of the car had been slashed. He started to shake with anger, but never made a noise. He banged his hands on the hood of the car furiously and stewed for a few moments. It was senseless. Who would slash his tires like this? Why would anyone slash his tires like this? He marched back across the street to the condominiums to confront the security guard, Terry, at the front desk.

"Hey! You! Somebody slashed my tires across the street. Did you see anything?" Jimmy asked.

Terry was playing with his cell phone. He had watched Jimmy come off the elevator and go across the street to examine the flat tires. He fully expected Jimmy to come back into the lobby. He calmly looked up from his cell phone at Jimmy.

"I'm sorry sir. I didn't see anything. Somebody slashed your tires?"

"Yeah, right there! My car parked over there across the street!" Jimmy said pointing to his car that was just visible outside through the glass front doors in the light of the street lamps.

"I'm sorry. I didn't see anything."

Jimmy lost control and spoke a little too freely.

"ARE YOU STUPID? YOU CAN SEE MY CAR FROM YOUR DESK. YOU'RE TELLING ME THAT YOU DIDN'T SEE ANYTHING? I CAN SEE THE SLASHED TIRES FROM HERE YOU IDIOT!"

Terry Combs was six feet six inches tall and weighed two hundred and eighty-five pounds. He was a security guard at the condominium high rise three nights a week, and a bouncer at a local bar three nights. During his time off, he liked to lift weights and wrestle with his pet Rottweiler. He was not an easy man to intimidate. Terry got up from his chair, rose to his full height and sauntered to the other side of the desk. He towered over the five feet, ten inches tall, one hundred and eighty pound Jimmy Demos.

"I-said-I-did-not-see-anything" Terry repeated in staccato as he poked his finger into Jimmy's chest. "And I don't think that I like your attitude. If you're going to shout in this building I'm going to have to ask you to leave."

The insane Jimmy Demos thought seriously about starting a fight with the huge security guard. Jimmy knew that Terry was lying. He tilted his head back and stared at Terry with a crazed look. Terry put his hands on his hips and stared right back at Jimmy. The two men stood facing each other, and neither one moved. It was a stalemate. Jimmy's insanity was balanced by Terry's sheer size and strength, but Jimmy eventually backed down and went back outside to his car. He pulled out his cell phone and called for a tow truck.

Jimmy Demos was a very strange man. His mood swings were extreme. He could be icy one moment and a flurry of rage the next moment. He was paranoid about maintaining control over his prostitutes. The absurdity of his confrontation with Sheila over Jenna was that he never once needed Sheila's confession. Jenna had a microchip implanted inside of her left armpit that sent a signal that was tracked by satellite. She knew nothing about the microchip. Jimmy had drugged her and had it implanted in her years ago. He tracked Jenna with his own cell phone any time that he wanted. When he was sitting on the couch, he had been tracking Jenna in just this way. When he noticed Sheila grab her own cell phone from the coffee table, he understood that she was going to try to warn Jenna. He did not beat Sheila to get her to confess. He beat her to teach her a lesson. When you are a pimp, you cannot let your whores ever think that they can get the best of you. If you do, they will lose their respect for you, and you will lose your control of them. When you are a pimp, you must make certain that your whores are terrorized from time to time so that they fear you. That is how you keep control. He pulled out his cell phone again and found Jenna's location on a map. She was still down by the railroad tracks to the south, but was slowly moving north. He could tell that she was on foot. Jimmy wondered what was happening to her, but he could do nothing about the situation. He leaned against his car and waited for the tow truck to come. Whatever Jenna was doing, he was going to have to wait until the next day to find her.

Terry Combs snickered to himself while he watched Jimmy Demos outside by the car. He went over to the telephone recorder, pulled the

---

disk with the recorded message and put it in his shirt pocket. Then, he strutted over to the elevator and smiled as he pushed the button for Sheila's floor.

Chapter Twenty

The thin and dirty drug addict came closer to Jenna. His shirt was unbuttoned all the way down. Even in the weak light of the lamp post, Jenna could see his bony chest. His pants were filthy, and ripped. His shoes were untied. He moved erratically with a bad limp in his right leg. He was only about ten feet away from Jenna. She was crouching behind the lamp post desperately wishing that he was too high to take notice of her. He came closer with his herky-jerky walk stumbling a little to his left and then to his right.

"Please go by. Please go by. Please go by." Jenna thought to herself. She was not that lucky. The drug addict noticed her hiding behind the lamp post. He stopped immediately and shouted at her.

"HEY! WHAD YOU DOIN'? HEY! HEY WHITE GIRL! HEY! WHAD YOU DOIN'?"

Jenna clutched at her purse with the file that she took from Rameesh's office. She was shaking with fear and pretended not to hear the man shouting at her.

"HEY! THERE'S A WHITE GIRL HERE!" the addict shouted down the street to his friends.

Jenna was rocking back and forth with her eyes closed. She did not know what to do. "Please just go away." She thought.

"HEY! OVER HERE! THERE'S A WHITE GIRL."

Three more drug addicts from down the street walked towards the lamp post. Jenna was terrified. All she could think about was being gang raped by these four disgusting men. She wanted to move, but it seemed like she was paralyzed. The men were coming closer and closer. She could see their faces in the light of the street lamp. They were ugly and mean like rabid animals.

"Oh yeah—that's a nice white girl."

"Gonna hit dat."

"Oh yeah. Oh yeah."

Jenna was surrounded on three sides by the drug addicts. The locked door to Rameesh's office was behind her. She had nowhere to hide or run. The only thing between her and the four drug addicts was the lamp post. She managed to stand up and started to back away from the men. She was hyperventilating, and her heart was beating out of control. There did not seem to be any way out. Jenna could see the lust in their eyes. One of the men was licking his lips. They wanted to rip her apart and inched closer to her as she backed up towards the office door.

"You got any crack cocaine?" one of the addicts asked in jest.

Instantly, Jenna remembered the vial of cocaine that Sheila had given her. In desperation she reached into her purse, pulled it out, and held it over her head.

"I have some cocaine. You want it?"

"Wha--?"

"SHE GOT DA CRACK!"

"GO GET IT!" Jenna yelled as she tossed the vial up into the air towards the four men.

"DAT'S MINE!"

"GIMME DAT!"

The four men rushed for the cocaine and fought over it. They were like puppets on a string, or slaves chained at the neck. Their master called to them from the vial. He ordered them to take the cocaine or else live in misery. They could not resist him. They did his bidding and served his purposes. He was a proud master. "I will ascend to the Most High!" he boasted, but he was only a pretender. Like all pretenders, he demanded that the truth conform to him instead of conforming himself to Truth. The illusion of happiness created by drugs was his natural playhouse.

Jenna ran pass the addicts as fast as she could down the street. She kept running. She ran at full speed, never stopped and never looked back. After two blocks, she turned north and ran another six blocks until she saw a corner gas station about one hundred yards ahead of her. The well lit station seemed like an oasis among the dark streets of this dangerous neighborhood. Between Jenna and the gas station, however, two prostitutes were working the street. They stood on the sidewalk and shouted and waved at passing cars. Jenna had been so focused on the gas station that she did not even notice the two women until she almost had run into them. One of the prostitutes was wearing a blonde wig and was dressed in glittering gold shorts, and a matching tube top. She had curvy hips and a large chest. Her pale skin was marked here and there with large purple bruises. The other prostitute had a darker complexion and was small. She wore a dark pink dress that barely covered her body.

"Well looky here. You lost honey? Huh? What you got in your purse?"

Jenna was startled by the women. She tried to go past them, but they blocked her way.

"You think you're too good to talk to us? Huh? Right, bitch? You think you're better than us?"

Jenna tried to go around the women to the left, and then to the right, but they purposefully moved to stop her from going anywhere.

"Leave me alone!" Jenna begged.

"Aw—are you scared? Look she's scared." the whore in the gold shorts gibed.

"Ha, ha—yeah, she's scared of us." The other whore agreed.

"Why are you so scared, bitch?"

"I just want to get by."

One of the streetwalkers grabbed Jenna by the arm.

"Gimme that purse."

"LEAVE ME ALONE!"

Jenna wrestled her arm free, pushed the woman aside and ran away towards the gas station.

"YOU'RE NO DIFFERENT THAN US BITCH!" one of the whores yelled. She then picked up a stone and threw it at Jenna just missing her.

Tears of fear were streaking down Jenna's face. She was sweating through her shirt in the heavy air. Her hair was wet with perspiration, and her whole body ached from running so hard, and so long. She just wanted to get away. She wished that she had never left her nice warm condominium. When she made it to the gas station, she tried to open the front doors, but they were locked. The clerk inside the station furiously banged on the bullet proof glass that separated him from the customers.

"THE STORE IS LOCKED! YOU HAVE TO PAY THROUGH THE DRAWER! USE THE DRAWER!"

Jenna looked at the clerk who was pointing towards the security drawer at the payment window. Could he not see that she was in trouble, and that she was not there to buy anything?

Suddenly a scraggly looking man walked up to the window, and put a card in the security drawer. He was wearing a dirty baseball cap and had a greasy shirt with a nametag on the front. He had a patchy beard and large yellow teeth.

"Yeah, gimme five lottery tickets." He said to the clerk.

The clerk rang up the lottery numbers for the customer while Jenna looked on. The customer noticed Jenna looking at him and turned towards her.

"You looking for a man? Huh? I'm a man. Huh? Huh? I got some weed in my car. You want some? We can go to my car."

Jenna turned away, and ran off halfway down the block.

The station clerk gave the scraggly customer the lottery tickets through the payment drawer.

The scraggily man took his tickets from the drawer and watched Jenna run off. "Now dat is what I need." He said out loud to himself.

At that moment, he heard the two streetwalkers Jenna previously had passed shouting at the cars as they drove by, and he looked in their direction. Like a man at a fork in the road, he looked towards Jenna, and then back at the two prostitutes. Either way he went, it was a wide path that he was choosing. Sorry that he could not travel both and be one traveler, he decided that soliciting a whore took less effort than rape, and he went towards the two streetwalkers taking the wider of the two paths.

Jenna was having a difficult time trying to catch her breath. She waited for the scraggily customer at the gas station to leave before she went back towards the station's reassuring lights. How was she going to get out of this neighborhood? Where was she going to go? What was she going to do? She needed a place to stay for a few days, but she knew that Jimmy would take out any money that she had in her bank account. She took out her cell phone and checked her account; it was empty. Jimmy already had taken the money out. She could not pay for a hotel. She could not even pay for a taxi cab. She was stranded. She had no family, or friends, and nowhere to go. She was all alone. "Why? Why?" She kept asking herself. "Oh God—why?" It was too much. She squatted down where she was and burst into tears. She felt like her mind had been put in a blender. Everything was mixed up. She did not know what to do. After a few moments, she stood up and tried to collect herself. Somehow she was reminded of Simon Bosse. She was like a drowning swimmer who was thrown a life preserver. Simon could save her. She had not spoken with him for over a week, but he was her only hope. How could she possibly convince him to come and pick her up? How could she ask him to help her after she had been so cold to him? There was no time to try to think about it, or prepare an excuse. She would have to improvise. She had no other option. She dialed his number on her cell phone and hoped.

Chapter Twenty-One

Simon Bosse did not have many possessions. He owned his trailer home outright, but he did not possess much of anything else. Simon did, however, have hope. He had learned that there is always hope, and that despair is a lie--a sin, even. Despair doubts the goodness of God while hope is a voice in the desert that knows that water can come from a rock. Simon had hope; with hope came fortitude, and with enough fortitude success was certain. He had made peace with the fact that Jenna did not want to hear from him anymore. He was happy for her—at least he wanted to be happy for her. She must have had her reasons for dumping him. Whatever those reasons were, he only wanted good things for her. Simon was getting ready to go out to the bar, hoping to meet a woman that he could love, who would love him back. He felt confident. As he splashed on some cologne, his cell phone rang. He could not believe the name that he saw when looked at the screen. It was Jenna. He paused for a moment. This was so ridiculous. He had called her maybe a hundred times in the last week, and now she was finally returning his calls? Just now after he had resigned himself to give up on her? What could her excuse possibly be? He thought about it for a while before he pressed the "receive" button and answered the call.

"Hello this is Simon?"

"Simon! Simon. It's Jenna."

"I didn't think you ever wanted to talk to me again."

"I'm sorry about not calling you back, Simon. I can't explain about it right now. I'm so sorry."

"I—

"Simon listen—

"I think—

"Simon, please listen. Could you come pick me up? Please, it's an emergency. I really need your help. Please! Please!"

A thousand thoughts were running through Simon's mind. Why was Jenna calling now? What did she want from him? What kind of trouble was she in? Why should he pick her up after she had dropped him? There were so many questions, but it was this last one that was at the top of his list. Why should he pick her up? Their relationship was over. She did not want to be with him—was that not obvious? Why not just make a clean break of it, and never see her again? Why torture himself like this? It was against all reason--except that she was a human being in need and asking him for help. This was the only reason that there was. Jenna had worth if for no other reason than that she was human. This was the lesson Simon had learned about Geraldine when he had talked to the pilot. It would be a difficult thing for him to unlearn it. Even if Jenna did not want to be with him, she needed his help. His feelings were such that he did not care if she wanted him or not. He wanted to help her.

"Please! Please! Simon! Please! I need you! Please!" Jenna begged.

"Okay, okay--I'll come and get you. Don't worry."

"Thank you. Thank you so much, Simon. Thank you so much."

"Where are you?"

Jenna looked at the street signs on the corner.

"I'm at the gas station at exit 34 off of 610."

"What the hell are you doing down there?"

"Please Simon. I can't explain right now. Please just hurry and come and get me out of here."

"Okay. I'm going to leave right now. I'll be there in about thirty-five minutes."

"Oh, thank you. Thank you, Simon. Thank you so much."

"I'll see you."

"Hurry! Please!"

Simon let out a sigh as he hung up the telephone. He bit his lip and contemplated the entire situation. What would come of all this? He did not know, but at least he was going to see Jenna again. It felt good just to have the chance to see her once more and talk to her. He grabbed his car keys and went out the door.

The gas station was not difficult to find, and Jenna was waiting by the curbside when Simon pulled up in his car. She quickly jumped into the passenger seat when he stopped the car in front of her. Before Simon could even say a word, she kissed him on the mouth in gratitude.

"Thank you so much. I can't tell you how much I owe you for this."

"Yeah." Simon replied quietly. He did not know how to react. Jenna was a mess. She was sweating all over, and her hair was wet and matted down. He pulled away from the curb, turned around and started to go back the way he came. For a while, he did not speak. He did not want to embarrass Jenna, but he was too curious, and he and could not resist the temptation to ask Jenna about what was going on.

"What are you doing out here anyway?"

Jenna was silent. She had been so scared that she had not thought to come up with a lie to tell Simon. Like all great liars, she told him half the truth and left the other half to his imagination.

"I'm—I'm trying to find out who my parents were. You know? And there was this guy down here who had these records that would help me. So I came down here to get them, and then I left and all these terrible people came--"

Jenna stopped. She was exhausted.

Simon listened to her carefully. He could hear the stress in her voice, and he felt bad for her.

"Well, you could not have picked a worse place to be stranded. This is the neighborhood where my brother was killed." Simon said.

"What?" Jenna asked in astonishment.

"My brother was killed somewhere around here at a donut shop."

"Oh my God."

"It's dangerous. That's why I asked."

They were quiet again for a moment.

"So where's your car?" Simon asked.

"I—I took a cab."

"Why?"

"My car's not available."

"It's broken down?" Simon asked.

"Yeah." Jenna lied.

"So where's the cab?" Simon asked.

Jenna wanted to change the subject fast so that she would not be exposed.

"Look. Here's the file the guy gave me." She said trying to offer proof of her story.

Jenna showed Simon the file that she was carrying. It did not change his feelings. He knew that he was not getting the whole story. Jenna was soaked with sweat. Her make up was running down her face from crying. Her hair was messed. It was obvious that she was not telling him everything. He thought of all the questions that he could have asked her. "Why didn't you have your roommate come and get you? Why did you call me? Who did you come down here to see in the middle of the night?" He could have pressed the matter with her, but he did not want to. He had no interest in watching her squirm. He was happy to be with her again if only for the short time that it took to drive her back to her condominium.

"I'll get you out of here." Simon smiled serenely.

Jenna could see that Simon was letting the issue drop, and she was very relieved. She did not have a good lie cooked up, and it was impossible to tell him the whole truth. She could not let the façade fall and reveal herself to him. She said the only thing she could say in response to his graciousness.

"Thanks."

Simon pulled onto the expressway. He started to head towards the America Center when Jenna realized where he was going and stopped him.

"I can't go back home, Simon. Please, I need to stay at your place."

Simon gave her a weird look. Picking her up in the middle of the night after she had dumped him was bad enough. Now she was asking him for a place to stay for a while? He slowed the car down and pulled over to the side of the road.

"Jenna—" Simon started, and then he stopped. He looked into Jenna's sad brown eyes that were red from crying. She looked so desperate and vulnerable. Her small frail frame was shaking She was beautiful and delicate, but there was something dark about her too. Should a man ask a rose why it has thorns, or simply accept them and admire its beauty? Simon did not know. He only knew that he felt drawn to her. She was a dark flower. She was a book that he could not put down; she was a riddle that he loved.

"I love you."

Simon had shocked himself. Did he just say that? He could not believe that those words came out of his mouth. He did not know how or why they did. But they did. For all his doubts, Simon realized that he really loved Jenna. He had spoken from his heart.

Jenna was stunned. She looked at Simon in disbelief. No one had ever loved her before. She had never known love. She had no parents. She had no brothers or sisters. She had only one friend, Sheila, but she would not say that their friendship rose to the level of love. Simon had touched her heart. Jenna was full of joy. The parked car was silent for a moment, and then Jenna started to cry.

"Oh—oh please don't do that. It's okay. I'm sorry." Simon started.

"Oh, Simon!" Jenna whimpered.

She undid her safety belt, and hugged Simon tightly around the neck. She was so thankful. Simon felt the warmth of her hug. She was shaking. He was glad that he had answered her call. Even if he never saw her again. He did not care. Just to have her hug him like this was enough. He had to pry her arms from his neck to make her stop.

"You can stay at my place." Simon said softly.

"Thank you so much. Thank you." she whispered. He had been so kind, and gentle. He had saved her. He loved her. She gazed into his eyes for a long time. She felt quiet and secure. She was warm all over. Was this what love felt like? She did not know. She had never felt this way before. She slowly eased back into her car seat, and Simon pulled the car out into traffic.

When they finally came to Simon's trailer, Jenna was so tired that she fell down on Simon's couch and fell asleep instantly. Simon stood over her, smiled and shook his head. What a strange girl she was. He took her shoes off and put a blanket over her.

When Jenna woke up early the next morning, Simon was cooking in the kitchen.

"I'm making scrambled eggs. You want some toast?" he asked.

Jenna sat up on the couch and yawned.

"It smells great. Yeah, I'll have some."

"Have a seat at the table."

Jenna went over to the kitchen table and sat down. Simon put a glass of orange juice in front of her and came back with two dishes of scrambled eggs and toast.

"I'm so hungry." Jenna said.

"Me too."

Jenna looked at Simon and smiled. He smiled back, and they ate quietly together. The whole situation was awkward. Neither one of them knew what to say. Jenna really wanted to explain things to Simon. In her mind, she was running over various ways to tell him the truth in a way that would soften the blow. There did not seem to be a good way to do it. Luckily, Simon broke the silence himself and went a different way with the conversation.

"So did you find out who your parents were?" Simon asked.

Jenna remembered the file that she had taken from Rameesh's office. For a moment, she wondered if anyone had discovered his body. Did his boss go to his office to get the report? Would anyone even go to Rameesh's office until Monday? Would Rameesh's wife be waiting for him and send someone to the office? Jenna was lost in thought about all these things.

"Jenna?"

"What?"

"Did you find out who your parents were?"

"Oh my God. I never looked at my file. Where is it?"

"Is that it by the couch?"

Jenna saw the file on the floor next to her purse by the couch where she had passed out the night before. She went over to the folder, brought it to the table and opened it up. It was a medical dossier of sorts, but it did not look official. There were a few pages of notes from a medical examination dated ten years earlier, and another set of notes from another exam an additional five years earlier. The only other documents inside the file were a birth certificate and an old newspaper clipping. All the documents were photocopies. There were no originals.

Simon finished his eggs and toast as he watched Jenna thumb through the papers in the file and examine them.

"What's it say?" Simon asked.

"I'm not sure what this means."

"What is it?"

"It's a birth certificate."

"That ought to have the name of your mother and father on it. You've got it! You know now. What does it say?"

"It says 'Jenna Phelps'"

"Who is Jenna Phelps?" Simon asked.

Jenna gave Simon a dazed look. She was stunned.

"I think I am..." Jenna closed her eyes momentarily and quietly contemplated the matter. Then she looked at the birth certificate again. "It says that she was born on New Years day...12:02am...Baby New Year... and she was born in Dallas."

Jenna handed the certificate to Simon and walked towards the window.

"There's no name for the father?" Simon asked.

"I know. Look at the birth date."

"I can't tell if this is an '8' or a '0' here. She's either 10 or 22. There's no way to tell from this." Simon thumbed through the other pages of medical notes in the file. "Not much here. I can't even read the handwriting on these notes."

Jenna came back towards Simon, pulled out the old newspaper clipping and showed it to him. There was a picture of man and a little girl watching a parade. The man had his back to the photographer, but the little girl was looking directly at the camera and waving.

"Look at this." Jenna said.

"That's you?"

"Yeah, that's me."

Simon read the caption under the picture out loud, "'Little Jenna and her Uncle Rick enjoy the festivities.' Uncle Rick?"

"He wasn't my real uncle. I think he was a foster parent that I lived with once. I barely remember him."

"The mother on this birth certificate is Clarissa Phelps." Simon said.

He got up from his chair, took his empty plate to the sink, found his cell phone and brought it over to the kitchen table. He fiddled around on the screen for a moment until he found a public records directory on the internet.

"C-L-A-R-I-S-S-A P-H-E-L-P-S"

Simon typed the name into his cell phone and waited for the public records directory to return the information for anyone named Clarissa Phelps in Texas. After a moment, he frowned and shook his head.

"It says she's dead. No relatives given. Not a sister, or brother or anything. That's pretty young to die—47 years." Simon wrinkled his forehead and handed the file to Jenna. He thought for a moment, "Give me that doctor's name."

"Daniel Hoyniman."

Simon typed in the name, "There it is. He's seventy-five."

"He's still around?" Jenna asked.

"You should just call this guy up. Ask him if he remembers delivering Jenna Phelps on New Years Day 22 years ago. He might remember delivering a baby on New Years Day like that. Maybe not, but it's worth a try."

"What's his number?" Jenna asked.

"It's—wait a minute....Can't do it. It says it's unlisted." Simon said, "Just his address in Lubbock."

Simon could see that Jenna was worried.

"What's wrong?" he asked.

"Look at the picture."

Simon looked at the picture, but did not see anything special about it.

"What about it?"

"It's Lubbock. Look—" Jenna pointed to a building in the background of the picture. The storefront sign read "Lubbock Collision Repair"

Simon rose from his chair, and went over to Jenna, who was standing next to the kitchen table with her arms folded. He walked up to her and rubbed her shoulder to comfort her.

"So the doctor is from Lubbock, and the picture is from Lubbock, so what? Who gave you this file?" Simon asked.

Jenna shivered a little. She could not even look at Simon. She pretended like he had never asked.

"I think I--." Jenna said.

"There's an easy fix to this." Simon said earnestly.

"I think that I'm Jenna Phelps. Somebody lied--" Jenna started.

"Listen to me." Simon interjected.

"It's so obvious. I'm Phelps. They—

"Listen!"

"It's right there..."

"Listen to me." Simon insisted, "I know what it's like to be all alone. I know what it's like not to have your parents, or any family left. It hurts. I know. But this is easy. Let's just go over to this guy's house and ask him. We can do it right now. Lubbock's what...four hundred miles? It's my day off. I've got nothing going on. I can drive you there, and we can ask this guy and come back."

"What if he's out? We're going to drive all that way. He could be out of town."

"So what? We'll make a day of it. If he's not there, you can write him a letter or something." Simon pointed at the screen on his cell phone that showed Hoyniman's address. "This says he's seventy-five years old. He'll be at home."

"Would you really do that for me? Go all that way with me to see this guy?"

"I know what it's like not to have any family. I know. And, I'm not doing anything. We'll just go, and get it over with. It will give us a chance to talk anyhow."

Jenna had tears in her eyes she was so thankful. This is what it was like to be loved? She buried her face in Simon's chest. He embraced her and rubbed her back. He wanted to help her. He wanted to give to her even if it meant that he had to sacrifice a little of himself in the process. They hugged each other lovingly for a while; then, they left the trailer to drive to Lubbock and visit Daniel Hoyniman.

Chapter Twenty-Two

It was a hot and dry day on the drive to Lubbock to visit Dr. Hoyniman. The car seats that were heated by the sun were stinging hot. Jenna was thankful that she was wearing her jeans. They made a stop between Houston and Dallas to get some gas, and buy some soft drinks to cool themselves down and then continued on. The air conditioner in Simon's car was not working, and they drove the entire way with the windows open. The noise from the air rushing by the windows made it difficult to carry on a conversation. Simon loved the way Jenna's hair was tossed about by the wind, and he could not help smiling at her from time to time. Jenna turned the radio up loudly and started singing along with the music. Simon laughed like a little kid. Jenna was such a bad singer.

"Are you laughing at me?" Jenna asked.

"You sound like a hurt duck."

Jenna tried to look shocked and offended, but she was really laughing inside. She knew that she was bad.

"Well let's hear you." She challenged Simon.

Simon smiled coyly. He knew the song that was playing and happily took up the challenge. He was awkward. Periodically, his voiced cracked at the high notes, and he sometimes had difficulty with the melody.

"Oh my God. And you're laughing at me? Wow!" Jenna joked.

"I didn't say that I was Sinatra or anything."

"You can say that again."

"Well, you sounded like someone was hurting you—pinching your arm or something."

Jenna laughed. She felt so good being with Simon.

"I'll show you whose arm is getting pinched."

Jenna reached over and pinched Simon on the arm.

"Hey!"

"Go ahead; sing while I'm pinching."

Again, Simon took up the challenge. Jenna pinched him in the arm again and again while he tried singing along with the radio. He started off fine, but when Jenna pinched harder he let out a yap at a part in the song where the singer hit a particular high note. The timing was comical.

"Not so hard." Simon smiled as he rubbed his arm.

Jenna roared with laughter, and Simon joined her.

They drove along not talking about anything in particular. They made fun of the people in the cars that they passed. It was such a wonderful time just to be with each other and talk. They were each reaching outside of themselves in mutual self-giving for the other person's benefit. This is what love really is, and it felt so good. They stopped again just outside of Dallas to eat some lunch.

It was a small restaurant with a cowboy theme. The waitresses looked silly wearing cowboy hats. Jenna shared her meal with Simon and fed him a few bites from her plate. Simon did the same for her, and they decided to switch orders. Jenna was feeling giddy. It was so nice to be around Simon again. He was so laid back. He never scolded her, or accused her. She felt so relaxed around him. Simon was pleased with her company as well. She was smart and pretty. He enjoyed the talk. It was easy and natural. Nothing was contrived. And they laughed. It seemed like everything was funny—only to them though. No one else could understand. The waitress was funny. The food was funny. Why was everything so funny? They did not care. They were there in the restaurant together, and they were happy. Simon paid the tab, and they walked out holding hands. They almost forgot why they were even on this trip to begin with.

On the trip west from Dallas to Lubbock, they did not talk much. It was a long drive. They had turned off the radio. Jenna stared out of the passenger window in a daze. The clap of the air going by filled her ears and hypnotized her. The lack of conversation gave Simon time to think, and his thoughts did drift to the purpose for their trip. He did not really think that they would learn anything about Jenna's past from the doctor—if they were even able to meet him. It was just an excuse to be with her. There was something about her that was so compelling, and it was not just her looks. She was so complicated, and that made her appealing to him somehow. Nevertheless, he did want to ask her about why she had dumped him. She never had offered an explanation. He had never asked. Was now the time?

He went over the matter in his head a number of times as he looked over at Jenna, who was resting her head against the half open window. How could he breach the subject with her politely? Would she feed him some story? Should he interrogate her about it and risk an argument? He really wanted to know, but he did not want to spoil this time they had together. What could she say that would make him feel any better anyhow? What was the point in spoiling the great time that they were having together? "Well, there was a point." He thought. If their relationship was going to be honest—that is if they were going to even have a relationship—it could not be so if Jenna was hiding some massive secret. No, it would never work out if she was hiding something from him. Even so, if there would come a time and place where she could open up, and let him know more about herself, that time and place was not now. The more he thought about it, the less important it seemed at the time. He was with her again, and they were happy together. He was going to enjoy the moment.

Jenna closed her eyes on the long drive west towards Lubbock and rested her head. It had been such a great time so far, but she kept wondering if Simon would ever start asking her about not returning his telephone calls, or about her emergency. She ran over various cover stories in her mind, but she could not come up with anything that was believable. Her plan was to tell Simon that she just was not sure about the two of them during that week when he was calling her all the time—that she was mixed up in the head, and confused for that week. She did not have any story to tell him about the night she had called him. There was nothing that she could think to say that sounded good enough about any of it. She could only hope that Simon would not ask. All the while on the trip to Lubbock, she waited for him to start questioning her. She could hardly believe it, but he never asked her about her strange escapade. It was such a relief. They rode together in peace all the way to Lubbock where they found Dr. Hoyniman's address and met him as he was watering his garden in the front of his house.

Dr. Daniel Patrick Hoyniman was a very peculiar man. He was the kind of man that made a point to wear bow ties—not because he necessarily liked the look of a bow tie, but because he wanted to stand out from other people. He felt like he was smarter than other people, and in his warped mind wearing a bow tie was his little way of showing it. He had been born in Rhode Island and attended public schools through college. After college, however, he attended Harvard Medical School, and graduated second in his class. He did his internship and residency at The University of Pennsylvania Hospital, and then he accepted a lucrative position in Dallas where he finally settled down and practiced obstetrics and gynecology for thirty years. He married a woman, Phyllis, in Dallas, and had two children, who eventually both married. He finally retired in Lubbock, Texas when he was offered a part time teaching position at the university there. By all worldly measures, he was a successful man. On paper, he could not have been a more solid citizen if he had tried; however, for the people who worked closely with Dr. Hoyniman over the years, there was always something twisted about him. His mannerisms were strange. He had a sinister sounding laugh that was cartoonish, and always had bad breath. As he got older, his eyebrows became overgrown, and they curled up and out from his forehead making him look like he had horns. With his large toothy smile and pinkish complexion he almost looked like the devil. Even so, professionally speaking, he had a golden touch. He always knew the right people to know. He always sat on the right committees, and in any work related dispute or controversy he always was on the winning side. By the time he was fifty years old, he was very rich and could have retired. He owned or partially owned a number of very successful businesses, and he had a soaring stock portfolio. He could have retired on the liquidation of his real estate holdings alone. But he liked his work, and he continued full time as an obstetrician and gynecologist until he was sixty-five years old before he took the teaching position in Lubbock.

Dr. Hoyniman liked to spend his Saturday mornings watering his elaborate flower beds with a garden hose in front of his plush house. He liked pruning the flowers and trimming the grass and bushes to fit his idealistic conceptions of beauty. His house reflected the same disposition. It was on a large corner lot on the top of a small hill that was beautifully landscaped. From all outward appearances, the house was a model of style and design like something out of an architectural magazine. It was impeccably decorated, and nothing was ever out of place. It was an impressive façade of perfection that many people in this world aspire to, but few ever obtain. The house was a perfect representation of Dr. Hoyniman's own obsession with worldly perfection.

Dr. Hoyniman was watering his flowers when Simon Bosse, and Jenna Park pulled up in Simon's car and parked across the street. Right away, the doctor frowned when he saw them park their car. They were out of place for the neighborhood. They were young, and messy. Simon's car was old, and missing a hub cap. What were "these" people doing here? They did not belong here. Like most men, however, the doctor was stunned by Jenna's appearance. For the doctor, Jenna's proportions were a kind of curiosity. She seemed to him to be almost perfect—almost. She was too short, and too skinny, and too busty, and too wide at the hips. Her eyes were too big, and her waist too dainty. Her legs were too long for her torso, and her butt was too round. But all these things had one thing in common, they were too much of a good thing. Combined, the sum was greater than the individual parts, and in Dr. Hoyniman's eyes Jenna was an archetype of female eroticism.

As they got out of the car, Simon saw the doctor watering the flowers, and approached him with Jenna at his side.

"Excuse me, sir. Are you Dr. Daniel Hoyniman?"

"Yes." Dr. Hoyniman replied without emotion.

"That's great. Doctor, my name is Simon Bosse. This is Jenna Park. She was born in Dallas twenty-two years ago."

"And what does this have to do with me?"

"And...well let me just show you this."

Simon pulled out the birth certificate for Jenna Phelps and handed it to the doctor.

"That's the birth certificate for 'Jenna Phelps.' We can't tell if she was born twenty two years ago or ten because this number looks like it could be an '8' or a '0.'"

"I think it's an '8'" the doctor observed.

"Yeah. Maybe. Anyhow, according to the certificate you were the doctor who delivered her. See here." Simon showed Dr. Hoyniman his name on the certificate.

Dr. Hoyniman did not show any reaction. He simply continued to look down at the certificate.

"The important thing is that this birth certificate showed up in a file with some of Jenna <u>Park's</u> personal papers. We wondered if there may be any connection." Simon waited a moment to let the doctor absorb this information.

"Jenna, here, was given up for adoption at birth, and is trying to track down her parents. We saw that you were the doctor named on the certificate, and we wondered if you might remember anything about the babies you delivered that day, and could maybe shed some light on all this stuff."

"I see." The doctor said.

"Do you remember delivering Jenna Phelps?" Jenna asked.

Hoyniman replied with his strange grin, "I have delivered thousands of babies over the years. I really cannot remember. That's what happens when you get old. You cannot remember things. It's terrible."

"You don't remember delivering Jenna Phelps on New Years day? I mean the certificate says she was born at 12:02am. She had to be the first baby of the new year. Are you sure you don't remember?" Simon asked.

"Please doctor." Jenna begged.

Dr. Hoyniman simply smiled and shook his head, "I'm sorry. I just don't recall. I've had lots of Baby New Year's over the years. One year, I

---

even had ten!" Dr. Hoyniman laughed his strange cackle at this thought. It was so weird. Jenna and Simon looked at each other in disbelief.

"Even if I could remember her, there are laws about these kinds of things. I could not reveal private medical information even if I wanted to. Do you understand that?" Dr. Hoyniman asked.

"I guess." Simon said.

"What about Clarissa Phelps? Do you remember her?" Jenna asked.

"The situation is the same. Even if I remembered her, I couldn't give you any private—

"But we don't want any private information. We just want to know if you remember her, and what— Jenna started.

"I'm so, so sorry. I am very sorry. I don't have any information for you." Hoyniman cut her off.

There was a pause. The silence was broken only by the sound of the water trickling onto the ground out of the garden hose that Dr. Hoyniman held in his hand. Jenna was perplexed. She folded her arms in frustration and walked back to Simon's car. Simon took the certificate back from Dr. Hoyniman.

"Doctor, do you know an Uncle Rick?" Simon asked. He did not expect the doctor to answer. He only threw the question out there to get the doctor's reaction—the same way he had confronted the pilot over Geraldine.

Simon looked at the doctor closely, very closely, and searched his face.

Dr. Hoyniman was a very intelligent, wise, experienced, educated and composed man. It would be a difficult thing to outsmart him. He did not move, and showed no expression on his face.

"I'm sorry, son. I don't recall that name." he replied.

Then, almost like ripple on some calm water, Hoyniman's eyes went down while he blinked and shook head. It was such a slight little move-- almost completely imperceptible. If Simon had not been looking so closely, he never would have seen it. But he did see it. He saw that little head move, and downcast of the eyes, and he knew that the doctor was lying.

"Thanks anyhow, doctor."

"Have a nice day you two. It's a hot one." Hoyniman waved back with his wide smile.

Simon turned back to the car and tried to comfort Jenna. They both got into the car and drove off. Dr. Hoyniman waved goodbye before he turned around and walked back towards his house.

"What a waste." Jenna said as she and Simon drove away.

"He's lying." Simon said.

"How do you know?" Jenna asked.

Simon looked at her and then stopped the car. He did a u-turn at the intersection and went back towards Dr. Hoyniman's house. Simon stopped short of Hoyniman's house a little ways, parked the car and got out.

"Hurry!" he called to Jenna.

Jenna quickly got out of the car and ran up the hill with Simon towards the back of Hoyniman's house. They crouched down behind some bushes near the garage that was separated from the main house by about twenty yards. There was a sun room in the back of the house with a screen door on the side. A little ways from the screen door on the side of the house, there were some metal garbage cans, and a few recycling bins.

"What are we doing?" Jenna asked.

"Be quiet. Let's just wait here a few minutes." Simon whispered.

Almost as soon as Simon spoke, Hoyniman came out of the back door of his house and threw a big bag of shredded paper into a garbage can and then went back inside.

"Wait here." Simon told Jenna.

He quietly ran up to the garbage can, took the bag that Hoyniman had just thrown away and went back to get Jenna.

"Let's go!"

Simon grabbed Jenna by the hand, and they ran together back to the car. He threw the bag of shredded paper in the back seat and they drove off.

"What do you think is in the bag?" Jenna asked Simon.

"I don't know, but we're going to find out."

After a few minutes of driving around, Simon found a local library and pulled into the parking lot. He and Jenna got out of the car with the bag of shredded paper and went inside. There was hardly anyone in the library. Some women were mulling about the children's section with their toddlers. The librarians sat at the check out desk and read the internet on their computers. Nobody even noticed Simon and Jenna when they walked in. Simon found a table in a quiet corner where he and Jenna could reassemble the shredded documents undisturbed.

"How do you know this stuff has anything to do with me?" Jenna asked Simon as she helped him pull the shredded paper out of the bag and onto the table.

"I'm just taking a guess. If the guy was hiding something about Jenna Phelps, there must be something criminal about it. My brother always said that all criminals have something in common. They're all selfish. They always look for a shortcut and won't do things the right way. That's why their criminals. I just figured that if this guy was a criminal, then he wouldn't get rid of the evidence the right way and would just toss it in the trash, or something stupid like that."

It was taking too long to put the strips of paper together in the right order. Most of the typing was nothing more than columns of numbers on a page. There were some handwritten notes here and there, but the writing was so illegible that it was useless. They spent an hour piecing the strips of paper together and had about a page and a half fully assembled. Jenna felt that they were wasting their time trying to make the strips fit together perfectly.

"Simon, this is useless."

"Don't give up."

"I'm not, but I—All these numbers don't mean anything. We need a name, or something. An address...anything. Just look for something like that and forget about trying to fix this like a jig-saw puzzle."

"What about this?" Simon asked triumphantly. He handed Jenna a small and short strip of paper that had some bold typing on it. It had not been shredded very well, and was still mostly intact. "I think this is a prescription."

Jenna looked at the paper. She agreed.

"It is. For someone with a name beginning in C-L-."

"Clarissa?" Simon asked.

It seemed like a stretch, but Jenna's hope was increasing.

"Keep looking for the others like this one." She said.

They sifted through the pile of shredded documents for another thirty minutes until they found another prescription. It was a prescription for someone with a last name ending in "e-l-p-s."

Jenna jumped up from her chair, went over to Simon and threw her arms around him.

"You were right! It's for Clarissa Phelps. I don't believe it."

"This is wrong." Simon said.

"Yeah. That bastard lied to us."

"No, no, no."

Simon took out his cell phone, pulled up the screen for the public records database and searched Clarissa Phelps.

"According this web page, Clarissa Phelps died six month's ago."

Jenna looked at him for the point that he was trying to make.

"Look at the date on this. This prescription is only three week's old. Why would you write a prescription for pain relievers for someone who has been dead for five month's?"

Jenna was silent. She had no answer.

"What do you think?" she asked.

"I think we should find out where Clarissa Phelps lives." Simon said with a broad smile.

Simon and Jenna searched the rest of the bag of scrap papers, and found an address on an old receipt, but it did not have the name Phelps anywhere on it.

"Levelland?" Jenna asked.

"I've heard of it. I've only been there once, though. It's about twenty-five miles west of here. There's nothing there but oil and cotton fields--miles and miles of cotton fields. It's worth a try. We've come all this way."

Jenna and Simon gathered the shredded paper back into the bag and left the library for the parking lot. They got into the car and went west towards Levelland, Texas to find out who Clarissa Phelps was. They had no idea what they would find, but for the first time in her life Jenna felt like she was in control of the direction of her affairs. She had always been so managed over the years—controlled. The state, foster parents and then Jimmy...someone else was always in control of her life. She finally felt like she was setting the agenda, like she was free.

About an hour east of Jenna and Simon, Jimmy Demos was chasing after them in his car. He had his cell phone mounted on his dashboard. It was set to the map that tracked the signal of Jenna's implant. He was annoyed and frustrated. Jenna was causing him so much unnecessary effort. He had lost control of her. She did not fear him anymore, and he had to change that situation. In his mind, he was plotting all kinds of elaborate tortures for Jenna that would cause her the most terrible and prolonged pain. In his imagination, he had her tied up to a spring mattress, and was electrocuting her. Then he was fantasizing about beating her bare back with an electric extension cord. And then his thoughts turned to whoever her companion was. He knew that she had found someone to help her and drive her all this way. He was quite decided that he would have to kill that person. He drove with a determination to resolve the whole mess in one day. Jenna was not going to get away with this. He was going to teach her a hard lesson.

An hour to the west, Simon and Jenna smiled at each other as they drove the car to Levelland. They held hands. Despite their pasts, despite the strangeness of the whole situation, despite everything that was wrong in their lives and the rest of the world, they were able to forget it all and just enjoy being with one another. Simon was so happy to be with Jenna. She made him laugh and forget his loneliness. He wanted to bare his soul to her—to reveal his true self to her. Jenna was so thankful that Simon was helping her. She hated keeping her background a secret from him, but she still did not trust him enough to let him know that she was a prostitute. She thought he might leave her if he knew the truth about her prostitution. So it was different for her. She was still holding back—not ready to completely open up to him. She did not want to lose him. He was the only person in the world who ever treated her like a human being. He made her feel the opposite of the way that she felt when she interacted with Jimmy. He made her feel like she had worth—not as a commodity, but as another human life.

Chapter Twenty-Three

Levelland, Texas is known for two things—oil and cotton. It is a boring little town of around 13,000 people about twenty miles west of Lubbock on the west end of Texas, and in August it is relentlessly hot. The people of Levelland are divided into two main groups. There are Catholic Hispanics who work in the cotton fields, and there are Protestant Whites who work in the oil industry. There are a few shops and restaurants in the little downtown, but not much else. People in Levelland spend their time either at work, watching television, or drinking beer. From all outward appearances, there never is much happening in Levelland, and that is the way they like it. Simon and Jenna drove west on route 114 from Lubbock and went through the tiny Levelland downtown until they came to route 1490 where they turned north. Simon studied a map of the town on his cell phone. He had typed the address from the receipt into the map. He had it marked on the map, but it did not seem like there was a house anywhere nearby. There was nothing but cotton fields all around.

"We're right on top of it, but I don't see anything, do you?" Simon asked.

Jenna took the cell phone from Simon. She looked at the receipt that they had pieced together with some transparent tape.

"It has to be here." She remarked.

Simon pulled the car over to the side of the road and stopped. Rows and rows of cotton bordered each side of the small two lane black top road. He got out of the car and looked in all directions, but did not see any houses. Jenna got out of the car as well and stretched.

"I don't understand." Simon said as he studied the map more closely.

Jenna looked at Simon and almost felt like she was looking at some sort of alien being from another world. He never complained. He had all the right in the world to be angry with her; instead, he was sincerely trying to help her. She had dropped him the way Jimmy had told her to. She had completely rejected him, and yet here he was in the middle of this cotton field. He never even had pressed her about that week of ignoring his calls. He never had berated her—like she knew she deserved —about calling him for help in the middle of the night. She looked at him, and could not figure him out. He was a mystery.

"Simon?"

"What?"

"Don't you— Jenna stopped herself. She wanted to ask Simon if he wanted to know what had happened to her for a week, but she was not sure if she wanted to bring up the subject. It was like picking a scab. She looked at Simon, who was smiling at her, and for the first time in her life she wanted what was best for another person despite any pain that it might cause her. Simon deserved an explanation even if it meant that she might lose him. She felt a lump in her throat, but found the courage to ask him what he must have been asking himself all this time.

"Don't you want to know why I didn't return any of your calls? Or, don't want to know what I was doing when I called you in the middle of the night for help last night?"

It was done. She had opened herself to the possibility of being exposed. Her heart was pounding hard, and she was nervous. She had opened the door for Simon to shout at her. She waited for the words, "Yes! Yes! Where the hell were you? Were you dumping me? Are you just using me now? What are you hiding?"

Simon, however, never spoke these words. He thought them. Certainly, a part of him wanted to scream at her, but he did love her. He was not sure why he loved her, but he knew that he did because he did not mind picking her up in the middle of the night like she had asked. He did not mind driving over 400 miles to help her find who her parents were. He had forgotten the fact that she had not returned his calls for a week. He was glad just to have her back. He was happy just to be with her.

"I would be lying if I said that I hadn't thought about it. I won't say that. I just—I don't know. It doesn't seem to be that important anymore. I want to know, but...I don't know. Before I thought that I would never see you again, but now I'm just glad that you're here. I can't explain it."

Jenna was astonished. She never had been treated this well before in her life. It puzzled her. She could not put her mind around it. If Simon had screamed at her, or slapped her around, she would have understood. As it was, she could not make sense of it. It was as if she had seen an apple come loose from a branch and float upwards instead of falling down to the ground. Simon had forgiven her, and this was a foreign experience for Jenna. She wrapped her arms around his neck and kissed him. He had been so kind.

"Looks like this was all a waste of time, though." Simon said when Jenna let him go.

Jenna smiled as she looked lovingly into his eyes. "Maybe not a complete waste of time."

They got back into the car, turned around and headed back towards downtown Levelland. As they drove, they came upon a little grassy road that led into the cotton fields. It was a service road of two ruts of dirt. Simon stopped the car just short of this road and turned to Jenna.

"You want to give it a try? We've come all this way. It can't hurt."

Jenna grabbed Simon by the hand.

"Yeah, Let's try it."

Simon turned onto the little road into the cotton field. He went slowly over the rough ruts. The car jostled about from side to side. About a half mile into the cotton field, the road opened up into a wide space cut out of the crops. In this space there was a medium sized one story ranch house, and a much larger garage for farming equipment. The garage was about one hundred feet long and had four large service doors. All the buildings were at the bottom of a small rise in the land that hid them from the main road. Simon stopped the car and turned to Jenna.

"This has to be it."

Jenna nodded her head.

"Are you ready for this?"

Jenna let out a sigh.

"What's wrong?" Simon asked.

Jenna hesitated. It seemed safer to stay in the car. Now that she might really meet her mother, she was not sure that she wanted to know her. What kind of a mother could she be? She probably did not even care if Jenna was alive or dead. Jenna looked at Simon. He smiled at her, and somehow that smile relieved her doubts. She smiled back and got out of the car.

The ranch looked well maintained. The roof looked new, and the white vinyl siding was clean. The front porch was neatly decorated with hanging plants and had two decorative rocking chairs on it. Behind the rocking chairs, there was a large bay window. There was no landscaping around the house, and the front lawn was marked with patches of dirt. Simon and Jenna walked up to the front door of the ranch. Simon knocked repeatedly, but nobody answered. Jenna looked through a front window, but did not see anything.

"I don't think there's anybody home." Jenna said.

"Just hold on a second." Simon said. He started to walk around to the back of the house, and Jenna followed him. He looked through one of the bedroom windows facing the backyard. Inside, there was someone sitting in a lounge chair, but their back was turned to the window, and Simon could not see if it was a man or a woman. "Look, there's somebody in there."

Simon picked Jenna up by the waist and held her so that she could see through the window.

"Hello? Hello?" Jenna called as she banged on the window. The person inside the house did not move, however.

"Let's just go inside, and see who he is." Simon said.

They tried to open the back door of the house that led into the kitchen, but it was locked so they went around to the front of the house and tried the front door. It opened. Jenna looked at Simon questioningly as he slowly opened the door.

"Hello?" Simon called into the open door, "We're looking for a Clarissa Phelps." Nobody answered. Whoever was in the chair was apparently all alone in the house.

Simon and Jenna went inside and walked towards the back of the house to the bedroom where they had seen the person sitting in their chair. They stopped at the bedroom door.

"Do you want to go in alone?" Simon asked.

"Please come with me." Jenna said looking down at the floor.

Simon was about to lead the way into the bedroom, when Jenna stopped him with her arm.

"Wait a second," she started. She paused a moment to collect her thoughts. In the next room could be her birth mother—where her life began. What would it reveal to Simon? She did not want to lose him.

"Simon, I have a weird past. I have a weird life. I—Sometimes I want..."

Jenna was trying to confess to Simon about her prostitution and sleazy history, but she just could not find the courage to come clean to him. She had no idea why she had picked this moment, but she really wanted to tell him. She did not want to pretend with Simon anymore. She wanted to share her most intimate self with Simon, but how? How could she explain that she had been a prostitute since she was thirteen? It was impossible. Her life was too dark, and she could not bear to expose it to the light.

"Jenna, don't worry. Everything is going to be alright."

Simon had misunderstood Jenna. Simon had thought that she was simply getting nervous about possibly finding out who her mother was. Jenna knew that he had not followed her words. She went along with it, nodded her head in agreement and followed him into the bedroom.

Inside the bedroom, sitting on the overstuffed lounge chair was an incredibly fat black woman. She was wearing a moo-moo, and was in a deep sleep. She had a mustache and terrible acne all over her face, and her hair was a tangled mess of dreadlocks. Her hips were as wide as the large chair itself, and her massive breasts drooped over her belly like two saggy beach balls.

"I don't think that she's your mother." Simon observed dryly.

Jenna saw the humor in the whole matter and started to laugh.

"No, I don't think so either."

Simon and Jenna shared a laugh for a moment. It was silly that they had come all this way and had been so serious about the moment only to find this old black woman. Simon noticed a bottle of prescription pills on the end table next to the bed. He picked it up and read the label.

"But she is Clarissa Phelps."

Simon handed Jenna the bottle and showed her the label. Dr. Hoyniman's name was clearly printed on the front.

"Hoyniman?" Jenna asked.

"Yeah."

Simon went over to the woman and tried to wake her up by gently shaking her arm, but she was heavily sedated. He shook her more vigorously, but it became immediately apparent that it would be impossible to wake her; so he gave up.

"I don't know what kind of drugs those are, but she's not waking up any time soon." He said.

"What the hell is going on here?" Jenna asked.

Simon looked around the room, but there was nothing out of the ordinary. The bed was made and everything was tidy. He opened a closet, but there did not seem to be anything special inside. He opened the dresser drawers, but there was nothing there either. In fact, if there was anything peculiar about the room—indeed the entire house—it was that it seemed so ordinary. Everything appeared so normal. Simon stopped looking.

"There's nothing here. Let's go." Simon said.

He led Jenna back outside the house.

"Why did the doctor lie to us? What is this woman doing alone out here all drugged up?" Jenna asked while they stood on the front porch. "Maybe we can talk to the farmer?"

Simon thought for a moment.

"Yeah. We can do that. Why not? We'll go find him. But first, I need to use the bathroom so bad. Wait here for me."

Jenna nodded her head while Simon went back inside the house to use the bathroom. As she waited on the front porch for Simon to come back, an old man came around the corner of the house and surprised her.

"What are you doing here?" he asked.

Jenna did not know what to say. She had been taken completely off guard. She looked back at the house and wished that Simon would come out soon.

The old man was in his sixties. He wore an old worn cowboy hat with the brim pulled out to protect him from the sun. He was tall and lanky, and he had bony hands, but the only thing special about him was that his eyes were flawed somehow. He was looking directly at Jenna, but it seemed like his left eye was focused over her right shoulder and two feet away. Both eyes were cloudy with cataracts.

"Come with me to the back of the garage and help me start packing those boxes into the van." He said to Jenna.

Obviously, the old man had mistaken Jenna for someone else. She did not want to alarm him, however. Instead, she went along with him to the garage and kept looking back for Simon, hoping that he would come out of the house soon.

At the back of the garage, a large moving van was parked with its back end near a garage door that was closed. Next to the garage door was a normal sized entrance that the old man was heading towards. When he got to the door, he passed his right hand over a plate mounted on the side, and the door unlocked. Jenna immediately remembered the lock that Rameesh had opened to retrieve her file. She knew that there was a connection and that there was something more to this garage and kept looking back for Simon.

The old man opened the door, and Jenna followed him into the garage. There were numerous boxes piled by the door ready to be loaded into the moving van outside. Without saying a word, the old man pointed to the boxes. He pushed a button that opened the garage door so that Jenna could load the boxes into the parked van. Then, he continued on his own towards a cinder block wall that partitioned a section of the inside of the garage off from the rest of the space. At the cinder block partition there was another door with another plate mounted on the side. The old man passed his hand over the plate to unlock the door. Jenna watched him open the door to the partition, prop it open with a heavy weight and disappear inside the other room. She turned around to run out of the opened garage door and almost ran into Simon, who had come looking for her and was standing just outside by the van.

"Hey! What's going on?" he asked.

"Hurry! Come on in." Jenna whispered.

Simon walked into the garage and looked around. It was huge, but mostly empty except for about two dozen banker's boxes packed for moving.

"Some old man let me in."

"Why are we whispering?" Simon asked.

"Because he's in the next room."

"Why did he take you here?"

"He thought I was someone else. I don't think that he can see very well."

"What the hell is all this stuff he's moving?"

"I don't know, but I think that old man might have some information about me."

"Did he say anything?"

"No, but he opened this door like Rameesh."

Simon did not understand what Jenna was talking about, "Who is Rameesh?"

"It doesn't matter. But look, I think there's more in that other room where he went...Over there."

Jenna pointed to the cinder block partition, and the door that the old man had propped open that led into another room.

"Well, let's go in and get it over with." Simon said.

He took Jenna by the hand, and started to lead her towards the other room, but she pulled away.

"I don't know, Simon."

"What?"

"This is too weird. I don't know."

"We'll just talk to the farmer and ask him about Clarissa Phelps. He has to know. We can show him the birth certificate."

Jenna looked sideways at the door that the old man had walked through. She was doubtful.

"Come on." Simon encouraged her.

Jenna looked down and sighed and let Simon lead her towards the door.

Chapter Twenty-Four

By the time that Simon and Jenna were pulled over on the side of the road 1490 in the middle of miles and miles of cotton fields looking for Clarissa Phelps's address, Jimmy Demos was only twenty-five miles to the east of them, and was just arriving in Lubbock. He could see on his cell phone exactly where Jenna was, and he was as anxious and angry as he had ever been in his life. He was barely in control of his mind. His face was contorted into a strange scowl that made him look like a gargoyle. He was not afraid that Jenna would escape from him. He knew that he would always be able to track her down by her implant. He was angry that she was being so rebellious, and risking the potential ruin of everything that he had built up over the years. Jimmy did not go directly to Levelland. He had understood Jenna's purpose from the moment that he saw that she was headed to Lubbock. He knew that he had to make the same stop in Lubbock that Jenna had made. He parked his car across the street from the beautiful white house sitting on top of a hill with a neat front lawn and handsome garden. He walked up to the front door, and rang the doorbell. Hoyniman came to the door, and instantly sized Jimmy up.

"You're here about Jenna, aren't you?" Hoyniman asked.

Jimmy nodded his head, "Yes, I have a little problem."

Hoyniman gritted his teeth in anger. He did not like being inconvenienced like this.

Simon held Jenna's hand, and told her not to worry as they walked towards the cinder block partition. They would just explain to the old man why they had come. If he became angry that they were on his property, then they would leave and forget about the entire expedition. Simon was not afraid, but Jenna was visibly scared. Simon put his arm around her shoulders and rubbed her back to encourage her. When they walked together into the next room, they were both astonished to find

---

that the old man was not there. There was no exit from the room except the door that Jenna and Simon had just come through.

"Where did he go?" Jenna asked.

"Down." Simon said as he pointed. In the corner of the room there was a small rectangular trap door where a set of stairs led downwards below the concrete floor of the garage. They were barely visible in the dim light. Simon and Jenna went over to the stairs to take a look. A light could be seen at the bottom of the stairs, and it was apparent that they led to a fairly large space beneath the garage.

"I don't like this. Let's get out of here." Jenna said.

Simon looked around the room, and took a closer notice of the objects surrounding him. Some of the boxes on the floor were opened at the top, and Simon could see some of the contents. There were graduated cylinders, glass beakers and tubing, and Bunsen burners. There was a metal wash tub in the corner, and an electric scale, and some test tubes—all the accoutrements of a chemist. Why would a cotton farmer have all this equipment out here in the middle of nowhere? It seemed obvious to Simon that this was no cotton farmer. He was standing in the middle of a drug laboratory. He felt a lump in his throat, and the thought of being caught by a group of drug dealers terrified him. The urgency of the situation suddenly dawned on him.

"This guy's a drug dealer. He'll kill us if he finds us."

Jenna was really nervous now. She nodded in agreement.

"We have to get the hell out of here." Simon said.

"Yes, please let's go." Jenna pleaded. She did not want to die. She wanted to be with Simon.

"UNCLE RICK? UNCLE RICK?" someone shouted from the next room.

Jenna and Simon looked at each other in shock. The old man farmer was Uncle Rick! They could hear footsteps coming from the steps that led underneath the garage. Simon grabbed Jenna by the waist and abruptly pulled her next to himself against the wall where it was very dark. Uncle Rick came up the stairs and shuffled passed Simon and Jenna without seeing them. They watched him walk through the door into the main part of the garage out of their sight.

"Let's just run to the car. They won't have any time to do anything about it." Simon whispered.

Jenna nodded

They came away from the wall, and started to walk towards the door. Jenna happened to look down the stairs, and stopped immediately at the edge of the opening going down. Simon walked ahead without noticing that Jenna had stopped. At the bottom of the stairs looking up at Jenna, there was a small girl who was about ten years old. She stared up at Jenna without any expression, and they both stood motionless for a moment. The light was dim in the room, and from the top of the steps, Jenna could barely see the girl. Even so, there was something immediately familiar about her to Jenna. The little girl turned around and retreated into the room beneath the garage. Mesmerized by the familiarity of the little girl, Jenna totally forgot about Simon and the dangerous situation that they were in and followed the little girl down the stairs.

When she came to the bottom of the staircase, Jenna could see that there was a very large room below the main floor that continued through almost the entire length of the garage. There were lighted fluorescent lights hanging overhead at the bottom of the staircase, but the basement was mostly dark. Far down the room, however, Jenna could see the form of the little girl, who was standing by a series of tall cabinets. The flicker from the light of a television set behind the little girl defined her silhouette. There appeared to be a small separate room in the corner where the television was.

Upstairs in the cinder block room of the garage, Simon was just about ready to dash when he turned around and noticed that Jenna had disappeared down the trap door. He quickly ran to the door, and went down the stairs after Jenna. She was standing still and looking down the room towards the other end.

"Jenna!" he whispered as he came up next to her. "We have to go now!"

Jenna pointed towards the little girl at the other end of the room. Simon had not noticed her at first, but he saw her distinct silhouette.

"I think I know her." Jenna said.

"Jenna, we're dead if we stay down here. We have to go."

Jenna did not say anything.

"I know that this is important to you. I know. I told you. I understand, but we're going to get killed down here if we don't leave now."

Jenna looked up at Simon with her large brown eyes full of tears. She was shaking with emotion. She wanted to see the little girl. She wanted to make this connection to her past, whatever it was. Simon could see that and relented.

"Just hurry, and come back quick."

Jenna turned away and walked towards the little girl.

Above them, on the main floor, Uncle Rick was at the open bay of the garage where the moving van was parked. He turned to his "niece" who

---

was standing by the boxes and was annoyed because she had not loaded them into the van.

"I thought I told you to start loading those boxes." He said.

"No you didn't."

"Don't contradict me child! I told you to move these boxes. You haven't done a damn thing!"

"You didn't tell me to do anything, Uncle Rick." The girl pleaded.

"DAMN IT! I told you by the house to come with me and help me move these boxes! Now move your ass!"

"Uncle Rick, I wasn't by the house. I only just got here from picking cotton."

Uncle Rick stared at the girl in disbelief. Then he heard the sound of a car outside near the house. He quickly shut the garage door.

"Stay here!" he ordered the girl, and went to see who was outside.

Simon stood by the bottom of the stairs and alternated between looking up the steps to see if anyone was coming, and looking at Jenna walk towards the little girl at the other end of the basement. He had done a foolish thing to come here with her like this. He was certain that he was going to die here. He had come to help Jenna find her past. It was what she wanted. Simon knew that she really wanted it, and he wanted to give it to her. But it was dumb, and now he was going to get killed in this basement. He began to think seriously about how he would confront Uncle Rick and began to search for a weapon. He found a light switch near the bottom of the stairs and flipped it on. A few more fluorescent lights came on overhead, and Simon could see the area around him more clearly. There were shelves against the walls with more laboratory equipment and large beakers. Next to one of the shelves, Simon saw a mop and grabbed it to use as a weapon.

At the other end of the long basement, Jenna was standing in front of the little girl in the very dim light. The girl was standing next to a large case, but did not move as Jenna slowly approached.

"I won't hurt you." Jenna whispered. "I just want to see you. I want to talk to you about Uncle Rick."

The girl looked behind her shoulder for a moment at the room with the television set that was partitioned off from the rest of the basement. She then turned back towards Jenna and looked up at the case.

Simon had had enough. They had to leave immediately. He did not want to die here. He had given Jenna all the time that he could. He hurriedly walked down the basement towards Jenna to grab her and bring her back up the stairs with him. As he walked, Simon noticed next to him some tall cabinets lined up against the length of the wall of the basement in a line. There was a musty smell in the air like fish. Simon could hear some swishing of liquid coming from the cabinets. "What is this place?" he asked himself. He kept moving along the wall until he came to Jenna.

"Jenna! Jenna!"

Jenna was kneeling in front of the little girl and did not say a word.

"Jenna!"

Again, Jenna did not move. In the darkness, Simon could see her gray form kneeling on the ground and shaking violently. He found a light switch near the wall, and flipped it on.

"JENNA! WE HAVE TO GO NOW! DID SHE TELL YOU ANYTHING?"

The fluorescent lamps overhead flickered on and off for a moment like they were struggling to fight against the surrounding darkness. They hissed and sputtered trying to light up. It was as if the darkness was too strong and held them back. Finally, the overhead lamps won the battle and pushed back the darkness to reveal the room. Simon stood with stone feet perhaps two yards away from Jenna as she cried out loud.

"I'M A CLONE! I'M A CLONE! I'M A CLONE!!!!"

Jenna's sobbing wail echoed in the large room like the howl of a wounded animal. When it died down, only the hum of the fluorescent lights could be heard.

In front of her, in a large glass case was a despicable abomination. The creation of lustful men with dark minds, and deep wants—boastful men, wicked men, men full of envy, murder, strife, deceit, malignity. They are men who demand what they have not earned and steal what is not theirs—ruthless, haughty, heartless and foolish men, haters of God. Men of endless ambition, they worship themselves and love the creation more than the Creator. In front of Jenna, in a large glass tank was the fully mature naked body of a woman suspended in liquid. Everything about the body was normal except that there was no head. Only a small portion of the brain stem poked out from above the neck. Along the wall, next to Simon going back towards the stairs, there were perhaps ten more such cases with more bodies in various states of maturity. Standing next to the case in front of Jenna and leaning against it, there was a small girl. She could have been Jenna's daughter. The resemblance was unmistakable. She was looking down at Jenna.

Suddenly, the clone without a head inside the glass case moved abruptly, and swished the liquid inside the case around.

"MY GOD! SHE'S ALIVE!" Simon gasped.

The naked clone moved around awkwardly with the tiny brain stem jiggling back and forth in a precession motion like the upper end of a top as it slowly stops its spin.

Simon tried to pick up Jenna from the floor, but she was hysterical.

"Come on! Come on!"

The little girl stared at them blankly.

Jenna could barely move, but Simon managed to get her to her feet. They started to move towards the stairs. Jenna was dragging, and clumsy. Simon dropped the mop and struggled to carry her towards the exit. He pulled Jenna along, and she was starting to gather herself and walk normally. Just then, the old man, Uncle Rick, appeared at the bottom of the steps, and turned on the rest of the basement lights. Standing behind him was Dr. Hoyniman, and Jimmy Demos.

Chapter Twenty-Five

"STOP!" Uncle Rick demanded. His voiced echoed in the large basement.

Simon held Jenna by the arm and led her backwards away from the three men. His instinct for survival was taking over. He started to look around for the mop that he had let drop to the floor, but he could not find it. Demos, Hoyniman and Uncle Rick closed in on them as Simon and Jenna moved towards the back wall.

"You have nowhere to go." Uncle Rick said.

Simon was looking around in a panic for a way out. They were being backed into a corner by the three men.

"Jenna, come here." Demos ordered.

Jenna was crying, and shaking badly. Simon looked at her in shock. The man knew her.

"You know this guy? Who is he?"

Jenna and Simon were completely cornered. Jenna could not speak. Simon was furious and desperate.

"TELL ME! WHO IS HE!" he shouted.

Jenna was red with anguish. She was in a pitiful state of abjection. The emotional pain on her face was transparent. It transformed her. The deep furrows on her brow, her severe frown and squinting eyes made her look like a different person. She had nowhere to go now, and nothing to lose—except her pride. She finally let the false facade of her life drop completely to reveal herself to Simon. She opened her soul to him for better or for worse and handed him the mask that she wore.

"He's my pimp. I've been with hundreds of men. I'm a whore."

Jenna collapsed to the floor, "I'm a whore. I'm a whore."

"You're my whore. Now get your ass over here." Demos demanded.

Simon was standing by himself. He continued to back up and look around for a weapon. He was numb. It was too much for him to process. He only thought about trying to find a way out now.

Seeing that Simon had been separated from Jenna, Demos pulled out his gun and prepared to shoot him.

Simon backed into a table. In desperation, he picked up a large glass jar full of liquid that was next to an opened safe. He held it over his head and was ready to throw it at Demos, who was only fifteen feet away.

"STOP! DON'T SHOOT!" Uncle Rick shouted.

Demos turned around and looked at Uncle Rick.

"Don't shoot!" Uncle Rick said again, and looked over at Hoyniman.

Hoyniman understood immediately. He slowly walked up next to Demos.

"Put the gun away, Jimmy." Hoyniman ordered.

Demos put the gun away and backed off. Hoyniman turned towards Simon.

"Son, put that jar down on the table."

Simon stood holding the jar above his head. It was ice cold in his hands. There was, in fact, a smaller jar within this jar. Simon was terrified and did not move.

"Put it down, son." Hoyniman said calmly. "Just put it down, and you can leave here. We'll let you go."

Simon regained some of his composure. He realized that he could use the threat of breaking the jar to get out of the situation.

"Back off, or I'll throw it." Simon demanded.

"Put the jar down." Hoyniman replied.

"I'll throw it."

"Put IT <u>down</u>." Hoyniman demanded pointing to the ground.

"I'll THROW IT."

"PUT IT DOWN!"

"I'LL THROW IT! I'LL THROW IT! BACK OFF! BACK OFF!" Simon screamed maniacally.

Shocked and a little scared, Hoyniman backed down and moved away.

Simon crept up to Jenna, who was slumped on the floor crying.

"Get up, Jenna. Get up."

Jenna slowly came up to her feet and held onto Simon. She was a wreck.

Simon started to move around towards the stairs making certain that he held onto the jar, and kept facing the three men. As he moved, he came to the open doorway of the room with the television set that was partitioned off from the rest of the basement. The little girl, Jenna's clone, was standing by the doorway watching him. Simon did not notice her and almost bumped into her. Startled, he momentarily looked away from Demos, Hoyniman and Uncle Rick into the little room. Inside, there were about six other children—clones--four boys and two girls. Not one of them was more than six years old. They were watching a pornographic video with the sound turned off. Some of them were naked, and were imitating the people on the video. They were being conditioned to be prostitutes. One of the little boys was on his knees.

Like a worm, Simon's anger was eating through his mind. The sight of those children—there were not sufficient words. He was furious, disgusted and depressed at the same time. Tears were coming down his face. He was like a beehive someone had thrown a stone at. He shook with rage as he turned towards Demos.

"YOU SICK BASTARDS! YOU—YOU—YOU'RE—YOU BASTARDS! YOU'RE GONNA FRY!!! YOU'RE GONNA FRY!!! YOU'RE SICK!!!"

Simon was crying hard now. He was losing his nerves from the shock of seeing such evil. His mind could not assimilate it all. The unexpurgated sight of abomination upon abomination was taking its toll on him.

Hoyniman let out a bored sigh.

Simon continued towards the stairs with Jenna. Hoyniman, Demos and Uncle Rick backed up out of the way.

"YOU'RE GONNA FRY!! THIS IS TEXAS YOU BASTARDS!!" Simon shouted as hard as he could.

"Nobody's going to fry." Hoyniman said matter-of-factly.

"OH YEAH. YOU ARE. YOU ALL ARE. YOU'RE ALL GONNA FRY."

The three men did not say anything. They only watched as Simon moved closer to the bottom step. They watched Simon start to walk backwards up the stairs with Jenna and let him reach the top.

"Wait! The door! There's a lock!" Uncle Rick yelled.

In all the tension of the situation, Uncle Rick had momentarily forgotten that there was a lock on the outside of the hatch that sealed the stairs from above. He motioned to Demos, who ran towards the stairs, but it was too late. Simon had enough of his senses to shut the hatch on the stairs. He noticed the bolt on the hatch, let Jenna fall to the floor, put down the jar, and managed to set the bolt before Demos could force the hatch open.

"YOU'RE GONNA FRY! YOU'RE GONNA FRY! YOU SICK BASTARDS!!! YOU'RE GONNA FRY!!! THIS IS TEXAS!!! THIS IS TEXAS!!!"

Simon bent over to grab the jar and took his first look at it. There was a label.

"ISS-104 embryos."

Simon realized that he was carrying a jar full of embryos. He held it tight to his chest. Jenna picked herself up from the floor. Together, they went out to leave the garage while Demos banged on the hatch trying to get out.

Chapter Twenty-Six

Simon and Jenna ran through the open garage door by the moving van and made their way to Simon's car. Simon put the jar of embryos on the hood of the car so that he could open the door for Jenna.

"Get in!"

"Nothing's going to happen to them." Jenna said in a monotone of despair.

"Get in! We'll go get the police right now."

"What are the police going to do?"

"They'll arrest them."

"No they won't. Do you know how many cops I've been with?"

"Just get in! You don't understand. There are judges and lawyers and—

"Ha!" Jenna laughed, "Do you know how many judges and lawyers I've been with?"

Simon grabbed Jenna by the arm, "Get in the damn car!"

"Who do you think they're breeding those kids for?"

Simon let go of Jenna's arm, crossed his arms and turned away from her.

"I know it's true. They did it to me. Nobody's going to stop them." Jenna's words were like the thud of a heavy weight falling to the ground.

"But they're just little boys?" Simon whimpered.

"They prostituted me out since I was thirteen." Jenna said stoically. "They cloned me, bred me--trained me for it."

Simon looked at Jenna with anguish. He knew that she was speaking the truth. He was furious. Inside, his sense of justice was burning. He could not let them get away with it. He was not going to let them get away with it. Their crime was like a toxic waste spill in the middle of a city. To leave it alone would be like allowing a cloud of death to creep throughout the population. Simon looked around. Parked on the side of the garage was a small farm tractor, and next to the tractor there were some gasoline cans.

"They'll fry. I'll do it myself." Simon said.

He reached into the glove compartment of his car and pulled out a pack of matches. Then, he started to walk towards the gasoline cans.

"COME ON!" he shouted back at Jenna.

Jenna jogged after him. There were two five gallon cans of gasoline. One was full, and the other was half empty.

"It's not enough." Jenna said.

"It is. There have to be some air vents to that basement. We put some stuff down the vents, pour some gas on it and light the match."

"What about those kids down there?" Jenna asked.

Simon stopped abruptly.

"Yes! What about the children?" a voice from behind Simon asked.

Simon whipped around; it was Demos with his gun drawn. He had it pointed at Simon. Behind Demos were Hoyniman and Uncle Rick. Standing next to Demos was a fifteen year old girl—a duplicate of Jenna

---

except for her right side. The clone girl's right eye looked like it was melting down her face. It blended in with her cheek, and upper lip. Two of the fingers of her right hand were fused together. Instead of having five fingers on her right hand, she had three normal fingers, and one gigantic middle finger. She walked with a mild limp in her right leg. She was some kind of mistake, a flaw in the cloning process. The clone looked back at her "mother," but she did not seem troubled. She had been conditioned to seeing duplicates of herself. It was not out of the range of her social norms.

This fifteen year old clone girl had been in the moving van loading boxes when Jenna and Simon had run out to the car. When she got out of the van, she had heard Demos trying to force open the hatch in the back of the garage and had gone to undo the bolt for him.

"Go get the jar and bring it back." Uncle Rick directed the clone girl.

She limped around Jenna and Simon to the car, grabbed the jar that was on the hood, came back and handed it to Uncle Rick.

Simon and Jenna stood pinned against the tractor. Demos pointed the gun at them from about ten feet away.

"I told you that nobody was going to fry." Hoyniman gloated.

"You can't do this to people."

"These aren't people." Hoyniman said pointing to the jar.

"They are." Simon insisted.

"No, these are just cells."

"No. They're people. I saw the label."

"And what did the label say? Huh? Tell me."

"Embryos."

"That's right. Embryos. Not 'people'—'embryos'" Hoyniman lectured.

"If they were just cells, you would not have been so scared that the jar would fall to the ground. You would not have it locked in a safe. You wouldn't fight over it."

Hoyniman was infuriated. The truth exposed him—convicted him. He hated the truth because in all his life he had never lived in accordance with it. In all his daily decisions throughout all the years, he had always done things his own way for his own purposes. The morality of it all was less important to him than getting his own way. After wronging thousands of people thousands of times—in school, in business, in private life--he had built a wall of rationalization and excuses around himself. What he had done was not his fault. What he had done was not really that bad. And now, to hear someone suggest that what he had done <u>was</u> really his fault, and <u>was</u> really bad was to have those walls of rationalization and excuses come crashing down. He turned red with anger and started to shake.

"Shut up! What do you know about it?" Hoyniman hissed.

"You're sick. You're turning those little kids into whores." Simon said.

"SHUT UP! SHUT UP!"

"Oh God. You screw little kids. Oh God! Oh God! You clone them and screw them."

"SHUT UP! SHUT UP! SHUT UP!" Hoyniman screamed as he covered his ears with his hands. "KILL HIM! NOW!" he shouted to Demos.

Demos looked at Hoyniman with a confused look. It was strange to see the doctor with his guard down and losing control of himself like this.

Simon was in tears and red with emotion.

"I saw the label..." he sobbed "...ISS--" Simon stopped. It was a revelation! He understood now. He understood it all.

"ISS" he knew those initials. Everyone in Houston—mission control—knew those initials. They stood for "International Space Station"

"Who are you people?" Simon squeezed.

"Son, you'll never know." Hoyniman said.

Demos pointed his gun at Simon and shot him in the head.

Simon's brains sprayed all over the tractor, and his body immediately fell to the ground.

Jenna broke down.

"NOOOOOO!!!!!! Oh my God! No! No! Please God! Ohhhhh! God! No. No. No. Oh God. No. No."

Chapter Twenty-Seven

In a polygamous society where men and women choose multiple mates throughout their lives without being held to any meaningful commitment, we can divide men and women into high and low prestige groups as described by William Tucker in his essay "Monogamy and Its Discontents" published in <u>The National Review</u> in 1993 as follows.

The high prestige male sits on the top of the pyramid of society like a male lion at the head of a pride. The high prestige male has the most money, power and independence, and can eventually obtain most of the material objects that he wants. Since human beings have unlimited wants, however, the high prestige male will find that he is never satisfied with what he has. He is like a little child that becomes bored with his toys and must constantly find new ones to play with. Anyone who might stand in his way is subject to his tantrums. If the person standing in the way is rich and powerful, this will probably mean a lawsuit. If he is poor and weak, it can mean something more violent for the person who is the obstacle to the high prestige male's wants. In any case, the high prestige male will not tolerate impediments to his agenda—like the pilot who helped Geraldine abort her baby.

Beneath the high prestige male is a varying array of relationships among people full of complicated emotions. High prestige females rank just below the high prestige male. Like Sonali's marriage to Rameesh, their marriage to a high prestige male is only nominal. They obtain a material wealth that they would otherwise not have possessed without the legal weight of a marriage certificate. In addition, they are able to enjoy their own liaisons as long as they do not interfere with their spouse's personal agenda. Their great dilemma in life is that their relationship with the high prestige male is a sham. Somehow they must reconcile this fact with their need for a more substantive basis of sustaining their social prestige. Maybe they use divorce as a threat against the high prestige male to keep him in line—like Sonali. Or, they might sincerely try to seek reconciliation with the high prestige male. Either way, they must fortify the tie that binds them to their mate, or face a humiliating degradation of prestige when the high prestige male decides that he can pay whatever price it will cost him to replace them.

Below the high prestige female are low prestige females. Poor or dumb and without couth, but sexually attractive in their own way, they are able to have access to a high prestige male that they would not be able to have in a monogamous atmosphere. Of course, because the relationship is only sexual, and they are really nothing more than a sex toy for the high prestige male, these women—like all toys—are eventually cast aside by the childish male without a care as soon as he gets bored with them. If they are like Geraldine Jankowicz, they find that their attachment to a high prestige male is a Faustian bargain, and that they will completely lose any chance at a normal and happy family of their own.

At the bottom of a polygamous society is the low prestige male. He is poor and unattractive. Without the material wealth to support a family of his own and unable to attract women by his looks, he is the loneliest and most unfortunate of individuals. Pornography and prostitutes may form poor substitutes for the real objects of his sexual yearnings. If he is able to find some woman to date him, like Simon's friend, Jerry, he is immediately faced with the prospect of competition from higher prestige males, who find it all too easy to lure a woman away from such a man. Forming a class of bachelors that sometimes lashes out in frustration, low prestige males can interject a lawlessness into society that threatens civil order.

The children of a polygamous society—like Roxanne's two little boys—emulate the behavior of their parents. As these children age, they become adults physically, but remain children emotionally. As they are too mentally immature to practice self discipline, and handle the responsibilities demanded of a modern civilization, they become incapable of reproducing that civilization themselves. Eventually, that civilization falls apart. As William Tucker in his essay "Monogamy and Its Discontents" published in The National Review in 1993 said "People who are incapable of monogamy, are probably incapable of many other things as well." The one thing the children of a polygamous society are capable of; however, is terrible crime--like the child murderer chewing on his dead mother's arm found by Pierre and Brommy in the house by the railroad tracks. Since these children have little control over their emotions, their daily interactions with others will erupt in numerous violent outbursts that inevitably result in sickening crimes.

In reality, this is of course an oversimplification of matters, and these descriptions are somewhat of a caricature. Emotional and spiritual influences play a large part in interpersonal relationships. Human beings have an inner life known only to them, and God. Their outer life is merely a mask for others to see that covers the true essence of their being. It is their pride, or lack thereof that impels them to wear the mask, or drop it. If they can change their inner self, or risk having their pride hurt, they eventually let the mask fall and become the person they were meant to be. They become more noble and selfless—more like God.

Paradoxically, men can have so much pride that they refuse to reform and are unashamed of their inner self. Such men may also let the mask fall and demand that the rest of the world accept their unrepentant self. They accuse anyone who does not accept their debauchery of being self righteous. In reality, these men are the truly self righteous. Instead of trying to humble themselves and repent of their ways and try to be more like God, they demand that God becomes more like themselves. Instead of conforming to the truth, and living in accordance with it, they demand that the Truth conform to them. Their insanity is a chaotic influence on society. In any case, only the truly good and the truly bad have no use for hypocrisy. The truly good have nothing to be ashamed of. The truly bad simply do not care. Everyone in between feels the need for a mask to show the outer world to protect their vulnerable inner self and is a hypocrite to some degree. The meaning of life—our purpose—is to become one of the truly good and become more like God, to have a heart like His heart—a crucified heart that is willing to sacrifice its well being for the sake of another (to truly love them) and lose the hypocrisy.

Ultimately, if polymorphous polygamous behavior becomes ubiquitous—if it becomes the norm--in a society of ever evolving social norms, that society will become a hellish place to live. Human life will be reduced to nothing more than a commodity and become nothing more than a means to an end—even little children and young girls become sex objects like the 8 year old mother "Betty" and her very young mother and grandmother. In such a world, the relationship between human beings becomes little different than the relationship between a pimp and his whores—a master and his slaves; it becomes a drain field of human misery. The happiness of family life, and the good fruit that comes from it will disappear. Like a world without the song of birds, society would become a cold and heartless place. Should technologies such as cloning and artificial wombs be introduced, the inevitable mass production of human life for pure consumption in medical research, recreational sex, spare body parts, use as soldiers in an army, or for whatever putrid purpose the warped mind of man can think of would be inevitable. It would be inevitable because humans have unlimited wants, and there will always be proud men who will seek the satisfaction of their unlimited wants by whatever means possible--even cloning and mass producing people--even creating transgenic offspring. They will use any and all rationalizations and excuses to justify their grotesque abuse of human life. They may even convince themselves that they are improving the human race. They would say that they are removing the genetic imperfections in humanity. But they reason badly when they think that what is weak proves itself to be useless. They only lie to themselves when they pretend that they can play God and manage human life like they were managing cattle. They would have their might be their right, and have no care for any moral objections to their obscene use of power. When this has happened to its fullest, and the preponderance of men have been lost to this terrible state of affairs, Satan will have his day in the sun. He will have eclipsed all that is decent and good like the moon coming in front of the sun, and he will have cast a dark shadow upon the world that can only be redeemed by the mercy of Almighty God. Satan will have turned God's good order upside down, and will have occasion to sing his hateful harangue against God and man.

Thou hated creation--

Thou timid and puny servant,

See the face that tends the night,

And oversees what was rightfully mine

Before thou were conceived of dust.

Thou cannot stay my temptations forever.

Even now I see thy virtue waning.

Soon it will only be a sliver on the horizon.

As I cut thou off from thy master,

Thou become a weakling!

Upon thy face, my shadow shines.

Oh Golden Knight, hast Thou come to find me?

Thy wretched ride hast come to an end.

Thy golden face no man can see,

And yet I see.

I see the fields Thou seek to tend.

And I corrupt them.

I take Thy seeds and sow my own,

And hear the tortured spirits groan.

And I laugh. And I hate Thee.

Thou puny servant,

Thou Golden Knight.

Shortly man will honor me,

And say what I say is "wrong" or "right."

For think he may, all night and day,

"What is truth?" No man can say.

But I can. And I say, the truth, I say,

The truth is but a lie!

And I am the father of it!

Jenna Park was crying and slouched on the ground next to the dead body of Simon Bosse. He had been the only man who had ever loved her, the only man who had ever treated her as a real person—a subject, not an object. But now he was dead, and her chance for true companionship was dead with him. She was all alone in the world without true love. She had nobody. She was all alone so she cried. Simon had been the only man that she felt that she could truly trust. He had not possessed a lot of money, or a fancy job. He had not been that smart; he had an athletic body, but his looks were plain. But she was willing to overlook his imperfections. She had abandoned the attitude that he was like a machine that was strictly there to serve her. She had been happy just to be with Simon because she knew that she could trust him, and that he sincerely cared for her. That was enough now. Jenna had changed.

She had become something better. Would she rather have struggled through the ups and downs of life with Simon than to live alone without him? Yes, she would have, and she would have been happy. If she could have, would she have given her life so that Simon could have his back? No, she did not have that kind of perfect love. Even so, her whole mindset had changed for the better. She would never let herself slip into the attitude that people were objects to be used for her own purposes and discarded when she was done with them, and she would never serve Demos again.

"Come on. Get up." Demos said as he stood over Jenna.

She looked up at him, "Who were my mother and father? Am I a clone?"

Demos ignored her question.

"Get up. It doesn't matter."

"Can't you just tell me the truth?" She pleaded with tears coming down her face.

"What is truth?" Demos mocked.

"I just—I just want to know the truth...please..."

"Get up!"

"Please..." Jenna whimpered.

"I am your mother and father." Demos replied.

"But you're my pimp. I'm just a slave to you."

Dr. Hoyniman interjected, "You are the clone of Jimmy Demos. You were implanted into Clarissa Phelps twenty-two years ago and born from her womb. Your birth name is Jenna Phelps, but you are actually Jenna Demos."

"Like I said, I am your mother and father." Demos said with a smirk.

Jenna Park—Jenna Demos—slumped over Simon's dead body.

Jimmy Demos hovered above her with the sun behind him and cast his shadow over her.

"Get up." he ordered.

Jenna looked at Simon with love, "No." she said.

"What?" Demos questioned her.

"I won't listen to you anymore." Jenna squeezed.

Demos frowned. She was not as weak as he thought. He knew that there was nothing he could ever do to change her mind so he shot her in the head. It was over.

--THE END